FLYING
DUTCH

FLYING DUTCH

Tom Holt

ORBIT

DEDICATION:
To Malcolm

An *Orbit* Book

First published in Great Britain in 1991 by Orbit Books,
a Division of Macdonald & Co (Publishers) Ltd
London & Sydney

A CIP catalogue record for this book is available from the British
Library.

ISBN 0 356 20111 2

Printed and bound in Great Britain by
BPCC Hazell Books
Aylesbury, Bucks, England
Member of BPCC Ltd.

Orbit Books
A Division of
Macdonald & Co (Publishers) Ltd
Orbit House
1 New Fetter Lane
London EC4A 1AR
A member of Maxwell Macmillan Pergamon Publishing Corporation

CHAPTER ONE

It's always a little startling to hear your name in a public place, and Vanderdecker froze. The beer in his glass didn't, and the froth splashed his nose. He put the glass down and listened.

'The story of the Flying Dutchman ...' the man opposite had said. Slowly, so as not to be seen to be staring, Vanderdecker looked round. His profession had trained him to take in all the information he needed to enable him to form a judgement in one swift glance, and what he saw was a plump young man wearing a corduroy jacket and a pink shirt with a white collar. Trousers slightly too tight. Round, steel-rimmed spectacles. Talking at a girl at least seven years his junior. American. Vanderdecker wasn't much taken with what he saw, but he listened anyway.

'Most people think,' said the plump young man, 'that Wagner invented the story of the Flying Dutchman. Not true.'

'Really?' said the girl.

'Absolutely,' the plump young man confirmed. 'The legend can be traced back to the early seventeenth century. My own theory is that it represents some misconstrued recollection of the Dutch fleet in the Medway.'

'Where is the Medway, exactly?' asked the girl, but the plump young man hadn't heard her. He was looking through her, as if she were a ghost, to the distant but irresistible vision of his own cleverness.

Vanderdecker knew exactly where the Medway was, and frowned. He disliked being referred to as a legend, even in his own lifetime. But the plump young man hadn't finished yet.

'The version used by Wagner — I say used, but of course

the Master tailored it to his own uses — tells of a Dutch captain who once tried to double the Cape of Good Hope in the teeth of a furious gale, and swore he would accomplish the feat even if it took him all eternity.'

'You don't say,' said the girl.

'No sooner had the fateful oath left his lips,' he continued, 'when Satan heard the oath and condemned the wretched blasphemer to sail the seas until the Day of Judgement, without aim and without hope of release, until he could find a woman who would be faithful until death. Once every seven years the Devil allows him on shore to seek such a woman; and it is on one such occasion ...'

'I always thought,' said the girl, 'that the Flying Dutchman was a steam train.'

This had the effect on the plump young man that sugar has on a full tank of petrol. He stopped talking and made a request that Vanderdecker, for his part, would have found it difficult to grant.

'Pardon me?' he asked.

'Or was that the Flying Scotsman?' said the girl, realising that the joke needed explanation before an American could understand it. She might as well have been speaking in Latvian for all the effect she had, however, and after a moment of bewilderment the plump man started off again with the details of the Daland-Senta plot from Wagner's opera. At this point, Vanderdecker let his attention drift back to his pint of beer, for he loathed the story. He had seriously considered taking legal action when the opera was first presented, but the problems of proving who he was would have been insurmountable.

By an odd coincidence, although not even Vanderdecker was aware of it, the plump young man was Vanderdecker's great-great-great-great-great-great-great-grandson; the final product of an evolutionary process which had started with a fleeting encounter with a barmaid in New England in 1674. And there was proof, if proof were needed, that the version of the story that Junior had just gone through was nothing but a pack of lies, for Vanderdecker had been off and away without waiting to see if the barmaid in question would be faithful until a mild cold, let alone death. He was younger then, of course — a stripling of one hundred and sixteen — and still obsessed with wild notions of having a good time every once in a while. Nowadays, on the rare occasions when he met them, he looked upon barmaids simply as people who were paid to sell him alcoholic beverages.

The girl looked at her watch for the third time in four minutes and said that they had better be getting along or they would be late for the curtain. Her companion said there was no hurry, he hadn't finished telling her the plot. She replied that she would just have to muddle through, somehow or other. Vanderdecker got the impression that she wasn't enjoying herself very much.

They got up and left, leaving the Flying Dutchman staring at his glass and wondering why, when so many things had remained basically the same through the centuries, the human race had chosen to muck about with beer quite so much. In his young days they slung some malt in a bucket, added boiling water, and then went away and forgot about it for a week or so. The result of this laissez-faire attitude was incomparably preferable to the modern version, he seemed to remember — or was that just another aspect of getting old? Not that he was getting old, of course; no such luck. He looked and felt exactly the way he did in 1585 — which was more, he reflected, than you could say for Dover Castle.

Melancholy reflections on the subject of beer led him to even more melancholy reflections concerning the great web of being, and in particular his part in it, which had been so much more protracted than anybody else's. Not more significant, to the best of his knowledge. His role in history was rather like that of lettuce in the average salad; it achieves no useful purpose, but there's always a lot of it. But this was by no means a new train of thought, and he knew how to cope with it by now. He finished his drink and went to the bar for another.

As he stood at the bar and fumbled in his pocket for money, he tried playing the old 'I-remember-when' game which had entertained him briefly about a century ago and which now only irritated him. I remember when money was real money, he said to himself, when it was made of solid silver and had lots of Latin on it. I remember when you could have bought all the beer in Bavaria, plus sales tax and carriage, for the price of half a pint of this. I even remember flared trousers. That dates me.

As he sat down to his drink, he tried to think of something that wouldn't set him thinking about how incredibly long he had lived, just for a change. He tried to think of what he was going to do next. But that, of course, wouldn't take him very long, because he knew exactly what he was going to do next. He was going to get pathetically drunk, crawl back to his hotel, and wake up with a splitting head next morning which would leave him in no fit state to go flogging round Hatton Garden selling gold bars. After he had sold the gold bars, he would traipse through the bookshops and buy up enough reading matter to keep him from going stark raving mad for the next seven years. Then he would do the rest of his shopping, which would only leave him just enough time to get pathetically drunk again before slouching back to Bridport and his bloody ship and his bloody, bloody shipmates. It wasn't that he didn't want to find a woman who would be true until death; he simply didn't have the time.

He was following the first part of this programme with almost religious diligence when, several hours later, the plump man and the girl came back for a last drink. Vanderdecker hoped that they would enjoy it, since it might make up for an otherwise completely wasted evening witnessing that puerile burlesque of his life story. For his part, as usual, Vanderdecker had come to terms with modern beer, and was rather better adjusted to the world in general. He no longer cared if he appeared to be staring. Staring was fun — at any rate, it was considerably more entertaining than what he had been doing for the last seven years — and a good long stare might help clear his head.

'The costumes,' said the girl after a long silence, 'were quite pretty.'

Her companion gave her the sort of look that should have been reserved for a tourist who goes to Rome just to

look at the gas works. 'What did you think,' he asked —
with obvious restraint — 'of the music?'

'I got used to it,' she replied, 'after a bit. Like a dripping
tap,' she added.

That seemed to wrap it up, so far as the plump young
man was concerned.

'Is that the time?' he said without looking at his watch.
'I must go or I'll miss the last train.'

'Must you?' said the girl. 'Oh well, never mind. I think
I'll just finish my drink.'

'See you tomorrow, then,' said the plump man. 'Perhaps
we can make a start on the July figures.'

Shortly afterwards, he wasn't there any more. Vanderdecker, however, continued to stare. If the girl was aware of
this, she gave no sign of it. She was reading her
programme. Presumably, Vanderdecker imagined, the
summary of the plot. The injustice of it made him
suddenly angry, although he recognised in his soul that it
was too late to do anything about it now. He finished his
drink and stood up to go. His route to the door and the
street led him past the girl's table and as he passed over
the top of her bowed head he heard himself speak.

'All that stuff,' he said, 'about angels and faithful until
death is rubbish. It was the smell.'

The girl looked up sharply, and just as Vanderdecker
was going through the door she caught a glimpse of his
face. Somewhere in the back of her mind she had a vague,
indefinable, inchoate feeling that she had seen him somewhere before.

'I remember,' said the stranger, 'when money was real
money.'

'That's right, mate,' said his new friend. 'Pounds, shill-
ings and pence.'

'And testoons,' said the stranger, 'and groats and placks
and angels and ryals and ducats and louis d'or and louis
d'argent ...'

'You what?'

'And nobles of course,' continued the stranger. 'I
remember when you could get pissed as a rat, have a really

good blow-out in a bakehouse, see the bear-baiting, and still have change out of a noble.'

The landlord turned his head very slightly. Drunks were no problem, but loonies he could do without.

'What are you talking about?' asked the stranger's new friend, in a tone of voice that suggested that their friendship might soon end as rapidly as it had begun.

'Before your time,' explained the stranger, twirling his beer round in its glass to revive the flagging head. 'Can't expect you to remember nobles.'

'Are you taking the ...'

'No,' said the stranger. 'Are you?'

Twenty years of keeping a pub in this particular district of Southampton had given the landlord a virtually supernatural instinct for the outbreak of a fight. Unfortunately he was at the other end of the bar, and before he could intervene the stranger's new friend had hit the stranger in the face, very hard.

'Christ almighty,' said the stranger's new friend. There was blood streaming from his lacerated knuckles, and the stranger was grinning.

'Go on,' he said, 'hit me again.'

Before this invitation could be accepted, strong and practiced hands had taken up both parties and put them out in the street. For his part the stranger landed awkwardly, staggered, lost his footing and fell extremely heavily against a parking meter. The parking meter broke, but not so the stranger. He simply gathered himself carefully to his feet, looked around, and set off in search of another pub he remembered in this part of town. When he got there, however, it was boarded up. It had been closed for the last seven years, ever since a party of Royal Marines had started a fight with a man they thought was trying to be funny, and which had ended with five very confused Marines receiving treatment for fractured hands and feet.

At this stage, of course, the Dow Jones was still buoyant, the Hang Tseng had never had it so good, the FT was climbing like a deranged convolvulus, futures were trading as if there was no tomorrow, and the only currency that wasn't performing too well was the Confederate dollar.

In an alleyway in the centre of Cadiz, a rather disreputable-looking cat was stalking an empty crisp packet.

Just as the cat had resolved to pounce, a puff of wind caught the crisp packet and blew it into the middle of the highway, along which an articulated lorry full of cans of tomatoes was travelling. The cat saw this, but decided to pursue its quarry nevertheless. He had been stalking it for over half an hour and he was damned if he was going to let it slip through his paws now.

The lorry driver, to his credit, did his best to brake, but the momentum of a heavily laden Mercedes lorry is not an easy thing to dissipate quickly. There was a thud, and the cat was sent flying across the road. The lorry-driver continued on his way, and soon put the incident out of his mind.

The cat wearily got to its feet and looked around for the crisp packet, but it was nowhere to be seen. At that moment an English tourist came running across to inspect the damage. The tourist was female and fond of cats.

When she saw the cat get up, she couldn't believe her eyes. She had seen the poor animal being run over by the lorry — it must have been killed. But it hadn't been. She came closer, and it was then that the smell hit her. She reeled back, with both hands over her face, and groped her way out of the alley.

The cat was used to such reactions, but that didn't make them any more pleasant. He sulked for at least ten minutes, until a discarded fruit juice carton caught his eye and he settled his mind to the serious business of hunting. In a very, very long life he had learned how to get his priorities right.

On her way back home to Maida Vale on the tube, the girl who had seen the Flying Dutchman was bored, for she had forgotten to bring a book with her to read on the journey. Not that she had ever doubted for one split second that she was coming home tonight — perish the thought! It had been simple forgetfulness, and the tedium of having nothing to entertain herself with but the posters and her opera programme was a fitting punishment.

After a random sample, she decided that the opera programme was marginally less dire than the posters, and she read the synopsis of the plot again. A modern version of the story, she decided, with the Dutchman doomed to spend the rest of time going round and round the Circle Line with nothing to read but vilely-phrased propaganda from the employment agencies, might have some possibilities, but by and large the whole idea was not so much tragic but silly. The daftest part, she reckoned, was the idea that Satan could get you just for expressing a determination to get round a traffic hazard — if that rule still applied, she said to herself, then you wouldn't be able to set tyre to pavement on the Chiswick Roundabout for souls in torment. Or perhaps the rule did still apply. It would explain the way some people drove.

The train stopped at Paddington, opened its doors, and sat very still. In the corner of the carriage there was a tramp with wild white hair and very distressing shoes, fast asleep with his head almost between his knees, but otherwise she was alone. The girl abandoned the legend of the Flying Dutchman and turned her thoughts toward the great web of being, with particular reference to her own part in it. I am an accountant, she said to herself, working mainly in banking. Why is it that, whenever I remember this fact, I want to scream?

Perhaps, she considered, the Dutchman story wasn't so silly after all. Perhaps Satan did hover unseen in the ether waiting to pounce on ill-considered sayings. She had only said one very stupid thing in her life — 'I want to be an accountant' — but of the various explanations for her present condition to which she had given consideration before, the Satan theory was as good as any. Was there such a person as Satan, by the way? Why not? Satan was no more incredible a concept than Mr Peters, the senior partner, and he undoubtedly existed. All one would have to do to make the gentleman in horns conceivable would be to get him out of those stuffy medieval clothes into a nice three-piece suit, and convert the Fires of Hell into a microwave. You could possibly get a Government grant for that.

The girl recognised that her train of thought was becoming alarmingly metaphysical, but when you are stuck in Paddington station at a quarter to midnight with nothing to read, you can afford to indulge flights of fancy. Plato would have loved the Bakerloo Line.

I may not be Dutch, she said to herself, but I'm positive I would hate to live for ever. She remembered that week in the middle of the summer holidays when she was young, that one, inevitable week when the joy of not being at school had worn off and the dread of going back to school had not yet taken hold. That week when there was no longer anything to do, when everyone else had gone off with their parents to Jersey, when there was nothing on the television except Wimbledon, and cousin Marian from Swansea came to stay. That week that was free of all the pressures of doing the things you hated doing, devoid of all the pleasures of doing the things you liked doing, that week that lasted at least a month and probably longer. No crime a human being could commit, however terrible, could merit a punishment as dreadful as another of those weeks of killing time. Perhaps she should stop thinking along these lines, before she found out just exactly how shallow her mind really was.

It was then she remembered hearing a voice somewhere above her head at some stage during the evening, which had said that the angels and the love interest were all rubbish, but that the smell had been the real reason — or words to that effect. It was peculiar, to say the least, that her brain should seek to filter out this scrap of jetsam from the rubbish that her memory was sorting and discarding; her mind, she reckoned, was like the little grill thing over the plug-hole which catches fragments of cauliflower and pasta shells when the washing up bowl is emptied. She was reckoning thus when sleep finally caught her out, and she slept through Warwick Avenue and only just woke up in time to scramble out of the train at Maida Vale and walk home the long way.

* * *

There is one pub in Southampton which it is impossible to get yourself thrown out of no matter what you do or say, and there the newcomer ran into someone he knew very well.

At first they tried to avoid each other, since it was three days yet before they had to go back to the ship, and then they would be together again, inseparable, for another seven years. But this plan broke down when the newcomer realised that he had run out of money.

'Antonius,' said the newcomer to his friend in Dutch, 'lend me a fiver till payday.'

Antonius felt in the pocket of his shirt and found a five pound note, which he gave to his companion. His companion's name, for the record, was Johannes, and he and Antonius had been born in the same village south of Antwerp over four hundred and thirty years before. Barring shore leaves like this, they had been out of each other's company for a period exceeding eight hours exactly once in four hundred and seventeen of those years, when Johannes' mother had suspected that her son had caught the plague and locked him up in the barn for a few days.

Neither of them would have chosen to have it this way, since they didn't get on very well and never had. Johannes was a short, noisy man with a hairy face and hairy arms, who liked drinking a lot and falling over. What Antonius liked doing best was standing quite still, unfocussing his eyes, and thinking of nothing at all. Each of them found the other remarkably uncongenial, and the only point on which they were united and could talk for more than three minutes without losing their temper with each other was their dislike of everyone else on board the ship, and in particular Captain Vanderdecker.

'After all,' said Johannes, a few minutes later, as they sat in a corner of the bar under the dartboard and drank their beer, 'he was the one got us into this in the first place.'

'That's right,' replied Antonius. 'All his fault.'

A dart bounced out of treble fifteen and point first onto Antonius' brown, bald head. He extracted it and handed it back to its owner.

'What the hell did he want to go drinking that stuff for

in the first place?' Johannes continued, picking a grain of
chalk dust out of his beer as he spoke. 'He should have
known it would end up all wrong.'

'He just didn't think,' Antonius agreed. 'No consideration for others.'

'And then dropping it,' said Johannes bitterly, 'into the
beer-barrel.'

'Typical,' said Antonius. It was a word he was very fond
of and saved for special occasions. He didn't want to wear
it out by overuse.

'This beer,' said Johannes, unconsciously echoing his
Captain, 'grows on you after a bit. You could get used to it.'

'It's got a taste, though,' Antonius asserted. 'You want
another?'

'Might as well.'

So they had another, and another, and two or three more
after that, and then they went outside to get some air. By
now they were feeling quite relaxed, and Antonius remembered the girl who lived round the corner. They decided to
go and visit her. They did this every time they came to
England, just as, every time, they forgot that she had died
in 1606 and that her house was now a car park. They
always left a note though, saying that they were sorry to
have missed her and would be sure to drop in next time.
Since the building of the car park they had taken to
sticking these notes behind the windscreen wipers of the
parked cars, and once they had left one on the car of an
avid and knowledgeable local historian, who had read it
and was quite ill for months afterwards.

The plump man, who was also an accountant, although a
vastly more important one than the girl, made himself a
cup of lemon tea and tried to forget that he had wasted a
performance of *The Flying Dutchman* at Covent Garden,
with Neustadt singing Senta, on a cultural void like Jane
Doland. Next to his career, he loved opera above all things
and a failure to appreciate it was a crime that could not be
forgiven. He opened his briefcase, switched on his calculator and put *Rienzi* on the CD player. Slowly, like the
return of spring, the wound began to heal.

CHAPTER TWO

The National Lombard Bank is situated in the very heart of downtown Bridport. It is the sort of location any red-blooded bank manager would give his heart and soul for, right in the epicentre of a triangle formed by the town's most beguiling attractions — the fish and chip shop, the Post Office and the traffic lights. In summer, whole families still make the difficult journey into Bridport from the surrounding countryside to stand and watch the traffic lights performing their dazzling *son et lumiere*; and although they now have a set of lights in Charmouth — a deliberate and cynical attempt to poach the holiday trade that has introduced much bitterness into the previously friendly relationship between the two communities — purists insist that the Bridport set has a purer green, a rosier red, a more scintillating amber than any others this side of Dorchester.

To a Sybaritic Londoner like Jane Doland, however, the Bridport Lights meant nothing more than another hold-up on her way to a not particularly pleasant assignment, and with the poverty of spirit that is the hallmark of the city-dweller she assumed that the small throng of children gathered round them were merely waiting to cross the road. She had no street-plan of Bridport to help her find the bank, but she located it nevertheless simply by looking straight in front of her as she drove in from the roundabout. A bank, she said to herself, what fun. This is well worth missing the London premiere of *Crocodile Dundee 9* for.

The causes of momentous events are often so bewilderingly complex that even highly-trained historians are at a loss to unravel them. Men wise in their generation have

gone grey, bald and ultimately senile in the great univer-
sities grappling with the origins of the English Civil War,
the Peasants' Revolt and the rise of Hitler, and it is
doubtful now that the truth will ever be known. In
contrast, the reasons why Jane Doland was in Bridport,
two years (give or take a week or so) since she had gone to
see *The Flying Dutchman* at the Royal Opera House, was
quite remarkably simple. A decree had gone out from
Caesar Augustus that all the world should be taxed, and
since this particular decree had had some viciously unexpected things in it about Advance Corporation Tax, all
leave was cancelled in the offices of the leading accountancy firm where Jane Doland occupied a trivial and
poorly-paid position, and accountants were dispersed like
dazed bacilli into the bloodstream of British commerce to
sort out the affairs of the National Lombard Bank, the
firm's largest and most complicated client. Since the
National Lombard has more branches than all the trees in
the New Forest, and the Bridport branch occupies roughly
the same place in the Bank's list of priorities as that
assigned to Leatherhead Rovers in the Football League, its
affairs were unhesitatingly entrusted to Jane Doland's
skill, expertise and highly-motivated commitment.

Jane was considering this when she parked her car
under a lime tree in that famous Bridport thoroughfare
which some unusually imaginative soul had christened
South Street. In fact the term 'nonentity' had been rattling
about in her brain like a small, loose bearing all the way
down the A303, and by the time she reached her destin-
ation she was in no mood to be pleasant to anybody or to
appreciate anything. This would go some way towards
explaining her lack of enthusiasm for the traffic lights,
which happened to be at their luminescent best this not
particularly fine morning.

Nevertheless, Jane said to herself as she walked through
the door of the bank. When trying to cheer herself up, she
never got further than nevertheless, but it was always
worth giving it just one more go. As she had expected, they
had looked out lots of nice accounts for her to amuse
herself with, and although they were all in such a hopeless

mess that Sherlock Holmes, with Theseus to help him,
Einstein to handle the figures and Escoffier laying on
plenty of strong black coffee, would have had a devil of a
job sorting them out. Jane told herself that it is always the
thought that counts. She could imagine the faces of the
bank staff when the news hit them that an accountant
from Moss Berwick was coming to visit them. 'Moss
Berwick, eh?' she could hear them saying to each other.
'Somebody hide the July returns while I shuffle the
invoices.'

After several false starts, the hour-hand of the clock on
the wall in the pleasantly intimate cupboard they had set
aside for her personal use crept round to one o'clock and
she made her Unilateral Declaration of Lunchtime. The
precious forty-five minutes that her contract of employment allowed her for rest, nourishment and the contemplation of the infinite was mostly dissipated in locating and
booking into the Union Hotel, which Jane was able to tell
from the public lavatories next door by the fact that the
roller towel in the public lavatories worked. By not bothering to unpack, Jane was able to dash down to the bar, fail
to get a drink and a sandwich before it shut, and sprint
back to the bank just in time to be three minutes late for
the afternoon session. The manager wasn't impressed, and
one of the cashiers gave her a look that nearly stripped all
the varnish off her nails. At about three-fifteen her pencil
broke.

Stay with it, girl, she said to herself as the office junior
came to tell her to go away because they were locking up
now, you've got four more days of this. Think (she said to
herself) of the Honour of the Firm. Think of old man Moss
hauling himself up by his bootstraps out of the slums of
nineteenth-century Liverpool, studying all the hours God
sent at the Mechanics Institute to pass his examinations,
qualify, meet up with old man Berwick and found the
greatest accounting firm the world has ever known. She
had read this stirring story in the recruitment pamphlets
they had sent her when she joined, and the recollection of
it never failed to arouse in her strong feelings of pure
apathy. Oddly enough, the pamphlet had been curiously

reticent on the subject of old man Berwick, preferring to concentrate on his more dashing colleague, and Jane often wondered where he had pulled himself up out of by his bootstraps. Harrow, probably.

A year or so back, the compilers of the same recruitment guide had been going round interviewing members of staff for the new edition, and they had asked Jane what the most satisfying, fulfilling, life-enhancing thing about working for the firm was, in her lowly opinion. She had replied, without hesitation, going home, and they hadn't included her in the guide or even the video, although she prided herself that she had the best legs in the department. Since the rest of the legs in the department belonged to Mr Shaw, Mr Peterson, Mr Ferrara and Mr Timson respectively, this was no symptom of vanity on Jane's part, merely the scrupulous accuracy and devotion to truth which marks an accountant out from his fellow creatures.

Since then, Jane had kept her opinion of her chosen career very much to herself; but, as if to compensate, she let it out of its cage pretty freely once she was alone with it. As she was now, for instance, on a cold Monday night in Bridport.

There are few excitements to compare with one's first night in a strange new town, and despite her weariness and a deplorable urge to take her tights off and watch 'Cagney and Lacey' on the black and white portable in her room at the Union Hotel, Jane set out to immerse herself completely in the town. After all, she reckoned, she might never come here again; live this precious moment to the full, crush each ripe fruit of sensation against the palate until the appetite is cloyed in intoxicating richness.

The cinema was closed when she eventually found it, what with it being half past September, and since she had no wish to be raped, robbed or murdered she didn't go into the White Hart, the Blue Ball, the Bunch of Grapes, the Prince of Wales, the Peacock, the Catherine Wheel, the Green Dragon, the Four Horseshoes, the Hour Glass, the Half Way House, the Bird in Hand, the Bottle and Glass, the Jolly Sportsman, the Dorsetshire Yeoman, the Boot and Slipper, the Rising Sun, the Crown and Cushion, the

Poulteney Arms, the Red Cross Knight, the Two Brewers, the Black Dog, the Temporary Sign, the Duke of Rochester, the Gardeners Arms or the Mississippi River-boat Night Club. Apart from these, the only place of entertainment open to the public was the bus shelter, and that was a touch too crowded for Jane's taste. She went back to the Union Hotel, had a glass of orange juice and some fresh local boiled carpet with gravy in the dining room, and went upstairs to catch the last ten minutes of 'Cagney and Lacey', which had been cancelled and replaced with athletics from Zurich.

Isn't it fortunate, Jane reflected, that I brought a good book with me. The only thing which can stop me enjoying my book is if the proprietors of this charnel-house forget to put a shilling in the meter. She picked the book out of her suitcase, opened it where her expired Capitalcard marked the place, and began to read.

This is not the right book, she said to herself as her eye fell upon the corduroy furrows of the page. This is the book I finished reading yesterday.

You can tell of your Torments of the Damned. You can, if you wish, allude to Sisyphus and the Stone. You can wax eloquent, especially if you are a television evangelist, about what is going to happen to the fornicators and the bearers of false witness when they finally come eyeball to eyeball with the Big G. But you cannot begin to describe, not if you speak with the tongues of men and of angels, the exquisite agony of being stuck in a fleabag hotel in a shut town with a choice between watching a load of tubby East Germans putting the shot in their underwear or reading a detective story every detail of whose plot is etched on your mind.

A berserk fury came over quiet, tranquil-minded Jane Doland. She pulled on her tights, picked up her room-key and went out into the gloomy corridor. Downstairs, in what was described with cruel irony as the residents' lounge, there might be a week-old newspaper or the July 1956 issue of *Woman and Home*. Or perhaps she might find a reasonably well-written telephone directory, or even a discarded matchbox with a puzzle on the back. There is

always hope, so long as life subsists. The beating of the
heart and the action of the lungs are a useful prevarica-
tion, keeping all options open.

She did find a matchbox, as it happens, but all it said
was 'Made in Finland, Average Contents Forty Matches,'
and after the third reading Jane felt that she had sucked
all the value out of that one. Disconsolate, she wandered
out to the reception desk. The sound of a television
commentator joyfully exclaiming that Kevin Bradford
from Cark-in-Cartmel had managed to avoid coming last
in the six hundred metres drifted through the illuminated
crack above the office door. Jane looked down and saw the
hotel register. Salvation! She could read that.

It was a fascinating document. For example, Jane
learned that in November 1986 Mr and Mrs Belmont from
Winnipeg had stayed three nights at the Union Hotel, and
although they had had breakfast, they had not had any
evening meals.

Why was that, she wondered? Had they spent every last
cent on the flight, and been reduced to eating their way
through all the individual portions of jam and marmalade
on the breakfast table to keep body and soul together
during their stay? Did they spend the evenings flitting
from casino to night-club to casino, scorning the Union's
prosaic cuisine? Perhaps they just didn't like the look of
the menu terribly much. She could sympathise with that.
And what had brought these globe-trotting Belmonts half-
way across the world, uprooting them from their cosy
timber-frame home among the wheatfields, beside the
immeasurable vastness of the mighty lake? Had they come
back in search of their heritage, or to pay their last
respects to a dying relative, resolving a twenty-year old
feud in a final deathbed reconciliation? Did they feel that
same restless urge that drove much-enduring Ulysses to
see the cities of men and know their minds? Or had they
simply got on the wrong coach?

Another thing that Jane discovered, and could well
believe, was that not many people stayed at the Union
Hotel, or at least not enough to fill up an optimistically
large register in a hurry. This one went back nine years, to

when a Mr J Vanderdecker of Antwerp had booked in for
two nights. Oddly enough, she noticed, another J Vanderdecker (or the same man that bit older and wiser) had
booked in seven years later. On neither occasion had he
risked the evening meal, but he had insisted on a room
with bath both times. A shy, private sort of man, Jane
imagined, who would rather die than have strangers see
him in his dressing gown and slippers wandering the
corridors at half-past seven in the morning.

The office door started to open, and Jane dodged guiltily
away from the desk. As she did so she barked her shin on a
low table, on which reposed a dog-eared copy of *Shooting
Times* and *Country Magazine*. She seized it, fled, read it
from cover to cover, finally fell asleep and had a nightmare
about a man-eating ferret.

'I spy,' said the first mate, 'with my little eye, something
beginning with W.'

Nobody took any notice. Even Jan Christian Duysberg
had guessed that one back in the 1740's, and he had been
thirty-four years old before he realised he was left-handed.

A seagull drifted across the sky, staggered in mid-air,
banked violently and flew off to the south-east. Cornelius
Schumaker clipped his toenails quietly in the shade of the
mast. Wilhelm Triegaart completed his seventy-ninth
crossword of the trip.

For some of the crew of the sailing-ship *Verdomde*
(which is Dutch for 'Damned') the second year of each
seven-year term was the worst. Just as Jane Doland often
felt at her most miserable on Tuesdays, because the
memory of the brief freedom of the weekend had already
faded without bringing Friday appreciably nearer, so it
was with the more impatient of Vanderdecker's command.
Others were content to take each year as it came, whiling
away the time with impossible projects — Pieter Pretorius,
for example, was building a scale model of the battle of
Lepanto inside an empty Coca-Cola bottle, while his
brother Dirk pushed back the limits of pure mathematics
by calculating the overtime claim he was going to put in
when the trip finally ended — while the remaining

members of the crew saw no further than the next watch. By now, the only man on the ship who even bothered trying to do something about the mess they were all in was the captain himself.

Captain Vanderdecker was a great reader of the *Scientific American*. He sat in his cabin with his feet up on the map-table and a relatively recent copy of that publication on his knees, trying to do long division in his head while he shook his solar calculator violently in a vain effort to make it work. Something important to do with the half-life of radium was on the point of slipping away from him for want of the square root of 47, and if it got away this time it might take him weeks to get it back. The fact that time was not of the essence was something he tried not to think about, for fear of giving up altogether. Vanderdecker generated artificial urgency with the same fatuous optimism that makes an eighty-year old woman dye her hair.

Ever since 1945, Vanderdecker had been fascinated by radiation. His original wild hopes had been dashed when he and the crew had lived through an early nuclear test in the Pacific and suffered nothing worse than glowing faintly in the dark for the next week or so; but he had persisted with it with a blind, unquestioning faith ever since he had finally been forced to give up on volcanoes. Not that he approved of radiation; he had read too much about it for that. For the rest of the human race, he thought it was a bad move and likely to end in tears before bedtime. For himself and his crew, however, it offered a tiny glimmer of hope, and he could not afford to dismiss it until he had crushed every last possibility firmly into the ground.

And so he read on, disturbed only by the creaking of the rigging and the occasional thump as Sebastian van Doorning threw himself off the top of the mast onto the deck. In 1964 the poor fool had got it into his head that although one fall might not necessarily be fatal, repeated crash-landings might eventually wear a brittle patch in his invulnerable skull and offer him the ultimate discharge he so desperately wanted. At least it provided occasional work for the ship's carpenter; every time he landed so hard he went right through the deck.

'The Philosophers' Stone?' the caption read. 'Break-through In Plutonium Isotopes Offers Insight Into Trans-mutation Of Matter.' Vanderdecker swallowed hard and took his feet off the table. It was probably the same old nonsense he personally had seen through in the late seventies, but there was always the possibility that there was something in it.

'It is rumored,' said the *Scientific American*, 'that experiments at Britain's Dounreay nuclear reactor will lead to a new reappraisal of some fundamental aspects of atomic theory. If recently published results by physicists Marsh-main and Kellner are vindicated by the Dounreay tests, the alchemist may shortly step out of the pages of histories of the occult and into European R&D laboratories. The co-ordinator of the new programme, Professor Montalban of Oxford University . . .'

Montalban. *Montalban*, for God's sake!

Over four hundred years of existence had left Vander-decker curiously undecided about coincidences. Some-times he believed in them, sometimes he didn't. The name Montalban is not common, but it is not so incredibly unique that one shouldn't expect to come across it more than once in four hundred years. Its appearance on the same page as the word 'alchemist' was a littler harder to explain away, and Vanderdecker had to remind himself of the monkeys with typewriters knocking out *Hamlet* before he could get himself into a properly sceptical frame of mind to read on. By then, of course, the lamp in his cabin had blown out, and rather than waste time trying to light it again with his original but clapped-out Zippo, he decided to go out on deck and let the sun do the work for once. With his finger in the fold of the magazine so as not to lose the place, he scrambled up the ladder and out of the hatch, just as Sebastian van Doorning made his ninth descent of the day.

Vanderdecker was knocked sideways and landed in a pile of coiled-up rope. As he pulled himself together, he saw his copy of the *Scientific American* being hoisted up into the air by a gust of wind and deposited neatly into the Atlantic Ocean.

'Sebastian.'

The sky-diver picked himself sheepishly off the deck. 'Yes, captain?' he said.

'If you jump off the mast ever again,' said the Flying Dutchman, 'I'll break your blasted neck.'

They didn't bother lowering the ship's boat, they just jumped; the Captain was in that sort of a mood. Eventually Pieter Pretorius fished the magazine out, and they tried drying it in the sun. But it was no good; the water had washed away all the print, so that the only words still legible on the whole page were 'Montalban' and 'alchemist'. Dirk Pretorius calculated the odds against this at nine million fourteen thousand two hundred and sixty-eight to one against, something which everyone except the captain found extremely interesting.

There, Jane said to herself, is a funny thing.

Do not get the impression, just because Jane is forever talking to herself, that she is not quite right in the head, or even unusually inclined towards contemplation. It was simply that, in her profession, there are not many people to talk to, and if one is naturally talkative one does the best one can. It is important that this point be made early, since Jane has a lot to do in this story, and you should not be put off her just because she soliloquizes. So did Hamlet. Give the poor girl a chance.

Extremely strange, she considered, and stared at the ledger in front of her through eyes made watery by deciphering handwriting worse even than her own. Undoubtedly there has been a visit from the Cock-Up Fairy at some stage; but when, and how?

It should not have been her job to look at the ledgers recording the current accounts; but an exasperating detail in quite ordinary calculation had gone astray, and she had, just for once, become so engrossed in the abstract interest of solving it that she had stayed with it for six hours, including her lunch break. Although she was not aware of it, she was pulling off a quite amazing tour de force of accountancy that her superiors would never have believed her capable of.

The reason why she had gone overboard on this one was a name. It wasn't a particularly common name, you see, and she had come across it once already. The name was Vanderdecker, J.

Vanderdecker, J had a current account with the National Lombard Bank. It contained £6.42. It had contained £6.42 for well over a hundred years.

A pity, Jane said to herself, it hadn't been a deposit account. The bank staff had stared at her as if she was completely crazy when she demanded the excavation of ledgers going back almost to the dawn of time. They had protested. They had assured her that the ledgers for the period before 1970 had been incinerated years ago. They had told her that even if they hadn't been incinerated (which they had), they had been lost. Even if they hadn't been lost, they were hopelessly difficult to get at. They were in storage at the bank's central storage depot in Newcastle-under-Lyme. Even if they weren't in Newcastle-under-Lyme, they were in the cellar. There were spiders in the cellar. Big spiders. A foolhardy clerk had gone into the cellar five years ago, and all they ever found of him was his shoes.

Until computerisation, all the ledgers were hand-written, and some of the handwriting was difficult to read. Jane's eyesight had never been brilliant, and too much staring at scrawly copperplate gave her a headache. She had a headache now; not one of your everyday temple-throbbers but something drastic in the middle of her forehead. Despite this, she was managing to think.

The logical explanation of the mystery — there is always a logical explanation — was that Vanderdecker, J had opened an account in 1879, lived his normal span of years and died, leaving the sum of £6/8/4d. In the anguish of his parting (Jane had read some deathbed scenes in Victorian novels and knew that people made a meal of such things in those days) the account had been overlooked. Inertia, the banker's familiar demon, had allowed the account to drift along from year to year like an Iron Age body in a peat bog, dead but perfectly preserved, and here it was to this day. Very salutary.

The only problem was the name J Vanderdecker in the register of the Union Hotel. Dammit, it *wasn't* a common name; and if J Vanderdecker was swanning around Bridport two years ago, and seven years before that, he couldn't have died in the early nineteen-hundreds, which was what the sensible theory demanded.

Anyone but an accountant would have told the sensible theory to stuff it and gone on with something else. But accountants are different. Legend has it that all accountants are descended from one Barnabas of Sidon, a peripheral associate of the disciples of Our Lord who had done the accounts for Joseph's carpentry business in Galilee. After receiving a severe shock at the Feeding of the Five Thousand, he had been present at the Last Supper but had missed all the fun because he was too busy adding up the bill and trying to remember who had had what. Like fish, accountants see things in a different way from people, and details which people find unimportant are their reason for existing.

Well now, said Jane to herself, what are we going to do about this? In theory, all she had to do was report her findings to the manager, who would say, Yes how interesting, have you got much more to do or will you be going soon? and then write the account off against arrears of bank charges as soon as she left the premises. Jane felt very strongly, for some reason, that this was not something that ought to happen. She had no idea why it was important, but it was.

The only other information she had about the account, apart from the name Vanderdecker, J and the sum of £6.42, was an address: Lower Brickwood Farm Cottage, Melplash, near Bridport, Dorset. It followed that if there was anything else capable of being found out about this mystery, it would have to be sought there. She would go there this evening, she resolved, and everything would be explained; there *would* be a simple explanation, and she would find it at Lower Brickwood Farm Cottage. In the meanwhile, she could get on with her proper work and put it out of her mind.

Came half-past six, and Jane was off in her W registration Ford Fiesta looking for Lower Brickwood Farm Cottage, a task marginally more difficult than finding the Holy Grail. Melplash is not on the street map of Bridport which the seeker after truth can buy at the newsagent; neither, if the truth be told, is most of Bridport itself. When it comes to Melplash, however, the stranger is definitely on his own. It is assumed that the only people who need have anything to do with Melplash are people who live there already, and of course they all know where Lower Brickwood Farm Cottage is. They have gone past it on their way to the pillar-box or the Green Man every day since they were six, and they don't know it as Lower Brickwood Farm Cottage; they know it as 'Davis's' or 'the old linney', or even, rather metaphysically, 'in over'. The postal address concerns nobody except the postman; and since he was up at half-past four this morning, he is presumably now in bed.

Jane was not one of those people who are too embarrassed to stop people and ask directions to places, but this facility wasn't a great deal of use to her. Of the six people she stopped and asked, two were retired Midlanders who had only been living in Melplash for a year or so, two were informative but completely incomprehensible, and one gave her a set of clear and concise directions which, had she followed them, would have taken Jane to Liverpool. The sixth informant was the landlord of the Green Man. He asked if she was from Pardoes and were they going to do the old place up at last? Jane remembered the name Pardoes from For Sale boards, and said yes for the sake of a quiet life.

By the time Jane got to Lower Brickwood Farm Cottage — which is, of course, about as far from Lower Brickwood Farm as you can go without leaving the parish — it was nearly dark. The directions she had been given led her down an unmetalled road to a yard containing five fallen-down corrugated-iron sheds, which looked for all the world as if they were used for storing the proceeds of plundering expeditions against the neighbouring villages. There were in addition a spectacular collection of damaged tractor tyres, a burnt-out Ford Anglia with a small tree growing

through the windscreen, several discarded items of farm
machinery and a derelict stone structure of great age.

Jane would probably have given up at this point, for she
was unused to such scenes; but she saw a crudely-painted
sign on the derelict stone structure which said 'Lower
Brickwood Farm Cottage' and decided that this must be it.
She walked up to the door and, being a well-brought-up
young lady, knocked. A voice in the back of her mind
called her an idiot, and she tried the door instead.

It wasn't locked; indeed, it gave a couple of inches before
coming to rest against something low and heavy and there-
after becoming immovable. It has previously been
recorded that the book Jane Doland had been reading
before she came to Bridport was a detective story, and it
should be noted that Jane was a devotee of this genre of
fiction. In many detective stories, the detective tries the
door of the lonely house to find it open but obstructed in
precisely this way. The obstruction, you can bet your sweet
life, will invariably turn out to be a dead body.

The last thing Jane wanted to find was a dead body.
However, the same inner voice that had called her an idiot
only moments before urged her to push against the door,
and when she did it opened. There was no dead body.
Instead, there was a heavy snowdrift of envelopes, most of
them extremely mouldy. Some of them had stamps with
the head of Queen Victoria on them. All of them had come
from the National Lombard Bank. Jane knelt down on a
century's worth of bank statements, invitations to take out
credit cards, insurance company mail-shots and encomia
of National Lombard Unit Trusts, and searched her
handbag for her torch.

A brief torchlight survey produced evidence that Lower
Brickwood Farm Cottage had not been inhabited for many,
many years by anything except small animals and birds.
It was extremely unpleasant, and Jane found herself
thanking Providence that she had been born with virtually
no sense of smell. She picked her way tentatively across
the floor to the middle of the one room that occupied the
ground floor and peered round.She saw that the staircase
had long since collapsed, along with large portions of the

ceiling. She decided that it probably wasn't terribly safe in here.

Just as she was about to leave, she saw a small tea-chest. It too contained envelopes. Having come this far and found so little, Jane made up her mind to investigate these. With extreme distaste, she fished out a handful of them and looked at them in the torchlight. They were all addressed to J Vanderdecker, and they contained invoices.

Whoever J Vanderdecker was, he had been a good customer of Jeanes' boatyard for a very long time. Each invoice was marked 'Paid with thanks' and related to some sort of repair done to a ship. A wooden ship, evidently; many references to tar, nails, boards, ropes, lines, sail-cloth, as well as a mass of nautical technical terms which Jane did not pretend to understand. The earliest invoice, which was so sodden with damp and rot that it fell to pieces in her hand, was dated 1704. The most recent one was exactly two years old. By the time her torch battery died on her, Jane had traced the invoices back in an unbroken line, from the present day to the reign of Queen Anne, at twenty-one year intervals.

Jane fumbled about in the dark looking for the door, and eventually she found it. Not the front door, with all the dead bank statements; the back door, which was also unlocked. Jane suddenly felt very nervous; something was going on, and from the facts she had at her command it looked as if it was something highly peculiar. Peculiar things, her common sense told her, are usually illegal. Perhaps she didn't want to know any more about it after all. Perhaps she should forget all about it and go back to London.

One thing was definite, and that was that she needed a drink, quickly. From what she had seen of it, the Green Man was fractionally less unpleasant than the snake-pit in a Harrison Ford adventure movie, but it was close and the landlord might tell her something else about Lower Brick-wood Farm Cottage. She went there.

'So they're selling the cottage, are they?' said the land-lord. 'They'll be lucky.'

The pub was virtually empty, and Jane wondered how

the landlord made a living out of it. She looked at him and decided that he probably did a little body-snatching on the side.

'Oh yes?' she said. 'Why not?'

The landlord looked at her. 'Haven't you been up there, then?' he asked.

'Yes,' Jane said, 'just now. But even if the building's all fallen down, the site must be worth something, surely.'

The landlord looked at her again, and Jane started to feel uncomfortable. 'You sure you went there?' he said.

Jane described what she had seen, leaving nothing out except the bank statements and the invoices. 'Is that the place you mean?'

'You didn't notice the smell?'

Jane explained that she had a truly abysmal sense of smell. The landlord burst out laughing. When, after a long time, he regained a semblance of coherence, he explained. He said that the place had been deserted for as long as everyone could remember because of the worst smell in the entire world. The story went that a foreigner with a funny name had rented it for a week or so, years and years back, before anyone now in the village had been born, and that ever since he left nobody had been able to stay more than ten minutes in the place, because of the smell. Everything had been tried to get rid of it, but it persisted. An attempt to use it as a pigsty had failed when all the pigs died. After being on the books of Messrs Pardoes for fifty-two years it had been taken off the market and forgotten about.

'Didn't they tell you that, then?' he concluded.

'No,' Jane said, 'they didn't mention it.'

'And you, not being able to smell, you didn't notice it.'

'That's right.'

'Well,' said the landlord, 'if that doesn't beat cock-fighting. That'll be a pound five, for the gin and tonic.'

Jane drove back to Union Hotel and went to bed. She didn't feel the lack of something to read. She was too preoccupied with thinking.

CHAPTER THREE

T he slight misunderstanding concerning the legend of the Flying Dutchman came about like this.

In the summer of 1839, a young German musician was sitting in a cafe in Paris drinking armagnac and thinking uncharitable thoughts about the regime of King Louis Philippe. It was a hot day, armagnac is by no means non-alcoholic, and the German was fiercely Republican by temperament, so it was perhaps understandable that the intensity of his reaction to the crimes against freedom that were going on all around him led him to speak his thoughts out loud. Before he knew what he was doing he was discussing them with the man sitting at the next table.

'Kings,' said the young German, 'are an anachronistic obscenity. Mankind will never be truly free until the last king's head is impaled on the battlements of his own palace.'

If the young German had bothered to look closely at the stranger (which of course he didn't) he would have seen a neatly-dressed weatherbeaten man of absolutely average height and build, who could have been any age between a gnarled twenty-nine and a boyish forty. There was just a hint of grey in his short beard, and his eyes were as sharp as paper can be when you lick the gum on an envelope. He considered the German's statement seriously, wiped a little foam off his moustache and replied that in his experience, for what it was worth, most kings were no worse than a visit to the dentist. The young German scowled at him.

'How can you say that?' he snarled. 'Consider some of the so-called great kings of history. Look at Xerxes! Look at Barbarossa! Look at Napoleon!'

'I thought,' interrupted the stranger, 'he was an
emperor.'

'Same thing,' said the young German. 'Look at Ivan the
Terrible,' he continued. 'Look at Philip of Spain!'

'I did,' said the stranger, 'once.'

Something about the way he said it made the young
German stop dead in his tracks and stare. It was as if he
had suddenly come face to face with Michaelangelo's
David, wearing a top hat and a frock coat, in the middle of
the Champs Elysées. He put down his glass and looked at
the stranger.

'What did you say?' he asked quietly.

'Please don't think I'm boasting,' said the stranger. 'I
don't know why I mentioned it, since it isn't really relevant
to what you were saying. Do please go on.'

'You *saw* Philip of Spain?'

'Just the once. At the Escurial, back in '85. I was in
Madrid with nothing to do — I'd just got rid of a load of
jute, you could name your own price for jute in Madrid
just then, I think they use it in rope-making — and I
thought I'd take a ride out to see the palace. And when I
got there — took me all day, it's thirty miles if it's a step —
Philip was just coming home from some visit or other. As I
remember I saw the top of his head for at least twelve
seconds before the guards moved me on. I could tell it was
the top of *his* head because it had a crown perched on it.
Sorry, you were saying?'

'How can you have *seen* Philip of Spain?' said the young
German. He never doubted the stranger's word for a
moment; but he needed to know, very badly indeed, how
this could be possible. 'He's been dead for two hundred
and fifty years.'

The stranger smiled; it was a very peculiar smile. 'It's
rather a long story,' he said.

'Never mind.'

'No but really,' the stranger said. His accent was very
peculiar indeed, the sort of accent that would always
sound foreign, wherever he went. 'When I say long I mean
long.'

'Never mind.'

'All right, then,' said the stranger. 'But don't say I didn't warn you.'

The young German nodded impatiently. The stranger took a pull at his beer and sat back in his chair.

'I was born in Antwerp,' he said, 'in 1553.' He paused. 'Aren't you going to say something?'

'No,' said the German.

'Funny,' said the stranger. 'I usually get interrupted at this point. I'll say it again. I was born in Antwerp in 1553. Fifteen fifty-three,' he repeated, as if he wished the young German would call him a liar. No such luck. He went on, '... And when I was fifteen my father got me a job with a merchant adventurer he owed some money to. The merchant was in the wool trade, like most people were then, and he said I could either work in the counting-house or go to sea, and since handling raw wool brings me out in a rash I chose the sea. Funny, isn't it, what decides you on your choice of career? I once knew a man who became a mercenary soldier just because he liked the long holidays. Dead before he was thirty, of course. Camp fever.

'Well, I worked hard and saved what I earned, just like you're supposed to, and before I was twenty-seven I had enough put by to take a share in a ship of my own. Not long after that I inherited some money and bought out my partners, and there I was with my own ship, at twenty-nine. Dear God, I'm sounding like one of those advertisements for correspondence courses. Excuse me, please.

'Anyway, soon I was doing very nicely indeed, despite the wars and the Spanish taxes — the Spanish were pretty well in charge of the Netherlands then, you remember, what with the Earl of Leicester and the Duke of Parma and all that — and I was all set to retire at thirty-five when I had a stroke of bad luck. Two strokes of bad luck. The first was the bottom falling out of jute, just when I'd got a ship crammed with the stuff. I'd put every last liard I had into jute, and suddenly you couldn't give it away. I hawked it all round Spain and Portugal and people just stared at me as if I was trying to sell them tainted beer. It was amazing; one minute you had perfect strangers accosting you in the street begging you to sell them some jute, the next thing you know jute is out. I'm not even sure that I know what jute is. I'm absolutely positive I don't care.

'And then I had my second stroke of bad luck, which happened just off Cadiz. I happened to run into the celebrated Francis Drake, who was on his way to singe the King of Spain's beard. You've heard of Francis Drake? Oh go d.

'When I said you couldn't give the stuff away I was exaggerating, because actually that's exactly what I did. I needed some persuasion, mind, but I think it was the way Sir Francis drew up alongside and said that if I didn't surrender my cargo he'd blow me out of the water that tipped the scale.

'Well, after that there was nothing much I could do except wait until Sir Francis had finished messing about in Cadiz harbour and go for a drink. Even that wasn't easy, what with the bombardment and so forth — one of the depressing things about licensed victuallers as a class is the way they dive for cover at the first little whiff of gunpowder — but eventually I found a tavern that wasn't actively burning down and where they were prepared to sell me fermented liquor.'

The stranger paused and looked at the bottom of his glass, but the young German didn't take the hint. He appeared to be spellbound, and the stranger carried on with his story.

'I'd been sitting there for a while, I don't know how long, when this man came in and sat down beside me. It's odd the way people sit down beside me in liquor-shops — no disrespect intended, of course, perish the thought. Anyway, he had this huge box with him, a sort of junior crate, and he was obviously worn out with lugging it about. Tall chap, thin, nose on him like an umbrella-handle, about your age or maybe a year or two older. I thought he was Spanish, or Italian, or he could have been French at a pinch. Anyway, a Southerner. Well, he looked even more miserable than I felt, which would have made him very miserable indeed, and I remember wondering if his trunk was full of jute. Incidentally, I've often wondered what Sir Francis did with all that good stuff he took off me. I bet he had no trouble shifting it at all.

'Do excuse me, I tend to get sidetracked. This Southerner came and sat down in this tavern, and I offered to
buy him a drink. He seemed offended.

' "I can afford my own drink, thank you very much," he
said. "That's the least of my worries." Brittle sort of bloke,
I thought, highly-strung.

' "All right then," I said. "You can buy me one."

'He looked at me, and I think he must have noticed that
I was still in my sea-boots and general working clothes,
because he suddenly became very much less hostile.

' "If you could tell me where I could find a ship to get me
across to England," he said, "I'd buy you as many drinks
as you like."

' "England!" I said. "You don't want to go there. The
English are a load of thieving bastards, they'll kill you for
the buttons on your doublet."

'He shook his head. "Better than being burnt alive," he
said. "And that's what's going to happen to me if I stay
around here much longer. I've got to get to a Protestant
country double quick."

'I didn't like the sound of this, but he wasn't going to
give up. "If you find me a ship that'll take me to England,"
he said, "I'll pay you a hundred pistoles, cash."

'To a refugee from the jute trade, this sounded too good
to pass up, even if the man was clearly three sols short of a
livre tournois, as we used to say when I was a boy. "What
would you pay me if I could provide a ship myself, then?" I
asked.

' "Think of a number," he replied, "then double it. I can
afford it, rest assured."

' "Who are you, then?" I asked.

' "Does it matter?" he said.

' "No," I replied, "I'm just incurably nosy." Which is
true, as it happens.

' "My name's Juan de Montalban, but I trade as Fortunatus Magnus," he said, with just a hint of pride. "You've
probably heard of me."

'I mumbled something about how out of touch you get
in my business, but I could see he was disappointed. It's

truc, though; you do lose track of things when you spend most of your life surrounded by hundreds of miles of open sea. Oh yes.

' "Well", he said, "if you must know I'm an alchemist."

' "You mean cures for headaches and things?" I said.

' "Certainly not," he replied. "I am a philosopher, and I have discovered the answer to the riddle of transmigration of the elements."

'I was startled. "Base metal into gold and all that sort of thing?" I said. He sneered slightly.

' "That's transmutation, not transmigration," he said. "Vulgar party trick, though it pays the rent, I'll grant you. I do that, too."

'Suddenly I could understand why he wanted to get out of Spain in such a hurry. Apart from being incredibly hard on heretics — and alchemists are heretics by definition — the Spanish had a peculiar horror of anything which might disrupt the nice little monopoly on gold and silver they'd been enjoying ever since Cortes came back from the Americas. Have you ever been to America? Funny place. You can't get a decent boiled egg for love nor money.

' "Be that as it may," he said, "I'll give you five thousand pistoles for a ride to Bristol. Good Spanish coin," he added, "I wouldn't try and palm you off with the home-made stuff."

'By now my natural scepticism was telling me that alchemists you meet in taverns at the end of a long, difficult day may well turn out not to be alchemists at all, particularly if they end up trying to borrow money or sell you a lump of cut-price gold; but there was something unusually convincing about him — probably the way he wasn't trying to convince me. Do you see what I'm getting at, by any chance?'

The young German nodded. He saw only too well.

'So,' continued the stranger, 'I said that if he showed up at the quay next morning with five thousand pistoles I'd take him to England with the greatest of pleasure, and then I went off to get drunk in slightly less eccentric company. I was so successful in this — getting drunk is one of the things I'm best at — that I didn't get up till quite late the next morning, and I reckoned that even if he'd kept the appointment he'd have given up and gone away long since. But when I got down to the quay at about half-past ten — I had some business to see to in the town first — there he was, looking extremely nervous and asking what the hell had kept me.

'I explained about my bad headache, but he didn't seem terribly interested. He did, however, seem extremely anxious to show me a large number of very genuine-looking gold coins, and I decided that even if he was a lunatic he was a rich lunatic, and that if he wanted to go to Bristol then I wanted to take him there, before any unscrupulous character turned up who might exploit the man's mental frailty by asking for six thousand pistoles.

'My crew were by no means overjoyed to be off again so soon, and when I told them that we were going to England they made some very wounding remarks about my intelligence. They pointed out, perfectly accurately, that Sir Francis Drake was English, and so were John Hawkins and Black Jack Norris, and that a country capable of producing such unsavoury characters was somewhere they were in no hurry to visit. In fact, so determined were they that I had to take the unprecedented step of promising to pay them before they would do any work at all.

'Their fears turned out to be absolutely groundless. Sir Francis and his fellow merrymakers were far too busy chivvying honest businessmen off Puental to bother us, and an unusually obliging wind took us right up to the mouth of the Bristol Channel.'

The stranger hesitated for a moment. 'You don't really want to hear the rest of this,' he said. 'I think it would be much better if we go back to discussing kings. Take Charlemagne, for instance. Did you know that Charlemagne didn't learn to read until he was forty?'

'Never mind Charlemagne,' said the young German. 'Go on with what you were saying.'

'I'd really much rather talk about Charlemagne,' said the stranger, 'if it's all the same to you. Believe me, I have very good reasons.'

The young German said something vulgar about Charlemagne, and the stranger shrugged and went on.

'It was then,' he said, 'that things started to go wrong. The unusually obliging wind went away again, leaving us stranded in mid-sea with nothing to do but look at the coastline of Wales, which is not something I would recommend unless you have an overwhelmingly keen interest in geology. To make matters worse, something unsavoury got into the ship's beer, and when you put twenty Dutchmen on a ship — did I mention we were mostly Dutch? Well, we were — when you put twenty Dutchmen and a *Scot* on a ship in the middle of the sea with nothing to drink but cloudy beer, then you have a recipe for unpleasantness on your hands.

'Halfway through the second day we were starting to feel more than usually thirsty, and by that evening the ship was alive with parched mariners in search of hidden caches of the right stuff. Me among them, I might add; I had an idea that the answer to the riddle of the transmigration of matter wasn't the only thing Fortunatus Magnus had in his luggage. You see, he was the only person on board who didn't seem worried about the beer crisis. When the first mate told him about it, all he said was "So what?" Suspicious, you'll agree.

'As soon as I'd got his big trunk open — it didn't take more than five or six blows with the axe — my suspicions were confirmed; there was this huge glass bottle arrangement, carefully packed with straw and about half-full of the most delicious-looking tawny-yellow liquid you ever saw in your whole life. I closed what was left of the lid of the trunk and went in search of privacy and a tankard.

'The tankard was no problem at all; but more or less the only privacy you can find on my ship is in the crow's nest, which is why I tend to spend a lot of time there. Even then, I wasn't going to take any chances, since the crow's nest is directly above the beer-barrel — we keep it permanently on deck, where everyone can see it; just knowing it's there can be a great help at times of stress — and there was a crowd of indomitable optimists gathered round it trying to fine the repulsive mess with Irish moss and fishmeal. I pulled the rope ladder up after me, uncorked the bottle, and poured myself a drink.

'It tasted odd to start with, but it had a certain some-thing, and after the third tankard I was feeling much more relaxed and in tune with the music of the spheres. Just then the alchemist appeared on deck, looking absolutely livid, like a sort of manic cormorant. I reckoned I knew why, but by then of course I couldn't care less.

'He started yelling about how someone had broken into his trunk and stolen something of great value, and of course I was grinning all over my silly face with pleasure. Nobody was taking much notice of him apart from me, because a couple of the crew had just put another cupful of Irish moss in the beer-barrel and were peering anxiously at it to see if it would do any good. Funny stuff, Irish moss — I think it's made up of ground-up fish bones, and I haven't the faintest idea why ... Sorry, you're right, I do tend to wander off the subject from time to time. It's probably subconscious.

'I imagine the alchemist must have lost heart, because he stopped shouting after a while and went and leaned sullenly against the rail, muttering to himself in Latin and breathing heavily through his nose. Did I mention he had a big nose? Oh, well, anyway, what with the drink and the general *stimmung*, and it was extremely wrong of me, I admit, but I suddenly felt the urge to let the alchemist know exactly what had become of his precious hoarded treasure. After all, selfishness is a major sin, and the creep hadn't offered any of us so much as a sniff of the cork. I leaned over the edge of the crow's nest, waved the flagon at him, and jeered.

'Given the quantity of its contents which I had consumed, waving the flagon was a bad move. It was, as I said, a big thing, and as soon as I lifted it up so that the alchemist could see it, I felt it slipping through my fingers. I made a desperate attempt to grab it back, but all I succeeded in doing was spilling its contents, which went soaring off into the air in a magnificent golden wave, like a sort of proof rainbow. A moment later I followed it, since I'd completely lost my balance; and that is a foolish thing to do in a crow's nest. Shall we talk about Charlemagne now? All right, please yourself.

'It's a very, very strange feeling to fall from a great height, I can tell you, and not something I would recommend to anybody who isn't employed by the Revenue. It seems to take a long time, and it isn't actually particularly frightening, even though the logical part of your mind is telling you that when you land you are definitely going to die. Of course I did land — eventually — and very unpleasant it was, too. Only I didn't die. I didn't even break anything. I just lay there on my back feeling an utter fool, with the crew gathered round staring at me as if I'd just grown an extra ear.

'After a while I got up and walked round the deck a few times, and my loyal crew seemed to lose interest. They muttered something about some people being born lucky, looked back a couple of times to make sure I was still alive and hadn't been fooling them, and went back to the beer-barrel. The only person who seemed to want to talk to me was the alchemist, and since I had a fairly good idea of what he was likely to say I kept plenty of deck between him and myself. He was gaining on me steadily when a terrific cheer went up from the vicinity of the beer-barrel.

'I pushed my way to the front and saw the most miraculous sight. That beer was actually clearing; the Irish moss must have done the trick after all. There was a very short interval, while everyone dived for vessels of any description, and then an orgy of sploshing noises while twenty involuntary abstainers made up for lost time. I had to use all my authority as captain to get close enough to the barrel to dip a tin cup in.

'In the general excitement I had forgotten all about the alchemist, and when I emerged from the ruck round the barrel he was standing over me with a face only marginally more pleasing to the eye than Sir Francis Drake's culverins. The only thing to do, I thought, was try to jolly him along.

'"Now look," I said, "I'm sorry I pinched your beer but there's plenty for everyone now. Grab a jug and get stuck in."

'"It wasn't beer," he said.

' "Porter, then," I replied, "perry, ale, whatever. Does it matter?"

' "Yes," he said. "That was my elixir."

' "Your what?" I asked.

' "My elixir," he replied. "The philosopher's stone. The elixir of life. The living water."

'I frowned. I hate beer snobs, don't you? "All right," I said, "so it was better than ship's beer, but let's not get carried away. They say you can get a very nice pint in Bristol."

' "It wasn't beer," he said solemnly. "It was elixir."

'Then something clicked in my brain and I remembered something. I remembered that I had just fallen out of my own crow's nest onto a deck of hard oak plants without suffering so much as a nosebleed.

' "Elixir?" I said.

' "Yes," he said. "E for Enrico, L for Lorenzo, I for Iachimo, X for Xeres, I for Iago, R for Roderigo, elixir. And you drank it."

'I felt unwell. "Is it safe?" I asked.

'He grinned. "I don't know," he said, "but it definitely works."

' "Does it?" I asked.

' "I think you just proved that," he said, "by falling out of the crow's nest. Or how would you interpret it? Luck? A sudden gust of wind? Dry rot in the deck? What do you expect if you drink the elixir of life?" '

The stranger fell silent and drew the tip of his finger round the rim of his glass. 'Anyway,' he said at last, 'that's how I came to acquire eternal life, for what it's worth. All this talk of beer has made me thirsty. Can I get you one?'

The young German replied in a small, awed voice that he would like another armagnac, and the stranger entered into an oral contract with a waiter for an armagnac and a half-litre of Stella Artois. Once the contract had been discharged to the satisfaction of both parties, the stranger continued.

'Not only me,' he said, 'my whole crew as well. You see, when I spilt the rest of the stuff in the flagon, just before my untimely descent from the crow's nest, it landed in the beer-barrel, rendering the beer free from impurities and immortalising everyone who drank it. The alchemist saw it happen, and once he had calmed down he explained it all to us. I don't think we were really convinced until he drank a half-pint of the beer and shot himself. Then we were all profoundly convinced. Especially the first mate; it was his pistol the alchemist borrowed, and when he pressed it to his head and pulled the trigger, the barrel burst. The first mate was livid, of course, but when he tried thumping Fortunatus Magnus all he did was squash his wedding-ring. The man was completely invulnerable. So were we all. As soon as it had sunk in, we all went completely mad and started belting each other about with our swords and roaring with laughter until there wasn't anything larger than a paperknife left on the whole ship. Mind you, we had all been drinking rather heavily.

'As for Fortunatus, he cheered up very quickly. It turned out that he had been lugging this elixir of his around with him for years but had never found anyone brave enough to test it out on, and he was damned if he was going to risk it himself, since he was petrified of possible side-effects. Naturally we asked him what possible side-effects, but all he would say was that so far as he knew there weren't any but we were bound to find out sooner or later, weren't we? The only living thing he'd ever given any to, he told us, was a stray cat in Cadiz, and the contrary thing had escaped before he could do much in the way of properly-organised tests. Mind you, I don't think he had intended to drink any himself, even when he saw that it hadn't killed us outright. He just got caught up in the general spirit of adventure and wanted to justify his discovery to us. Common or garden scientific vanity. Well, there we are.

'The next morning we got a breeze that took us straight into Bristol, where Fortunatus was immediately arrested as a Spanish spy and thrown in prison. He went very quietly for an invulnerable man, but when we offered to rescue him he said no, he'd much rather go quietly, since he had a lot to think over and prison seemed as good a place as any. So we left him to it and set out to spend five thousand gold pistoles on refreshments and riotous living.

'We were all fairly well pleased with ourselves, as you can imagine, what with suddenly being made immortal and having five thousand gold pistoles. At first, we couldn't see beyond the immediate benefits, such as being able to clean up on extremely dangerous wagers involving tall buildings, loaded firearms and ravenous bears; but even after the first wave of euphoria had worn off and nobody would bet us any more, we reckoned that we had done all right for ourselves, all things considered. For example, being immortal we were incapable of starving to death, which meant a tremendous saving on food; we could drink as much as we liked without the slightest danger of damaging our health; and since we were completely immune from what was then described as the Pox ... Anyway, we felt we had every reason to be cheerful, one way or another. My only regret was that the morning before we left Cadiz I had wasted five pistoles taking out a life assurance policy, which was now obviously of no use whatsoever.'

As the stranger stopped speaking again the young German caught sight of his face. It was a terrible sight, completely indescribable, and the young German looked away quickly. He could still see it behind his eyelids days later. He felt a sudden urge to discuss the career of Charlemagne, but before he could do this the stranger resumed his narrative.

'However,' said the stranger, 'there were side-effects. Shall I tell you about the side-effects? Do please say if you'd rather I didn't. We could talk about Gustavus Adolphus if you like.'

'Tell me,' said the young German, 'about the side effects.'

'We spent a fortnight in Bristol drinking to excess and laying up a cargo — wool, I think, and tin ore, and a bit of salt fish, definitely no jute — and then we left. We would have liked to stay longer, but we had somehow made ourselves unpopular in Bristol and most of the taverns had banned us — and that took some doing in Bristol, even then. So we set sail for Flanders, and we made good headway for a day or two, until the wind dropped again.

But we didn't care; we had plenty of beer now, and no
killjoy alchemist on board. It was then we noticed it.'

'Noticed what?'

'The smell. The nastiest, most sordid, least pleasant
smell you ever came across in all your born days. Nothing
more unlike the scent of dewy roses could ever exist this
side of Plato's Republic. And the smell was coming from
us.'

The stranger finished his drink and looked through the
empty glass at something the young German couldn't see.
The young German decided that that was probably just as
well.

'After a day of frantic and hysterical washing,' continued
the stranger, 'which only seemed to make it worse, one of
us hit on the idea of consulting the alchemist's notebooks,
which he had left behind on the ship when he got arrested.
Sure enough, we found the answer, in a passage where our
old buddy Fortunatus was describing his experiments on
the cat in Cadiz. He had done his best to get round the
problem by fiddling the recipe here and there, and he was
pretty positive he had fixed it, which I suppose explains
why he drank it himself after we'd done his guinea-pig
work for him.'

'Well,' said the young German, 'that was fascinating. I
really ought to be getting ...'

'I really wish,' said the stranger, 'I could describe that
smell for you now. Try to imagine, if you possibly can, a
muck-heap on which someone has placed the decomposing
bodies of three hundred and thirty-three dead foxes. Next
to this muck-heap try and picture an open sewer. Not just
an ordinary open sewer, mind — this one collects the
effluent from an ammonia works on the way. The muck-
heap is, of course, in the back yard of a cholera hospital ...
No, don't bother. Just take it from me, it was an absolute
zinger of a smell.

'Anyway, it soon became painfully obvious that unless
and until we found some way of toning this odour down a
bit, the only place we could be was as far out in the middle
of the ocean as we could possibly get. So we set sail for
nowhere in particular, rationed the beer, and waited. We

waited and we waited and we waited. Occasionally something would happen to relieve the monotony. A Barbary corsair would creep up on us and attempt to board us, which was good for a laugh. One of us would go for a swim, and an hour later you couldn't see the surface of the water for dead fish. Not to mention the run-in we had with what you would know as the Spanish Armada; boy, did we have some fun with them! Oh, don't get me wrong, there were the occasional highlights. But most of the time it was dead boring.

'After three months we were all so crazy with boredom and mutual loathing that we decided to blow up the ship and ourselves with it. It didn't do any good, of course. The ship blew up all right, but we didn't. We floated, and after a while the number of dead fish got so embarrassing we decided we'd better swim on a bit before we wiped out the livelihood of every fisherman in the Atlantic Ocean. After a day or so of nonchalant doggy-paddling we ran into another ship. They must have been downwind of us, because before we'd got within two hundred yards of them they'd taken to the boats and were rowing away as fast as their arms could work the oars. That sort of thing really dents your self-confidence, you can imagine. You begin to despair of making those lasting relationships with people that add the interest to life.

'Well, after we'd made the new ship comfortable — painted out the name and got it nice and squalid — we sailed on a bit longer and a bit longer still, and we came to a decision. The time had come, we decided, to try and do something about it, rather than tamely giving in. That's the way we are in Holland; every brick wall you come to has big red marks where people have been beating their heads against it. Now it so happened that when we blew the ship up I had old Fortunatus' notebooks in the pocket of my doublet, and although the ink had run in a few places they were still legible — I think he'd written them in some kind of incredibly clever new ink, and it makes you wonder why he ever bothered with turning base metals into gold when he had such a fantastically commercial proposition at his fingertips. Anyway, we read through those notebooks until we knew them by heart. We discussed them, argued about them, tried experiment after experiment, even tried reading them upside down; all totally useless, needless to say, but at least it passed the time, and although we didn't discover an antidote to the elixir we did find out some extremely interesting things along the way. Extremely interesting ... I'm sorry, I'm wandering off again. I do tend to do that, I'm afraid. It comes of having nothing to do for long periods of time but talk; it makes you extremely wordy.

'Where was I? Oh yes. One morning, exactly seven years after we'd first drunk the elixir, we all woke up to find that the smell had actually gone. It was amazing. We were still invulnerable and immortal, of course, but at least we didn't niff quite so much, and the first thing we did was set course for the nearest land-mass, which happened to be Le Havre. We had all assumed that one of our numerous experiments had finally worked, and that we'd cracked it.

'We spent the next month getting thrown out of every tavern, inn and brothel in Le Havre, predictably enough, and we were just on the point of saying goodbye to each other and going our separate ways — as you can easily appreciate, after all that time on the ship and what with the smell and everything, we all hated each other so much you wouldn't credit it — when the first delicate whiff of the Great Pong came filtering through and we knew that we weren't home and dry after all. We spent a frantic afternoon buying up every drop of beer, every chess-set, every book and every piece of chemical apparatus that we could lay our hands on, and we got back to the ship just before a mob of extremely savage Frenchmen with handkerchiefs in front of their faces threw us into the sea.

'We were still kidding ourselves that we had found an antidote and that it had worn off, and so we carefully recreated all the experiments we had done in the last seven years, and made scrupulous notes in proper joined-up writing in a big leather-bound book. But when we'd tried everything and nothing had worked, we lost heart and spent a whole year playing shove-ha'penny all round the coast of Africa. We did land once or twice, but only for hours at a time, and there is — or was — a tribe in Madagascar that worships us as gods; pretty ceremonies, very heavy on the incense. Now then; seven years after our brief visit to Le Havre, the smell stopped again, and we scrambled into Tangier to do our shopping — we wasted a week getting there, what with contrary winds — knowing full well that we had exactly a month before we had to leave. We were right, of course. Three weeks later, the smell came back, and seven years later it went away again. That's the way the pattern works, and once we'd spent forty-nine years reading up on alchemical theory we all knew why, it was blindingly obvious.

'We were all pretty good alchemists by then, incidentally, and that's how we make our living. For eighty-three months in each seven years we turn base metal into gold, and in the remaining month we spend it. That's the problem with alchemy; it works all right, but compared with simply taking a pick and a shovel and digging the stuff out of the ground it's hopelessly inefficient. There I go again, digressing. Do please excuse me.'

There was a very, very long silence, during which the young German tried to recapture the use of his brain.

'So you've been alive since 1553?' he said at last.

'Yes,' said the stranger, 'that puts it very neatly. And also in perspective. Is there anything else you want to ask me?'

'No,' said the German. 'No, I think you've said quite enough.'

'Oh well,' said the stranger. 'I seem to have that effect on people. Not,' he went on, 'that I tend to tell my story much these days. In fact, you're the first person in over thirty years I've told it to.'

'Well ...' the young German started to say; then he thought better of it and decided to stare horribly at the stranger, like a man in one of Hieronymus Bosch's less cheerful paintings. The stranger seemed to find the silence awkward, and to break the tension he started to speak again.

'Oh yes,' said the stranger, 'I've had some interesting experiences in my time. Well, fairly interesting. Now you mentioned Napoleon a moment ago. The only time I met Napoleon ...'

The young German suddenly jumped up, screamed, and ran away, very fast.

Vanderdecker shook his head and went to the bar for another drink. It had been roughly the same the last time he told the story, when he had landed in Porlock and met the man who was on his way to a wedding. That, he had said to himself, is the last time; but the pleasure of talking to someone new after seven years with Antonius, Johannes, Pieter and Cornelius had gone to his head.

In case you were wondering, the young German made a moderate recovery, after two or three months of careful nursing, and went on to become the composer of such celebrated operatic masterpieces as *Lohengrin, Götterdämmerung* and *Parsifal.* To his dying day, on the other hand, his manner was always very slightly unsettling, particularly to strangers, and if anyone happened to mention Philip II of Spain he would burst out into maniacal laughter which could only be cured with morphine injections. Unlike Vanderdecker's earlier confidant, however, he never became addicted to narcotics, and the rather garbled version of the story which he embodied in his opera *The Flying Dutchman* can probably be attributed to nothing more serious than artistic licence or a naturally weak memory.

CHAPTER FOUR

The plump young man is now two years older and an inch and an eighth plumper, and he has become a partner in the firm of Moss Berwick. Oddly enough, there were no comets seen that evening nine weeks ago when Mr Clough and Mr Demaris told him the wonderful, wonderful news; the only possible explanation is that it was a cloudy night, and the celestial announcement was obscured by a mass of unscheduled cumulo-nimbus. These things happen, and all we can do is put up with them.

Although they had made the plump young man (whose name, for what it is worth, was Craig Ferrara) a partner, they had not seen fit to tell him about The Thing. Or at least, they had not told him what it was; they had hinted at its existence, but that was all. For his part, Craig Ferrara had been aware that it existed for some time, ever since he had been allowed access to the computer files generally known in the firm as the Naughty Bits.

Moss Berwick's computer was a wonderful thing. It lived, nominally, in Slough; but, rather like God, it was omnipresent and of course omniscient. Unlike God, you could telephone it from any one of the firm's many offices and even, if you were a show-off like Craig Ferrara, from your car. You could ask it questions. Sometimes it would answer and sometimes not, depending on whether it wanted to. Not could, mark you; wanted to. It would take a disproportionate amount of ingenuity to think up a sensible question that the computer couldn't answer if it wanted to, up to and including John Donne's famous conversation-killers about where the lost years are and who cleft the Devil's foot — and this despite the fact that the Devil is not (as yet) a client of Moss Berwick.

But in order to ask the computer high-rolling questions like these, you have to be the right sort of person. Only someone with a Number can get at that part of the computer; all that earthworms like Jane Doland can get out of it are a lot of waffle about the Retail Price Index for March 1985. Not that Jane Doland hadn't been trying, ever since she came back from Bridport. That, although he didn't know it, was the main reason why Craig Ferrara had become a partner.

Craig Ferrara was only human, and so he would dearly have loved to find out what The Thing was. However, it had been made unequivocally clear to him that he didn't really want to know by Mr Clough and Mr Demaris; and although in law he was now a sharer of their joys, sorrows and financial commitments, he was not so stupid as to believe that a mere legal fiction made him worthy to loosen the straps of their sandals, should they ever behave so uncharacteristically as to wear such things. His relationship to The Thing was that of ignorant guardian. If any member of his department started showing an unhealthy interest in anything to do with Bridport, he was to report directly to Mr Clough and Mr Demaris, who would take the necessary action. What that action might be Mr Ferrara knew not, but he had a shrewd notion that it would be the terror of the earth.

A brief glance at the computer's call-out sheet told Mr Ferrara that Jane Doland, the girl with the tin ear, had made a large number of Bridport-related enquiries of the computer in the last few months, most of them at times of day when she could normally be relied on to be hanging from one of those Dalek's antennae things in a compartment in a Tube train. This was exactly the sort of thing Mr Ferrara had been told to keep an eye out for, and he felt a degree of pride at having immediately succeeded with the project his betters had entrusted to him. Find us a mole, Clough and Demaris had said, and here one was. For such a fiercely, passionately corporate man as Mr Ferrara, it was roughly the same as discovering insulin.

But accountants are not hasty people. They do not out

with their rapiers the moment they hear rats behind the arras. Smile and smile and smile and be an accountant is the watchword. Before calling in Clough and Demaris, Mr Ferrara resolved to try one more, utterly diabolical test. He would give Doland the RPQ Motor Factors file.

The RPQ Motor Factors file, it should be explained, was where failed accountants went to die. How the affairs of a relatively straightforward small business had come to get into such a state of Byzantine complexity nobody really knew; it had just happened, like the British economy, and the more people tried to straighten it out, the more it wrapped itself round its own intestines. Just reading through the horrible thing was enough to make most young accountants run away and become wood-turners, but trying to sort it out was an infallible cure for sanity. Jane Doland was henceforth to be its custodian; furthermore, she was to be given a month to produce a balance sheet and profit-and-loss account.

Although a degree of sadism went into the decision — Ferrara could never forget that Jane Doland was the girl who didn't appreciate Wagner — it was mainly a shrewd piece of tactical planning. Anyone with a month to sort out the RPQ Motor Factors file wouldn't have time to brush their teeth, let alone ask the computer awkward questions about Bridport or The Thing. By the time Jane Doland had either succeeded or failed with RPQ, she would be so sick of sorting things out and investigating anomalies that she could safely be entrusted with the expenditure accounts of the CIA.

Mr Ferrara dictated the memo, smiled and started to hum the casting scene from *Die Freischutz*.

It is galling, to say the least, to have been to every place in the world and then not know where somewhere is. It's rather like having a doctorate in semiconductor physics and not being able to wire a plug. You begin to wonder whether it's all been worthwhile.

Vanderdecker, typically, blamed himself. Instead of frittering away his time and money on beer and scientific journals, he should have remembered that he was, first and foremost, a ship's captain and got some decent charts. Quite a few of the ones he still used had bits of Latin and sea-serpents in the margins, and he defended his retention of them by saying that: (i) he was used to them, (ii) they looked nice and (iii) in the circumstances, what the hell did it matter anyway?

Since his crew generally lacked the intellectual capacity to argue with a man who spoke in bracketed roman numerals, he had managed to have his own way on this point, but the short-sightedness of this attitude was coming home to him at last.

He had heard of Dounreay; he had an idea it was somewhere in Scotland, on the coast. That, however, was as far as his memory took him. After four hundred years of existence, one's powers of recollection become erratic. Just as, when a stamp collector has been going for a year or so, he will discard all the used British definitives his elderly female relatives have been clipping off envelopes for him and start buying choicer specimens, so Vanderdecker was becoming selective in what he chose to keep in his head.

He rummaged around in his map-chest and dug out a chart he hadn't tried yet. Unfortunately it showed Jerusalem as being at the centre of the world, and he put it back with a sigh. The next one he found was extremely noncommital on the topic of Australia, and that too was discarded. As it happened, Vanderdecker had been the first European to set foot on Australian soil. He had taken one look at it, said 'No, thank you very much' and gone to New Guinea instead. Subsequent visits had not made him review his opinion.

There was, he said to himself, only one thing for it. He would have to ask the First Mate. Not that Antonius would know the answer; but it would at least put his own ignorance in some sort of respectable context.

Antonius was playing chess with the cook on the quarter-deck. Vanderdecker saw that of Antonius' once proud black army, only the King remained. This was by no means unusual. Antonius had been playing chess for three or four hours a day for four centuries and he still hadn't won a game.

'Antonius,' he said, 'do you happen to know where Dounreay is?'

Antonius looked up irritably. His expression suggested that he had been on the point of perfecting a sequence of manoeuvres which would have resulted in victory in four moves, and that his captain's interruption had dispersed this coup to the four winds.

'No,' he said. 'Is it in Italy?'

'Thanks anyway,' said Vanderdecker.

'I know where Dounreay is,' said the cook.

Vanderdecker stared. It was remarkable that anything should surprise him any more, but this was very much out of the ordinary. The last time the cook had been deliberately helpful was when Sebastian van Doorning had gone through a brief wrist-slashing phase and the cook had lent him one of his knives.

'Do you?' Vanderdecker asked.

'Yes,' replied the cook, affronted. 'It's on the north coast of Scotland.'

Vanderdecker frowned. 'How do you know that?' he asked.

'I was born there,' said the only non-Dutch member of the crew. 'They've built a power station over it now. Typical.'

Well yes, Vanderdecker said to himself, it is rather. Miserable things tended to happen to the cook, probably because they were sure of an appreciative welcome.

'So you could tell me how to get there?' he asked. The cook shook his head.

'No way,' he said. 'I'm a cook, not a pilot. I couldn't navigate this thing if you paid me.' The cook frowned. 'That reminds me . . .' he said.

'All right, all right,' said Vanderdecker. 'But you'd recognise it if you saw it again?'

'Maybe,' said the cook, 'maybe not, how the hell should I know? Like I said, they've built a bloody fast-breeder whatsisname on top of my poor granny's wee croft, so there's probably not a lot of the old place left to see.'

'Thanks anyway,' Vanderdecker repeated, and wandered off to have a stare at the sea. It was his equivalent to beating his head repeatedly against a wall.

On the other hand, he said to himself, as he let his eye roam across the grey waves, the number of nuclear power stations on the North Coast of Scotland is probably fairly small. All one would have to do in order to locate it is to cruise along keeping one's eyes open for three-headed fish and luminous oysters. And God knows, we're not in any hurry. We never are.

He walked back along the deck, feeling that he had earned this month's can of Heineken. As he passed by the cook (who had finally and irretrievably checkmated the First Mate, who seemed very surprised) he stopped and said thank you.

'Forget it,' growled the cook, in the tone of one who firmly believes that his request will be acted on.

'Just one more thing,' said Vanderdecker. 'How did you know they'd built a nuclear power station on your granny's wee croft?'

'I saw it last time we were there,' said the cook. 'Last February, I think it was. I seem to remember it rained.'

Vanderdecker didn't say, Then why the bloody hell didn't you say so earlier. He said thank you. Then he went to have another good look at the sea.

Jane was feeling pleased with herself. Just when she had begun to think that her career was going nowhere and that she might soon be looking for another job, here she was with an important new file to look after.

Not that she was particularly fond of her career, but it did help pay the rent, and she was enough of a realist to know that it was probably the only one she was likely to have, what with the vacancy of Princess of Wales having been filled and so many O-Levels being needed for pearl-diving these days.

She knew for a fact that the RPQ Motor Factors file was something of a mixed blessing. Look at Jennifer Cartwright. Look at Stephen Parkinson. In fact, you would need binoculars if you wanted to do this, since both of them had left the firm and gone to work in Cornwall after a week or so with RPQ. A hot potato with the pin out, as Mr Peters would say.

Of course, it would mean less time to try chasing up that strange thing she had come across in Bridport, but that was no bad thing. Ever since she had got back to the sanity of London, she had been seriously doubting whether she had actually seen all those curious and inexplicable things. There is nothing like a few trips up and down the Bakerloo line to convince you that nobody can live for ever, and the fierce determination to get to the bottom of it all had waned after the first few cracks at the computer.

It stood to reason that if there was anything to find out, it would come up on the wire from Slough. Slough — figuratively speaking — was brilliant. You could ask Slough anything and the answer would be waiting for you before you had time to blink twice. But she had found nothing, which must surely mean that there was nothing to find and that the Vanderdecker nonsense must all have been a figment of her imagination.

The coffee machine was going through one of its spasmodic fits of nihilism, during which it produced cups of white powder floating on cold grey fluid, and Jane decided to have tea instead. The tea came from a device which looked like a knight's helmet, and generally tasted as if the knight hadn't washed his hair for a long time, but Jane could live with that now that her future seemed slightly more secure. It is remarkable how quickly ennui evaporates when faced with a rent demand. Her Snoopy mug filled, she returned to her desk and opened the RPQ file.

She read for about half an hour, and found that she was almost enjoying it. Jane had a perverse curiosity about the people who had left the firm shortly before she had joined it. Had they still been there and she had got to know them, she would doubtless have filed them away in her mental portrait gallery under Poison Toads and that would have been that. But knowing them only from their letters and file notes, she was able to recreate them as they should have been. She knew most of their names, but some were no more than initials or references, and of course these were the truly glamorous ones. She would, for example, have loved to know more about RS/AC/5612, who had passed briefly and intriguingly through the RPQ story like a Hollywood star playing a three-minute cameo, dictating four letters and disappearing into the darkness like the sparrow in the mead-hall. She pictured him — it had to be a him — as a tall, cynical man with hollow eyes and long, sensitive hands who had eventually turned his back on accountancy, started to write the Great Novel and died of consumption. At the other extreme there was APC/JL; an old man, broken by frustration and disappointment, struggling to keep his job in the face of relentless youth and seizing on the RPQ file as his last chance to make his mark. There was a pathetic dignity in his last letter to Johnson Chance Davison, and the dying fall of his 'we thank you sincerely in anticipation of your reply' moved her almost to tears.

Jane suddenly stopped dead in her tracks. She instinctively knew that the paper in front of her was different. For a start it was hand-written, and the handwriting was erratic. It read as follows:

THE VANDERDECKER POLICY

This has nothing to do with RPQ. This is a warning, in case they do it to you too.

I found out about the Vanderdecker Policy, which is the proper name for The Thing. It's a safe bet, whoever you are, that you've found out about it too or you wouldn't have been given this file.

The Vanderdecker Policy is important. It's so important that anybody who finds out about it gets given the RPQ file. That's how important it is. Sorry if you can't read my writing, but I daren't have anybody type this out, in case they find out. That's why I've put this message here, in the RPQ file, because it's the only place nobody would ever think of looking. Except you, and you're only looking at it because they've found out that you've found out. Which is why they gave you the RPQ file.

I can't risk doing anything about the Vanderdecker Policy. I can't tell you where to look or what I've found out. I'm getting out and starting a new life a long, long way away, where they won't find me.

Whatever you do, don't let them know that you know
that they know. For God's sake stay with it, for as long as
you can stick it out. Someone's got to blow the whistle on
it sooner or later, it just can't go on like this much longer,
it all has to stop.

So just carry on, pretend you don't know they know,
do something about it. If you've read this, please tear it
out and burn it.

Jane looked round, then tore the sheet off the treasure tag,
folded it up and stuffed it into her pocket. Her heart was
beating like a pneumatic drill.

Somehow she survived the rest of the day and took the
train home as normal. Every few minutes, in the intervals
of looking over her shoulder for murderers, she tried telling
herself that this was just some poor fool who'd finally
flipped after doing too many bank reconciliation statements, but the name Vanderdecker was too big and too
noisy to ignore.

She packed everything she thought she could possibly need,
plus a pot of marmalade and her hot water bottle with the
woolly tiger cover, into her car and drove. At the first
National Lombard cash dispenser she saw, she stopped and
withdrew all the money the machine would let her have. If
only she'd been sensible, she told herself, and not been put
off by all those idiotic white horses in their advertising cam-
paigns, she could have had a bank that wouldn't betray her
whereabouts to Slough every time she made a withdrawal.

The question was where to go, but the answer wasn't
easy. She thought of her parents' house, but the thought
made her shudder; her father had succumbed to National
Lombard Unit Trust propaganda nine months after
retiring to the Sussex coast. Surely they wouldn't do
anything to hurt her parents? Better not to think about that.

Where else, then? Her sister had a National Lombard
Home Loan, so that was out. Ever since she had left the
world behind and taken to accountancy she had alienated
all her friends by boring them to tears with accountancy
stories. That only left. . .

No.

Yes, why not? It's a long way from London. Even idiots have their uses. Even obnoxious, repulsive, pathetic little gnomes. She found a call-box and fished out her diary. Fortunately, the local vandals had spared the dialling codes section and she located the code for Wick. The phone started to ring. It was answered.

'Is that you, Shirley?' she asked. Shirley said yes, it was.

Jane took a deep breath. Even when her life was quite possibly at stake, this was extremely distasteful.

'Look, Shirley,' she said — the very words were like a live worm in her mouth — 'I'm going to be up near you for a week or so, can I come and stay?'

Shirley said, 'Well, it's a bit short notice, isn't it?' Jane's fingernails were hurting the palm of her left hand. She fought herself and won.

'Look, Shirley, I'm in a call-box, I haven't got much change. Will it be all right? I'll be with you tomorrow afternoon some time. See you.'

She slammed down the receiver quickly and jumped back into the car.

Maybe being murdered would be better after all.

Fair stood the wind for Scotland, which made a pleasant change. Indeed, it was nice to be going somewhere, as opposed to just going, and Vanderdecker found the crew rather less tiresome than usual.

The first mate climbed up onto the quarter deck. He was going to ask the captain a question. Vanderdecker could hear his brain turning over like a coffee-mill before he so much as reached the foot of the stairway.

'Captain,' said the first mate, 'we aren't going to land, are we? When we reach wherever this place is we're going to.'

'Yes,' said Vanderdecker, cruelly. As he had expected, this was beyond the first mate's understanding. Antonius stood very still for a while as the coffee-mill approached maximum revolutions.

'Yes we are,' he finally asked, 'or yes we aren't?'

'Yes we are,' Vanderdecker said. 'We're going to land.'

Antonius considered this reply and then looked at his watch, just to make sure. 'But captain,' he remonstrated, 'we can't do that, it isn't time yet.'

'So what?' Vanderdecker said, 'we aren't going to have a good time and get drunk. We're going to see if we can find that blasted alchemist.'

'But won't they just run away?'

'Possibly,' Vanderdecker admitted. 'But it's worth a shot, isn't it? If we wait another five years we may be too late. They may all have gone away anyway by then.'

'Oh,' said Antonius, relieved to have been given an explanation even if he couldn't understand it. All he needed to know in order to feel reassured was that there was a reason and that somebody was in control of it. Vanderdecker envied him.

'After all,' Vanderdecker went on, 'we've got absolutely nothing to lose, have we?'

'I don't know, do I?' said the first mate truthfully. 'That's why I asked.'

'Take it from me,' said Vanderdecker firmly, 'we've got nothing to lose. If we're lucky it could be the answer to the whole mess. If not, well, it makes a change, doesn't it?'

The first mate nodded and went away. The coffee mill was still turning fitfully, but it would soon be still again. Vanderdecker, for his part, was beginning to have his doubts. What if the smell did drive everyone away as soon as they came within smelling distance of the plant? And presumably it wasn't going to be all that easy getting to see Montalban even if he was still there. He knew that all self-respecting Governments are less than happy about the thought of members of the public tripping lightly round nuclear power stations, or even coming near them in a disconcerting manner. Now there was something about the sailing ship *Verdomde* that many people found highly disconcerting, and although its crew were invulnerable, the ship wasn't. Not that he felt any great sentimental attachment to his command — far from it; he hated every timber in its nasty, clinker-built frame — but if the *Verdomde* got blown out of the water by some over-excitable patrol boat, they might have problems in finding another one; or at least one sufficiently primitive that it ran on wind and not oil. Oil is hard to come by when you spend all your time in the middle of the ocean and smell perfectly horrible.

Vanderdecker was still busy worrying himself to death (so to speak) with these and other misgivings when the look-out sighted Duncansby Head. This was Vanderdecker's cue to get out his charts and his sextant, since there were other perils to navigation in these waters besides patrol-boats; for one thing there were rocks, and also sandbanks, eccentric and malicious tides and sundry other hazards to navigation. It was refreshing to be doing some real sailing again, and the Flying Dutchman's mind soon became far too full with getting there to contain any worries about what he was going to do as and when he succeeded in this aim.

'If I remember right,' said the captain to the first mate, 'there's a little cove around here somewhere that we can hide up in.'

It was getting dark, and Vanderdecker was worried about shoals. They hadn't progressed very far with their inch-by-inch search for Dounreay, but progress was necessarily slow because of the need to keep out of sight. Now a good skipper can plot a course that keeps him from being seen from the shore; or he can hug the coastline in such a way as to render himself almost invisible from the open sea. But not both at the same time. As it turned out, the *Verdomde* was seen by several ships and a fair number of landsmen, but none of them took any notice. They naturally assumed that the fish finger people were filming yet another commercial, and carried on with their everyday tasks.

Vanderdecker found the cove in the end, just before it became too dark to see anything at all, and the anchor slithered down and hit the water with its usual dull splosh. The crew settled down to sleep, but Vanderdecker was too restless to join them. Somewhere out there he might find the answer to his problem, and although common sense told him that the power station was not something he was likely to overlook, he felt an urge to get off the ship and go and have a look about. He licked his finger to reassure himself that the wind was still out to sea, lowered the boat, and rowed ashore.

A brisk climb brought him to the top of the low, shallow

cliff, and he walked down the slope on the other side. To his dismay, he saw a building with lights in the windows, and the wind was changing. No good at all. He set off briskly in the other direction.

How it happened was always a mystery to him. One minute he was walking along the tarmac road, the next minute a car came round the sharp bend, failed to stop, and slammed into him. He went over the bonnet, bounced on the roof, and slid over the hatchback rear end to the ground. The car screeched to a halt (and why the devil couldn't you have done that in the first place, said the Flying Dutchman under his breath), the door flew open, and the driver came running towards him. Vanderdecker groaned. Whoever this road-hog was, he was going to get the shock of his life just as soon as he next breathed in. Served him right, too.

It wasn't a he, it was a she. Very much a she, bending over him and looking extremely worried.

'Oh God,' she said, 'are you all right?'

Vanderdecker stared in disbelief. Even he could smell it, and he had long since stopped noticing the smell, except when it was at its most virulent. For some reason, contact with dry land tended to make it even more rank and offensive than usual. But this girl didn't seem to have noticed, or else she was being quite incredibly polite.

'I'm fine,' Vanderdecker said, and stood up to prove it. 'Look, no broken bones or anything. You may have shortened the life-expectancy of my trousers a bit but ...'

A horrible thought struck him. He had forgotten to change. He was wearing his old, comfortable clothes, which were very old and very comfortable indeed. The girl seemed to be having enough difficulty in coming to terms with his invulnerability. As soon as she saw he was dressed in sixteenth century seafaring clothes, she would probably have hysterics.

Fortunately it was dark, too dark to see anything but silhouettes. Vanderdecker dusted himself off and started to back away. But he wanted to know, very much, why this girl couldn't smell the smell.

'Are you sure you're all right?'

'Positive,' he said. 'Sorry to have frightened you. My own silly fault.'

'Can I give you a lift anywhere?' the girl persisted. Vanderdecker remembered that they have funny little lights inside cars that switch themselves on when you open the door. He refused politely and said that he was nearly there. She didn't ask where, thank God.

'I still can't understand how you aren't hurt,' said the girl.

'Luck,' replied the Flying Dutchman. 'Fool's luck. Look, can I ask you a question?'

'Yes,' said the girl doubtfully.

'Can you smell anything?'

'*Smell* anything?'

'That's right,' Vanderdecker said. He hadn't meant to ask, it had just slipped out. But now that it had, he might as well know the answer.

'No,' said the girl. 'But I've got a really rotten sense of smell, so I'm not the best person to ask.'

'I see,' Vanderdecker said. 'Sorry, I thought I could smell something. Can you tell me the way to Dounreay nuclear power station, by any chance?'

'I'm sorry,' said the girl, and Vanderdecker could tell she was staring at him despite the darkness. 'I don't come from around here, actually. I've got a map in the car ...'

Vanderdecker remembered the little light. 'That's all right,' he said. 'Well, I mustn't keep you. Bye.' A moment later and the darkness had swallowed him.

Jane Doland stared a little more, realised that such an act was futile, and got back into the car. She still had twenty-odd miles to go, and it was late. She had missed her way at Lybster, or had it been Thurso, just before she had got behind the milk-tanker that was behind the tractor which had been trying to overtake the JCB ever since Melvich, and she knew that her obnoxious cousin Shirley went to bed at about half-past six. As she drove, she tried to work out what was really unsettling her; believe it or not, it wasn't the fact that she had just run into a fellow human being at forty miles an hour, or even the remarkable lack of effect the collision had had on her victim. It was the vague but definite notion that she had met him before. Not seen him, heard him, a long time ago.

An hour later, she pulled up in front of Cousin Shirley's bungalow in the picturesque but extremely windy village of Mey, put on the handbrake and flopped. She needed a moment to pull herself together before meeting her least favourite kinswoman again. She had hoped that when Shirley married the burnt-out advertising executive and went off with him to Caithness to keep goats and weave lumpy sweaters that they would never meet again this side of the grave. She remembered something from an A-Level English set book about something or other that made vile things precious, but she couldn't remember what the something was and let it slip by.

She was just bracing herself to go in and have done with it when the door of the car opened. She looked round, expecting to see Shirley, but it wasn't Shirley. Perhaps you are now in a position to judge the significance of the fact that she would far rather have seen Shirley than the person she actually saw.

'Jane Doland?' said the mystery door-opener. A tall, fat man with grey hair and a face that did nothing to reassure her. She looked round quickly at the passenger door, but that had been opened too.

'My name is Clough,' said the door-opener, 'and this is my partner Mr Demaris. We want to talk to you about Bridport.'

The cat arched its back by way of acknowledgement to the sun, and curled up to go to sleep. It had had a long day chasing cockroaches in the shunting yard, and if it didn't get forty winks now and again it was no good for anything. The live rail was pleasantly warm against its head, and the sleepers were firm under its spine. An agreeable place to sleep.

The 16.40 from Madrid is an express, and it doesn't usually stop before Cadiz. It stopped all right this time, though. It stopped so much that all the carriages jumped the rail and didn't stop slithering until they reached the foot of the embankment. It was a miracle nobody was seriously hurt.

The cat took it in its stride, the way cats do. It wasn't in the least nonplussed by waking up to find an express train running over its head, and when the last sprocket had bounced off its ear and gone spinning away into the air it got up, licked its paws and set out to find somewhere a bit less noisy. On the way it caught a large brown rat, which offered remarkably little resistance. It just curled up in a ball and squeaked once or twice. That had happened a lot in the last four hundred years, and the cat found that it took all the fun out of hunting.

Three days later, some men in gas masks lured it into a cage with a saucer of milk and some catnip and took it away to a large building with lots of clean white paintwork and scientific equipment. It was dull there, but the food was good and you didn't have to chase it if you didn't want to. The men in gas-masks tried to get the cat to play some very silly games with funny lights and big metal cylinders that went round and round, but after a while they gave up. A day or so after that, they put the cat in a basket, took it to the airport and put in on a flight to Inverness.

Everyone was amazed that a man could exist and survive to maturity who would willingly marry Cousin Shirley; but since the idiot groom proposed to take her off to the northernmost tip of Scotland as soon as he had finished getting the rice and the confetti out of his hair, everyone kept extremely quiet — Aunt Diana, in fact, attributes the arthritis in her fingers to keeping them crossed throughout the six months of the engagement. On the other hand, it seemed to everyone that Julian was a nice young man once you got used to him, and it really wasn't fair, and they ought to tell him. But they didn't. Shirley was a sullen bride, and when Julian fumbled putting the ring on her finger she clicked her tongue so loudly that her mother thought all would yet be lost. But the service proceeded to its tragic close, and Shirley went away. To judge by the wedding presents she received — a tin opener from her parents, a reel of cotton from Jane, three paper-clips from Paul, Jenny and the twins, a paper bag from Uncle Stephen — it seemed likely that contact would not be maintained between the newly-weds and the rest of the House of Doland. Distance, however, is a great healer, and everybody remembered to send Julian a card on his birthday.

Jane had, obviously, never been to see Mr and Mrs Regan in their new home-cum-workshop only a long mortar-shot from the romantic Castle of Mey, but she could guess what it would be like inside. Miserable. It was.

Cousin Shirley's greeting to Jane and the two senior partners of Moss Berwick was nothing if not characteristic. 'You're late,' she said. 'Wipe your feet.'

Mr Demaris was a tall man in his late forties with the face of a debauched matinée idol. He had charm, which on this occasion thoroughly failed to have any effect. His partner Mr Clough, just as tall but alarmingly fat, thatched with a sleek mat of senatorial grey hair and blessed with a voice that they could probably hear in Inverness, also had charm. Astoundingly, Cousin Shirley seemed to like him, for she gave him a pleasant smile. The three were permitted to enter.

Jane noticed that Julian, who was sitting by the fireside weaving something, had changed since the wedding, in roughly the same way as a slug changes when you drop it in a jar of salt. In another year, Jane reckoned, you would be able to see right through him. His reason for giving up a thriving career in advertising in order to make primitive garments out of goats' wool had not been a desire to test the theory that a fool and his money are soon parted, but a feeling that the pace of life in the rat-race was wearing him out. Lord, what fools these mortals be.

Jane considered, just for a moment, throwing herself on Julian's protection and asking him to send the nasty men away, but a glance at her cousin-in-law disillusioned her. His reaction to the intrusion of two startling strangers into his living room was to say hello and go on weaving. Mr Clough sat down in the least uncomfortable chair, Mr Demaris leaned against the mantelpiece, and Jane subsided onto the footstool. She noticed that Cousin Shirley had left the room, and thanked Heaven for small mercies.

If Jane had expected an awkward silence she was wrong. Men who charge over three hundred pounds an hour for their time are rarely silent for longer than it takes to breathe in.

'You weren't at the office today, then,' said Mr Clough.

'No,' said Jane. 'I had some holiday coming.'

'That's fair enough,' said Mr Demaris. 'Next time, though, perhaps you should clear it with Craig Ferrara first.'

'You didn't come all this way,' said Jane shakily, 'to tell me that. Or were you just passing?'

Cousin Shirley was back in the room again. She had brought Mr Clough a cup of tea. Just the one cup. She hadn't stirred it, and the milk lay about a quarter of an inch under the surface like a grey cloud.

'We're flying back to London tonight,' said Mr Demaris. 'We'll give you a lift, if you like.'

'That's very kind,' Jane said, 'but I don't want to put you out in any way.'

There was a shuffling noise and Cousin Shirley was with them again. She was offering Mr Clough a plate of very hard biscuits. He took one without looking down at the plate, popped it into his large mouth and said, 'You've done well on the Bridport matter, but I think we should work together on it from now on.' Then he reached out, took another biscuit, and smashed the one already in his mouth into powder with one movement of his powerful jaws.

'I do think that would be best,' said Mr Demaris, 'don't you? Don't get me wrong, we're very impressed with how you've handled it, but this is something where we have to be very careful, don't you think?'

Jane had intended to fight, but her willpower had melted like a candle in a microwave. 'How did you find me?' she asked.

'Right then,' said Mr Clough, standing up and smiling, 'now that's settled we'd better be on our way. Thank you for the tea, Mrs Regan, and we'll be in touch about that other matter in due course.'

This remark jerked Jane out of her comatose state. 'What other matter?'

Cousin Shirley gave her a look of pure scorn. 'Mr Clough is our accountant,' she said.

'We're thinking of making the business into a limited company,' said Julian unexpectedly. 'But George thinks we should wait another year, because of the tax implications.'

That, as far as Jane was concerned, was that. She went quietly.

Mr Clough explained it to her on the drive to the airport. It was very simple. Moss Berwick were the accountants for the advertising agency where Julian had worked, and since the agency was such an important client, Mr Clough had acted for them personally; at least, he let his subordinates do the work but personally attended the more important lunches. When Julian had decided to get out of advertising and into authentic knitwear, he had mentioned this fact to Mr Clough over the nouvelle cuisine. Mr Clough, whose greed for clients was pathological, immediately appointed himself accountant to the projected enterprise, obtained a cheque for a thousand pounds on account of initial costs, and handed the matter on to the YTS girl. Accordingly, when Mr Clough turned up on the doorstep half an hour before Jane's arrival and started talking loudly about rollover relief and Section Thirty elections, Julian and Shirley hadn't been at all surprised. They simply handed him a cheque for another thousand pounds and believed everything he told them, the way people do when they talk with their professional advisers.

'So now what?' Jane said.

'Mr Gleeson will explain,' said Mr Demaris.

Jane stared and was incapable of speech. Mr Gleeson was the senior partner. Mr Gleeson, it was widely rumoured, did the accounts for God. In fact, so the story went, it was Mr Gleeson who first gave God the idea of organising the Kingdom of Heaven into a properly inte-grated group of holding companies. The idea of actually talking to him was more than Jane's mind could hold.

'Really?' she said.

'He's waiting for us at the airport,' said Mr Clough.

While Jane's mind did another series of forward rolls, Mr Demaris was considering something. 'I've heard people say,' he said, 'that you've got no sense of smell. Is that true?'

Jane admitted that her sense of smell was none too good. Mr Clough looked at Mr Demaris.

'I think it's about time we reviewed your salary,' he said.

CHAPTER FIVE

'Can I speak,' Vanderdecker shouted, 'to Professor Montalban?'

In a long life, reflected the Flying Dutchman, I have come across many bloody silly ideas, but two of them are in a class of their own for pure untainted idiocy. One was the Court of King Ludwig of Bavaria, and the other is the privatised British telephone service.

A long way away, definitely in another continent and quite probably in another dimension, a little voice asked him to repeat the name.

'Montalban,' he said. 'M for Mouse . . .'

The lovely part of it was that he was standing in a telephone kiosk within sight of the gates of the power station he was telephoning. If he was to shout just a little bit louder they'd be able to hear him without using the phone at all.

'Who's calling, please?' said the voice.

'My name's Vanderdecker,' Vanderdecker said.

'I'm sorry,' said the voice, 'I didn't quite . . .'

'*VANDERDECKER* . . . Oh I'm sorry, I didn't mean to shout, it's not a very good line . . . Oh I see. When do you expect him back?'

'Professor Montalban has gone to Geneva,' said the voice, 'we don't expect him back for a week or so. Will you hold?'

'No, no,' said the Flying Dutchman, 'that's fine, have you got a number for him in . . .'

'Could you speak up, please?' the voice said, 'it's rather a poor line.'

'Have you got a number where I can reach the professor in Geneva?' Vanderdecker enunciated. The voice said no, she didn't, could she take a message? Vanderdecker thanked her and hung up.

Even on his antiquated maps, Geneva was clearly marked as being a long way from the sea. Not from water, but from the sea. All in all, it would be foolish to risk trying to reach him there. Vanderdecker pressed the little lever, but no change came cascading down into the tray marked Returned Coins. There would be nothing for it, he said to himself, but to put out to sea for a while until the good professor came back.

For about the seven thousandth time, Vanderdecker assured himself that the alchemist would be as keen to see him as he was to see the alchemist. If Montalban was even remotely concerned with the same field of research as he had been in the reign of His Most Catholic Majesty Philip II, it stood to reason that he would welcome a chance to examine his very first human guinea pigs. His reading of scientific journals had taught him a lot about the way scientists think. They like to have plenty of data. Vanderdecker had a ship full of data; noisome, foul-smelling data, it was true, but ...

At this point, a thought entered into Vanderdecker's mind. During the short time it stayed there, it made its presence felt in more or less the same way a hand grenade would assert itself in a glassworks.

If Montalban had drunk exactly the same stuff as he had, presumably Montalban had been subject to exactly the same side-effects. Yet here the alchemist apparently was, spending a week here, a fortnight there, completely surrounded by human beings. It was by no means unlikely that he had gone to Geneva in an aeroplane, and that while there he would stay in a hotel. If he was able to do these things, it necessarily followed that he didn't smell. How was this?

In Caithness, many of the postmen still ride bicycles. If without any warning they get downwind of a member of the crew of the sailing ship *Verdomde*, they tend to ride these bicycles into trees. The sound of a postman's head making contact with a Scots pine brought Vanderdecker out of his reverie. He was being antisocial again. Time to move on.

While he had been away, the crew had passed the time

by going for a swim in the sea. Complete immersion in
seawater did nothing to impede the communication of the
smell, but it did make you feel better. Now the water
around Dounreay has been declared completely safe by
NIREX, which may be taken to mean that it's about as
safe as a gavotte in a minefield; but from the point of view
of Vanderdecker's crew, this was a point in its favour. They
could bathe in it with a clean conscience if it was polluted
already.

By some strange accident of chance, it was Antonius,
the first mate, who noticed it first; and this in spite of the
fact that the odds against Antonius noticing anything at
any given time are so astronomical as to be beyond calculation. The next person to notice it was Sebastian van
Doorning. He only noticed it because after his ninth
attempt to drown himself he was so short of breath that he
was inhaling air like a vacuum-pump. Then Pieter and
Dirk Pretorius noticed it, and they pointed it out to Jan
Christian Duysberg. He in turn mentioned it to Wilhelm
Triegaart, who told him that he was imagining things. In
short, by the time Vanderdecker returned, everyone was
aware of it. They all decided to tell their captain at the
same time.

'Hold on, will you?' Vanderdecker said. There was a
brief but total silence, and then everyone started talking
again.

'Quiet!' A man who has just spent five minutes talking
into a British Telecom payphone is not afraid to raise his
voice. 'Sebastian,' he said, choosing someone at random,
'can you please tell me what's going on?'

'It's the smell, captain,' replied the spokesman. 'It's
gone.'

Vanderdecker stared. Then he sniffed so violently that
he almost dislocated his windpipe.

'When did this happen?' he asked quietly.

'Must have been when we were all swimming in the
water, captain,' Sebastian said.

'You don't say.' Vanderdecker closed his eyes, buried his
nose in Antonius's doublet and concentrated. There was still
a whiff of it there, but it was very faint. 'This water here?'

'That's right,' several voices assured him. Others urged him to try it for himself. They didn't want to be rude, they said, but he smelt awful.

Vanderdecker needed no second invitation. He pulled off his shirt and trousers and jumped into the sea.

'I do believe you're right,' he said, a quarter of an hour later. They were back on board ship again by this stage. The ship itself was as bad as ever, but what could you expect? 'It's definitely still there, but it's faded a hell of a lot.'

'What d'you think's happened?' asked the first mate anxiously. 'What's going on?'

Vanderdecker had a shrewd idea that it wasn't a coincidence. He didn't know much about these things, but it stood to reason that the sea next to a power station absorbs quite a fair amount of any escaping vapours or things of that sort. Until a few days ago, Professor Montalban had been doing experiments inside that very same power station. If that's a coincidence, Vanderdecker said to himself, then I'm not a Dutchman.

An hour later, it had worn off. The cloud of avaricious gulls which had formed over the ship suddenly evaporated. The fumes from Wilhelm Triegaart's repulsive pipe were once again the sweetest-smelling things on the ship. Because he had had his immersion later than the others, Vanderdecker was slightly more wholesome than they were; only slightly. He would still have been barred from any fashionable sewer as a health hazard.

Vanderdecker said, 'Get me all the empty barrels you can find. Then fill them up in the sea where you lot were all having your swim.'

Antonius, who was a conscientious man, felt it his duty to point out to Vanderdecker that you can't drink seawater. Vanderdecker ignored him politely. He was thinking again.

It no longer matters, he said to himself. Geneva can be on top of the Alps for all I care — if we can keep ourselves from smelling for just a couple of days, we could make it to Geneva and go see Montalban.

While we're on the subject of coincidences, how else would

you account for the fact that the Dow Jones' second biggest
slide in twenty years started that same afternoon?

The most direct route by sea from Dounreay to Geneva, so
to speak, is straight down the North Sea and into the
Channel. Vanderdecker, however, was extremely unhappy
about going anywhere near the Channel now that it was so
depressingly full of ships. He made for Den Helder.

Yet another of these wretched coincidences; MV *Erdkrieger*, the flagship of the environmentalist pressure group
Green Machine, left Den Helder at exactly the same time
on the same day that Vanderdecker left Scotland. It was
headed for Dounreay. Its progress was slightly impeded by
its cargo of six thousand tons of slightly wilted flowers,
contributed by Green Machine's Dutch militant sister
organisation Unilateral Tulip, which the *Erdkrieger*'s crew
intended to use to block the effluent outlets of the newly-
built Fifth Generation Reactor whose construction and
installation Professor Montalban (better known in environmentalist circles as the Great Satan) was presently
supervising. As a result, the *Erdkrieger* was not her usual
nippy self. She was going about as fast as, for example, a
sixteenth century merchantman under full sail.

'Now then,' said Mr Gleeson, 'the Vanderdecker Policy.'

Mr Gleeson was not what Jane had expected, but then
she shouldn't have expected him to be; not if she'd thought
about it for a moment. What she should have expected was
an extraordinary man; and for all his shortcomings, he
was certainly that.

He was short; maybe half an inch shorter than Jane,
who was a quintessential size 12. He was round but not fat,
and his head had hair in more or less the same way a
mountain has grass — sparse and short and harassed-
looking. He had bright, quick, precise eyes and a smile
that told you that he would make jokes but not laugh at
yours. As to ninety per cent of him he looked like somebody's nice uncle. The other ten per cent, you felt, was
probably pure barracuda.

'I don't know,' said Mr Gleeson, 'how much you've found

out for yourself, so I'd better start at the beginning. Would you like something before we start? Cup of tea? Gin and tonic? Sherry?'

Jane had never been in Mr Gleeson's office before, and she didn't feel at all comfortable. It was an unsettling place — just comfortable enough to make you start to feel at home, and just businesslike enough to make you suddenly realise that you weren't. Jane had the perception to understand that this effect was deliberate.

'No, thank you,' she said. Her mouth was like emery paper.

Mr Gleeson reclined in his chair and looked at his fingernails for a moment. 'The Vanderdecker Policy,' he said, 'is the single most important secret in the world. I don't want to worry you unduly, but when you leave this office tonight you'll be taking with you enough information to wipe out every major financial institution and destabilise every economy in the world. I just thought you ought to know that. You can keep a secret, can't you?'

Jane mumbled that she could. Mr Gleeson nodded. He accepted her word on this point. He was a good judge of character, and could read people.

'Actually,' he continued, 'the risk involved in telling you this is minimal, because if you leaked it to anybody they wouldn't believe you. I'm not sure they'd even believe me. Or the President of the United States, for that matter. When you actually come face to face with the true story, it's so completely incredible that you could publish it in the *Investor's Chronicle* and it wouldn't make a blind bit of difference. What we've been trying to cover up, ever since long before you were born, is not what the secret is but that it exists. And mainly, of course, we're trying to deal with the actual problem, so that by the time it does get out — it will one day, it must, there's no stopping it — we'll have solved it and that will be that. Now then.'

Mr Gleeson scratched his ear slowly and gently, as if this was a very delicate and difficult feat to perform and required all his concentration. Then he leaned forward.

'So that you can understand what I'm going to say,' he continued, 'I'd better just fill you in on the history of this

firm's most important client. You don't need me to tell you
that that's the National Lombard Bank. It's a very old
bank; in fact it's the oldest Bank of all. To be honest with
you, nobody knows exactly when it was founded; it started
off as a large number of silver pennies in a sock belonging
to an Italian merchant who was too fat to go to the
Crusades in person, but was alive to the fantastic commercial opportunity they presented. These silver pennies bred
so many other silver pennies during the Siege of Jerusalem
that the sock was too small to contain them all, and the
Italian merchant, or his grandson or whoever it was, built a
bank instead and kept them in that. Spiritually, however,
the whole organisation remained a sock, and a sock it is to
this day. Remember that, and you'll understand a lot about
how banks work.

'For reasons best known to itself, the sock left Lombardy
early in the fourteenth century and migrated to the cities
of the Hanseatic League, where it went to live with some
people called Fugger. They were kind to the sock and fed it
lots of silver pennies, until almost all the silver pennies in
the world were either in the sock permanently or else inde-
feasibly linked to it by a series of binding legal agreements.
The more people tried to take money out of the sock, the
more money ended up in there, and although everyone
complained bitterly about this state of affairs, none of
them realised that the only way to break the vicious circle
was not to take money out of the sock in the first place.
Even now,' said Mr Gleeson, 'the lesson has not been
learned which is why the economic infrastructure of the
developed nations is completely up the pictures.'

'Anyway,' continued Mr Gleeson, 'the Fuggers were
industrious men, and they weren't content to let the sock
do all the work. They were forever trying to think up new
ideas for getting even more silver pennies from people, and
one of them hit on a very simple but extremely effective
concept. It was basically a form of gambling, and it went
something like this.

'The Fuggers would think of something that was
extremely unlikely to happen, and then they would persuade someone to wager them money that it would. Now the

proper term for this arrangement is a sucker bet, but the Fuggers wanted to find a respectable name for it, so they called it Insurance. It caught on, just as they knew it would, and soon it became so respectable that they were able to get people to make a new bet every year, and they called this sort of bet a premium. But although everyone was soon convinced that the bets were totally respectable, the Fuggers were perfectionists and wanted to make absolutely sure, so they took to writing the bets out on extremely long pieces of parchment, frequently in Latin. This practice survives to this day; we call them policies, and usually they're so completely and utterly respectable that it takes a couple of trained lawyers to understand what they mean.'

Jane nodded instinctively, for she had just renewed her car insurance. Mr Gleeson went on.

'Well,' he said, 'if we can just fast-forward for a bit, the House of Fugger became Fugger and Company, which in turn became the Lombard National Bank, which turned into the National Lombard Bank plc. The name has changed, but the sock remains the same. In fact, you would be forgiven for thinking that the sock is the only truly immortal entity in the world. You would be wrong.'

Mr Gleeson paused and opened the top drawer of his desk, from which he extracted a packet of digestive biscuits. He offered one to Jane, who refused, and then ate one himself. Once he had cleared his mouth of crumbs, he continued.

'Back we go to the sixteenth century. We are in Cadiz, one of the most important seaports in the world. If you are tired of Cadiz, you are tired of life and so on. Naturally, there is a Fugger office in the High Street, offering low-interest overdrafts, mortgages (the word mortgage literally means 'dead hand', which I find terribly evocative, don't you?), bottomry loans, whatever they were, and the inevitable life insurance. It is a Thursday.

'Into the Fugger office walks a relatively prosperous sea captain in his early thirties. He has become rather concerned about the risks involved in his profession now that the seas are full of English pirates, and he wants to

take out some insurance on his ship. This is perfectly
natural, because his ship is his living, and if somebody
puts a culverin ball through its bows, our sea-captain will
be out of a job.

'The manager of this particular Fugger office is well
versed in the basic tenets of his trade, and the fundamental rule of insurance is, Don't take bad risks — that,
by the way, is what an insurer calls a sucker bet when you
offer it to him. There is a severe risk that what the sea-
captain fears so much will actually come to pass. Therefore, regretfully, the manager has to refuse to insure the
ship. But he is nothing if not a tryer; it hurts him severely
if someone walks out of his office without making at least a
small bet, and so he suggests to the sea-captain that he
might do worse than take out a little life insurance.'

Again Mr Gleeson paused, and Jane noticed to her
amazement that he was quivering slightly. Mr Gleeson
must have noticed her noticing, for he smiled.

'This is the good bit,' he said, 'don't go away. I remember
when I was told it. By rights, of course, I should never have
been told it at all. You see, the story is handed down from
generation to generation of managing directors of the
House of Fugger or whatever they're calling it this week.
Fortunately, the managing directors of the Bank had
always died in their beds with plenty of notice from the
medical authorities, and so there was always time to pass
the story on. The way I got to hear it was extremely fortui-
tous, a complete break with tradition, you might say. You
see, I was at Oxford with the son of the then managing
director, and I was staying with the family one long vaca-
tion. We all went out rough shooting and there was a
terrible accident, the old man got shot. No time to get a
doctor, he just rolled over and with his dying breath
blurted the whole horrible thing out. I happened to be
there, and so of course I heard it. I wasn't even qualified
then, but of course I became the bank's chief auditor on
the spot, just as my friend became the next managing
director, because of what we had heard. You see, the
system is that the whole board knows there's a secret, but
only the MD knows what the secret is. I've introduced the

same system at Moss Berwick, but it doesn't seem to have worked so well there.'

'So what is the secret, exactly?' Jane asked.

'I'm coming to that,' said the senior partner. 'I was just trying to put it off for as long as possible, because it's so ... so silly, I suppose is what you'd have to call it, if you were going to be savagely honest. I've lived with this for thirty years, my entire life and phenomenal successes in my career are built around it and I've never ever told anyone before.'

Jane looked him in the eye. She was sorry for him. 'Go on,' she said.

'Thank you,' said Mr Gleeson. He was probably quite nice when you got to know him, should you live that long. 'The policy that the manager sold Captain Vanderdecker — the sea-captain's name was Vanderdecker — was a perfectly standard policy specially designed to meet the needs, or rather the gullibility, of sea-captains. You had the choice of paying regular premiums or a single lump-sum premium — the sea-captains found it difficult to pay regular premiums in those days, you see, because they rarely knew where they'd be at any given time from one year's end to the next — and in return you got an assured sum on death. It wasn't exactly a fortune, but it would tide your nearest and dearest over until the plague or the Inquisition finally finished her off, and since there was no income tax in those days it was guaranteed tax free.

'The sting in the tail was this. Because sea-captaining was such a risky job in those days, it was a virtual certainty that the policyholder wouldn't make sixty years of age. This is where the sucker-bet part of it comes in. Because of this actuarial semi-certainty, the policy contains the proviso that the sum assured — the payout — will increase by fifty per cent compound for every year that the life assured — the sucker — survives over the age of seventy-five. Seventy-*five*, mark you; those Fuggers were taking no chances. It made a marvellous selling point, and the age limitation only appeared in very tiny script on the back of the policy, just underneath the seal where you wouldn't think of looking. They sold tens of

thousands of those policies, and for every one sucker that
made seventy-six, there were nine hundred and ninety
nine that didn't.'

Mr Gleeson stopped talking and sat very still for a
while, so still that Jane was afraid to interrupt him. It is
very quiet indeed in a soundproofed office on the fifteenth
floor of an office block at two in the morning.

'Talking of sucker bets,' Mr Gleeson finally said, 'this
one was the best of the lot. You see, Captain Vanderdecker
didn't die. He just went on living. Nobody knows why —
there are all sorts of far-fetched stories which I won't bore
you with, because your credulity must be strained to
breaking-point already. The fact remains that Vanderdecker didn't die. He is still alive, over four hundred years
later. Please bear in mind the fact that the interest is
compound. We tried to calculate once what it must be now,
but we couldn't. There is, quite literally, not that much
money in the whole world.

'So, you see, if Vanderdecker dies, the whole thing will
go into reverse. All the money which has gone into the sock
— and that's every penny there is — will have to come out
again, and it will all go to Mr Vanderdecker's estate. This
is of course impossible, and so the Bank would have to
default — it would have to welch on a sucker bet. And that
would be that. End of civilisation as we know it. You know
as well as I do that the economies of the major economic
powers are so volatile that the markets collapse every time
the Mayor of Accrington gets a bad cold. The faintest hint
that the National Lombard was about to go down and you
wouldn't be able to get five yards down Wall Street without
being hit by a freefalling market-maker. And that is the
basic story behind the Vanderdecker Policy.'

That same long, deafening silence came back again,
until Jane could bear it no longer.

'But surely,' Jane said, 'if Vanderdecker is going to live
for ever, he'll never die and the problem will never arise.'

Mr Gleeson smiled. 'Who said he was going to live for
ever?' he replied. 'All we know is that he hasn't died yet.
It's scientifically impossible for a man to live for ever. Logi-
cally, he must die eventually. And every year he doesn't

die, the problem gets inexpressibly worse. You see the problem we're in. We can't afford for him to die, any more than we can afford for him to live any longer. Fifty per cent compound. Think about that for a moment, will you?'

Jane thought about it. She shuddered. 'So where is he now?' she asked.

'We don't know,' said Mr Gleeson. 'We lost track of him in the 1630's, and then he kept turning up again. He turns up once every seven years or so, and then he vanishes off the face of the earth.'

Suddenly Jane remembered something. 'You mean like the Flying Dutchman?' she said.

'Vanderdecker is the Flying Dutchman,' said Mr Gleeson. 'The very same.'

'I see,' Jane said, as if this suddenly made everything crystal clear. 'So where does Bridport come in?'

'I was coming to that,' said Mr Gleeson, 'just as soon as I'd given you time to digest what I've just told you. Obviously you've got a remarkable digestion. Or you think I'm as mad as a hatter. Bridport comes in because that's where Vanderdecker was last recorded in this country. He opened an account at the bank's Bridport branch in 1890-something. I believe you found it.'

'I did,' Jane confirmed. 'Why on earth haven't you closed it?'

'Easy,' replied Mr Gleeson, 'we can't close it without either his instructions or sight of his death certificate. Rules are rules.'

Jane was astounded. The last thing she had expected was integrity. 'But what about bank charges?' she said. 'Couldn't you just write it off against those?'

'No bank charges in eighteen ninety-thing,' replied Gleeson. 'It wouldn't be right. There would be an anomaly which would have to be noted in the accounts. As the Bank's auditor, I would have to insist on it.'

'I see,' Jane said again. 'I didn't realise the rules were so strict.'

'All we can do,' said Mr Gleeson, 'is keep very quiet about it. The only people who know the significance of that account are me, the chairman of the bank, and now you.

Obviously the local manager doesn't know. And if anyone finds out apart from us, of course, we hound them to insanity and have them locked up in a mental hospital.'

'That's within the rules, is it?'

'I've read them very carefully,' Mr Gleeson replied, 'no mention of it anywhere. Therefore it stands to reason it must be legitimate.'

'In that case,' Jane said slowly, 'why haven't I . . .'

'Because,' replied Mr Gleeson, 'you have no sense of smell.'

For the third time, Jane asserted that she saw. She lacked conviction.

'Let me explain,' said Mr Gleeson. 'There's one other thing we know about the Flying Dutchman. He smells. Awful. You've heard of the *Marie Celeste?*'

Jane said that she had.

'National Lombard were part of the syndicate insuring her, so it carried out its own investigation. It found the only survivor.'

'Ah.'

'Well might you say Ah,' replied Mr Gleeson. 'As soon as the managing director found out what was going on, he cleared everyone else out of the way and spoke to the man personally, just before he died of acute bewilderment. He reported how they were all sitting there minding their own business when this old-fashioned sailing ship came alongside. There was this smell, the survivor said. It was so bad, he said, everyone jumped into the sea and was drowned. Except him. The old-fashioned ship picked him up just before he was about to drown and took him on board. He was on the ship for three weeks before it dropped him off. He described the smell in detail; that bit of the report runs to four hundred and seventy-nine pages, so you can see it made quite an impression. Anyway, it turned out that the name of the ship's captain was Vanderdecker. Since the name is not common and the survivor said the whole crew were in sixteenth-century costume, it's a fair assumption that it was him. There have been other incidents since which corroborate the story, but the names won't mean anything to you because they happened in remote places and the bank managed to cover them up in time. It is an undoubted fact that Vanderdecker smells so horrible that nobody in the world can bear to be in his presence for more than a few seconds at a time. This,' said Mr Gleeson, 'is where you come in.'

'I see,' Jane said, for the fourth time.

'What we want you to do,' said Mr Gleeson, 'is find Vanderdecker and reason with him. Tell him he can't take it with him. Negotiate with him to surrender the policy in return for an annuity — a million pounds a year for life or some such figure. It'd be worth it, the bank can afford it. You'd be on commission, naturally.'

'But how do I find him?' Jane said. 'If it was possible, surely you'd have done it by now.'

'We haven't dared try,' Mr Gleeson replied. 'In order to find Vanderdecker, we'd have to let too many people in on too much of the secret. Far too risky. Sucker bet. Only someone like you can do it, because you know already. And you only know because I've told you, and I've only told you because you have no sense of smell. Do you follow me?'

'I think so,' Jane said, 'more or less. Actually, I might have a lead already.' And she told him about Lower Brickwood Farm Cottage, and the invoices. When she had finished, Mr Gleeson nodded and smiled, a you-can-call-me-Bill sort of smile that he usually reserved for Prime Ministers.

'Will you help us, then?' he said. 'If you succeed, you can name your own fee.'

'Well ...' Jane hesitated, genuinely doubtful. If she accepted the job, she would have to find some way of coming to terms with what she had just been told, and that would not be easy, not by a long way. On the other hand, and bearing in mind all the material circumstances, with particular regard to the section of the Rules which said nothing at all about locking people up in lunatic asylums, she felt she didn't have much choice.

'Yes,' she said.

Mr Gleeson grinned at her. 'That's the spirit,' he said. 'May the Sock be with you.'

CHAPTER SIX

'Cheer up, for God's sake,' said the other man in Quincy's, with his mouth full, 'you're putting me off my asparagus quiche.'

His companion scowled at the little cardboard square under his glass. For reasons which it would be counterproductive to rehearse, he knew that the jolly little cartoon on the beermat of a Viking warrior drinking lager was completely inaccurate, but that wasn't the thing that was upsetting him.

'I don't want to cheer up,' he said. 'Cheerfulness would be very strange behaviour just now, don't you think?'

Suspense is a legitimate literary device only if responsibly handled. Know, then, that the other man's name is Gerald.

'You always were a gloomy sod,' said Gerald, his jaws temporarily free, 'even when we were kids. You had this knack of always looking on the black side. And what good does it do? Tell me that.'

'It enables me,' said Gerald's friend, 'to harmonise with my karma. My karma is presently as much fun as a traffic-jam on the M6. Therefore I am gloomy. If I were to cheer up now, I could suffer severe spiritual damage.'

'Funny you should mention the M6,' Gerald replied. 'I was three hours — three whole hours out of my life — getting between Junctions Four and Five the other day. And you know what caused it all? Changing the light bulb in one of those street-lamp things. Pathetic, I call it, absolutely bloody pathetic.'

'Tell me all about the M6,' Gerald's friend said savagely. 'I'm sure it's incredibly relevant to my getting the sack.'

'You have not got the sack,' Gerald said. 'How many times have I got to tell you? You've been moved sideways, that's all. It happens to everyone. I got moved sideways last year, and it's been the making of me.'

'Gerald,' said his friend, 'how long have we known each other?'

Gerald's friend thought for a moment. 'Good question that,' he said. He put down his fork and began to count on his fingers. 'Let me think. Seventy-three, was it? Seventeen years. My God, how time flies!'

'I've known you for seventeen years?'

'Looks like it.'

'Why?'

Gerald frowned. 'What do you mean?' he said.

'Why?' said his friend angrily. 'I mean, what has been the point? Seventeen years we've been meeting regularly, sending each other postcards from Santorini, inviting each other to parties, having lunch; you'd think it would count for something. You'd think it would go some way towards creating some sort of mutual understanding. And now you sit there, drinking a glass of wine which I paid for, and tell me that getting transferred from Current Affairs to Sport is a sideways move.'

'Well it is,' said Gerald. He had grown so used to this sort of thing that he took no notice whatsoever. 'More people watch sport than current affairs, it's a known fact. Call it promotion. Will you be able to get me seats for Wimbledon, do you think?'

'What's Wimbledon?' asked his friend.

Gerald frowned. He didn't mind Danny trying to be amusing, but blasphemy was another matter. 'Doesn't matter if it's behind a pillar or anything like that,' he said. 'It's the being there that really counts.'

Danny Bennet ignored him. 'Anything but Sport,' he said, 'I could have taken in my stride. "Songs of Praise." "Bob's Full House." "Antiques Roadshow." Take any shape but this and my firm nerves shall never tremble. Sport, no. At Sport I draw the line.'

'You never did like games much,' Gerald reflected, as he cornered a radish in the folds of his lettuce-leaf. 'Remember the lengths you used to go to just to get off games at school? You just never had any moral fibre, I

guess. It's been a problem with you all through life. If only
they'd made you play rugger at school, we'd be having less
of these theatricals now, I bet.'

'Have you ever tried killing yourself, Gerald? You'd
enjoy it.'

'If I were in your shoes,' Gerald continued, 'I'd be over
the moon. Plenty of open air. Good clean fun. What the
viewer really wants, too; I mean, quite frankly, who gives a
toss about politics anyway? Come to think of it, maybe
you could do something about the way they always put the
cricket highlights on at about half past three in the
morning. I'm not as young as I was, I need my eight hours.
And it's all very well saying tape it, but I can never set the
timer right. I always seem to end up with half an hour of
some cult movie in German, which is no use at all when I
come in from a hard day at the office. My mother can do
it, of course, but then she understands machines. She
tapes the Australian soaps, which I call a perverse use of
advanced technology.'

'Isn't it time,' Danny said, 'that you were getting back?'

Gerald glanced at his watch and swore. 'You're right,' he
said, 'doesn't time fly? Look, I hate to rush off when you're
having a life crisis like this, but the dollar's been very iffy
all week and God knows what it'll get up to if I'm not there
to hold its hand. You must come to dinner. Amanda's
finally worked out a way of doing crême brulée in the
microwave, you'll love it. Thanks for the drink.' He
scooped up the remaining contents of his plate in his
fingers, jammed the mixture into his mouth, and departed.

With Gerald mercifully out of the way, Danny was able
to enjoy his misery properly. He savoured it. He rolled it
round his palate. He experienced its unique bouquet. It is
not every day that a living legend gets put out with the
empty bottles and the discarded packaging; in fact, it
would make a marvellous fly-on-the-wall documentary. For
someone else.

Perhaps, Danny said to himself, I am taking it rather
too hard. Perhaps they were right, and I was getting a bit
set in my ways in current affairs. Perhaps it will be an
exciting   challenge   producing   televised   snooker   in

Warrington. Perhaps the world is just a flat plate spinning
on a stick balanced on the nose of the Great Conjuror, and
my fortunes are so insignificant as to be unworthy of consideration. Perhaps I should pack it all in and go work for
the satellite people.

In the three years since his story (the details of which
are not relevant hereto) Danny had often considered
leaving the BBC and signing on under the Jolly Roger, but
only when he was in no fit state to make important decisions. He had come as close as typing his letter of resignation on that day which shall live in infamy when they told
him that they had no use for his searing revelations of
corruption in the sewage disposal department of a major
West Midlands borough, provisionally entitled 'Ordu-
regate'. That same letter had been typed and stamped
when 'Countdown to Doomsday,' his mordant exposé of the
threat posed by a popular brand of furniture polish to the
ozone layer, had ended up on the cutting room floor; while
a third edition brushed the lip of the postbox after the top
floor suspended filming of the script which would have
unmasked a hitherto-respected chiropodist in Lutterworth
as the Butcher of Clermont-Ferrand. But he had never
done it. The final Columbus-like step off the edge of the
world and through the doors of the South Bank Studios
was not for him, and he knew it.

The fourth edition of his resignation letter, therefore,
remained unwritten, and when he left Quincy's he
returned to the studios and went to see the man who was
going to tell him everything he needed to know about
sports broadcasting in twenty-five minutes.

'The main thing,' said the expert, 'is to turn up on the
right day at the right place and keep the sound recordists
out of the bar. Leave everything else to the cameramen,
and you'll do all right. That's it.'

Is it like this, Danny asked himself, in death's other
kingdom? 'That's it, is it?' he said.

'Yes,' said the expert. 'Apart from the commentators, of
course. They're a real pain in the backside, but there's
absolutely nothing you can do about them, so don't let it
worry you. It's basically a question of hanging on and not

letting it get to you.'

'Even if they say "Well, Terry, it's a funny old game"?'

'That, my son,' said the expert, 'will be the least of your worries.' He paused and looked at Danny curiously. 'Aren't you that bloke who did the thing about the buried treasure?'

'That's right,' Danny said. The expert grinned.

'I saw that,' he said. 'Load of old cobblers. You're lucky you've still got a job after a stunt like that.'

'Oh yes?' Danny said.

'Listen,' said the expert. 'I've been in this game a long time. The average viewer doesn't want all that. No goals. No big girls. No car-chases. We're living in the age of the video now, just you remember that and you won't go far wrong.'

'Thank you,' Danny said, 'for all your help.'

Now that he knew everything there was to know about producing sports programmes, he felt that he was ready to take on his first assignment. He was wrong.

'For God's sake,' he exclaimed. 'You can't be serious.'

'Someone's got to do it,' he was told.

'They said that about Monte Cassino.'

'What,' came the reply, 'is Monte Cassino?'

'Be reasonable,' Danny urged. 'Quite apart from the fact that it's a fate worse than death, it must be a highly difficult technical assignment. Stands to reason. I've got no experience whatsoever. I'll have no end of problems.'

'That's right, you will. But you'll cope.'

'I don't want to cope,' Danny blathered, 'I'm a perfectionist.'

'And look where it's got you.'

Danny paused, but only because he had spoken all the breath out of his lungs. As he breathed in, a terrible thought struck him.

'This is deliberate,' he said. 'Of course, why didn't I realise it before? You've given this to me just so as I can cock it up and you can fire me.'

'You and your conspiracy theories.'

'Stuff conspiracy theories,' Danny snapped, 'this is my career at stake. You can't do this to me. I have friends.'

'Name one.'

Put like that, it wasn't easy. The life pattern of a television producer is not conducive to the forming of friendships. The only one he could come up with was Gerald, and he probably wouldn't count for much.

'Contacts, then,' Danny said. 'I have contacts. All I'd have to do to get my own show on Channel 4 is snap my fingers.'

'All *I'd* have to do to get a show on Channel 4 is snap my fingers,' his interlocutor pointed out reasonably. 'Look, stop being such a pain about it and go and film some yachts. You'll like it once you get there. They tell me the trick is not to lean backwards too far or you'll fall off the boat.'

'What boat?'

'You have to film it from a boat,' he was informed. 'That's how you film boats. They tell me.'

Danny fumed, like a cigarette discarded on flame-proof furniture fabric, and then said, 'All right, you win. Where do I have to go?'

On the other side of the desk a very faint grin started to form, and out of it came the word 'Bridport.'

'Bridport? Where the bloody hell is Bridport?'

'Bridport,' said the context of the grin, 'is where the Bridport Old Ships Race starts from. Beyond that, I must confess I know very little. Mandy in the front office has an atlas, ask her.'

Mandy in the front office did indeed have an atlas, which was so up to date that it showed all the principal towns in the Belgian Congo. It also showed Bridport.

'You going there, are you?' she asked.

'No,' Danny replied, 'I just needed reassuring it was still there.' He sighed and went to sort out his briefcase.

Aboard the protest ship *Erdkrieger,* all was not well.

'Woher,' someone said, 'kommt der Geruch?'

Someone else asked what the hell that was supposed to mean, and a third party translated for her.

'Where's the smell coming from?'

'That's the trouble,' remarked the second party from behind her handkerchief, 'with being on a goddamn multilingual ship.'

Wherever the smell was coming from, it was not pleasant. Some of the ship's company compared it to a Zellophanpapierfabrik; others got halfway through saying Exkrementeverarbeitungswerk before the vapours got into their lungs and reduced them to spluttering hulks.

'Sewage farm,' explained the translator.

'I guessed.'

In any event, it was a horrible smell, and horrible smells out in the middle of the sea can only mean one thing to the crew of an environmental patrol vessel.

'We'd better get those guys, whoever they are,' said the imperfect linguist. 'You fetch the handcuffs and I'll go connect up the fire hoses.'

The translator, a short, weatherbeaten New Zealander, refused to budge. She was happy where she was. It might be cramped and wet and full of discarded foodstuffs, but it was out of the way of the terrible breeze that was carrying the Geruch in from wherever it originated. Her companion started off full of scorn, but came back rather quickly.

'Jesus,' she said, 'it smells really awful.'

The captain, a tall, blond German, was going round issuing gas masks. They helped, but not all that much; they had only been designed to cope with relatively minor environmental pollution, such as mustard gas. Nevertheless, their morale value at least was sufficient to enable the imperfect linguist and a few other diehards to scramble out of hard cover and take stock of the situation.

Through the misted eyepieces of their masks, they could dimly make out a ship creaking slowly towards them across the whale-road. It was slow, and it was unnaturally quiet. But the imperfect linguist, whose name was Martha and who came from Bethlehem, Pa., knew what that signi-fied.

'This is something big,' she said to the New Zealander.

'Is it?'

'I read about it,' she replied. 'There's some new kinds of waste so volatile they daren't put them on conventional ships because of the danger of combustion; you know, sparks from the electrics, that kind of thing. So they use these sail-powered ships.'

'I never heard that.'

'Well you wouldn't, would you,' Martha said. 'It's secret.'

That made sense, and the New Zealander scurried off to tell the captain, whom she eventually found inside one of the lifeboats, with a tarpaulin over his head.

The captain's appeal for volunteers was truly a call for heroes, for the mission that was proposed called for selfless dedication to the cause. It demanded the sort of sacrifice that ought once and for all to sort out who were the real friends of the earth and who were the ones who just dropped in now and then for a cup of coffee and a chat. So rigorous was this selection process that the result was two people only. As the outboard motor of the dinghy finally fired and propelled the frail craft towards the poison ship, the New Zealander set her jaw and tried to think of the rain forests. It wasn't easy.

'For Chrissakes, Jo, you nearly had us over,' remarked her fellow martyr, as they bounced off a rather bumptious wave. 'This isn't Indianapolis, throttle back a bit.'

Jo throttled right back while Martha checked the handcuffs with which they were going to chain themselves to the side of the poison ship. Deep down in the unregenerate parts of her brain, there was a tiny hope that the handcuffs would fall to bits and they could go back to the *Erdkrieger* with honour.

'They seem to be taking it very calmly,' she muttered as they came within fifty yards of their target.

'You what?'

'They seem to be taking it very calmly!' Martha yelled. Jo shrugged. By and large, she was thinking to herself, she was regretting that she hadn't become a dentist like her family wanted her to. Dentists also have their part to play in the Great Society, and they don't have to chain themselves to extremely smelly ships.

'If they turn the hoses on us,' Martha continued, 'just try and kinda roll with it.'

'They don't look like they've got any hoses, Martha,' Jo replied. 'Looks a bit on the primitive side to me.'

'That's just a front,' Martha replied confidently. She had been in this game long enough to know that all the masks of the enemy are fundamentally weird.

'Are those cannons sticking out the side?' Jo asked.

'Could be,' Martha said. 'They sure look like cannons. Probably the pipes they pump the stuff out of, though.'

At last they could make out a human being on the ship. Two human beings, two human beings leaning against the rail looking mildly interested. They seemed entirely oblivious to the smell.

Martha seized the grappling-hook while Jo swung the tiller. There didn't seem an awful lot you could get a handcuff round on the gleaming oak sides of the ship, but she owed it to herself to try.

'Hello there,' said a voice from above her head. 'Are you lost?'

Martha blinked. 'Are we what?'

'Lost,' repeated the voice.

'Don't try that one with me, buster,' Martha said. 'We're coming alongside, and don't bother trying to stop us.'

The taller of the two men gazed at her with a puzzled expression. 'Do you really want to come alongside?' he said.

'Yes.'

'Takes all sorts,' replied the taller man. 'Shall I drop you a line?'

Martha was about to say something, but Jo explained that it was also a seafaring term. 'He wants to lower us a rope,' she whispered.

'What?'

'He wants to lower us a bloody rope!' Jo shouted.

'That's right,' said the man on the ship, 'I want to lower you a rope. If you'd like me to, that is. I'm not bothered one way or the other.'

Martha only had a few seconds to decide whether this was simple or duplex treachery. She decided on duplex.

'Lower away, sucker,' she replied. 'See if I care.'

'Your friend isn't very polite, is she?' said the man on the ship. He threw a rope to them, and Martha grabbed it and made it fast. Together, she and Jo hauled themselves level with the ship. With the best will in the world, there was nothing — absolutely nothing — to handcuff them-

selves to short of the rail that ran round the side of the
ship. Martha thought of acid rain and the whales, and
started to scramble up the rope.

'Hold on,' said the man on the ship, 'it's wet, you'll slip.'
He was right.

Several other men had joined him now. There was snig-
gering. But no hoses. Martha was not enjoying herself. She
was at home with hoses, she knew where they were coming
from. But nobody seemed to be taking her seriously.

'Come on, Jo,' she panted as she hauled herself up into
the dinghy again and seized the rope. She was feeling
angry, frustrated, humiliated and above all wet, and a little
voice in the back of her mind was saying that it really was
about time the whales learned to look after themselves, or
what the hell was the point of evolution, anyway? She
dismissed it with the contempt it deserved. 'Scared, are
you?'

'No,' Jo replied. 'I'm going up the ladder.'

'What ladder?'

'The one they've just lowered,' Jo replied, and stepped
out of the dinghy.

Vanderdecker had just managed to say the 'What can I
do' part of 'What can I do for you?' when the smaller of the
two visitors deftly and entirely unexpectedly manacled
herself to the ship's rail. The second — rather unwillingly,
Vanderdecker felt — followed suit.

'Is something the matter?' he asked.

On the bridge of the *Erdkrieger,* the captain observed
the scene aboard the poison ship and felt ashamed in his
Teutonic heart. His Kameradinen had dared to go where
he had been afraid to go, and that was not good enough.
He proposed the motion — it was a fundamentally democratic ship — that they lower the other boats, and that they
jump to it.

'Why,' Vanderdecker was asking, 'have you two ladies
chained yourselves to the rail of my ship? Sorry if that
sounds nosy, but ...'

'Because,' Martha replied, 'we are sisters of our mother
Earth.'

There was a brief silence, and then the first mate spoke.

'Captain,' he said, 'if they're her sisters, how can she be their mother?'

Vanderdecker smiled patiently at his first mate. 'Not now, Antonius,' he said. 'I'll explain later. Environmentalists?'

'That's right,' Martha said. 'So ...'

'So why are you chained to the railings of my ship? Practice?'

Martha sneered, although Vanderdecker couldn't see because of the gas mask. 'Don't act innocent with me. We know what you've got on this ship.'

'What have I got on this ship?' Vanderdecker said. 'Go on, you'll never guess.'

'Extremely hazardous toxic chemical waste,' came the reply, in chorus. Vanderdecker shook his head.

'No,' he replied, 'you're wrong there. Apart from a few tins of supermarket lager we got in Bridport last time, that is. It's true what they say, you get what you pay for. I'm sorry,' he said, noting a certain hostility. 'You were guessing what I've got on this ship.'

'If there's no toxic waste on this ship,' said Jo sardonically, 'how do you explain the smell?'

Vanderdecker shrugged and turned to the first mate. 'All right,' he said, 'which one of you forgot to buy the soap?'

'Very funny,' Martha snarled. 'We know you've got that filth on board, and we're not unchaining ourselves until you turn back to where you came from.'

'I promise,' Vanderdecker said solemnly, 'there's not so much as a thimbleful of toxic waste on board. You can look for yourselves if you like.'

Martha laughed. 'What, and unchain ourselves? You'd really like that, wouldn't you?'

Vanderdecker frowned irritably. 'Look, miss,' he said, 'if you think I'm getting any sort of thrill out of seeing two females in wetsuits and gasmasks chained to a railing, you're working the wrong pitch. Try Amsterdam. And if you're so damned nosy as to want to go poking about looking for seeping oildrums, then be my guest. If not, then please excuse me, I've got a ship to run.'

The two women stood firm and scowled at him. Just

then, Sebastian drew his attention to the other four dinghies making their way across from the *Erdkrieger.*

Their arrival solved what could have developed into a very tedious situation. Once the raiding party had been over the *Verdomde* inch by inch, molesting the ship's stores with Geiger counters and sticking litmus paper into the beer barrel, they had to admit that it was clean as a whistle. But smelly, nevertheless.

'Tact,' said Vanderdecker in German to his opposite number from the *Erdkrieger,* 'is clearly not your strong suit. I admit we aren't all lavender bags and rosewater, but we have been at sea for rather a long time.'

'But this ship,' said the German. 'It's so peculiar. Why are you sailing in a galleon?'

'Living archaeology,' Vanderdecker replied. 'We're reconstructing Magellan's circumnavigation of the world.'

As he said this, Vanderdecker was conscious of a puzzled noise behind him. It was the first mate.

'So that's what we're doing, is it?' he said. 'I was beginning to wonder.'

The smile reappeared on Vanderdecker's face. Over the centuries it had worn little tracks for itself, and its passage was smooth and effortless.

'That's right, Antonius,' he said. 'I'll explain later.'

'Who was Magellan, captain?'

'Later!' Just for a split second, the smile was disrupted; then it smoothed itself back. 'We're doing it in aid of the rain forests,' he said to the German, to whom this remark, astonishingly, made sense.

'Oh,' he said. 'That's very good. Sorry to have bothered you.'

'Not at all,' Vanderdecker replied. 'I mean, we're on the same side, aren't we? All Greens together, so to speak.'

The captain nodded enthusiastically, so that the hose of his gas-mask clunked on his muscular stomach. Vanderdecker winced, but imperceptibly.

'So,' he asked, as casually as he could, 'where are you off to then?'

'Dounreay,' said the German cheerfully. 'We're going to sabotage the nuclear power plant.'

'Jolly good,' said Vanderdecker. 'But isn't that a bit counterproductive? Blowing up a nuclear plant?'

'Who said anything about blowing it up?' said the German. 'We're going to stuff tulips up the drainpipes.'

'What a perfectly splendid idea,' Vanderdecker said, through his Antonius smile. 'Very best of luck to you. Got enough?'

'Enough what?'

'Tulips.'

'Ja, ja, we have Uberfluss of tulips.' He waved proudly at the distant profile of the *Erdkrieger.* 'Our whole ship,' he said, 'is full of tulips.'

'Isn't that nice,' Vanderdecker said, afraid for a moment that the corners of his Antonius smile would meet round the back of his neck and unzip his face. Then an idea occurred to him. 'If you're going to Dounreay,' he said, 'you could do me a small favour.'

'Certainly,' said the German.

'Have you,' Vanderdecker said, 'got any paint?'

'Ja, naturlich. Uberfluss of paint.'

'Red aerosol paint?'

'Ja,' said the German. 'Humbrol.'

'Then,' said Vanderdecker, 'I don't suppose you could see your way to painting a little message for me on the walls somewhere. I'll write it down for you if you like.'

Thus it was that when Martha, Jo and the German were finally bundled off in vans by the Sutherland and Caithness Constabulary, they left behind them a crudely-inscribed but extremely visible message on the perimeter wall of Dounreay power station.

ALL THAT GLITTERS IS NOT GOLD, it read. YOU SMELL, MONTALBAN. YOURS, VANDERDECKER.

CHAPTER SEVEN

G erald — you remember Gerald — was puzzled. He squashed the plastic cup in his hand into a spiky ball and dropped it in the waste-paper basket, where it bounced off a heap of shareholders' circulars and rolled onto the floor under his swivel chair.

Actually, Gerald wasn't the only person in the City of London that morning who was seriously puzzled, and we only single him out because we have already been introduced to him and know what a level-headed sort of fellow he usually is. If Gerald can't understand it, it must be odd.

It was. Something extremely unpleasant was happening to the dollar, and Gerald didn't like it. His relationship with the dollar was rather like Heathcliffe's relationship with Cathy, although which of them was which at any given moment it was generally difficult to decide. But if something bothered the dollar, it bothered Gerald. It was like telepathy.

At the next desk, Adrian was getting into an awful tangle with the Deutschmark, while Imogen had washed her hands of the yen and was having a quiet sit down and a cup of lemon tea. In fact, virtually all the occupants of the glass tower that housed Marshall Price Butterworth were behaving like ants whose queen has just died; there was a great deal of activity and absolutely no unified purpose. And over the whole organisation hung the dreadful possibility that if this went on much longer they were all going to have to miss lunch. It was as bad as that.

Black Thursday, as it has since come to be known, started in the usual way. The breakdown of Middle East peace talks took some of the shine off oil and vague fears on Wall Street about the possibility of the restoration of the

Jacobites caused the pound to fall two cents in early trading, but good figures from the banking and insurance sector helped the FTSE to perk up a bit, and only the lost, violent souls whose business it was to follow the vertiginous progress of the Hang Seng were having anything but a perfectly average day. Then it happened. Somewhere in the ether through which the faxes hurtled invisible the notion was spawned that something too ghastly for words was about to happen to the National Lombard Bank. Nobody knew where it came from, but such instances of parthenogenesis are so commonplace in the Square Mile that nobody ever bothers to ask. Consult anyone who has had anything to do with the markets since they introduced the new technology and they will tell you that all such rumours originate with a little man who lives in a converted railway carriage in Alaska and phones them through to the newspaper seller at Liverpool Street station. It may not be true, but it provides a much-needed focal point for baffled indignation.

Once the rumour had started, it grew. Nobody believed a word of it, of course — nobody ever does — but as custodians of the trust of countless small investors they saw it as their duty to wipe as many millions off the price of everything as they possibly could, and so the process was set in ineluctable motion. In the short time it takes for a message to bridge the Atlantic on fibre-optic wings the rumour had hit New York, and from there it moved on, faster than light and considerably faster than thought, to Tokyo, Hong Kong, Sydney, Paris, Geneva and all the other financial capitals of the world. So swift was its development and transmission that within two hours of its immaculate conception it was prompting market-makers in the Solomon Islands to get out of cowrie shells and knocking the bottom out of the reindeer futures market in Lapland.

Gerald took another long, unfriendly look at the screen, scratched his ear with his left index finger, and decided to take an early lunch. The dollar, he decided, was only doing it to attract attention to itself, and if he ignored it then it would stop playing up and return to normal. It was not,

perhaps, the view that Keynes or Adam Smith would have
taken, but it made about as much sense as anything else.
He picked up his personal organiser, scribbled a note
saying 'Sell' on his scratch pad to remind him when he
came back, and tottered off to the Wine Vaults.

All the time in the world, said Vanderdecker to himself
through teeth clenched tight as masonry, we've got all the
time in the world, so let's not get all over-excited about a
little puff of wind in the North Sea.

The gale howling through the shredded canvas of the
mainsail was so loud that Vanderdecker was compelled to
stop talking to himself and shout to himself instead. All
around the *Verdomde*, waves as high as towers were
forming and collapsing, like those speeded up films which
show you a rosebud forming, flowering and withering away.
The rain meanwhile was lashing horizontally into his eyes,
so that even if it hadn't already been as dark as midnight
he wouldn't have been able to see anything anyway.
Nothing unusual, he screamed at his subconscious mind.
Normal business hazard. Slight electric storm in the North
Sea.

Out of the tiny corner of his eye which was still opera-
tional, Vanderdecker noticed something, and he edged out
from under the insufficient shelter of the beer-barrel.
'Sebastian!' he yelled, 'pack it in, will you? This is neither
the time nor the place.'

As soon as the first bolt of lightning had split the velvet
sky, Sebastian had hurried on deck with a great lump of
magnetic iron ore in his hands. He kept it specially for
thunderstorms, and although he had so far failed to attract
a single skyborne volt with it there was always a first time.
Up to a point, Vanderdecker admired the man's ingenuity,
to say nothing of his tenacity, but he wasn't in the mood for
a swim if a baffled thunderbolt went straight down
through the soles of Sebastian's invulnerable feet and
reduced the *Verdomde* to woodshavings.

'Take in all sail!' Vanderdecker shouted, but nobody was
listening, as usual. That's what's wrong with this bloody
ship, mused its captain as a wave broke over the side and

tried to pull all his hair out, too much bloody apathy. Nobody cares if all the sails get ripped into dusters. So what? We weren't going anywhere anyway. Only this time they were going somewhere; they were going to Geneva to see Professor Montalban, with five barrels of radioactive deodorant safely lashed down in the hold. The one time I want to get somewhere, I run into the worst storm in fifty years. Tremendous!

Just then there was a horrible rending sound; timber, grievously maltreated, giving way. The yard arm of the mainsail had cracked under the pressure of a freak gust, and its own weight was dragging it down on a hinge of splintered wood. Down it came with shattering force on the back of Sebastian van Doorning's head, crushing him onto the deck like a swatted cranefly. Old instincts die hard; before he knew it, Vanderdecker sprang forward and knelt over his fallen crewman, shielding his crumpled body from the violence of the storm.

'Is that you, skipper?'

'It's all right,' Vanderdecker said, as Sebastian's large eyes slowly opened. 'You're going to be all right.'

'Am I?'

'Yes,' Vanderdecker promised.

'Oh, for crying out loud,' Sebastian exclaimed, picked himself up, and shuffled away through the driving rain, muttering something about it just not being fair. Vanderdecker shook his head and retreated back to the cover of the beer-barrel.

When, eventually, the storm had blown itself out, Vanderdecker hadn't the faintest idea where they were. By a miracle — or sheer force of habit — the ship had stayed in one piece, but only just. The sails were in tatters, the mainmast was completely useless, and the whole structure of the vessel had been so badly knocked about that it was patently obvious that major repairs would be needed just to keep her afloat. Just my luck, Vanderdecker raged in the silence of his mind, just my perishing luck.

Ironically, there was now no wind whatsoever; the ship sat there like a rubber duck in a bath all the rest of the day, and when darkness fell the stars were clear and bright in a

cloudless sky. With their help, Vanderdecker worked out
more or less where he was and then faced up to an agonising decision.

The first mate's report on the damage forced him to
admit that a change of plan was inevitable; unless it was
patched up pretty damn quick, the ship would be going
nowhere except down. And there was only one place, in the
whole wide world, that the ship could be patched up. No
alternative. Pity the place was such a dump, but still.

Vanderdecker called the crew together on deck and told
them. We are no longer going to Geneva; instead, we are
going to Bridport. As the all-too-familiar chorus of groans,
complaints, accusations and other going-to-Bridport
noises reached its crescendo, Vanderdecker walked away
and opened the last can of Stella Artois. He needed it.

Man's reach must exceed man's grasp, or what's a heaven
for? For twenty years Marion Price had dreamed of a nice
little cleaning job at a chicken-plucking factory somewhere, and here she still was, running the tourist information office in Bridport.

Every year, when the clouds close in and Aeolus lets slip
the sack wherein the four winds are pent, about a hundred
thousand miserable-looking holiday-makers with children
dangling from their wrists traipse in from West Bay and
demand to be informed as to what there is to do in Bridport when it's wet. To this question, there is only one
answer. It rarely satisfies. Nothing shall come of nothing;
speak again. Sorry, ladies and gentlemen, but that's all
there is to it. There is absolutely nothing to do in this
man's town in the rainy season except grow your hair.

You don't put it like that, of course. You suggest that
they go and take a look at the Bridport Museum, or the
Rural Crafts Exhibition, or the Working Water Mill. You
draw them little plans on the backs of envelopes to show
them how to get there. They stand there, dripping, and
stare at you, as if you were keeping from them the secret of
the location of King Solomon's Mines, and finally they take
a few Glorious Dorset leaflets and go away. On your way
home in the evening, you retrieve the Glorious Dorset leaf-

lets from the litter bin on the corner and reflect on the
vanity of human wishes.

Some of them, however, refuse to go away until you come
up with something that sounds at least bearable, and these
poor fools are generally advised to go and visit Jeanes'
Boatyard. As a cure for optimism, Jeanes' Boatyard,
which is open to the public from 10 till 3 Mondays to
Fridays all year round, has few rivals. In the interests of
research, Marion has been there once. Never again. There
is a hackneyed quip about such-and-such being as interesting as watching paint dry. The paint-drying shop is the
highlight of a visit to Jeanes' Boatyard.

Here is Marion Price, and she is talking to a pair of
hopeless, incorrigible, dyed-in-the-wool optimists and
their seven-year-old offspring.

'Boatyard?' says the male optimist.

'The oldest working boatyard in Dorset,' replies the tape
recording that lives inside Marion Price's larynx. 'Boats
are built there as they have been for the last five hundred
years. Traditional crafts are lovingly kept alive by master
shipwright Walter Jeanes and his two sons, Wayne and
Jason. Nowhere else in Dorset can you more perfectly
recapture the splendours of Britain's age-old maritime
heritage. A wide range of refreshments and souvenirs are
also available.' And the very best of luck to you, my
gullible friends. Why don't you just go back home to
Redditch and redecorate the spare room?

A long silence. Jean-Paul Sartre would have savoured it.
'How do we get there, then?' says the female optimist.

'Let me draw you a map.' Nimble, practised cartogra-
pher's fingers that have long since sublimated the last
dregs of guilt draw a plan of the most direct route. The
optimists depart. The rain falls. Time passes.

Jane Doland, being properly brought-up, wiped her feet
before walking into the tourist information office. It was
her last hope; she had tried the phone book, the post office
and the hotel desk. If they couldn't tell her here, she would
give up and go back to her room.

'Excuse me,' she said, 'can you tell me where I might
find Jeanes' Boatyard?'

'Certainly.' The woman behind the desk smiled at her.
Thank God. It was wonderful to find someone actually
helpful in this dismal place. 'Shall I draw you a map?'

'If you wouldn't mind,' said Jane. 'I always forget directions, in one ear and out the other. Is it far?'

'Oh no,' said the woman behind the desk, drawing
busily without seeming to look at the paper, like one of
those machines in hospitals that draw charts of people's
heartbeats. 'Have you been to Bridport before?' she asked.
Jane said yes, once.

'It's a lovely little town, isn't it?' said the woman behind
the desk. 'Some people just keep coming back time and
time again.'

Very true, Jane reflected, you don't know how true that
is. 'This boatyard,' she asked, 'is it very ... well, old?'

'Yes indeed,' the woman replied brightly. 'Boats are
built there as they have been for the last five hundred
years.'

'As old as that?' Jane asked. 'That's quite a record, isn't
it? Well, thank you very much.' She looked at the map.
'Which way is north?' she inquired. The woman pointed,
and smiled again. Clearly she enjoyed her work. Just now,
Jane envied her that.

As she waded through the puddles in South Street, Jane
cast her mind over the events of the past week, starting
with the slump on the markets. As soon as she had seen
the report of the attempted sabotage at Dounreay and
what had been painted on the wall there, she had set off for
the North of Scotland as quickly as she could. It was no
problem getting to see the protesters who had done the
painting; she simply called the Inverness office of Moss
Berwick and they fixed it, using their contacts with the
lawyers who were defending them. It had not been an easy
interview. None of the Germans spoke A-level German,
only proper German (which is a quite different language)
and all of them were clearly confused as to why they
should be talking to an accountant when they were facing
criminal damage charges. But the story had slowly coagu-
lated there in the lawyer's interview room, and when all
was said and done, it didn't get anyone terribly much

further forward. All that Jane could say for certain was that one place that the Flying Dutchman was likely *not* to be was the North of Scotland, since he had just left there.

She arrived at West Bay at the same time as a television van, and the sight of it made her heart stop. For a terrible moment, she thought that the van might be there for the same reason as she was — after all, the link between the couple of sentences in the newspaper about goings-on at Dounreay and the dramatic slide on the world markets had yet to be sorted out; had some sharp-nosed ferret of an investigative journalist found out about the Vanderdecker policy? But the little mayfly of terror was soon gone as Jane remembered what she had heard on the car radio about some idiot boat-race at West Bay in the next day or so, and she dismissed it from her mind.

It was, she admitted to herself as she parked in front of the boatyard, a long shot, a hunch — or, if you preferred English to the language of the talking pictures, a very silly idea. It had started as she sat on the flight back from Inverness, trying to think of good reasons why she shouldn't follow the Montalban lead. This had not been easy; it was, after all, the logical next step, to go to Geneva, find this Montalban, dream up some pretext for talking to him, and find out what he knew. But for some reason best known to herself — natural diffidence, probably, with a large slice of embarrassment and laziness thrown in — she didn't want to go to Geneva. Her mind had been floating on the meniscus of this problem when she saw a paragraph on the back page of someone else's newspaper about terrible storms in the North Sea. It occurred to her that Vanderdecker would be somewhere in the North Sea at this precise moment, on his way to wherever he was going when he met the *Erdkrieger* (Holland, probably; after all, he was Dutch) and that he might have got caught up in this storm. With unaccustomed boorishness she leaned forward and studied the other person's newspaper, and saw that the storm (the worst for fifty years, so they reckoned) had been off the Dutch coast. Well then, she said, Vanderdecker's ship is very old and probably very fragile. If he's been out in that, he may well need repairs. And where does

he come to get his boat fixed? Bridport, of course. A long
shot. A hunch. A very silly idea. We shall see.

'Sorry,' said the sound recordist. 'I didn't see you there.'

Danny Bennet looked at the sleeve of his suede jacket,
then at the sound recordist, and said something very
quietly which nobody was supposed to hear. His debut in
the field of sports coverage was not going well, mainly
because he hadn't the faintest idea of what was going on.

It was still raining outside, and from that point of view
the inside of the scanner van was as good a place to be as
any. It was dry, there was a thermos of at least luke-warm
coffee, and no cameramen. That, however, was about it as
far as the attractions of the venue went. On the other
hand, there were the monitors, and Danny didn't like them
at all.

So far as he could make out, his job was to direct oper-
ations in such a way that the viewer at home got the best
possible view of the proceedings from the best possible
angles. In order to manage this, Danny had to make sure
that the little motor boats with his camera crews in them
were in the right place at the right time. Since he hadn't
the faintest idea where they were, this was of course
impossible. All he could see were the pictures on the
screens. There was another minor difficulty to face up to;
he was entirely ignorant of the rules of old ship racing,
which meant that he didn't have a clue what the pictures
on the screens were supposed to look like. Racing, as far as
he understood it, meant a number of competitors trying to
go faster than each other; but all the old ships went quite
remarkably slowly. This was confusing, like a boxing
match between two pacifists. There was no way of knowing
whether he was doing it right or not.

Usually in these situations the wise thing to do was to
leave it all to the cameramen and not get under their feet.
Cameramen have invariably done it all before and know
precisely what they are supposed to be doing; their Aatens
would be glued to the centre of the action all the time, and
all the producer would have to do is sit in the van and stay
awake. Unfortunately, this was the first year that the BBC

had seen fit to televise this stirring maritime spectacle, and so everyone was as ignorant as he was. For the first time in his television career, cameramen were asking him things instead of telling him. It should have been a moment to savour. It wasn't.

At least he had the radios. He could shout into them. It didn't improve matters — in fact it seemed to make them worse — but it made him feel better.

'Chris,' he yelled, 'can you hear me, Chris?'

Chris replied that he could hear him perfectly well, thank you.

'Chris,' Danny said, 'what the hell am I meant to do with this close-up of a seagull you're giving me? This isn't bloody 'Naturewatch', you know.'

Not unreasonably, Chris asked what he should be filming instead, and Danny was at a loss for a reply. Then he had an inspiration.

'Chris,' he yelled, 'use your bloody common sense, will you? This is supposed to be a boat race, right?' Then he switched to another frequency quickly, before Chris had a chance to argue.

'Don't let's play silly buggers, Terry,' he was saying now, glorying in this marvellous new formula he had found, 'this is meant to be a boat race, okay? Just use your common sense and get on with it.' Click. 'Derek, can I just remind you we're supposed to be filming a boat race here?' It was as easy as that.

Then a horrible thought struck him. Perhaps it wasn't meant to be a boat race, or at least not yet. He pulled off his earphones and leant back to talk to the man from the brewery which was sponsoring the event, and who seemed to know more about it than anybody else. 'Excuse me,' he asked, 'have they started yet?'

The brewer shook his head. 'Not for five minutes,' he said. 'Everyone's just getting into position.'

'Oh.' Danny drove his fingernails into the palm of his hand. 'What's the starting signal, then?'

'They fire off a cannon,' said the brewer. 'From that big white yacht.'

'I see,' Danny said. 'Which big white yacht?'

The brewer shrugged. 'The starter's yacht, naturally. Shouldn't you have a camera on it, by the way?'

Danny cast a frantic eye over his bank of monitors. No big white yacht. 'Haven't I?' he said.

'No.'

Danny grabbed the headphones and jammed them on. 'Terry!' he shouted. 'Stop arsing about and get a shot of the starter's yacht. Don't you realise they'll be starting in five minutes?' Then he switched frequencies as quickly as a rattlesnake. Miraculously, a big white yacht appeared on one of the monitors. It worked!

Danny turned back and smiled at the brewer. 'Amateurs!' he explained. The brewer looked at him but said nothing.

'Chris,' Danny was off again, 'I can see the seagull, pack it in, will you — Dear God, what's that?'

On one of the monitors there was the most remarkable ship Danny had ever seen. It wasn't just another reconstruction of a tea-clipper or overgrown yacht; it was a whacking great galleon, like a pirate ship or something left over from the Armada Year. It was extraordinary.

'Phil,' Danny bellowed, 'zoom in, I want a closer look. What is that?'

Phil did what he was told, and Danny could see little men in funny costumes running up and down rope ladders. The ship looked like it was in a bad way; its sails were in rags, and some of the wooden bar things the sails were supposed to hang down from were broken off or dangling precariously from frayed ropes. Surely they weren't proposing to enter it in the race?

Danny was aware of someone sitting beside him. It was the brewer. He was staring.

'Odd,' he said. 'I don't remember that being on the list of competitors.'

Danny stared too; there was something magnetic about this very old-looking old ship. He tried to think if any film companies were releasing spoof swashbucklers this year, and were trying to crash the race to get coverage. But the ship didn't look as if it was trying to attract attention to itself; if a ship can have an expression, it was looking more

embarrassed than anything else, as if it had come to the
party wearing the wrong thing. Which it had, at that.

'Phil,' Danny said, 'get in closer.'

'All right then,' Vanderdecker shouted, 'if any of you
bloody intellectuals think you can do any better, you're
welcome to try. Come on, then, who's going first?' Total
silence. 'Right then, let's have a bit less of it from now on.'

Righteous indignation is a useful thing; it was galva-
nising Vanderdecker into an uncharacteristically assertive
display of authority at a time when, left to himself, he
would be curled up in his cabin wishing it would all go
away. But, because the crew were all muttering about him
and calling him names behind his back, in spite of the fact
that he had managed a quite spectacular feat of seaman-
ship in just getting his shattered ship this far, here he was,
doing his best. It probably wasn't going to be good enough,
but that was just too bad.

They had started shipping water badly just off the Isle
of Wight, and soon after that it was clear to Vanderdecker
that he was going to have to be very clever and even more
lucky to get this miserable remnant of a sailing-ship to
Bridport in one piece. There would be no time to lie up and
sidle into their usual sheltered and discreet cove under
cover of darkness; they were going to have to go in in broad
daylight, and the hell with it. That's if they could get that
far. For the last six hours it had been touch and go, and
Vanderdecker had amazed himself with his own brilliant
resourcefulness and skill in managing to cope. Nobody
else was impressed, of course; they all seemed convinced
that it had been his fault to start with. But that couldn't be
helped.

Vanderdecker had groaned out loud when he saw all the
ships in West Bay; there was no way they could make
themselves inconspicuous now. So far they hadn't been
intercepted, but it couldn't last. He had considered not
using the deodorising water from Dounreay, so that the
smell would keep them at bay, but he recognised that that
would cause more problems than it would solve. Better to
get it over with.

* * *

Danny Bennet got up from his place in front of the monitors. He felt that peculiar tingling at the base of his skull that meant 'story'.

'Julian,' he said, 'I'm just popping out for a minute. Film the race for me, will you?'

Julian said something, but Danny chose not to hear it. Partial deafness ran in his family. The brewer got up too.

'Are you going to have a look at that ship?' he said.

'Yes,' Danny replied. 'Coming?'

The brewer nodded. 'They aren't on the list of competitors,' he said. 'My company is very strict about things like that. For all I know, it could be demonstrators or something.'

Danny jumped down from the van and called to a cameraman who was sitting on a packing-case reading a newspaper. They hired a boat and set out to take a closer look.

For the record, Julian filmed the race, and he did it very well. Remarkably well, considering that he had only dropped in to take orders for pizzas. Even D.W. Griffiths had to start somewhere.

'Right then,' said the Flying Dutchman, 'gather round, let's get a few things straight before we go in to land.'

It wasn't a particularly brilliant speech — not in the same league as King Henry's address at Harfleur or something by Churchill — and it got the reception it deserved. Vanderdecker wasn't in the least surprised.

'You will have noticed,' he continued, 'that the bay is full of boats. What you may have overlooked is the fact that most of them are sailing-boats, not motor-boats. I think we've been lucky, and pitched up in the middle of some sort of yacht-race or regatta or something, so if we act naturally and mind our own business, perhaps nobody will take any notice of us. Meanwhile, it's quite important that we should get this ship over to Jeanes' Boatyard in the next half hour, because if we don't we're all going for a swim. Got that?'

A rhetorical question. With an exquisitely fine mixture of apathy and contempt the crew of the *Verdomde* slouched back to their positions and got on with their work. They were going to make it, but only just.

'Captain,' Vanderdecker turned round to see the first mate behind him, looking worried.

'Not now, Antonius,' Vanderdecker said.

'But Captain ...'

'Please,' Vanderdecker said, as gently as he could, 'I know you mean well, but just now ...'

'Captain,' Antonius said, 'there's a boat coming alongside.'

Vanderdecker stared at him for a moment in horror. 'What?'

'I said there's a boat ...'

'Where?'

Antonius pointed proudly at the boat, which was about thirty yards away and closing fast. 'There,' he said, as if he was pointing out a new star in the Crab Nebula. 'I saw it just now.'

'Oh God,' Vanderdecker muttered, 'not now, we haven't got time.'

'Haven't we?' Antonius said. Vanderdecker had almost forgotten he was still there. 'Time for what?'

'That's bloody marvellous,' Vanderdecker went on, mainly to himself. 'We've got to get rid of him somehow, and quickly.'

Antonius beamed. 'Leave it to me, skipper,' he said, and disappeared down the companionway before his commanding officer could stop him. He was heading towards the gun deck, where the ship's entirely authentic sixteenth-century culverins were lined up. Vanderdecker called after him but he didn't seem to hear. He had thought this one up all by himself. It was his big chance.

'Fire!' he shouted down the hatch.

'You what?'

'Fire!' repeated the first mate impatiently, 'and less lip off you.'

'Please yourself,' said the voice, and a moment later there was the unique sound of an entirely authentic but hopelessly corroded sixteenth century culverin blowing itself to shrapnel, followed by disappointed oaths from Sebastian van Doorning.

In the bay, the competitors in the Bridport Old Ships Race jumped to their positions and cast off. The motor-boat, which contained Danny Bennet, a representative of a leading brewery, a cameraman, the boat's owner, thirty thousand pounds worth of camera equipment and a roundshot from an entirely authentic sixteenth-century culverin, sank. As the water closed over Danny's head, he suddenly remembered that he had forgotten something. Swimming lessons.

'You've got to do something,' the brewer said. 'I'm telling you, they shot a cannon at us. They were trying to kill us.'

The coastguard smiled a sort of 'well-yes-quite-possibly smile'. 'What exactly happened, then?' he asked.

The brewer shuddered and pulled the blanket closer round his shoulders. 'I went out with the producer in a launch — he wanted a close-up of the ship, and I wanted to see their entry form. They weren't on the list of competitors. We came in alongside and bang! They shot at us.'

'Shot at you,' repeated the coastguard. 'With a cannon.'

'With a cannon, yes.' The brewer had the feeling that his word was being doubted. 'They shot a hole in the boat and we sank. We swam back to shore.'

'I see,' said the coastguard. 'And which ship exactly was that?'

The brewer scowled. 'The galleon,' he said. 'The Tudor galleon.'

'Excuse me,' said the coastguard, 'but there isn't a Tudor galleon anywhere on the schedule.'

'Exactly,' said the brewer.

'Exactly what, sir?'

'Look,' said the brewer, who had not expected Socrates, 'you ask the rest of them, they'll say exactly the same thing.'

'I might just do that, sir,' said the coastguard. And he did.

The cameraman said that he'd heard a bang, sure. What

he wanted to know was who hired that perishing boat in the first place, when it was obvious that the man driving it was as pissed as a rat. He must have been, or he wouldn't have run into that buoy. The buoy we collided with. Just before we sank.

The owner of the boat said that he had almost certainly heard a bang, and he would be sueing the BBC for every penny they'd got. It was definitely the last time he hired his boat out to film people. They should have warned him that all that electrical gear was liable to blow up when it got water on it. Some people have no consideration for others. They just don't think.

Danny Bennet didn't say anything. He wasn't there. He was on the deck of the *Verdomde*, drinking a can of Skol and thinking 'Oh no, not again.'

CHAPTER EIGHT

Never a particularly dressy man, Vanderdecker had not taken much trouble choosing an appropriate outfit to visit Jeane's Boatyard. He hadn't even stopped to consider whether his shirt went with his trousers; he'd just flung open the lid of his sea-chest and grabbed. As a result, he was wearing a good, solid herringbone overcoat which had blossomed on the loom when George V was on the throne, a pair of flared slacks, a coarse Venetian doublet from the early seventeenth century, and Hush Puppies.

Jane Doland, on the other hand, didn't share this lilies-of-the-field attitude to clothing. By nature and inclination she was very much a baggy pullover and pleated skirt person, but she had realised quite early on that account-ants are not as other women are; that it stands as an edict in destiny that unless you wear a suit nobody will believe you can add up. She therefore affected the imitation Austin Reed look, and wore her light grey dogtooth check as if it had broad arrows running down the sleeves.

Most people who frequent Jeanes' Boatyard either buy their clothes in the army supplies shop or find them in the corners of fields. As a result, both callers at the yard looked rather out of place.

The problem of dealing with the House of Jeanes had been a constant source of worry to Vanderdecker for longer than he could remember. Usually he only went there once every generation, so there was no danger of being recog-nised and rebuked for not being dead yet; on the other hand, there was the equally difficult job of explaining himself from scratch every time he called. By now the words flowed out of his head without conscious thought; but the worry was still present, like a submerged rock.

The speech, as perfected over the centuries, went like this:

'Mr Jeanes? My name's Vanderdecker, I wonder if you can help me. I have this very old ship, and it needs some work doing on it.'

So far, so good. Mr Jeanes is expecting, at the worst, something that was last a tree in the 1940s. He says something non-committal, like 'Oh.' Although it was completely wasted on him, Vanderdecker had over the years acquired enough research material to write a definitive study of heredity among the seafaring classes; the only part of which that had registered with his conscious mind was the fact that every Jeanes since 1716 had said 'Oh' in precisely the same way.

'Yes,' Vanderdecker now replies. 'She's down in that cove half-way to Burton at the moment. Do you think you could come out and look at her?'

The invariable reply to this suggestion is 'No.' If by some wild sport of genetics a stray proton of politeness has managed to get itself caught up in the Jeanes DNA this quarter-century, the 'No' will be coupled with a mumbled excuse concerning pressure of work, but this is not to be taken too seriously. The truth is that deep down in their collective unconscious, the members of the Jeanes tribe believe that the world outside the Yard is populated by werewolves, particularly if you venture out beyond Eype, and consequently they try to go out of the curtilage of their fastness as infrequently as possible. Once a week to the bank is plenty often enough, thank you very much.

'Right then.' Vanderdecker replies, 'I suppose I'd better bring her in. There's not a lot needs doing, actually,' he adds, 'just a general looking-over, if you could manage that.'

This rarely gets a reply from a Jeanes, and Vanderdecker goes away and comes back with a sixteenth-century galleon. This is where the fun starts.

'Here she is,' Vanderdecker will now say. Jeanes will stare out of small, ferretlike eyes and say nothing. We have reached the unsolicited explanations stage, the trickiest part of the whole undertaking. The knack to it is not to look as if you have anything to explain, and it is best achieved by seeming to boast. The preferred gambit is something like 'bet you haven't worked on anything like *this* before?'

A flicker of a Jeanes eyebrow will communicate 'no', and we're away. We explain that the *Verdomde* is either: (a) a film prop; or (b) a rich man's toy; or (c) part of a ten-year project by the University of Chicopee Falls History Faculty to prove that Columbus was a liar; or (d) the entire naval strength of Monte Carlo; or (e) a fish fingers advertisement; depending on what this particular Jeanes is likely to believe. From then on, it's just a matter of waiting for the work to be done and parting with an extremely large sum of money at the end of it.

The presence of so many Old Ships in West Bay dictated that it was rich man's toy time once again, and Vanderdecker quietly rehearsed some patter about how he had been all set to wipe the eyes of those cocky Australian so-and-so's with their fibre-glass hulls when the storm hit him, and now look at her. It wasn't perfect, but it ought to do well enough to get him out of here in one piece. Another consistent feature of the House of Jeanes throughout the ages is a notable lack of intelligence, which probably explains why they are still in the boat-building business after all these years.

With that characteristic shrug of the shoulders that you see so much of among fighter pilots and professional lion-hunters, Vanderdecker walked towards the yard entrance and put his hand on the gate. As he did so, he saw a face that he recognised. Not an everyday occurrence for the Flying Dutchman.

The last time he had seen it had been in Scotland, on the A9 near Dounreay. The time before that, his memory rather irrelevantly informed him, was in a pub in Covent Garden. I never forget a face, lied his memory smugly, but he wasn't listening.

The girl was staring, and Vanderdecker's heart froze. It wasn't a friendly stare. For a part of a second that only a scientist could accurately quantify there was silence and stillness. Then, very softly, the girl spoke.

'You're standing,' she said, 'on my foot.'

Many years ago now, when he had still been a force to be reckoned with in the jute business, Vanderdecker had been condemned to death. He couldn't remember the details — something about exceeding the permitted tariff in a Hanseatic League town in election year — but he could remember the flood of relief when the jailer came into his cell on what he had been led to believe was going to be his last morning on earth and told him that the sentence had been commuted to a seventy-groschen fine. Ironic, really, when you thought of what was going to happen to him a few years later; but the feeling had been just like coming up after being underwater for rather too long. The same sensation caught Vanderdecker somewhere in the windpipe, while his brain registered the apparent fact that the girl hadn't recognised him after all. When his respiratory system started working again, he apologised and lifted his foot.

'Sorry,' he said, 'how clumsy of me.'

'That's all right,' said the girl slowly. She was looking at him again, and as soon as her eyes met his, Vanderdecker realised how he would have reacted if on that cold morning in the 1540's the jailer had gone on to wink and say, 'Sorry, son, I was just kidding.'

The logical thing to do, said a part of Vanderdecker's mind that was still functioning, is to get out of here quickly. Vanderdecker noted this advice but took no steps to act on it. He was looking at the girl's face. A nice face, if you like them slightly on the round side. Some words bubbled up into his mouth, like nitrogen into the brain of a diver with the bends.

'Is this Jeanes' Boatyard?' he asked.

'I hope so,' said the girl. 'I've been looking for it all morning.'

She had noticed the doublet. Perhaps, suggested the voice of optimism, she's thinking what an idiot I look. Perhaps not.

Had Vanderdecker been able to get inside Jane's mind, he would have seen a brief replay of her sixth-form History of Art classes, and heard the words 'I've seen that shirt

somewhere before.' Jane didn't know it, but she had, in a
painting by Tiepolo. A hint to people who are contem-
plating living for ever; never have your portrait painted,
even if it only costs a couple of soldini, because there is
always the risk that centuries later the scruffy-looking
artist who did the painting will have turned into an Old
Master and be studied in good schools.

Come to that, said Jane to herself, I've seen that face
before; but where? Meanwhile, her voice started to work,
out of pure reflex.

'They gave me a map at the tourist information place,
but it can't be very accurate. Or maybe it's just that I'm
hopeless with maps.'

'Me too,' Vanderdecker lied. 'Let's see.'

Jane fished the folded glorious Dorset leaflet out of her
bag, and the two of them examined Mrs Price's cartog-
raphy with exaggerated diligence.

'If that's the Post Office over there,' Jane started to say;
then something fell neatly into the right place in her mind.
The clothes he's wearing, she said to herself, come from
different periods. He looks like a tramp who's robbed a
theatrical costumier. Jeanes' Boatyard. Different periods
of history. Surely not . . .

'Well,' the man was saying, 'if that's the Red Lion, then
that over there must be north. Try turning the map the
other way up and then we'll see.'

Jane thought for a moment. It was worth a try.

'So that's the Red Lion,' she said. 'I wonder what was
there before.'

'A butcher's shop,' Vanderdecker replied. Then he lifted
his head and stared at her.

'And when would that have been?' Jane said. Her voice
was quiet, slightly triumphant, and more than a little bit
frightened. The Red Lion had been built, according to the
smugly-worded inn sign, in 1778.

'Before your time,' Vanderdecker replied.

'But not yours.'

'No', said the Flying Dutchman. 'Not a lot is. Have you
been looking for me?'

'Yes,' Jane replied sheepishly.

'Then,' Vanderdecker said through a weak smile, 'you've made a pretty lousy job of it. This is the third time we've met. Small world, isn't it?'

Jane seemed to shrink back from even this tiny display of aggression, and Vanderdecker suddenly felt a great compacted mass of fear sliding away from him. It was like having your ears syringed; you could perceive so much more without it. Jane said nothing for a long time, and then looked at him.

'I imagine,' she said carefully, 'that someone in your position would think so.' She felt that she ought to add 'Mr Vanderdecker' at the end of the sentence, but that would be too much like a detective story. She waited for a reply.

'Too right,' he replied, and the smile began to solidify, like wax dropped on a polished table. 'Small and extremely boring.' He paused and took a deep breath. 'Just to make sure we're not talking at cross purposes, do you know who I am?'

'I think so,' she said. 'I think you're Julius Vanderdecker.'

For some reason, he had expected her to say 'The Flying Dutchman.' It was a nickname he had always hated — Dutchman yes, perfectly true, but why 'Flying', for pity's sake? — and the fact that she used his proper name was somehow rather touching.

'And you've been looking for me?' he asked.

'That's right.'

'I see.' His face seemed to relax, as he said, 'Will you just bear with me while I go and see about my ship? Then we can go and have a drink and talk about it.'

'Fine,' Jane said. Very matter-of-fact. Very civilised. Noel Coward saying it's a fair cop, but do let's be *adult* about it. 'Mind if I come too?'

'Be my guest,' Vanderdecker said. 'You can watch a master liar at work, if you don't mind being an accomplice.'

'Doesn't worry me,' Jane replied, 'I'm an accountant.'

Very slowly and cautiously, Danny Bennett peeled back the blanket from over his head and looked about him. He was not one of those shallow people who judge by first impressions; he needed more data before he could responsibly start to scream.

A man in a threadbare woollen doublet, patched hose and a baseball cap walked past him and gave him a friendly smile, which Danny did his best to return. Then the curiously-dressed one started to climb the rigging of the ship. After a long climb he reached the unrailed wooden platform (was that the crow's nest, or was that the little thing like a bran-tub at the very top? Briefly, Danny regretted not reading the *Hornblower* book his grandmother had given him when he was twelve); then he waved, took a deep breath, and jumped.

Danny's eyes instinctively closed; the tiny muscles of his eyelids were perfectly capable of taking that sort of decision without referring back to the central authority between his ears. As soon as his conscious mind had reasserted its authority he looked for a broken mush of flesh and bone-splinters. Instead, he saw the badly-dressed man picking himself up off the deck, apparently unharmed, and shouting to someone else. Someone else was also dressed like one of those comic relief characters in *The Merchant of Venice* whose names Danny could never remember, except that he had a Dire Straits tee-shirt instead of a doublet, and a baselard and dusack hung from his broad leather belt. A production of *The Merchant of Venice* at the Barbican, he decided.

'Hey!' shouted the sky-diver, 'I want a word with you.'

The heavily-armed man turned his head. 'You talking to me?' he said.

'Too right I'm talking to you.' The sky-diver pointed to one of the many tears in his doublet. 'Look at that.'

'I'm looking,' replied the other man. 'What about it?'

'That's your fault,' said the sky-diver angrily.

'Really?' The other man didn't seem impressed. 'How do you make that out?'

'Look,' said the sky-diver, 'you're meant to be the carpenter on this ship, it's down to you to make sure there's no nails sticking up where people can tear their clothes on them every time they take a jump.'

The other man laughed scornfully. 'Listen,' he said, 'if

you didn't keep on jumping, I wouldn't have to keep on
fixing the damned planking, so there wouldn't be any
nails. Would there?' And he thrust his head at the sky-
diver, until their noses were almost touching. For some
reason Danny was reminded of the Sistine Chapel, except
that that had been fingers, not noses.

'Don't give me any of that crap,' said the sky-diver. 'I've
had it up to here with your shoddy workmanship, and ...'

'Are you,' said the armed man quietly and furiously,
'calling me a bad carpenter?'

'Yes.'

With a movement of the arm so swift that Danny only
saw the arc it described in the air, the carpenter whipped
out his dusack and brought it down with sickening force on
the sky-diver's head. This time, Danny's eyelids stayed
where they were. So, incredibly, did the sky-diver's brains.
Just then, another of these peculiar people came hurrying
up. He too was dressed in a thought-provoking manner,
but Danny didn't even bother to analyse it.

'Cut it out, you two,' said the third party. 'Can't you see
we've got visitors?'

The two combatants turned round and smiled sheepishly at Danny, who reciprocated. 'It's all right,' the third
party called out, 'they're just kidding about, same as
usual.'

It was the 'as usual' that really worried Danny. He could
feel his mouth open and his chin melt into his neck;
always a bad sign.

'That's fine,' he said. 'Don't mind me.'

The three of them looked at him for a moment. Then
they walked over to him. He tried to shrink back, but he
was already tight up against a large coil of rope and there
was no scope for further withdrawals.

'I'm Danny Bennett,' he said, 'I'm with BBC sports.'

This remark had slightly less effect than an air rifle in
an artillery duel, and Danny wished he hadn't said
anything. The three peculiar people looked at each other.
Then one of them extended a large hairy-backed hand,
which Danny took. The skin on its palm felt like coarse-
grain sandpaper.

'Pleased to meet you,' said the third party, the one who had broken up the fight. 'I'm Antonius, this' — indicating the sky-diver — 'is Sebastian, and this' — the homicidal maniac with the big sword — 'is Jan.'

Danny smiled, a sort of railway-buffet tea smile. He felt he would be able to remember the names.

'So', said Antonius. He was leaning forward, with his hands on his knees. 'Sorry about your little boat.'

'My boat?' Danny asked.

'Your little boat,' said Antonius. 'We sank it, remember?'

'Oh,' said Danny, 'that boat. Yes. No hard feelings.'

Antonius smiled warmly. He was obviously a man who gave due credit for magnanimity when it came to sunk boats. 'Television,' he said.

Danny nodded, and then said, 'What?'

'You're with television,' Antonius said, 'aren't you?'

Danny nodded again, deeply relieved. For a while he had thought he was among pagans.

'Television,' Antonius went on, 'is a wonderful invention. We all watch it when we're on shore leave. "Coronation Street".'

'I beg your pardon?' Danny said.

'"Coronation Street",' repeated Antonius. 'That's television. We like that.'

'Really?' Danny narrowed his eyes, as if trying to see a single cell without bothering with a microscope. He felt that the conversation was drifting away from him again.

'Of course,' Antonius went on, 'we find it hard following the plot.'

'I know what you mean,' Danny started to say, but Antonius carried on over him, like a streamroller over a shrivelled apple. 'You see, we only get to see it once every seven years, and a lot changes.'

'Oh I don't know,' Danny said. 'Why every seven years?'

'We spend a lot of time at sea,' said Sebastian, 'don't we, Antonius?'

'That's right,' Antonius confirmed, 'because of the smell.'

Danny saw Sebastian kick Antonius on the shin, and for a moment he expected swords to start flying. But instead

Antonius looked sheepish and said, 'Of the sea. We love the smell of the sea, we Dutch. It's in our blood.'

Whatever's in your blood at this precise moment, Danny thought, it's sure as hell not seawater. However, he kept this comment to himself.

'No,' said Antonius, 'I dunno what we used to do before there was television. We played the flute a lot more than we do now, of course, and danced galliards and went to bear-baiting, but you can get sick of that sort of thing, can't you?'

'Yes,' Danny said. It was a good, non-commital thing to say, in the circumstances.

'The skipper, of course,' Antonius went on, 'he's got his alchemy. Apple?'

'I'm sorry?'

'Would you like an apple?'

'No thanks.'

'Please yourself. The skipper, he's never happier than when he's got his nose in some alchemy book or other. Can't see what he sees in it. Tried to read one myself once. No pictures. Just funny little line drawings. But he seems to like it, and I suppose it's better than ships in bottles. You ever tried that?'

'No,' Danny confessed.

'Don't bother,' said Antonius sagely, 'Waste of time. At least there's something at the end of the day with alchemy, so they reckon.'

'Is there?' Danny said.

'Course there is,' Antonius replied. 'But it wouldn't suit me, not all that reading and stuff you've got to do. It's all right when you're stuck in the middle of the sea, maybe, but the skipper doesn't stop there. He even does it on shore leave. I remember one time in New Amsterdam ...'

'New York,' Sebastian interrupted him. 'They call it New York now.'

'Do they?' Antonius looked surprised. 'What a daft name. New York, then. Miserable place, that. You ever been there?'

'Yes,' Danny said.

'Do they still have that law where you can't get a drink anywhere?'

'How do you mean?' Danny asked.

'You can't get a drink in New Amsterdam,' Antonius explained, 'It's against the law. Same in the whole of America, come to think of it.'

'Hang on,' said Danny. 'When was this?'

'Year or so back,' Antonius said, 'when we were last there. Didn't they have that law there when you went?'

'No,' Danny said. 'No, they didn't.'

'Anyway,' Antonius went on, 'there we all were, shore leave coming up, everyone as dry as the bottom of a parrot's cage, and where does the Skip take us in to? New bloody Amsterdam, just so's he could go and look something up about alchemy in a library there. We were not pleased, I can tell you. I mean, what would you have thought?'

Danny shuddered very slightly. If he tried very hard, perhaps he could nudge what he had just heard into some dark, damp corner of his mind where his subconscious could hide it and build a protective layer of mother-of-pearl over it until it wasn't quite so uncomfortable any more. 'I'd have been livid,' he said.

'We were,' Antonius went on. 'Sick as parrots, the lot of us. And then there was that other time, when we all had to go to Easter Island to see Halley's Comet. That was all to do with alchemy, he said. Something about magnetism. There is nothing, absolutely nothing, to drink on Easter Island except water. Mind you, the skipper's completely nuts on Halley's Comet. Never misses it.'

That word 'never' was a problem, Danny thought. Do what we may, we will not get the mother-of-pearl to stick on that one.

'Really?'

'Obsessive, I call it,' said Antonius, disgustedly, 'I mean, comets are all right, but once you've seen one, you've seen them all, and Halley's Comet's just another comet, right? But to hear the skipper talk, you'd think it was free beer and Christmas all rolled into one. Every time it pops up, there's no talking to him for weeks. Not unless you want your head bitten off, I mean. God knows I don't mind a man having a hobby, but there's such a thing as taking it too far.'

Danny glanced at Sebastian out of the corner of his eye, just in case there was a clue to be gleaned there. After all, it was possible that Antonius was the sole loony on this ship and that everyone else was reasonably sane. But Sebastian only looked bored.

'What was all that you were saying about alchemy?' Danny asked Antonius. 'About your captain, and it being a hobby of his?'

'Oh, he's serious enough about it,' Antonius replied. 'You interested in that sort of thing, then?'

'Yes,' Danny said. 'Not that I'm an expert or anything, but ...'

'Pity you missed the captain, then,' said Antonius. 'Tell you what, though, you could have a word with old Cornelius. He's not alchemy mad like the skipper, but he helps him a lot with the actual cooking of the stuff. He could show you the crucible and all that, if you like.'

Cornelius, it turned out, was only too happy to show the visitor the crucible, perhaps because the alternative was playing chess with Antonius. He led the way down to the rear gun-deck. There were no guns on the rear gun-deck; instead, there was a large stone basin with a sort of stove arrangement under it backing onto a bulkhead, with five or six shelves behind it. Half of these shelves had small, dark jars with handwritten Latin labels, while the other half contained books. Some of the books looked very old, but most of them were shiny new paperbacks, and when Danny glanced at the spines he saw that they were scientific textbooks. Because he had spent his science lessons daydreaming of scooping the big Board of Governors corruption scandal for the school magazine, Danny couldn't tell whether they were really as high-powered as their titles suggested, but he was prepared to bet that 'Elements of Quantum Mechanics' wasn't in his local library, and neither were 'Properties of Fissile Materials' or 'Sub-Atomic Particle Dynamics'. Unless Fissile was rotten proof-reading for fossil, that was something nuclear, while

Atomic spoke for itself. Nuclear! Suddenly, very far off, Danny began to see a chink of light.

'So you do a bit of this yourself, then, do you?' Cornelius's voice broke in on his reverie. It was a loud voice, rather jolly, filtered through a lot of facial hair.

'A little bit,' said Danny cautiously. 'Quantum mechanics, fissile properties, that sort of thing.'

'Huh.' Cornelius was not impressed, apparently. 'All that modern crap the skipper's so hot on. Boring. Give me the old ways any time.'

'Good, are they?' Danny asked. Cornelius grinned.

'Good?' he chuckled. 'Watch this.'

He produced a Zippo from the battered leather pouch that hung from his sword-belt and opened the stove door. Then he messed about with a few of the jars. 'Don't tell the skipper,' he said, 'he gets all snotty if I use his gear. But I've done it lots of times, it's like falling off a log.'

'Dangerous, you mean?'

'Easy,' said Cornelius. 'You got anything metal on you?'

Danny had a sudden flashback to a children's party when he was six. There had been a conjuror, and he had ended up with a lot of coloured flags being pulled out of his ears. He pulled himself together and reached in his pocket for his car keys. 'Will these do?' he said.

'Fine,' replied Cornelius. He took them and tossed them into the crucible before Danny could stop him. There was a flash of white light and a faint humming noise, like the sound you hear when you stand under an electric pylon.

'Takes about thirty seconds to do all the way through,' Cornelius said. 'Beats your fission into a cocked hat, if you ask me.'

Thirty seconds later, Cornelius reached under the stove and produced what looked like a solid gold ladle. With this he extracted the car keys from the crucible and held them under Danny's nose. They were glowing with the same blue light, and they seemed to have been turned into pure gold. Pure gold car keys. It reminded Danny of the time Gerald had taken him round the Stock Exchange.

'There you go,' Cornelius said, and tipped them out onto Danny's hand. 'Don't worry, they aren't hot or anything.'

Danny winced, but he could feel nothing. The blue light
faded away. The keys felt unnaturally cold and heavy.
Solid gold. What did solid gold feel like?

'Impressive, huh?' said Cornelius.

'Very,' Danny said. He stared at his car-keys. In his
mind, a strange and terrible alchemy of his own was
taking place. All this meaningless garbage was turning
into a story; a story about unlicensed, clandestine nuclear
experiments on a weird ship manned by lunatics. Story.
Story. Story. If only he could get off this dreadful ship and
get to a telephone, he would be through with even the
distant threat of sports reporting for ever and ever. Until
then, however, there was investigative journalism to be
done.

'Tell me something,' he said, as casually as possible.
What was that man's name? The arch-fiend of the nuclear
lobby, the man behind all those goings-on at Dounreay.
There had been a protest, he remembered.

'What?'

'Do you know someone, a guy called Montalban?
Professor Montalban? He's into all this alchemy, isn't he?'

Cornelius' face split into a huge laugh. 'Too right I know
Montalban,' he said. 'He's the one who got us into all this
mess to start with.' Then something seemed to register
inside Cornelius' head. He looked at Danny again; eyes not
friendly, not friendly at all. 'How come you know
Montalban?' he said.

Fortune, it has often been observed, favours the brave.
At that particular crucial moment, two boats were
approaching the *Verdomde*. On one, coming in to the star-
board side, was Vanderdecker and Jane Doland. On the
other side was a small motor-boat, containing a couple of
stray newspaper photographers who thought the ship
looked pretty and reckoned some of the glossies might be
able to use a photograph. Because the bulk of the *Verdomde* was between them, of course, neither could see the
other.

Danny spotted the motor-boat through an open gunport. On the one hand, he said to himself, I cannot swim.
Never mind.

'Where do you think you're going?' Cornelius roared at him, and tried to grab his arm; but it was too late. Danny had already squeezed his slight shoulders through the gunport. A moment later he was in the water, bawling for help and thrashing about like a wounded shark. The motorboat picked him up just before he drowned.

The first thing he saw when his eyes opened was a camera-bag with lots of lenses and rolls of film in it. 'Press?' he gasped.

'Well, sort of,' said one of his rescuers. 'Freelance. Does it really matter, in the circumstances?'

Swing low, sweet chariot, said Danny's soul inside him. 'Listen ...' he said.

CHAPTER NINE

'There you go,' said Mrs Clarke, 'I've brought you a nice cup of coffee. Don't let it get cold.'

She put the cup down on the table, next to the other two cups. They were all full of cold coffee, with that pale off-white scum on the top that right-thinking people find so offputting.

'Thank you,' said the man at the table without looking up. He reached out, located a cup by touch, lifted it to his mouth and drank half of its contents. It was one of the cold ones, but he didn't seem to notice. Mrs Clarke shuddered and went away. Although she was not a religious woman, she knew where people who let hot drinks go cold went when they died. Back in front of her typewriter she shook her head sadly and wished, not for the first time, that she'd taken the job at the plastics factory instead.

Had Professor Montalban, who had recently returned from Geneva, realised how much pain he was inflicting on his secretary, he would have taken care to drink the hot coffee. He was by no means a callous person. Just now, however, his powers of concentration were directed elsewhere. His mind was centred on a small area of the table, which contained a foolscap pad, three pencils (sharpened at both ends), a calculator and ten or fifteen books, all open. He had a headache, but that was not a problem. He had had the same headache for three hundred and forty two years, and he knew it was caused by eyestrain. Because of the elixir, it was impossible for his eyesight to deteriorate, however much he abused it, but it didn't stop him getting headaches. He also knew that the optician in Cornmarket Street could fix him up in ten minutes with something that would cure his headache forever. It was just a question of finding the time. Tomorrow, perhaps, or the next day.

Ironic, really, time was one thing that Professor Montalban had plenty of. Genius he most certainly lacked; he didn't even have that little spark of intuition that the scientist so desperately needs if he is ever going to get anywhere. He was nothing more than a competent and careful follower of the proper scientific procedures. But, because he had plenty of time, this didn't matter. He could do everything by a process of elimination. This may sound haphazard, but the true test of any scientific method is results, and Montalban's results were quite astoundingly spectacular, if you chose to look at them that way. Every major scientific discovery from gravity to the electric toothbrush was based on the work of Professor Montalban. Every breakthrough, every quantum leap, every new departure he had either initiated or, more usually, carried through himself to the verge of publication. In every case, someone had come in at the last moment and stolen all the credit, but that was what the professor wanted. He had reasons of his own for not wanting to make himself conspicuous.

Suppose a Neolithic cave-dweller had wanted to put some shelves up in his cave. All he has is a tree. What he must do is invent the refinement of metals, the saw, the plane, the chisel, the drill, the screwdriver, the screw, the rawlplug, sandpaper, polyurethane varnish, the spirit level, the carpenter's pencil and, finally, the marble-look Formica veneer, and then he can set to work. Nothing intellectually taxing about it all, but it takes a lot of time.

Professor Montalban had not set out to discover electricity, nuclear fission, or the circulation of the blood, just as the caveman has no great urge to pioneer the Stanley knife: they were just tiresome and necessary stages in the quest for the final overriding objective, in the same way as modern mathematics is a by-product of Richard the Lion-Heart's desire to recapture Jerusalem. Professor Montalban's objective was, in his eyes at least, infinitely more important than the little side-shows on the way, such as splitting the atom: Professor Montalban was searching for the Ultimate Deodorant.

That had not always been the objective. When he was young, he had been more interested in the secret of eternal life and the transmigration of elements, which was how he had got into this mess in the first place. He now regarded his earlier ambitions in the way the managing director of a major multinational might review his childish intention to be an engine-driver. If he had any philosophy of life, it was that everything happens by accident, and that at any given time, ninety-nine-point-nine-five per cent of the human race are a confounded nuisance.

He worked on, as he had been doing for so many years, until his headache became so insistent that he could concentrate no longer; and by that time, of course, the optician had shut up shop and gone home. So the professor put on his jacket and took a stroll round the college yard to clear his head. It was a cool evening, and if Montalban hadn't been so engrossed in a fallacy he had detected in the theory of Brownian motion he would probably have enjoyed the sunset. As it was, he wandered into the college bar without thinking and sat down at one of the badly-scarred chipboard tables in front of the television. He didn't take any notice of what was on the screen — a sports programme of some sort — and let his thoughts wander back to the interplay of random particles. Then he became aware of somebody yelling something loudly in the very furthest part of his mind.

'Look!' it was yelling. Professor Montalban looked. On the screen, in the far corner of the picture but unmistakeable, he saw something he recognised. It was a ship.

'And?' Jane asked.

'And,' Vanderdecker said, 'that's about it, really. I have had other experiences, but none of them germane to the point at issue. Which reminds me.'

'Yes?'

Vanderdecker smiled, and lifted his glass to his lips. 'What is the point at issue? Why were you looking for me?'

Despite the recent reform in British licensing laws, the only place you can get a drink at half-past three in the afternoon in West Bay is the Rockcliffe Inn. It is hard to imagine a thirst powerful enough to drive a person into the Rockcliffe Inn. It can therefore be taken as read that Vanderdecker was not smiling at his beer, which was thick, cloudy and infested with little white specks that reminded him of the stuff you find in the corners of your eyes after a long sleep.

'Because of the insurance policy,' Jane said.

Vanderdecker looked up. 'What insurance policy?' he asked.

'The Vanderdecker policy,' Jane said.

'Don't let's be all cryptic,' Vanderdecker replied, 'not when the beer's so foul. If you want to be cryptic, I demand Stella Artois at the very least.'

'Who's Stella Artois?'

'Barbarian.'

'Sorry.'

'Stella Artois,' said Vanderdecker, 'is a brand of beer. I'm sorry, that was very rude of me. I shouldn't have called you a barbarian just because you've never heard of it. Are you sure you've never heard of it?'

'Yes,' Jane replied. 'I don't like beer very much, I'm afraid.' afraid.'

'Then you are a barbarian. What's the Vanderdecker policy? Go on, it's your turn.'

'Your life insurance policy,' said Jane. 'With the House of Fugger.'

Vanderdecker was just about to object when two tiny leads connected in his memory. 'My life insurance policy?' he repeated.

'That's right.'

'Oh.' He frowned. 'That's all?'

'Yes.'

Vanderdecker put down his glass. 'After four hundred and fifty years,' he said, 'you want to sell me life insurance. Don't you people ever give up?'

But Jane was shaking her head. 'We don't want to sell you any life insurance,' she said, 'we want to buy it.'

As she stared at him, a tiny germen of a thought thrust a green blade through its shell in the back paddock of her mind. It was an extraordinary thought, but it was there.

'Why?' Vanderdecker said.

Jane said, 'Surely that's obvious,' but her heart wasn't in it. She could feel an enormous, colossal wave of laughter welling up inside her. Her entire body wasn't big enough to contain it. Meanwhile, Vanderdecker was talking.

'Are we talking about the same thing?' he was saying. 'I remember taking out a policy with the Fuggers, sure, but that was years ago. Hundreds of years ago, come to that. I haven't paid a premium for centuries; I mean, what was the point?'

'But you've still got the policy?' Jane could feel the laughter crashing against her teeth like the Severn Bore, but she kept it back.

'I don't know,' Vanderdecker said. 'I'm hopeless with things like that. Hang on, though.' He paused, and felt in the pocket of his overcoat. 'I usually put important documents in here,' he said, and he pulled out a big sealskin envelope. 'Not that I have all that many important documents, after all this time. Let's see.' He lifted the flap and started to rummage about. 'What's this? Alchemical notes, that's not it. Birth certificate, passport, the receipt for my electric razor, book of matches from Maxim's, what's this?' He peered at a curled yellow scrap of paper. 'No, that's not it. Ah, we're in luck. Is this it?' He fished out a folded sheet of vellum with the remains of a crumbled seal attached to it.

'I don't know,' Jane said. 'I can't read it.'

'Can't you?' Vanderdecker glanced at the tiny, illegible sixteenth-century script. 'I suppose you can't,' he said, 'it's in Latin. Yes, this is it. Is it important?'

'Have you ever read it?' Jane said. Of course, she realised, she shouldn't be doing this. She should have got hold of it and destroyed it, and so saved the world. But the pressure of the laughter against the sides of her skull was too much for her; she had to let him in on the joke.

'To be honest with you,' Vanderdecker said, 'no, I haven't. I can't be doing with all that legal-financial mumbo-jumbo.'

'You should,' Jane said.

Vanderdecker looked at her. His face had a tired, harassed look, as if this was starting to turn into a

problem. 'Let me guess,' he said. 'You're after me for four
hundred and fifty years unpaid premiums. Well, you can
forget that, because I just don't have that sort of money.'

That was too much for Jane; she started to laugh. She
laughed so much that the afternoon barmaid of the Rockcliffe Inn withdrew her attention from the Australian soap
opera she was watching on the bartop portable and stared
at her for at least three seconds. She laughed so much that
her body ached with the strain, and her lungs nearly
collapsed. Vanderdecker raised an eyebrow.

'What's so funny?' he said.

With a Herculean effort Jane stopped laughing, just for
a moment. 'Read it,' she said. 'Read it now.'

'If it'll stop you making that extraordinary noise,' said
the Flying Dutchman, and started to read. When he had
finished, he looked up and said 'I still don't get it.' Fortunately, Jane was incapable of further laughter.

'I'm sorry,' she said.

'So you should be,' Vanderdecker said, 'it's very embarrassing. You've no idea how conspicuous it makes me feel.
Do please try and keep a hold of yourself.' He folded the
policy up and put it away again, along with his birth certificate and the receipt for his electric razor.

'Are you from the insurance company?' he asked.

'Yes,' Jane said. 'It's a bank now, of course, as well as an
insurance company. And I'm not actually with them; I'm
an accountant.'

'So you said.'

'So I did.' Jane wiped the tears from her eyes with a
corner of her handkerchief.

'Do you know,' Vanderdecker said, 'you remind me of
someone.'

'Do I?'

'Yes.' Vanderdecker looked faintly embarrassed, as if he
didn't want to say what he was saying. 'Someone I used to
know, years back. In fact,' he mumbled, 'that was her
address on that piece of paper you saw just now. She must
have been dead for three hundred years now.'

'Go on,' Jane said.

'Greta,' said the Flying Dutchman, 'from Schiedam.

There's nothing to tell, actually. We met at a dance and just seemed to hit it off. I told her a joke, I remember — actually, it wasn't a joke as such, just something that had happened to me that she thought was funny — and she laughed so much she spilt wine all down my trouser leg. Anyway, it turned out that she was leaving for Bruges the next day, and it was the last day of my shore leave. She gave me her address. I wrote to her, seven years later, and seven years after that I picked up her reply from the poste restante in Nijmegen. Apparently she'd met this man, and perhaps he wasn't the most wonderfully exciting human being there had ever been but by all accounts he was going to be very big in worsteds one day, and of course she would always think of me as a very dear friend. Undoubtedly for the best,' he went on, 'things being as they are. Still.'

'And I remind you of her?' Jane asked.

'Only because you laugh so damned much,' replied Vanderdecker austerely.

'I see,' Jane replied. 'Can I get you another drink?'

Vanderdecker swirled the white specks round in the bottom of his glass. 'Yes,' he said. 'Only this time I'll try the mild.'

'Is that good?'

'No,' he said.

Shortly afterwards, Jane came back with the drinks. 'If it's nasty,' she said, 'why do you drink it?'

'Because it's there,' Vanderdecker replied. 'What's so special about my life policy, then? Do try not to laugh when you tell me.'

Jane took a deep breath. She was, she realised, gambling with the financial stability of the entire free world. On the other hand, it didn't seem like that, and the strange man had turned out not to be all that strange after all. 'Before I tell you,' she said, 'do you mind if I ask you something?'

'Be my guest,' Vanderdecker replied.

'Mr Vanderdecker,' she asked, 'what exactly do you want out of life?'

Vanderdecker smiled; that is, there was an initial movement at the corners of his mouth that developed into a ripple just under his nose and ended up with a full display of straight, white teeth. 'What a peculiar question!' he said.

'Yes,' Jane admitted, 'and as a rule I'm not into this soul-searching stuff. But you see, it is quite important.'

Vanderdecker was surprised. 'Is it?'

'Yes, actually,' Jane said, 'it is.'

'Well then,' Vanderdecker said, composing himself and looking grave, 'The way I see it is this. After all this time, and bearing in mind the things I've told you about, I would have thought it was more a question of what the hell it is life wants out of me. Blood?'

'I see,' Jane said. If she'd had a notebook, she would probably have written it down. 'So you've never had any urge to rule the world, or anything like that?'

'What, me?' Vanderdecker said. 'No, I can't say I have. It would be nice to change some things, naturally.'

Jane leaned forward and looked serious. 'Such as?'

Vanderdecker considered. 'I don't know,' he said, 'now you come to mention it. I can't actually think of anything that even remotely matters. You get such a wonderful sense of perspective at my age.'

'You look about thirty-three.'

'Thirty-five,' Vanderdecker replied. 'And you flatter me. Aren't we getting a bit sidetracked, or is this all relevant?'

'It's sort of relevant,' Jane said. 'So you would say that you're a relatively balanced, well-adjusted person?'

'Perhaps,' said the Flying Dutchman. 'When you consider that I've lived for over four hundred and fifty years, and seven-eighths of those years have been mind-numbingly boring, I think I've coped reasonably well. What do you think?'

'I think,' said Jane with conviction, 'that I'd have gone stark staring mad in the early fifteen-sixties.'

'I tried that,' Vanderdecker reminisced. 'It lasted about eight hours. You can't go mad running a ship, which is what I do most of the time. You simply don't get an opportunity. Just when you're starting to work up a good thick fuzz of melancholia, someone puts his head round the door to tell you that the cook and the bosun are fighting again, or that some idiot's lost the sextant, or we appear to be sixty leagues off the Cape of Good Hope and weren't we meant to be going to Florida? There's all sorts of things I was always meaning to get around to learning to play the flute, calculating the square root of nought, going mad — but I just didn't have the time. After a while you give up and get on with things.'

'But don't you ever feel ...' Jane searched for the right words, only to find that she'd forgotten to bring them. 'Don't you feel sort of different? Important? Marked out by Destiny?'

'Me?' Vanderdecker said, surprised. 'No. Why should I?'

'I'd have thought you might,' Jane said. 'What with being immortal.'

'That's not what it feels like,' Vanderdecker said. 'May I put it bluntly?'

'Please do.'

'It's hard to feel special or important,' he said, staring at the table in front of him, 'let alone marked out by Destiny, when you smell quite as bad as I usually do. I trust I make myself clear.'

'Perfectly,' Jane said.

'Good.' Vanderdecker lifted his head and grinned. 'Do I get to hear your story now? About this life policy of mine?'

'If you like,' Jane said.

'Fire away.'

So she told him.

'Look,' Danny said to the telephone, 'what you obviously fail to grasp is ...'

The pips went, and Danny fumbled desperately in his trouser pocket for more small change. What he found was five pennies, a washer and a French coin with the head of Charles de Gaulle on it which he had somehow acquired at Gatwick Airport. He made a quick decision and shoved the French coin into the slot. Remarkably enough, it worked.

'What you obviously ...' he said. The voice interrupted him.

'No, Danny,' it said. 'What *you* fail to grasp is that you're supposed to be filming a boat race. Anything not germane to high-speed navigation is therefore off limits. Keep that principle firmly before your eyes and you won't go far wrong.'

Danny dragged air into his lungs, which were tight with

anger. He forced the same air out through his larynx, but
he sublimated the anger into determination.

'All right,' he said. 'You leave me with no alternative.'

'You're going to film the race?'

'I am not going to film the race,' Danny said. 'I am going
to telephone Fay Parker at the *Guardian*.'

Coming from a man with five pennies and a washer in
his pocket, this was clearly an idle threat. But of course
the voice didn't know that, and just for once it said nothing.

'And you know what I'm going to tell her?' Danny went
on. 'I'm going to tell her the truth about the Amethyst case.'

The voice wasn't a voice at all any more. It was just a
silence.

'I'm going to tell her,' said Danny to the silence, 'that the
person who recommended to the Cabinet Office that the
Amethyst documentary should be banned wasn't the
Prime Minister or the Home Secretary or even the
Minister of Defence. It was the head of BBC Current
Affairs, who wanted it banned so that he could get himself
hailed as a martyr to the cause of press freedom and then
nobody would dare sack him on the grounds of gross
incompetence. Do you think she could use a story like that?'

The silence carried on being a silence, and Danny was
terribly afraid that Charles de Gaulle would run out before
it became a voice again. 'Well?' he said.

'Bastard,' said the voice.

Danny glowed with pleasure. 'Thanks,' he said, just as
the pips went.

'Really?' said Vanderdecker.

'Cross my heart and hope to die,' Jane replied, rather
tactlessly. 'That's why I was looking for you.'

'Oh,' Vanderdecker said. 'Do you know, that's rather a
disappointment.'

'Is it?' Jane queried. 'Why?'

Vanderdecker scratched his ear. 'Hard to say, really,' he
replied. 'I suppose it's just that I've been half expecting
people to be looking for me for a long time now, and for
other reasons.'

'That's a bit paranoid, isn't it?'

'Maybe,' said Vanderdecker, shrugging his shoulders. 'I just had this notion that what I was doing — being alive after so long and all that — was — well, *wrong*, somehow, and that sooner or later somebody was going to find out and tell me to stop doing it. Act your age, Vanderdecker, that sort of thing. And since I couldn't stop even if I wanted to, I wasn't keen to be found. I have this feeling that somehow or other I'm breaking the rules, and that's not my style at all.'

'What sort of rules?'

'The rules,' Vanderdecker said. 'Maybe you don't understand, let me try and explain. Do you remember the first time you went abroad?'

Jane shuddered. 'Vividly.'

'Do you remember that awful feeling of guilt,' Vanderdecker said, 'that you felt — I assume you felt — as if you were breaking all sorts of local laws and violating all sorts of local customs without knowing it, and sooner or later one of those policemen in hats like cheeseboxes was going to arrest you?'

'Yes,' Jane replied. 'That's a natural feeling, I guess, from being a stranger in someone else's country.'

'Well then,' Vanderdecker said, 'that's how I feel all the time. I'm a stranger everywhere except on a ship in the middle of the sea. I don't think I've broken any laws — I don't think just being alive is actually illegal anywhere, except maybe in some parts of South-East Asia — but the thought of all the embarrassment if anyone ever asked who I was or what I was doing ... Do you see what I'm driving at? It means that I can't give a truthful answer to virtually any question I'm likely to be asked, for fear of being thought crazy or rude. It gets to you after a while, let me assure you. And of course there's the smell.'

'Yes,' Jane said. 'I could see that would be a problem.'

'It is,' Vanderdecker assured her. 'Decidedly.'

'If we could just get back to what I was saying,' Jane suggested tentatively. 'About your life policy.'

'You want me ...'

'No.' Jane couldn't understand why she was so definite about this. '*They* want you to sign it away. Assign it back to them, actually, but it amounts to the same thing.'

'I see,' said the Flying Dutchman. 'Why should I?'

Jane couldn't think of a single reason. Not good.

'Excuse me for muddled thinking here,' Vanderdecker went on, 'because I haven't even started to consider all the ramifications of this yet, but why the hell should I?'

'Well,' Jane said feebly, 'it's not going to do you any good, is it?'

'That,' said Vanderdecker, 'if you'll pardon me saying so, goes for all life policies. Correct me if I'm wrong, but the prerequisite for collecting on the blasted things is being dead, and I remember hearing something somewhere about not being able to take it with you.'

'Exactly.'

'Exactly what?' said Vanderdecker, confused.

'You can't take it with you,' Jane said. 'So it's no good to you. On the other hand, it's putting the financial stability of Europe in jeopardy.'

'So what's so wonderful about the financial stability of Europe?' Vanderdecker said.

Jane felt that she could explain this, being an accountant: but while she was deciding where to start, Vanderdecker continued with what he was saying.

'Let me put it this way,' he said. 'If what you say is true, I'm in a position to tell all the money men in the world what to do. I have the power, the actual and useable power, to introduce a little bit of common sense into the economic system of the developed nations. In other words, I could save the world.'

'Do you want to?' Jane asked.

Vanderdecker considered for a moment. 'No,' he said.

'Why not?' Jane asked. 'Sounds like a good idea to me.'

'No it doesn't,' replied the Flying Dutchman. 'That's why you were asking me about whether I'd ever suffered from megalomania or a desire to rule things. To which the answer is still no. I mean, it's all very fine and splendid to think that I could sort out interest rates and conquer infla-tion and send the rich empty away and all that, but that's not me at all. Damn it, I couldn't even understand the jute market back in the fifteen-eighties. I'd just make things even worse than they are now.'

'So why not do what they want?' Jane said. 'It would make things easier for you as well.'

'Would it?'

'It could,' Jane said. 'All you'd have to do is think of the right price.'

'Go on.'

'Something like,' Jane said, 'an index-linked annuity starting at two million pounds a year, plus all the co-operation and protection you need. Passports, nationality papers, a new ship, bits of paper signed by presidents and prime ministers to shove under the noses of customs men and coastguards. Everything necessary to make life easy for you. No more of this skulking about, hiding, getting your ship fixed up by Jeanes of Bridport because there's nowhere else you dare go to. You could demand anything at all. A new identity. No questions asked. You could even start enjoying life. You wouldn't have to spend all your time in the middle of the sea, come to that.'

'What about the smell?'

'Demand that they build you a special massively air-conditioned bunker in the heights of the Pyrenees. A hundred special bunkers, one in every country. Real Howard Hughes stuff. That really wouldn't be a problem.'

Vanderdecker thought for a moment, then grinned. 'That's very kind of you, and I appreciate the offer, but no thanks. I think we'll just leave matters as they are.'

Jane felt as though someone had just pumped sand in her ears. 'Why?' she said.

'I don't know,' Vanderdecker confessed. 'Instinct, mainly. Look,' he said, putting his chin between his hands, 'I remember reading somewhere about these tramps, people who'd been living rough for years and years, who finally were persuaded to come in out of the wind and the rain into a nice clean hostel. Clean clothes, beds, hot food. After a week or so, they all started sleeping on the floor, wearing the same clothes all the time and eating the scraps out of the dustbins. The staff couldn't understand it at all, but the tramps just couldn't trust the beds and the clothes and the food; they reckoned they must be some sort of trap

and they wanted nothing to do with it. You get that way
after a while.'

'I see,' Jane said. 'So I've failed, have I?'

'Looks like it,' Vanderdecker said. 'Sorry.'

Jane considered for a moment. 'How about as a personal
favour to me?' she asked. Vanderdecker stared at her.

'Come again?' he said.

'As a personal favour,' she said, 'to help me out of a jam.'

'But ...' Vanderdecker's voice trailed away, and he
looked at her. Perhaps he saw something he hadn't seen for a
long time. 'You mean, just because I like you or something?'

'Just,' Jane said, 'because you're a nice person. Like
letting someone through in a stream of traffic, or giving up
your seat in the Underground.'

'I hadn't looked at it from that angle,' Vanderdecker
admitted.

'Try it.'

Vanderdecker drew in a deep breath. 'Did I mention,' he
said, 'about my adventures in the real estate business?'

'No,' Jane said. 'Are they relevant?'

'Fairly relevant, yes.'

'Oh,' Jane said. 'Fire away, then.'

'Right.' Vanderdecker leaned back in his chair and
closed his eyes. 'Many years ago,' he said, 'many years ago
even by my standards, I bought some land in America.
Don't know why; it was cheap, I had some capital for once,
I thought I'd invest it. My idea was to build a little place
out in the middle of nowhere but next to the sea, where I
and my crew could be sure of some privacy and a glass or
two of beer when we came in to land. That sort of thing.
Anyway, before I could start building, I met this man in a
pub who was down on his luck. He was Dutch, too, and I
felt sorry for him. He had a dreadful story to tell, about
how he'd been chased out of Holland because of his religious beliefs, forced to sell his farm and his stock and
come out to the New World and start all over again, and
how he hadn't got anything like the right price for his
property back home and the fare out here had taken up a
large slice of that because all the carriers were profiteers,
and on top of all that the weevils had got into the seed-corn

and three of his cows had got the murrain and how he was going to afford enough land in America to support a wife and three children he really didn't know. So I asked him how much he had and he told me and I offered to sell him my land for exactly that much. It was very cheap indeed, and he accepted like a shot. And I did it because I'm a nice chap, and of course it didn't matter a hell of a lot to me, considering how I was fixed.'

'And?'

'And what I sold him was the island of Manhattan,' said Vanderdecker, sadly. 'Error of judgement, wouldn't you say?'

Jane didn't say anything.

'Of course,' Vanderdecker went on, 'I wasn't to know that then. You never do. But that's the thing about eternal life; you have to live with your mistakes, don't you? Like when I met the Spanish Armada.'

'You met the Spanish Armada?'

'Pure fluke,' Vanderdecker said. 'It was just after the coming of the Great Smell, and we were lying off Gravelines, becalmed. Suddenly the sea is covered with Spanish ships. Marvellous. Then all the Spaniards become aware of the Great Smell, and before their commanders can stop them they're all casting off and making for the open sea with their hands over their noses. Result; they lose the weather-gauge and get shot to bits by my old jute-trading contact Francis Drake. Or what about Charles the Second?'

'Charles the Second,' Jane said.

'Exactly,' said Vanderdecker. 'There I was in this pub, having a quiet drink, when this tall man with a moustache asks me if he can hitch a lift as far as France. No problem. Cromwell didn't think so, but I didn't know that, of course. Dunkirk, there's another instance of exactly the same thing. If those German cruisers hadn't come downwind of me at exactly that moment, just as all those little boats were zooming across the Channel with no escort whatsoever ... You see the point I'm trying to make. I keep having these drastic effects on history. I don't try to. I don't even want to. I hate myself for it afterwards, but it keeps happening. You asked me if I thought I had a special destiny. I know I don't, it's just coincidence. Not coincidence, even; pure, calculable probability. If one man stays around long enough, just by his being there, important things are bound to happen to him or because of him sooner or later. Now there's nothing I can do to stop it, but I'm damned if I'm going to do it on purpose. It was bad enough that time with Napoleon ...'

'Napoleon?' Jane asked.

Vanderdecker scowled at her. 'Who do you think was the idiot who picked up a passenger on Elba in 1815?' he said. 'I met this man in a pub. "Where are you headed for?" he asks. "France," I tell him. "What a coincidence," he says, "so am I." Why is it, by the way, that they always want to go to bloody France? I tell a lie, though; Garibaldi wanted to go to Italy. Anyway, I've got to face the fact that history to me is little more than a horrible reminder of my own interference. Even now, I can't listen to the Skye Boat Song without cringing.'

Jane's eyebrows may have twitched up an extra quarter inch, but she said nothing. It was a good throwaway line, and she didn't want to know the details.

'You should write your autobiography,' she suggested.

'I did, once,' Vanderdecker said. 'It was very boring, very boring indeed. Lots of descriptions of sea-travel, with comments on licensed victualling through the ages. The hell with it. I'm sorry, but I don't think I can help you.'

'Oh well,' said Jane. 'It was nice meeting you, anyway.'

'So what are you going to do?' Vanderdecker said.

'Do?' Jane frowned. 'I don't know. Does it matter?'

'To me,' said Vanderdecker, 'yes. I mean, you aren't the sort of person who bears grudges, are you? I mean, you know a lot about me now; what I do, where I get my boat fixed, all that.'

'I see what you mean,' Jane said. 'No, you needn't worry on that score.'

'I believe you,' Vanderdecker said. 'And what are you going to do?'

'Good question,' Jane said. 'You see, I don't exactly relish the prospect of telling my boss that I didn't manage it after all.'

Vanderdecker thought for a minute. 'Am I right in

thinking,' he said slowly, 'that you said you have no sense
of smell?'

'Rotten sense of smell, at any rate,' Jane said.

'Well, then,' said the Flying Dutchman, 'would you like
a lift anywhere?'

'Anywhere where?'

'Anywhere,' Vanderdecker replied. 'I can assure you that
my ship is entirely free of etchings.'

'Etchings?' Jane asked and then said 'Oh I see,' quickly
and reflected that it was one way of putting it. 'I don't
know,' she said. 'I mean, you said yourself, it's quite boring
being at sea for seven years at a time.'

Vanderdecker smiled. 'Ah yes,' he said, 'but is it as
boring as being an accountant?'

Jane thought hard. 'Nothing,' she said, 'could possibly
be as boring as being an accountant. What was he like?'

'Who?'

'Bonnie Prince Charlie,' Jane said.

'Oh, him,' Vanderdecker replied. 'Just like all the others,
really.'

He stood up and went to the bar for another drink, just
as the barman put the towels over the pump handles.

Not for the first time, Danny was stuck for the right word.
As a result, he was feeling frustrated, and he gripped the
telephone receiver so tightly that it creaked slightly.

'You've got to look at it,' he repeated, '*globally.*'

'You what?'

'Take the *global* view,' Danny urged. 'Perspective-wise.'

'You do realise I haven't the faintest idea what you're
talking about?'

The slender umbilical cord connecting Danny to his
self-control snapped. 'What I'm talking about,' he said, 'is
the biggest story since Westlands. And you're prepared to
jeopardise it for the sake of the cost of hiring a boat.'

'What was Westlands?'

Danny made a noise at the back of his throat not unlike
an Irish linen sheet being torn into thin strips. 'Don't play
silly buggers with me,' he said. 'God, what a way to run a
television network! Don't you understand, all I want to do

is hire a bloody boat and go and shoot some pictures.'

'I understand that, yes. What I don't understand is why. That's where our communications interface appears to have broken down.'

'But don't you ...' Danny paused for a moment, and an idea sprouted in his mind like the first pure, simple snow-drop of spring. 'Stuff you, then,' he said.

'Sorry?'

'You will be,' Danny retorted, slammed the receiver down and retrieved his phonecard from the jaws of the machine. It was pathetically simple, he said to himself. I'll hire a boat myself. With my own money. Or, to be precise, put it on expenses. Alexander the Great, unable to untie the Gordian Knot, sliced through it with his sword. Similarly, Danny had reached the point where nothing was going to get between him and the story. When the time came for a documentary to be made about the making of this documentary, the actor portraying him would have plenty to work with in this scene. He strode out of the tele-phone booth and went in search of a boat.

It wasn't much of a boat, when he found it, but then again, by modern standards neither was the *Golden Hinde.* It was functional. It would do the job. He herded his camera crew onto it, indicated to the mariner in charge that it was time to go, and sat back to prepare himself.

About half an hour later, the mariner leaned across and said, 'You sure it was here?'

'Yes.'

'Well,' said the mariner, with the authority of a Pope, 'it isn't here now.'

'Then it must have moved,' Danny said. 'I suggest you look for it.'

'Where?'

'I don't know,' Danny snapped, 'use your bloody imagi-nation.'

The mariner shrugged and fiddled with his engine. The camera crew exchanged glances of a variety unique to members of a powerful trade union who are on overtime and are getting wet. Among such specialised social units, language ceases to be necessary after a while.

Three quarters of an hour later, the mariner suggested

that that just left West Bay. He said it in such a way as to suggest that West Bay was so unlikely a place to expect to find a ship that only a complete imbecile would bother looking, but Danny was too wrapped up in his own destiny to notice.

By sheer coincidence, Danny's boat entered West Bay just as the *Verdomde* was leaving it. The *Verdomde* wasn't the only one, at that; on shore, there was a sudden and unprecedented scrambling for cars and dropping of car-keys. People were getting out in a hurry, because of the smell.

Jane, for reasons which will not need to be explained, couldn't smell the smell; but everyone else could, including Vanderdecker. The effects of the enchanted seawater of Dounreay had worn off, about five minutes after the *Verdomde* had been declared seaworthy and money had changed hands, and thankfully the wind was in the right direction, at least for the purposes of navigation. Although Vanderdecker was extremely unhappy about setting off in broad daylight, he knew that he had no alternative except to take the chance. He might be conspicuous if he went, but he was going to be a great deal more so if he stayed. Once, in Puerto Rico, they had called out the fire brigade and turned the hoses on him, and that sort of experience leaves its mark on a man's psyche.

In later years, Jane often asked herself why she stayed on the ship. Occasionally she tried to tell herself that she hadn't yet given up hope of accomplishing her mission, but that was pure self-deception. Insofar as there was any rational explanation, it could only be that she couldn't stand the thought of the adventure ending. In her own defence, she could argue that she only had a five-hundredth of a second to decide, and even the clearest brains are likely to be pushed to make momentous decisions in the time it takes for the shutter of a camera to fall. Anyway, she said, 'Can I come with you?' and Vander-decker had agreed. At least, she assumed he agreed. Perhaps he hadn't heard her, being too busy giving orders to the crew. At any rate, she stayed.

Danny saw the ship about one second before he smelt the smell, but it must be borne in mind that he had a cold. Everyone else smelt the smell first. Then they told Danny

about it, just in case he hadn't noticed it for himself. They
suggested that the smell was extremely unpleasant and
that it might be prudent to go away. They expanded on this
point. They threatened to put Danny in the sea. Finally
they ignored him. He shrieked at them for a while, but
quite soon the sound of the ship's engine being revved to
death was so loud that he was quite inaudible.

'That boat,' Jane said.

'What boat?' Vanderdecker said. 'Not now, Sebastian.
Take it off.'

Sebastian van Doorning untied the anchor chain from
his leg and went back to his post, muttering. 'You were
saying,' said Vanderdecker, 'about a boat.'

The Flying Dutchman had that harassed look again. It
suited him by now, rather as a Savile Row three-piece with
Jermyn Street socks suits its wearer. It looked right on
him, somehow.

'I thought I recognised the man,' said Jane.

'Which man?' asked Vanderdecker.

'The man on the boat,' said Jane.

'Which boat?'

'Oh,' said Jane, 'never mind. Where are we going?'

'The long-term itinerary,' said Vanderdecker 'we can
discuss later. Right now, would the statement "Out to sea"
satisfy you?'

'No.'

'Tough,' said Vanderdecker. 'You see, the drill is to get as
far out of the usual sea-lanes as possible before anyone
sees us. Getting out of the usual sea-lanes in the English
Channel isn't easy, what with all the ships. Therefore we
tend to postpone the thinking part of it indefinitely.'

'Right.'

Vanderdecker deliberately slowed his brain down and
thought for a moment. 'What are you doing here?' he asked.

'Well . . .' said Jane, lucidly.

'Don't get me wrong,' he went on, 'it's not that you're not
welcome, far from it. It's just that we aren't scheduled to
land again until the mid 1990s. If you have anything urgent
lined up for the first part of the decade, now is the time to say.'

Jane hadn't thought of it like that. 'You mean you're just sort of going on?'

Vanderdecker nodded. 'It's what we do best,' he said.

'But what you were telling me,' she said. 'Montalban, the nuclear power station, all that. Aren't you going to follow it up?'

'Maybe it's not so important after all,' said Vanderdecker. 'I expect Montalban can wait another five years; he's waited long enough, God knows. That's something you learn when you're a sea captain, not to rush into things.'

'I think you should follow it up,' Jane said.

'Yes,' said Vanderdecker, 'perhaps I should. You sound just like my mother.'

Jane was startled. 'Do I?' she said.

'As far as I can remember,' replied the Flying Dutchman, 'yes. Why don't you take that job with the wool merchant? Don't you think it's about time you settled down and started making something of your life? You really ought to write to your uncle, Cornelius. I think that's what made me go to sea in the first place.'

'Oh.' Jane felt deflated. 'I'm sorry.'

Vanderdecker smiled sheepishly. 'So am I; I didn't mean to be nasty. It's just that I'm a trifle flustered, just like usual when I have to sail this blasted ship. You'd think that after all this time it would be second nature, but it isn't, quite. I reckon that if I had my time over again, I'd be a civil servant, something like that. Quiet. No need to be assertive or display qualities of leadership.'

Jane giggled. 'You'd hate it,' she said.

'Would I?' Vanderdecker shrugged. 'You seem to know an awful lot about me all of a sudden.'

Jane let that one go, and said, 'If you don't mind, I'll come along for the ride.'

'It'll be very boring for you if we don't go chasing Montalban.'

'Not half so boring,' said Jane firmly, 'as being an accountant.'

'That's a job,' said Vanderdecker, 'that I've always fancied. It was different in my day, of course. No computers, just little brass counters and exchequer boards. If you

got bored with doing the quarterly returns, you could rope
in another accountant and play draughts. Should I really
follow up the Montalban angle?'

Jane considered. To her surprise, she was not influenced
by personal motives in her choice of advice.

'I think you should, really,' she said. 'After all, that
seawater ...'

'You're right,' said Vanderdecker, 'of course, there's just
one problem.'

Jane looked at him. 'What's that?' she asked.

'The problem is,' said Vanderdecker, 'that I can't go on
land for another five years. Because of the smell. Doesn't
that rather hinder my freedom of movement?'

Jane smiled. 'Doesn't hinder mine, though, does it?'

'True,' said Vanderdecker, 'but of questionable relev-
ance. What's it got to do with you?'

Jane felt exasperated. 'Let me spell it out for you,' she
said. 'Watch my lips.'

'With pleasure.'

Jane ignored that. 'I will find Montalban, and pass on a
message from you. If you want me to, that is.'

'Would you really?' Vanderdecker said. 'That would be a
very great help to us. We'd appreciate that.'

'Right,' Jane said.

'And then,' Vanderdecker went on, 'we could meet up
somewhere later, and you could tell me what he said.'

'Right,' Jane said.

'If you're absolutely sure.'

'Sure I'm sure,' Jane said. 'What's the message?'

Vanderdecker didn't reply. Instead he knelt down and
picked up a short length of rusty chain.

'This ship is getting very untidy,' he said. 'Look at this,
junk everywhere. I'm not a naturally finicky person, but
after a while it does get to you a bit. The Flying Dutchman
I can just about handle. The Flying Dustman, no.'

'What's the message?' Jane repeated.

'Are you really sure?'

'Really *really* sure. What's the message?'

Vanderdecker hesitated, then smiled broadly. 'Right,' he
said. 'Listen carefully ...'

CHAPTER TEN

'What I need,' Danny said, 'is a helicopter.'
The voice at the other end of the telephone wire told him what, in its opinion, Danny really needed. It was not a helicopter.

'If I had a helicopter,' said Danny, mentally pigeonholing the recommendation, 'I could fly over the ship and the lads wouldn't be exposed to the waste fumes. That way, there'd be no problems from the health and safety at work angle. I take it that's what you're worried about.'

'To a certain extent, yes,' said the voice. 'Mostly, though, I'm worried about having a producer who's as crazy as a jay-bird loose in Dorset. I think it's probably about time you came home and did "Playschool" for a bit, just till you're feeling better.'

'Look,' Danny hissed, 'you remember our deal, right? About a certain cover-up? I don't want to have to remind you ...'

'Funny you should mention that,' said the voice. 'I've been chatting to a couple of other people over lunch, and I think you'll find they remember it rather differently. In fact, they seem to think you had quite a lot to do with that ... What did you call it?'

Danny felt his knees weaken. 'You *bastard*,' he whispered. 'You wouldn't dare stitch me up like that. I've got memos ...'

'So have I,' said the voice, casually. 'Very good ones, too. I wrote them myself, just now. I think it's time you came home.'

Suddenly Danny noticed that the hair on the back of his neck was beginning to rise. 'Just a moment,' he said. Then his phonecard ran out.

The phonecard revolution, like the French, American and Russian revolutions, is a phased phenomenon. In Phase One, they scrapped all the coin-boxes and replaced them with card-boxes. In Phase Two, whenever that comes about, they will start providing outlets where you can buy phonecards. We may not see it, nor our children, nor yet our children's children, but that is really beside the point. Every revolution causes some passing inconvenience to the individual. Ask Louis XVI and Marie Antoinette.

As he wandered through the streets (or rather street) of West Bay in search of an open Post Office, Danny was thinking hard. So there was going to be a cover-up, was there? A cover-up of the original cover-up. But what was this cover-up really covering up for? Not the original cover-up, surely; that was already well and truly covered, and nobody in his right mind would risk blowing the cover for anything so trivial as the cost of a few hours' helicopter hire. The only possible explanation was that this rather obvious warning to lay off was designed to get him off the story he was on; in other words, it was a sublimated or double-bluff cover-up. Despite his natural feelings of anxiety, Danny couldn't help licking his lips. It was the sort of situation he had been born to revel in, and revel in it he would, just as soon as he could get somewhere where he could sit down and get all the complications straight in his mind with the aid of a few charts and Venn diagrams. Then he would see about helicopters.

He found the camera crew in the Rockcliffe Inn, which had opened again shortly after Jane and Vanderdecker had left. Soon it would close again.

'Right,' said Danny briskly, 'drink up, we'd better get on with it while there's still some light left.'

They ignored him, but he was used to that. He changed a five-pound note, found the telephone in the corner of the pool room, and called a number in Shepherds Bush.

'Dear God,' said the voice at the other end, 'not you again. Do you ever do anything besides call people up on the phone?'

'Yes,' Danny replied. 'From time to time I make television programmes. That's when establishment lackeys aren't trying to muzzle me, that is. Lately, that's tended to happen rather a lot, which means I have to spend more time telephoning. Cause and effect, really.'

'Are you calling me an establishment lackey?'

'Yes.'

'Another one who gets his vocabulary from the Argos catalogue. Look, I couldn't care less what you think of me. I get called ruder things on "Points of View". But if you think I'm going to put up with you wandering round seaside resorts spending the Corporation's money on your idiotic persecution fantasies, then you're a bigger fool than I took you for. And that, believe me, would be difficult.'

'Cirencester,' said Danny.

There was a pause. 'What did you say?'

'I said Cirencester,' Danny said.

'I thought you said Cirencester,' replied the voice, 'I was just giving you a chance to pretend you'd said something else.'

'And what's wrong with me saying Cirencester?' Danny asked politely.

'Nothing, given the right context,' said the voice smoothly. 'In a conversation about Cotswold towns, nothing could be more natural. In the present case, though, a less charitable man than myself might take it as proof that you've finally gone completely doolally.'

The pips went, but Danny was ready for them. He shoved in another pound coin. 'I said Cirencester because I know you know what it means,' he said.

'Thank you,' said the voice, 'that's the nicest thing anyone's ever said about me. What are you gibbering on about?'

'About the Cirencester Group,' said Danny, trying to sound cool and failing. 'About your being a member of it.'

There was another pause. A long one, this time. 'So?' said the voice. 'What of it?'

'I was thinking,' Danny said, 'just now, when you were trying to muzzle me. I thought, why is this man trying to muzzle me? Then it hit me, right between the eyes. Cirencester. It's not you that's trying to muzzle me, it's the whole bloody lot of you. The Group.'

'What possible connection is there between a select private literary society and you not making very silly documentaries?'

'I like that,' Danny said. 'Select private literary society. On that scale of values, the Third Reich was a bowls club. I know what you lot get up to in that neo-Georgian manor house on the Tetbury road.'

It must be pointed out at this juncture that Danny hadn't the faintest idea what went on there, although this was not for want of very strenuous trying. But the silence at the other end of the wire made it obvious that he had hit on something here. The effect of his previous threat had been pleasant, but this was incomparably better.

'What was it you said you wanted?' asked the voice.

'A helicopter.'

'Any particular make?'

Danny was taken aback. 'How do you mean?' he asked.

'Gazelle? Lynx? Sea King? I believe Sea Kings are very comfortable.'

'That sounds fine,' said Danny. 'So I can hire one then, can I?'

'Wouldn't hear of it,' said the voice. 'I'll order you one myself. Much quicker that way.'

'Oh.' Danny frowned with surprise. 'That's very kind of you.'

'Not at all,' said the voice, 'no trouble whatsoever. What's the use of having a desk with six phones if you never use them? Where do you want to be picked up from?'

'Wherever suits you,' Danny said, not to be outdone. 'I don't know where the nearest airfield is, but . . .'

'Airfields!' said the voice, forcefully, 'who needs them? Go down to the beach and I'll get someone to pick you up there. Give me half an hour.'

The line went dead. Danny pocketed his remaining change and went to the bar for a drink, just as the towels went back over the pump-handles.

Cornelius and Sebastian rowed Jane ashore in the skiff. They had to land her at a rather remote spot for fear of making themselves conspicuous, and the walk to the road over rocky and troublesome country was not to Jane's liking, since she was feeling tired enough already. She had packed quite a lot into this one day already without gratuitous exercise.

It was all very well saying she would find Montalban, as if all she had to do was look him up in Thompson's Local under Alchemists. It was all very well saying that once she had found him she would pass on Vanderdecker's message. The reality might be somewhat trickier. And was he back from Geneva yet?

As she finally joined the road, she was nearly blown off it by the downblast of the blades of an enormous helicopter that roared by apparently only inches over her head. She said something very unladylike to it as it went past, but it was very unlikely that it heard her, what with the noise of the rotor blades and all. Probably just as well.

After a long walk she reached West Bay, unlocked her car and took her shoes off. Then she wrote down Vanderdecker's message on the back of an envelope, just to make sure she didn't forget it. Montalban. Who did she know who might know where to find him?

Oddly enough, it was just conceivable that Peter might know. There was not a lot, when all was said and done, that Peter did know. He wasn't particularly well up in female psychology, that was certain, and she had her doubts if he had a firm grasp of the basics of tying his own shoelaces, but he was a scientist. Scientist. He lived in a little white box in north central Oxford and did research into semiconductors, whatever they were. All she knew about them was that they had nothing to do with buses or orchestras.

That seemed to be a likely place to start off her enquiries, then. All she needed to do now was to locate his telephone number. This should be marginally easier than finding the source of the Nile, always supposing that she had remembered to bring her address book.

She found a telephone box and tried Directory Enquiries instead. Then she called Peter's number, which was engaged. Enough of this, she said to herself. Food.

By far the best way to get something to eat in West Bay is to go to Bridport, where they will gladly sell you a sandwich if you show them enough respect. Jane discovered this eventually, and over her sandwich and a cup of pale brown oil in the Cherry Tree cafe she considered her next move. Phone Peter, get Montalban's co-ordinates, go there, see him, deliver the message, be back home in time for the afternoon repeat of 'Neighbours'. It could be that simple. On the other hand, it might be a lot harder, and it would be wise to give some thought to possible complications. But Jane's mind was starting to wander, and she found herself thinking about something quite other.

What would it have been like to spend four hundred years on a boat? The same boat? The same small, rather uncomfortable and inconvenient boat? Would she have liked it? A lot would depend, she decided, on the company. It was hard to imagine anyone, however brilliantly entertaining, that you could cheerfully spend the post-Renaissance era cooped up on a boat with without going stark raving mad, but from what little she had seen of the Flying Dutchman's crew, it wasn't very likely that they had helped much in keeping Vanderdecker from losing his grip on sanity. And yet he had managed it, somehow. Remarkable, in itself. A fairly remarkable person, in a woolly, harassed sort of way. Or had he done something rather similar to what she and everyone else did in order to keep themselves going through a generally dull and bleak existence? Accountancy, in a way, is rather like sailing endlessly round the world, in that it offers few bright spots and those widely separated by broad, blue expanses of tedium. In order to get across those, you try not to think about them. You think about the weekend instead. Now in Vanderdecker's case, the bright spots came once every seven years rather than seven days, but once one had got used to it the principle was probably the same. Jane shuddered. It was depressingly similar to her own situation, only worse.

At least all Vanderdecker had to do was find Montalban, reverse the alchemical process and render himself marginally less smelly, and he would be fine. In order for her to get out of her own vicious circle, she was going to have to

do something immeasurably more clever, like win on the
Premium Bonds or marry a millionaire. Vanderdecker,
once he was adequately sanitised and had come to a
grown-up understanding with the House of Fugger, would
be able to live out the rest of Time in peace and luxury.
She hadn't even got around to organising her pension
scheme yet. Some people, she said to herself, have all the
luck. And if I had been able to persuade him to come to
that grown-up understanding with the Sock, perhaps I'd
be out of it and free too. But she let that thought go. If the
Flying Dutchman did decide to cash in his policy, then
good luck to him. He'd earned it, in a way, and she wasn't
going to be the one to bounce him into anything.

Jane dragged her mind back from its reverie and considered the crust of the sandwich and the gritty residue of her
cup of coffee. That more or less wrapped up the nutritional
side of things for the time being. It was time to try phoning
Peter again.

'Hello, Peter,' Jane said. 'Where can I find Professor
Montalban?'

'Hello, Jane' said a rather surprised voice; rather as one
would expect Rip Van Winkle to sound if someone had
woken him up in the early 1830's and asked him the time
of the next bus to San Bernardino. 'Is that you?'

'Yes,' said Jane. 'Montalban. Where?'

'*Professor* Montalban?'

'No, Archbishop Montalban. Where can I find him?'

'It's been ages since I heard from you,' Peter said. 'How
have you been keeping, anyway?'

Jane wanted to scream, but it was one of those phone-
boxes that aren't closed in. 'I've been keeping nicely, thank
you Peter. I put it down to the formaldehyde face-packs.
Professor Montalban. What's his address? Where does he
live? You do know, don't you?'

'No.'

Then why the hell didn't you say so, you furry-brained
clown? 'You don't?'

'No,' Peter said. 'Sorry.'

'That's a pity, Peter, really it is. You have no idea how
great a pity that is.'

'I could always look it up, I suppose.'

'Could you?'

'Oh yes.'

Give me strength, dear God. Not the strength to move mountains, perhaps; just enough to see me through the rest of this telephone call. 'What in, Peter?'

'Well, the faculty directory, of course.'

Of course. How silly of me not to have known. That sound you can hear is me slapping my wrist. 'And do you have a copy of it handy, Peter?'

'Naturally.' Peter sounded a trifle offended. 'It's right here on my desk now.'

'That's good, Peter, I think we're getting somewhere at last. How would it be if you opened it at the letter M.' She counted five under her breath, to give him time. 'You there yet, Peter?'

'Yes.'

'Montalban, Peter. At a guess I'd say it was somewhere between Mellish and Moore. Any luck?'

'Hold on, I've dropped it. Ah yes, here we are. Montalban. You want his address, you said?'

'That's right,' Jane said cheerfully. 'You must be a mind reader.'

'Well,' Peter said, 'It's ...'

'Hold on,' Jane squawked. 'I've got to get a pencil.'

The pips went. Just in time, Jane crammed a pound coin into the slot, then unearthed a pencil and the back of an envelope. 'Ready,' she said. 'Fire away.'

'It's Greathead Manor, High Norton, near Cirencester.'

'Thank you.'

'Gloucestershire.'

'Oh, *that* Cirencester. Do you know if he's back from Geneva? He is? Well, thanks a lot, Peter. How's the thesis coming along, then?'

'Not very well, I'm afraid,' Peter said. 'I keep having to go back and change the beginning.'

'Very difficult things, beginnings,' Jane said. 'Almost as difficult as middles and ends, in my experience. Stay with it, Peter. Remember Robert the Bruce and the spider. It's been lovely talking to you, must dash, bye.'

She retrieved her car, adjusted the rear-view mirror, put on her seat-belt and pulled out the choke. According to her AA book, you could get to Cirencester by way of the M4 and a number of other reputable main roads, and although it was her experience that road-maps generally tend to speak with forked tongue, particularly when dealing with the location of motorway service stations, it was certainly worth a try. As she turned the ignition key, something moved her to look out of the window and take one last glance at the little town of Bridport, where so much of such consequence had happened; the initial discovery at the bank, the visitor's book in the hotel, the curious ruined cottage, culminating in the dramatic meeting outside the boatyard and her irrational, as yet undissected decision to involve herself deeper still in this improbable but magnetic adventure. The sun gleamed on the windows of the Town Hall, and the traffic lights seemed to wink at her like old friends. Perhaps she would come back again one day, perhaps not. Perhaps she would never pass this way again, and this was to be the last time.

'Yippee!' she said aloud, and let out the clutch.

The cat woke up, uncurled its tail, and decided it would be nice to go for a walk. It got about three feet and discovered there were bars in the way.

Pleasant enough bars, as bars go. Quite probably there for its own good, to keep it from wandering too far and falling the short distance to the floor. If there were wolves about, it might keep them out for at least thirty seconds, provided they were not too hungry. The cat considered all these possibilities and rejected them. It yowled.

At the other end of the room, a man was playing a tall, elegant musical instrument, something halfway between a spinet and a harpsichord. It must be noted that he was doing so absolutely soundlessly, unless you counted the clattering of the keys under his rapidly-moving fingertips.

Hearing the yowl, he lifted his head and looked at the cage. He put down the lid of the musical instrument and walked across the room, stopping about halfway to pick up a dead mouse by the tail from a cardboard box of the kind that cream cakes come in.

'Here, pussy,' he said, in a rather embarrassed voice, for he was not used to addressing cats, small children or any of the other forms of sentient life who have to be spoken to in a silly voice. In truth, he wasn't accustomed to talking to anyone who didn't have a first-class honours degree, and it showed. 'Pretty pussy like a nice mouse, then?'

Pretty pussy yowled, and the man dropped the mouse down through the bars of the cage. The cat ducked and thereby avoided being hit on the head; it didn't look particularly grateful for the kind thought, either. The man made a selection of cooing noises and poked a finger at the cat, apparently by way of a friendly gesture. The cat appreciated that all right; it bit it, hard. The man winced slightly and withdrew the finger. It was undamaged. Heartened by this minor reprisal, the cat ate the mouse. The man stepped back and looked at his watch. Five minutes later, he stepped out of the room and called up the elegant Queen Anne staircase.

'Mrs Carmody!' he said. 'Could you come through into the study for a moment?'

A tall, grey-haired woman appeared in the doorway. She was wearing an apron over a fiendishly expensive Ralph Lauren original, and her hands were covered in flour.

'Well?' she said.

'Mrs Carmody,' asked the man. 'Does that cat smell?'

The woman sniffed carefully. 'No,' she said. 'Should it?'

'No,' said the man. 'Thank you, you've been most helpful.'

The cat looked at them both in astonishment, but they took no notice. The woman asked when she should expect the guests.

'I think they said about half-past six,' said the man.

'Then they'll have to wait,' the woman said firmly. 'You can't expect me to produce malt loaf out of thin air, you know.'

The man bowed his head, acknowledging his fault, then turned and sat down again at the spinet and began to play, as quietly as before. After about ten minutes, the telephone rang and someone read out the results of an experiment involving platinum isotopes. The man thanked him, said goodbye and put the receiver down.

Half an hour later, the man summoned Mrs Carmody again.

'Now does it smell?' he asked.

'No,' she said.

'Excellent,' said the man. 'You don't mind helping me like this, do you?'

Mrs Carmody thought for a moment. 'No,' she said. Then the man thanked her again and she left.

What the cat thought about all this is neither here nor there.

'Excuse me,' Danny asked, 'but aren't we going the wrong way?'

The pilot leaned back and grinned reassuringly. Obviously he couldn't hear a word, what with the roar of the engines and the earphones he was wearing. But he was going the wrong way.

'You see,' Danny shouted, 'we're going inland, and we should be going out to sea.'

The pilot removed one earphone. 'You what?' he shouted.

'Inland!' Danny shouted. The pilot nodded.

'Yes!' he shouted back.

'No!' Danny replied. 'Wrong way. Should be going out to sea.'

The pilot shook his head firmly. 'No,' he replied. 'Inland. Much better. Right way.'

All right, Danny muttered under his breath, even if you're hell-bent on going the wrong way there's no need to talk like a Red Indian. He shook his own head equally firmly and shrieked back, 'No. *Wrong* way. We want to go out *there!*'

He pointed at the English Channel but the pilot didn't even bother to look. He had put his earphone back on and was busily flying the helicopter. Danny tapped him on the shoulder.

'What is it?' shouted the pilot irritably, like a man who can take a joke if necessary but who'd really rather not have to prove it every five minutes. 'You'll have to speak up,' he added.

'We are going the wrong way,' Danny yelled slowly — it's not easy yelling slowly, but Danny managed it somehow — 'we should be going out to sea.'

Equally slowly, the pilot yelled back, 'No we shouldn't. Please sit down and stop talking.'

Then he leaned forward and switched on the wireless set; full volume, so that it would be audible above the ear-splitting noise.

'The Financial Times One Hundred Share index,' said the wireless, 'closed at nine hundred and seventy-six point eight; that's a slight fall of two points on yesterday's close. Government stocks were also down on the day, following a late flurry of activity shortly before the close of trading. The Dow Jones ...'

The pilot grunted happily, switched off the wireless and leaned back. For the first time, Danny noticed that he was wearing rather a natty lightweight grey suit and a shirt with a button-down collar under his flying jacket. 'Now,' he said, 'what were you saying?'

'Nothing,' Danny replied, 'nothing at all.' He sat down, looked out of the window and tried to remember the little geography he had learned at school.

Leigh Delamere service station is unquestionably the Xanadu of the M4. Bring us, it seems to say, your weary and oppressed, your travel-sick children, your knackered and your bored stiff, and we will make them a strong cup of tea and a plate of scrambled eggs. If only it had a cinema and some rudimentary form of democratic government, no-one with any sense would ever want to leave.

As she felt the vigour of the tea flowing through her bloodstream like fire, Jane began to take stock of her situation. It was all very well saying 'I will arise and go now and deliver Vanderdecker's message to Professor Montalban,' but there were imponderables. He might not be in. He might not wish to see her. She might not be able to find High Norton, let alone Greathead Manor. There might be danger, or at least profound embarrassment. In other words, she summed up, why am I doing this?

Good question, Jane girl, very good question indeed. As usual when faced with a thorny problem, Jane wondered what her mother would say. That was relatively easy to extrapolate; are you sure you're eating properly, Jane dear? Jane finished the last mouthful of her jam doughnut, and her conscience was clear. Yes.

Unfortunately, that left the original good question largely unanswered. Why are you doing this, Jane dear, and is it really terribly sensible? What are your employers going to say? Do you still have employers? What will become of you, you reckless, feckless child?

I used to be a bored accountant, she said, until I discovered Bridport. Then I got caught up in the destiny of mankind, and I became a sort of knight-errant for the Stock. Quite by chance. I tracked down the wholly improbable person I was sent to find, and I offered him the deal I was sent to offer him. He turned it down. I should now report back to my superiors and get back to doing some accounts. Except that my superiors have turned out to be rather spooky people, and I've got myself into such a mess now that it doesn't seem terribly prudent to go back. Don't ask me how this happened; it was none of my doing, and I suspect that I'm not cut out for this sort of thing, but it wouldn't do to think too closely about it for fear of suddenly going completely mad. Besides, I don't really want to be an accountant any more.

I am therefore going to a place called High Norton to see á very old alchemist and give him a rude message. What then? If I do all right, and whatever Captain Vanderdecker has up his sleeve works out, what then? When I suddenly decided to be on Vanderdecker's team, what was going on inside my silly little head?

Well, Jane said to herself, Captain Vanderdecker has lots and lots of money, in a rather peculiar way. If he manages to get what he wants from Professor Montalban, no doubt he could be persuaded to express his immense gratitude in fiscal terms. Then Jane can live happily ever after and won't have to go to work ever again. Provided that Vanderdecker really exists, of course, and this whole thing isn't the result of an injudicious bed-time cheese sandwich. And if it is, why then, we'll wake up and go to work as usual. Fine.

But that's not the reason, is it? Jane frowned at the space where the doughnut had been, and was forced to confess that it wasn't. So what the hell was? Could it possibly be Captain Vanderdecker's grey eyes? We consider this point, said Jane hurriedly to ourselves, only out of thoroughness and to dismiss it. Captain Vanderdecker is very old, he spends all his time on a ship in the middle of the sea, and by his own admission smells.

Ah yes, said the inner Jane, but if he didn't smell he wouldn't have to spend all his time in the middle of the sea. Don't get me wrong, it added hurriedly, I'm not suggesting there's anything in the grey eyes hypothesis as such, I'm just suggesting that it can't be rejected as easily as all that. Are you doing all this because you want to help Captain Vanderdecker out of his predicament? Be truthful, and write on one side of the paper only. Yes, of course that's part of the reason; but grey eyes needn't enter into that at all. Then why did you bring them up in the first place?

Let's leave the eyes on one side for a moment, as they say in the anatomy labs. Did you suddenly make up your mind to be a heroine because it seemed the right thing to do? Yes, mother, I did, of that I am sure. And because I hate being an accountant, and it seemed like a good idea at the time, and there might be good money in it. Because I wanted to.

Because it means that, whatever happens next, I will be a different Jane ever after, the sort of Jane who does that sort of thing. As for the realities of her situation, we will take a chance on the ravens feeding her. Talking of which, where is she going to sleep tonight? Even new Janes have to sleep and put on clean underwear in the mornings, and she is down to her last change of intimate garments. I may sympathise with Captain Vanderdecker, but I'm damned if I'm going to end up smelling like him.

But the voice of the new Jane had an answer to that, and told her that she would sleep in a hotel in Cirencester

and first thing in the morning she would buy herself new
underwear in the Cirencester branch of Marks and Spen-
cers. Then she would go and see Montalban, and after
that, who could say?

Feeling rather surprised and slightly frightened, Jane
thanked her new avatar for its guidance and finished her
tea. Whatever it was that had got into her seemed like it
was going to stay there for some time, and on the whole she
wasn't sorry.

'Mrs Carmody,' the man said, 'is everything ready?' The
elegant woman nodded. 'Please be so kind as to bring it
through, then, we mustn't keep our guests waiting.'

Shortly afterwards, Mrs Carmody wheeled in an old-
fashioned trolley with a porcelain cake-stand and a silver
tea-set on it. The man thanked her and asked her yet
again for her opinion of the cat.

'No,' she said.

'Thank you so much,' said the man. 'Would you just ask
Harvey to show them in?'

The man inspected the cake-stand and tried a slice of
the malt loaf. It passed muster. Then he closed the lid of
the spinet and leaned against it, waiting for his guests to
arrive.

The helicopter pilot was the first to enter. He had taken
off his flying jacket and he came into the room backwards;
not out of diffidence or perversity, but so that he could
keep the muzzle of his gun pointed at Danny's navel.
Danny came next, and after him the camera crew. The co-
pilot of the helicopter brought up the rear; he resembled
the pilot very closely, except that his suit was navy blue
and his gun was of a different make.

'Do sit yourselves down, gentlemen,' said Professor
Montalban. 'There should be enough chairs for you all. I'm
sorry you had such a long wait, but apparently the malt
loaf took rather a long time to rise.'

Danny, who had spent the last hour and a half in the
cellar listening to the opinions of the camera crew, was not
impressed. He hated malt loaf anyway. The barrel of the
pilot's gun suggested that he should sit down.

'Thank you, Harvey, Neville, please help our guests to some tea and cake,' said the professor. The pilot gave him a severe look and picked up a plate, while the co-pilot took charge of a cup and saucer with his free hand. The professor poured the tea and selected a slice of the malt loaf, and the two armed men delivered them to Danny, who accepted them with all the good grace he could muster, which was not much. Then Harvey and Neville repeated the same routine for the head cameraman, the assistant cameraman and the sound recordist. It all took a very long time, and more than a little tea ended up in the saucer.

When he judged that the polite thing had been done, the Professor introduced himself. 'My name,' he said, 'is Montalban. This is Harvey,' he said, indicating the pilot, 'and this is Neville.'

That, it seemed, was all the explanation that Danny was going to get, at least until the Professor had cleared his mouth of malt loaf. Danny waited, urging himself to stay calm and not do anything that could be construed as hostile or threatening. That wasn't too hard, in the circumstances; a Mongol horseman would find it difficult to make a threatening gesture with a cup in one hand and a plate in the other. He would also be hard put to it to eat the cake or drink the tea.

'And this,' said the Professor at last, 'is my personal assistant, Mrs Carmody. I trust you had a reasonable journey here.'

Danny nodded cautiously. His arms were aching from holding up the teacup and the plate, but Harvey's gun was still pointed at him.

'Mr Bennett,' went on the Professor, 'I must apologise for troubling you like this, but to a certain extent you did bring it on yourself. You see,' he explained, 'you did mention that you knew something about Cirencester.'

Danny's hand wobbled, spilling tea. 'Cirencester?'

'Exactly. And Harvey here felt that he had no option but to bring that fact to my attention.'

This time, Danny dropped his cup. '*Harvey!*' he exclaimed.

'That's right, Danny,' said Harvey sheepishly. 'We meet at last.'

Now that he came to think about it, of course, Danny never had met his superior in the flesh, however many telephone conversations they had shared. Nor had he ever asked what the H stood for. He had invariably asked the switchboard for Mr Beardsley, and prefaced his remarks with 'Look ...' It only went to show.

'I thought you were probably only bluffing,' Harvey went on, 'but you can't be too careful, and maybe you had finally managed to nose out something important, instead of all that crap about the Milk Marketing Board. So ...'

'Look,' Danny said, probably out of sheer habit, 'just what is going on?'

'You should know,' said Harvey, grinning. 'You're the ace investigative producer, you started it.'

'For crying out loud ... Harvey,' said Danny, 'put that bloody thing away and explain what all this is about. Are you trying to muzzle my story, or what?'

'What story?' Harvey asked. 'Oh, that load of old cock about nuclear dumping; no, not at all, but you were the one who dragged Cirencester into it, remember.'

'Actually,' said the Professor.

Harvey turned his head and looked at him. 'What?' he said.

'I'm sorry, Harvey,' said the Professor apologetically, 'there wasn't time to brief you in full. It was Mr Bennett's film of the Old Ships Race that made it necessary to bring him here.'

'Now wait a minute,' Harvey said, and Danny saw that he wasn't taking any notice of him any more. To be precise, the gun was pointing at the floor. Similarly, Neville had one hand full with a rather sticky slice of malt loaf, and was using the other to hold his plate under his chin to catch the crumbs. It was now or never, Danny decided. He sprang.

There was suddenly a great deal of movement, and we shall do our best to cover it sector by sector. Then we will join up the various parts to form a concerted picture.

The cat woke up, arched its back, and started to

sharpen its claws on the piece of chair-leg thoughtfully provided for that purpose.

The assistant cameraman hit Neville with a small padded footstool. Neville dropped his plate and fell over, and the assistant cameraman sat on him and removed his gun from his inside front pocket.

Mrs Carmody lunged for the trolley, retrieved the cake-stand and carried it out of harm's way. A slice of malt loaf toppled off it into the carpet and was ground into the pile by Danny's heel; but that comes later.

Danny grabbed Harvey's wrist and tried to bring it down on his knee to jar the gun out of his hand. Unfortunately, Danny wasn't nearly as strong as he thought he was, and a rather undignified tussle followed, during the course of which Danny slithered on the slice of malt loaf, lost his balance and fell over. In doing so, he nearly dislocated Harvey's wrist, to which he was still clinging, and jolted his trigger finger, firing the gun. The bullet hit Professor Montalban just above the heart.

Danny, sitting on the floor surrounded by the wreckage of a chair, stared in horror and relaxed his grip on Harvey's arm. Suddenly everyone was looking at the Professor, who did something very unexpected. He didn't fall over.

'Please, Mr Bennett,' he said, removing a flattened bullet from the lapel of his jacket for all the world as if it were a poppy on the day after Armistice Sunday, 'I must ask you to be more careful. There could have been an accident, you know.'

Harvey expressed himself rather more vigorously, and placed the barrel of his gun in Danny's ear. Gradually, everyone resumed their place, and the cat went back to sleep.

'Perhaps,' said the Professor, 'I had better explain.'

CHAPTER ELEVEN

'Not now, Sebastian,' said Vanderdecker, and instinctively ducked. The sound of an invulnerable Dutchman hitting oak planks suggested that Sebastian hadn't heard him in time.

It's quite a distinctive sound, and to tell the truth Vanderdecker was heartily sick of it. Day in, day out, the same monotonous clunking. Had he thought about it earlier, Vanderdecker reflected, he could have turned it to some useful purpose. For example, he could have trained Sebastian to make his futile leaps every hour on the hour, and then it wouldn't matter quite so much when he forgot to wind his watch.

Too late now, however, to make a bad lifetime's work good. With the sort of deftness that only comes with long practice, he put the irritating thought out of his mind and wondered how Jane was getting on. Had she succeeded in tracking the alchemist down yet? She had thought it would be quite easy, and perhaps it would be; after all, the name Montalban seemed to be familiar to other people beside himself these days. There was the lunatic the crew had fished out of the sea and shown the alchemical plant to, for example; apparently, he'd come up with the name all of his own accord. Certainly Jane had heard of him. So maybe all she'd have to do would be to look him up in the telephone book. Why didn't I ever think of that?

So let's suppose she's actually managed to deliver the message. What if Montalban wasn't interested? What if he didn't come? Come to that, what if he hadn't actually discovered an antidote to the Smell? That didn't bear thinking about; nor was it logical. If he was able to pass freely in normal human society, it stood to reason that he'd come up with something that dealt with the problem, even if it was only exceptionally pungent pipe tobacco. Except that they had all tried that, and it was a washout like everything else; and since Matthias had got to like the horrible stuff, there was something else they had all had to learn to put up with.

Now if there's one other thing we have all had to learn, Vanderdecker said to himself as he leaned on the rail and watched the seagulls veering away in shocked disgust, it's tolerance. With the exceptions of needled beer and country and western music, we've learned to tolerate pretty well everything on the surface of the earth. We don't mind being spat at, shot at, hosed down with water-cannon, exorcised and thrown out of Berni Inns. We can handle Sebastian's suicide attempts, Cornelius's snoring, Johannes's toenail-clipping, Pieter Pretorius's whistling, Antonius's conversation and chessplaying, pretty well everything about the cook, with nothing more than a resigned shrug and a little therapeutic muttering. In a world which still hasn't grown out of killing people for adhering to the wrong religion, political party or football team, this is no small achievement. A bit like Buddhism, Vanderdecker considered, without all that sitting about and humming.

And after all this time, what else would we do? Vanderdecker blew his nose thoughtfully, for this was something he had managed to keep from reflecting on for several centuries. What would it be like *not* being on this ship, or for that matter not being at all? The second part of that enquiry he could dismiss at once; it's impossible to imagine not being at all, and probably just as well. But suppose we can somehow get shot of the smell, what would we do?

The Flying Dutchman smiled. It's typical, of course, he said to himself, that I say 'we'; after so many years of all being in the same boat, we poor fools share a collective consciousness that you don't get anywhere else in the animal kingdom. True, we all dislike each other intensely, or tell ourselves that we do: but the arm probably hates the hand, and no doubt the toes say cutting things about the ankle behind its back. We are the creations, as well as the victims, of our common experience. I can't see us ever splitting up, or admitting anyone else to our society. Particularly not the latter; by the time we'd all grown used to the newcomer's own particular habits, he or she would long since have died of old age.

But that's what I've tried to do, Vanderdecker contradicted himself, by enlisting Jane as an ally. Well, someone had to do the job; we can't and she was prepared to do it, so don't knock it. On the other hand, it was no end of a pleasant change to say more than three words together to someone I hadn't been through the War of the Spanish Succession with. But what about when the novelty wore off? It's different talking to Antonius; in our various conversations over the years, we must have used every conceivable combination of the few thousand words that make up his simian vocabulary. I can predict exactly what Antonius will say in any given situation, and I have got through the phase of wanting to push him in the sea every time he opens his mouth. Nothing he can say can do more than mildly bewilder me. That's a rather comforting thought, in a way, and to a greater or lesser extent it goes for everyone else on the ship. Why throw all that away and jeopardise a unique relationship, just for the chance of a chat or two with someone who'll be dead and gone in another seventy-odd years? Seventy years, after all, is no time at all; it took Antonius longer than that to do his last jig-saw puzzle.

'Captain.' Talk of the Devil. 'I've been thinking.'

'Good for you, Antonius. How do you like it?'

Antonius looked at him. 'Like what, captain?'

'Thinking.'

The great brows furrowed, the massive boom of the beam-engine slowly began to move. 'How do you mean, captain?'

'Nothing, Antonius,' Vanderdecker said. 'Forget I spoke. What were you going to say?'

'Well,' said the first mate diffidently, 'me and the lads were asking ourselves, what's going to happen? If that Montalban actually has invented something. I mean, what do we all do then?'

Out of the mouths of babes and sucklings, muttered the

Flying Dutchman to himself, not to mention idiots. 'That's a very good question, Antonius,' he replied, 'a very good question indeed.'

'Is it?' Antonius looked pleased. 'Well, what *is* going to happen, then?'

'Has it occurred to you,' Vanderdecker said, 'that I don't know?'

'No,' Antonius replied, and Vanderdecker believed him. He discovered a lump in his throat that hadn't been there before. 'I mean,' said Antonius, 'it isn't going to change things, is it?'

'Certain things, yes,' Vanderdecker said.

'Oh.' Antonius' face crumbled. 'How do you mean?'

'For a start,' Vanderdecker said, 'more shore leave. Less getting thrown out of pubs. That sort of thing.'

Antonius' eyes lit up. 'I'd like that,' he said.

'Would you?'

'Yes.'

'Good.'

Antonius leaned forward on the rail, and Vanderdecker could hear him imagining what it would be like not to be thrown out of pubs. 'Antonius,' he said.

'Yes, captain?'

'Do you like ... Well, all this?'

'All what, captain?'

Vanderdecker made a vague, half-hearted attempt at a gesture. 'All this being stuck on a ship in the middle of the sea and everything.'

'I suppose so,' Antonius replied, 'I mean, it helps pass the time, doesn't it?'

'Yes,' Vanderdecker said, 'I suppose it does. Do you know, I'd never looked at it like that before.'

'Like what captain?'

'Like you just said.'

Antonius turned his head, surprised. 'Hadn't you?' he asked.

'No,' Vanderdecker replied. 'Not exactly like that. Well, thanks a lot, Antonius, you've been a great help.' Spurred on by a sudden instinct, Vanderdecker put his hand in the pocket of his reefer jacket. 'Have an apple?'

'Thanks, Captain' Antonius took the apple and studied
it carefully, as if weighing up whether to eat it now or wait
till it grew into a tree. 'I like apples, for a change.'

'That's what they're there for,' Vanderdecker said, and
hurried away before the first mate could ask him to
enlarge on his last remark. On his way to his cabin, he met
Sebastian.

'Hello there, Sebastian,' he said, 'how's things?'

Sebastian frowned. 'How do you mean?' he said.

Vanderdecker smiled. 'You know,' he said. 'How are you
getting on?'

'Same as usual, I suppose.' Sebastian's eyes narrowed.
'What are you getting at, skip?' he asked suspiciously.

'Nothing, nothing,' Vanderdecker reassured him. 'How
have the suicide attempts been going lately? Making any
headway?'

'No,' Sebastian replied.

'Never mind,' he said, 'Stick with it, I'm sure you'll get
there eventually. Not that I want you to, of course. Mind
how you go.' Then he slipped past and leaped up the steps
to his cabin two at a time. Sebastian stared after him,
tapped his head twice, and got on with his work.

Had Danny Bennett been there, he would have sympa-
thised. As it was, he was back down in the cellar, after an
entirely fruitless interview with the Professor.

Once the Professor had gleaned from him that he didn't
actually know the first thing about the Cirencester Group
(beyond the fact that it existed and a few fairly fundamental conjectures that a moderately intelligent laboratory
rat could work out for itself in about three minutes) he had
explained the dilemma he was in. Quite illegally, he had
kidnapped a BBC producer and imprisoned him, by force
of arms, in a damp cellar with an alleged rat. All he had
managed to achieve by this was to reveal to his captive
rather more about the deadly secret organisation he had
discovered than he knew already. So now either Danny
must join the conspiracy and work for it in some unde-
fined but lucrative capacity, or else ... well, there wasn't
really an else, since even Danny could see that Montalban

wasn't going to order his cold-blooded execution; and here
he was, taking up house-room and needing to be fed and
provided with clean laundry. It was all most aggravating,
and if Danny hadn't been in a hurry to get out of there and
start filming, he would have quite fancied the idea of
staying put for a good long time and making as much of a
nuisance of himself as he possibly could.

He was sitting on the floor thinking this over when
Neville, the stockbroker who moonlighted as second
murderer, appeared. He was holding his gun, as before,
and also a large, scruffy cat. He seemed put out about
something.

'Here you are, then,' said Neville, releasing the cat. 'I
hope you're satisfied.'

Danny stared. 'What are you doing?' he said. Although
he didn't know much about torture, he knew that it often
happened to prisoners of diabolical conspiracies, and
furthermore he didn't like cats.

'You said there were mice in this cellar,' Neville explained. 'So I was told to bring the cat down here. Satisfied?'

'Oh,' Danny said. 'I see. Thanks,' he added, belatedly.
But by that time Neville had gone, leaving the cat.

The cat roamed around for a bit, scratched at the door,
mewed querulously, and then went to sleep. It didn't seem
interested in mice, and who could blame it? Danny, being
of liberal views, was firmly opposed to racial and sexual
stereotyping, and the principle presumably applied to
species, too.

And that was it, for about half an hour. Then there were
footsteps on the cellar stairs again, which Danny hoped
had something to do with food. He looked round at his
camera crew. They were all fast asleep, just like the cat.

The door opened, and a girl came in. Behind her was
Harvey and Harvey's gun.

'In there,' Harvey grunted superfluously. The girl gave
him an unfriendly look and stepped in.

It was fairly dark in the cellar, and that would explain
why Jane, in normal circumstances a careful person, trod
on the cat's tail. The cat woke up, screeched, and moved.
So did Jane. She jumped about three feet in the air, lost

her balance, and fell against Harvey. For his part, Harvey reacted according to the instincts of generations of chivalrous ancestors and caught her, in doing so dropping the gun. Please follow what happens next carefully.

The gun fell on the stone floor, landed on its exposed hammer, and went off, shooting the cat. Danny, hearing the shot, dived for cover, only to find that there wasn't any. Harvey tried to let go of Jane, but Jane refused to be let go of and grabbed his ears, thereby rendering him helpless for a long enough period of time for Danny to wriggle over, grab the gun with his least trussed hand, and try and cover Harvey with it. Unfortunately, he was too trussed to be able to cover the right person, and Jane, observing yet another perfect stranger pointing a gun at her, shrieked and let go of Harvey's ears. Harvey stayed exactly where he was. He had had enough of all this fooling about with guns and locked cellars, and was going on strike.

'Right then, Harvey,' Danny said, 'the game's up.'

'Oh for crying out loud,' Harvey replied, for he hated clichés. Danny, however, had seen far more spy films than were good for him, and felt sure that he knew what should come next. 'Freeze,' he snarled. He enjoyed snarling it, and the fact that he was still pointing the gun at the wrong person was neither here nor there.

The recent spate of moving about had woken up the camera crew, who opened their eyes, took in what was going on, and started voicing their opinion that it was about time, too. Jane, feeling rather left out, introduced herself.

'I'm Jane Doland,' she said, 'I'm with Moss Berwick, accountants. Who are you, please?'

'Danny Bennett, BBC Current Affairs,' Danny replied. 'Pleased to meet you.' He wriggled his weight onto the funny bone of his left elbow and brought the gun level with Harvey's lemon socks. That would have to do.

'Can we go now, do you think?' Jane asked.

Danny thought for a moment. 'Yes,' he said.

'Oh good,' Jane replied. 'Come on, then.'

Danny remembered something. 'Perhaps you could untie me,' he suggested.

Jane looked at the ropes, and then at her fingernails.

She was not a vain person, but they did take an awfully long time to grow if you broke them, and the ropes looked rather solid. 'I'm hopeless with knots,' she said. 'Perhaps Mr ...'

'Harvey,' Danny said.

'... Would do it instead. Please?'

Harvey nodded. 'Hold on,' Danny said, 'not so fast.' He was secretly pleased to have an opportunity to say that, too, although because of the angle his body was at he didn't have enough breath to spare to be able to snarl it. 'Here, you take the gun and cover him.'

With a tremendous effort, he handed Jane the gun, which was heavy and rather oily. She didn't take to it much. Harvey untied the knots, and Danny got up.

'Here,' protested the sound recordist, 'what about us?'

Harvey untied them, too, until everyone was completely back to normal and the gathering resembled nothing so much as an unsuccessful drinks party. '*Now* can we go, please?' Jane said. But Danny had noticed something else.

'Hey,' he said. 'That cat.'

'Which cat?'

'The cat you trod on. It's still alive.'

Jane frowned at him. 'I only trod on its tail,' she said.

'Yes,' Danny replied, 'but when the gun went off just now, I'm sure the bullet hit it.' He stooped down and picked something up.

'Look,' Jane said, 'I'm sure this is all very interesting, but shouldn't we be getting along?'

'The bullet,' Danny said, displaying it on the palm of his hand. 'This bullet hit that cat.'

'Really? How interesting.'

'Look at it, will you?'

When people are being tiresome, Jane's mother always told her, it's usually easiest just to agree. She looked at the bullet. Its nose had been flattened, as if it had hit a wall or something.

'Maybe it hit the wall,' Jane suggested.

'No,' Danny said, 'it definitely hit the cat. Like the cat's ... invulnerable, or something.' Like the Professor was, in fact, he remembered.

Jane remembered where they were. 'It probably is,' she said. 'Look, I promise I'll explain, but I really do think we ought to be going. Otherwise ...' She recollected that she was holding the gun, and she turned and jabbed Harvey with it. 'Move,' she said firmly.

Now this is all very well; but what about the sound of the shot? Didn't Neville come running as soon as he heard it, with Montalban at his heels clutching a battle-axe and Mrs Carmody bringing up the rear with ropes and chloroform? Not quite. Neville, it seems, was outside checking the oil and tyres of his car when the gun went off, and didn't hear it. Professor Montalban heard it, but took it for a door slamming and dismissed it from his mind. What Mrs Carmody made of it is not known, but since no action on her part is recorded, we can forget all about her. Mrs Carmody is supremely unimportant.

So when Jane pushed Harvey up the stairs back into the scullery, there was no-one waiting for her. There was no-one in the hallway, either.

She asked Harvey to open the front door and go through it, and then she followed him. All clear so far. Then she caught sight of Neville, bending over the open bonnet of his car and wiping the dipstick on a piece of paper towel. She cleared her throat.

'Excuse me,' she said.

Neville looked up and saw the gun. He registered faint surprise.

'Would you please put your hands up?' Jane asked. 'Thanks.'

No-one asked him to, but Danny went and relieved Neville of his gun, which he found wedged rather inextricably in Neville's jacket pocket. The hammer had got caught up in the lining, and he had rather a job getting it out. Danny felt ever so slightly foolish.

'Right,' he said. 'Now let's get out of here.'

'What a perfectly splendid idea,' Jane said, 'why didn't I think of that? My car's just down the drive.' She prodded Harvey again, but he refused to move.

'You don't need me for anything now, do you?' he said.

'Look, chum,' Danny snarled, but Jane pointed out that

there wouldn't actually be room for all of them plus Harvey
as well in her car without someone getting in the boot, and
then she thanked Harvey for his help and said good-bye,
firmly. Harvey smiled thinly and walked back to the house.

'What the hell did you do that for?' Danny asked furiously.

'Oh do be quiet,' Jane replied. 'And put that thing away.'

Danny looked terribly hurt and Jane felt embarrassed at
being so uncharacteristically rude. It wasn't like her at all,
but he really was getting on her nerves.

'And anyway,' Danny said, 'where are we going?
Shouldn't we hold them here until the police come?'

Jane's guilt evaporated. 'Blow the police,' she replied
sternly. 'We don't want to go bothering them, do we?'

Danny looked at her. 'Why not?'

'Because ...' Because if Montalban is arrested and sent
to prison it will complicate things terribly, but I can't
possibly explain all that now. 'Oh never mind,' she said.
'Are you coming or aren't you?'

'We're coming,' said the sound recordist. 'Can you give
us a lift to the nearest station?'

They were still standing there when the door of the
house opened and the Professor came out, followed by his
two sheepish-looking henchmen. They all had their hands
in the air, which made them look like plain-clothes morris
dancers.

'Hold it right there,' Danny snapped, and waved his
gun. Even if nobody else was going to take this seriously,
he was. They ignored him. It wasn't fair.

'Miss Doland,' said the Professor, 'before you go, would
you like some tea?'

'Tea?'

'Or coffee,' said the Professor. 'And if you could spare
the time, there is a message I'd be grateful if you would
take to Mr Vanderdecker.'

Jane frowned. 'I thought you couldn't make any sense of
what I told you,' she said.

'I looked up some old records,' the Professor replied. 'So,
if it wouldn't put you out too much ...'

'Thank you,' Jane said, putting her gun in her pocket as
if it were a powder compact. 'Two sugars, please.'

CHAPTER TWELVE

'This,' said the Professor, 'is my computer.'

Danny, balancing his gun and a plate on his knee while he ate a sticky bun, looked up. Montalban was pointing at the harpsichord.

'Of course,' the Professor went on, 'it's rather an old-fashioned design. In particular, it has no screen; instead it prints out simultaneously.' He picked up what Jane had taken to be the sheet music and pointed to it. 'You see,' he said, 'when I first invented the computer in seventeen — sixteen ninety-four, the nearest approximation to a letter-free system of abstract notation was written music, and I adapted the principle for my own purposes. Minims, crotchets and quavers each have their own quantitative value in Base Seven, and as it happens it's an extremely powerful and flexible system: much better than the binary systems that I used in the first commercial models. Since I'd got used to it over the years, I never bothered to transcribe all my data resources into the new computer languages that have since been developed; I've simply tinkered with my original design as and when I needed to. So now my system is entirely sufficient for my needs, with the added advantage that nobody else in the world can understand it. Complete secrecy and immunity from the attention of ... Hackers, I think they're called.'

'That's right,' Jane said. 'That's very impressive.'

'Is it?' The Professor was mildly surprised. 'I certainly don't aim to impress. For virtually the whole of my working life, I've sought to do the opposite; to keep out of the limelight, so to speak. Absolutely essential, if I'm to be able to get on with my work in peace and quiet. Which is why I formed the Cirencester Group.'

'Ah,' said Danny.

'I originally founded it,' Montalban said, 'in seventeen — when was it, now? It was just after the collapse of the South Sea Company. Have some more tea, and I'll tell you about that.'

The tea was cold, but nobody mentioned it. Danny had put his plate and gun on the floor by now, and was taking notes.

'The South Sea Bubble,' said the Professor, 'was my doing. I needed an economic collapse, you see.'

'You needed one?' Danny said.

'Does that make me sound terribly selfish?' the Professor said. 'Well, perhaps I am. In order to get the resources I required, I had to get control of large financial and mercantile institutions. The best way to get control is to buy when prices are cheap, following a slump. I couldn't afford to wait for a slump, so I created one. First I built up a bubble and then I pricked it. It wasn't hard; I engineered certain changes in the national economy, by introducing new technology and new industrial processes. I put the capital I had built up by the practice of alchemy into the bubble, and the bubble grew; then I pricked it, as I said. The computer was invaluable, of course.'

'I see,' Jane said. 'And then?'

'And then I got on with my work, and left all that side of things to the computer. I had programmed it to handle the economies of the developed nations, and that's what it did. That, in fact, is what it still does.'

This time it was Neville's turn to look shocked. 'You never told me,' he said.

'I know,' said the Professor, 'and I do apologise. But if you'd known, I'm afraid you couldn't have resisted the chance to make very substantial sums of money for yourself. Instead, you have helped me, and by so doing merely made substantial sums of money. I think you have been reasonably treated, all in all.'

'Just a moment,' Jane said. 'This work of yours. What exactly is it?'

'Very simple,' said the Professor. 'You asked me if I smelled. I do not. That is my work.'

'But you don't,' Jane said. 'Have you finished, then?'

'Nearly,' the Professor said, 'but not quite. I discovered that the elixir which Captain Vanderdecker and I both drank fundamentally altered our molecular structures. The change was similar to the effect of bombardment with intense radiation — we had become, if you like, isotopes of ourselves. I hope I'm not being too technical.'

'You are a bit,' Jane said, 'but please go on.'

'Thank you. Recently, about sixty years ago, I discovered that intense radiation bombardment can partially reverse the effects of the elixir. Since then, I have been trying to construct a sufficiently powerful atomic generator to provide enough radiation for my purposes. Hence, I'm afraid, the nuclear industry. I must apologise for it, but there was no other way.'

'Quite,' Jane said, rather unsympathetically. 'Go on, please.'

'Basically,' said the Professor, 'if you put a person who has drunk elixir into the very heart of an atomic reaction, it adjusts the molecular structure. It loosens them up and jiggles them about. But the sort of jiggling I want — jiggling out the smell without jiggling the whole thing out of existence — isn't easy, and I haven't quite got it right yet. The obvious difficulty was that radiation is dangerous, and I wasn't keen on experimenting on myself; nor, for that matter, on anyone else, not even Captain Vanderdecker — even though he got me into this situation in the first place. But then I remembered the cat who had drunk the elixir when I first tested it out, and eventually I tracked it down and acquired it. After some experiments at Dounreay in Scotland, I found that the smell could be temporarily suppressed by prolonged exposure to intense radiation of a certain type; a bit like the modern process of food irradiation. The longest period it's lasted so far is a month, and soon Percy and I will have to go back for another dose.'

'Percy?'

Montalban flushed slightly. 'I call my cat Percy,' he said, 'short for Parsifal. The Holy Innocent, you see.'

Jane didn't see, but wasn't too bothered. She asked the Professor to continue.

'And that,' he said, 'is my work. That is all that concerns me. The Cirencester Group, which has operated from here ever since I first built the house, comprises all the people whose assistance I require — bankers, financiers, public relations people, industrialists, heads of Government agencies ...'

'Hold on,' said Danny, whose pen had just run out. 'Now, then. What came after bankers?'

'... And, of course, the most important of them all, the Controller of Radio Three. Without these people ...'

Danny had dropped his new pen. 'What did you just say?'

'Radio Three,' said the Professor. 'Without him, the whole system would break down, obviously. Now ...'

'Why?' Danny demanded.

'I'm sorry,' Montalban said, 'I thought I had explained all that. I said my computer used a system based on musical notation. Now, to all intents and purposes, it *is* musical notation. You can sit down at the piano and play one of my programmes with no difficulty at all, and usually (may I say, in all modesty) with great pleasure. In fact, I'd be prepared to wager that you know a great many of my programmes by heart. Of course, I wrote them all under several noms-de-plume ...'

'Such as?' Danny asked.

'Bartok,' replied the Professor, 'Mendelssohn, Sibelius, Chopin, Mozart, Elgar, Delius, Handel, Ravel, Schubert, Jelly Roll Morton ...'

Danny's mouth fell open. 'You did?'

'Yes indeed.'

'I don't believe it.'

The Professor smiled. 'You're prepared to believe that I invented the computer and the electric light, but not that I wrote the *Eroica* or *Rhapsody in Blue* — which is, as it happens, little more than a simple word-processing programme. Ah well, they say a prophet is never honoured in his own country. Let me give you a demonstration.'

The Professor got up and walked over to the rather impressive stereo system. He selected a compact disc and fed it into the machine.

'What's thirty-six,' he asked Danny, 'multiplied by the square root of nineteen, divided by five and squared?'

Danny started counting on his fingers and then gave up. 'I don't know,' he said.

'Here is a pocket calculator,' said the Professor. 'You work it out on your machine, while I do it on mine.'

Danny started pressing buttons, while Montalban played a short snatch from Handel's *Messiah*. Then he switched off the stereo and said 'Nine hundred and eighty-four point nine five nine nine seven. Am I right?'

'Yes,' Danny confirmed. The Professor nodded.

'As you can tell by the date of the composition,' he said, 'that was one of my first programmes, a simple calculating system. Catchy, though.'

Danny handed the calculator back in stunned silence, and the Professor went on.

'Hence,' he said, 'the need to be able to dictate what is played on Radio Three at certain times; it's my way of programming a number of other computers running my musical language in strategic positions all over the world. The consequences of the wrong thing being played at the wrong time can be catastrophic. For instance, the recent stock market slump was the result of some foolish person deciding to broadcast "The Ride of the Valkyries" at half-past five on a Friday afternoon. I didn't compose that, by the way, but by pure chance it's perfectly intelligible to one of my computers as an urgent command to sell short-dated Government stocks. I'm only thankful it wasn't the overture to *HMS Pinafore*.'

There was a very long silence, disturbed only by the assistant cameraman humming 'I Did It My Way', during which the Professor drank the rest of his tea. Then Jane rallied the remaining shreds of her mental forces and asked a question.

'So where does that leave us?'

'That depends,' said the Professor, 'on you. If you and your friends would be happy to forget all about what I've just told you, I can continue with my work until it's finished; after that, I intend to retire and keep bees. If you refuse, of course, I shall have to do my best to carry on regardless. No doubt you will broadcast your discovery to the world, and although I will naturally use all my considerable influence and power to prevent you, you may possibly be believed, and then the world will have to make up its mind what it wants to do with me. I cannot be killed, or even bruised. I can do incalculable damage before I'm got rid of — all I have to do to cause an immediate recession is to pick up the telephone and ask the BBC to play 'Sergeant Pepper's Lonely Hearts Club Band' at three-fifteen tomorrow afternoon. It will take hundreds of years of poverty and darkness to dismantle the structures that I have built, and the immediate result of my overthrow — for want of a better word — will be the destruction of the economies of the free world . . .'

'Not you as well,' Jane said.

'I beg your pardon?'

'Nothing,' Jane said wearily. 'Go on.'

But the Professor was interested. 'You said not me as well,' he said. 'Can I take it that you know about the Vanderdecker policy?'

'Yes,' said Jane. 'Do you?'

'Most certainly,' said the Professor. 'It's one of my most worrying problems.'

'One of your problems?' Jane repeated.

'Assuredly,' Montalban replied. 'You see, one of the first things I did after the South Sea Bubble collapsed was to buy up the Lombard National Bank.'

Danny Bennett felt better. He had found a television.

Although no umbilical cord connected him to the instrument, he could feel its reviving power soaking into him, like the sun on Patmos only without the risk of sunburn. Admittedly, there was nothing on except 'The Magic Roundabout' but that was better than no telly at all. As he sat and communed with his medium, an idea was germinating inside his brain, its roots cracking the thin, tight shell and groping forcefully for moisture and minerals. He could give the story to someone else.

Rather out of character? Very much so. A bit like Neil Armstrong saying to Buzz Aldrin, 'You do it, I think I'll

stay in and do the ironing,' but the fact remains that
Danny was seriously considering it. For all his Bafta-lust,
he knew that this was a story that had to be made, and if
he couldn't make it himself, he had no option but to give it
to someone else. But who?

There was Moira Urquhart; no, not really. Danny would
gladly have given his jewel to the common enemy of man,
but not this story to Moira. She lacked vision. She would
probably try and work cuddly animals into it, and that
would clutter up its flawless symmetry. Moira worked
cuddly animals into everything, even ninety-second clips
for 'Newsnight' about the European Monetary System.
Not Moira, then.

Or there was Paul. Let Paul do it. Good old Paul. The
Cirencester Group would really love that, because that way
the story could break once and for all and nobody would
take the slightest bit of notice. Such was Paul's skill at
grabbing the attention of the viewer that if he told you your
ears were on fire you'd be so bored with the topic you
wouldn't bother putting them out. Not Paul.

Which meant it would have to be Diana: a pity but there
it was. Just then, Danny noticed that Zebedee and Dougal
had yielded place to the news, and there was Diana on the
screen, surrounded by fallen masonry, telling the folks
back home about the situation in Lebanon. Since Danny
didn't have the Beirut phone-book and had little confidence in Lebanese Directory Enquiries, that ruled her out.
Not Diana, either. Not, apparently, anybody.

He stood up and switched the television off. There
must be something he could do, but he had no idea what it
was.

'Hello, Danny,' said a voice behind him, and there was
Jane, holding a cup of tea and a Viennese finger. 'Would
you like a cup?'

'No.' Danny said. 'Look, when are we going to get out of
here?'

'I don't know,' Jane replied. 'Nobody seems to have given
it any thought.'

'We can't stay here for the rest of our lives,' Danny said.

'You wouldn't have thought so, would you?' Jane

answered. 'But I don't think we're in any position to leave
without permission.'

'Permission!' Danny snapped. 'Haven't you still got that
gun, then?'

'Yes,' Jane admitted, 'but what does that solve? Even if I
were to shoot Professor Montalban, all that would achieve
would be a hole in his cardigan. Not that I think he'd try
and stop us just walking out — not by force, I mean — but
he did drop very strong hints that if we make nuisances of
ourselves it'll be Sergeant Pepper time, and personally I
don't want to take the responsibility for that.'

'So, what's happening?' Danny said. 'I mean, we can't
just sit here. Surely someone's planning to do something.'

Jane sipped some tea and sat down on a chaise longue.
'From what I can gather,' Jane said, 'we've really got to
wait for Vanderdecker to show up. He's the only person I
can think of who's got any sort of hold over the Professor.'

Danny frowned. 'How do you mean?'

'Well,' Jane said, 'first, it looks like when Montalban got
off Vanderdecker's ship all those hundreds of years ago, he
left some of his notebooks behind, with all sorts of calculations and results in them that he hasn't been able to
reproduce since. I think Vanderdecker's still got them, and
that's a start, isn't it?'

'Possibly.'

'And then,' Jane went on, 'there's the Vanderdecker
policy. If anyone ever finds out about that, then bang goes
the National Lombard Bank, and with it Montalban's
research funding.'

'But that's not really a threat,' Danny said, 'given that
that would achieve exactly the same result as Sergeant
Pepper, which is what I imagine we're trying to prevent.
Also,' he added, 'I don't think all that much of your first
angle, either.'

'You don't?'

'Try this as a threat. "Montalban," you say, "give up
your whole research project or we won't let you have your
notes on a small part of it back." Breathtaking. He's got us
all stuffed. Even I can't do anything.'

Jane forbore to comment on that one. 'Oh well,' she said,

'never mind. Have you actually asked yourself what's so utterly terrible about Montalban's conspiracy, or whatever it is?'

Danny stared. 'Are you serious?' he said. 'It's a *conspiracy.* It's a fundamental threat to the liberty of the free world. It's ...'

'It's the way things have been run for the last three hundred odd years,' Jane said thoughtfully. 'True, I never liked it much myself, but I don't think the fact that it's an organised scheme by a really quite pleasant old Spanish gentleman in Cirencester, rather than the accumulated megalomania and negligence of generations of world statesmen, makes it any the more terrible, do you? I mean, Montalban isn't planning to overthrow democracy or annexe the Sudetenland, he's just trying to get rid of a smell. Will it really be so awful if he succeeds?'

'But ...' Danny spluttered. He knew exactly why it was so pernicious and so wrong, but he couldn't quite find the words. 'But he's just one man, one selfish individual, and he's controlling the lives of millions and millions of people. You can't do that. It's not right.'

'I see,' Jane said. 'So if we have third world poverty and nuclear weapons and East–West hostility and economic depressions, but all brought about by means of the democratic process, then that's all right, but if just one man is responsible then it's tyranny. Sorry, I never did history at school, I don't understand these things.'

'Don't be stupid,' Danny said, 'you entirely fail to grasp ...'

'Very likely,' Jane said sweetly. 'But before you found out about Montalban, you would have given your life to defend the fundamental basics of our society and our way of life against the Montalbans of this world; the status quo, you'd probably call it. And now it turns out to be all his doing, you suddenly realise it's evil and it's got to go. Please explain.'

Danny glared at her and drew in a deep breath. 'So you're on his side now, are you? I see.'

Jane shook her head. 'I'm not on anybody's side. You make it all sound like hockey matches at school. I don't

care at all whether Montalban gets rid of his smell or not
— or rather, I do; I think it must be rather awful to smell,
and besides, if he finds a cure for it then Vanderdecker will
be cured too, and I ... well, I like him. And I also don't
want to see some sort of dreadful Wall Street Crash, and
everybody jumping out of windows the length and breadth
of King William Street, because that isn't going to help
anyone, now is it? Whereas —' Jane suddenly realised that
she'd used the word "whereas" in conversation, and didn't
know whether to feel ashamed or proud — 'whereas if
everybody's sensible and we all act like grown-ups, we can
all sort things out and everyone can have what they want.'

'Can they?'

'I don't see why not,' Jane replied. 'Vanderdecker can
swap the Vanderdecker Policy for the antidote to the smell
and a cash lump sum, he can give the Professor his recipe
back, the Professor can wind up his various businesses —
he just wants to retire and keep bees when he's finished
his work, so perhaps he could put it all into some sort of
gigantic trust fund for the Ethiopians or something like
that. And perhaps we'll insist that he finds a substitute for
atomic power and a replacement for petrol and things —
to judge by his track record, he shouldn't have any trouble
with that — and ...'

'And everybody will live happily ever after?'

'Yes,' Jane said. 'And why not?'

'So you fancy this Vanderdecker, do you?'

It was Jane's turn to stare. 'What did you say?'

'Well,' Danny said, 'it's obvious, isn't it? You're prepared
to sell the whole of Western civilisation down the river for a
man who's old enough to be your great-great-great-great-
...'

Jane got up and brushed crumbs of Viennese finger off
her skirt. 'Good morning, Mr Bennett,' she said.

'Where are you going?'

'To ask Harvey and Neville to tie you up and put you
back in the cellar,' she said. 'With the rat.'

'Mouse.'

'Rat,' Jane said firmly, and left.

Although she wouldn't admit it to herself, Danny's

suggestion had made Jane very cross indeed, and she felt
that she needed some fresh air. She walked out through the
front door and round the back of the house, where there
was a huge lawn, the sort of thing the early Edwardians
used to play cricket on.

Suddenly she looked up. There was a clattering noise. A
helicopter was coming down to land. Jane groaned from
the soles of her feet upwards. Now what?

And then she was aware of something — very horrible
and unfamiliar, but extremely faint and far away. It was a
smell; a smell so pungent and horrible that even she could
smell it.

The helicopter hovered for a moment over the immaculate turf and flopped down like a tired seagull. Out of it
jumped a man in a gas mask. He was running for all he
was worth, but another man — Sebastian, the suicidal
maniac — was after him, caught up with him and brought
him to the ground with a low tackle. The man in the gas
mask seemed to give up and tried to bury his head under
his body.

Then someone else jumped out of the helicopter; and
Jane, who was able to ignore the smell, ran to meet him.

'Hello,' she said, 'what on earth are you doing here?'

Vanderdecker was looking surprised. 'Did you just kiss
me?' he said, as if a nun had stopped him in the street and
sprayed whipped cream in his ear from one of those
aerosol cans.

'Yes,' Jane said. 'You need a bath, mister.'

'This is very forward of you,' Vanderdecker said.
'Usually I never kiss people I haven't known for at least
three hundred and fifty years.'

'We'll go into all that later,' Jane said, feeling suddenly
foolish. 'Look, what *are* you doing here? What's going on?'

'There's trouble,' Vanderdecker said.

'Yes,' Jane said, 'but ...'

'No,' said the Flying Dutchman, 'a different sort of
trouble. Where's Montalban?'

'In there,' Jane said, pointing to the house. 'Where did
you get the helicopter from?'

'Well,' Vanderdecker said, 'there was this destroyer, and

when we sailed up alongside, all the crew ran to the side and jumped off into the water. Luckily we managed to fish out one of the helicopter pilots and intimidate him into bringing us here. Have you ever been in one of those things? They're awful. Like being inside a Kenwood mixer.'

'What did you do to him?'

'Well,' Vanderdecker said, 'Sebastian threatened him.'

'With a gun?'

'No,' said Vanderdecker, 'with a sock.'

'A sock?'

'Yes,' said Vanderdecker. 'One of the socks he was wearing. Threatened to take it off and put it inside the fellow's gas mask. After that he was extremely co-operative. Look, I've got to see Montalban.'

'But how did you know where to come?' Jane demanded.

'Simple,' said Vanderdecker, 'I phoned Directory Enquiries. Isn't that what you did?'

'I think he's in his study,' Jane said. 'Follow me.'

CHAPTER THIRTEEN

'Oh,' Montalban said. 'Oh, that is most unfortunate. Would you care for some more tea?'

'Not just now, thanks,' said the Flying Dutchman. 'Have you got official notice yet?'

'Let me see.' The Professor stood up and walked over to an elegant Jacobean chair in the corner of the room. He pressed a knob on the carved side, and a telex printer appeared through the seat.

'Ah yes,' said the Professor. 'It's just come through this minute. You were right. Dear me, this is most regrettable.'

'Regrettable!' Jane said. 'Isn't that putting it rather mildly? I mean, the Dounreay nuclear power station is about to blow up and take half of Northern Europe with it, and you say . . .'

'Extremely regrettable, yes,' said the Professor. 'Unfortunately, the telex doesn't give details. Perhaps I should telephone somebody.'

'Good idea,' said Vanderdecker. 'You go and do that.'

The Professor wandered away, and Jane turned to Vanderdecker. Her face was white.

'It was lucky we were there,' Vanderdecker said. 'We were just sailing along the Bristol Channel, minding our own business, when we happened to bump into the *Erdkrieger* again — you remember, that nuclear protest ship I told you about, with all those terribly earnest young people on it. They'd just come from Dounreay, and they were seriously worried. They'd seen this sort of glow on the water, and they didn't like it one little bit. They'd tried to radio in to warn everyone, but of course nobody believes a word they say on that particular subject. So I asked them exactly what they'd seen, and when they explained I guessed that there'd been some awful accident. And then we saw the destroyer, which was following the *Erdkrieger*, and the rest you know.'

'But ...' Jane started to say.

'Sorry?'

'I mean,' Jane said, 'no offence, but what can you do?'

Vanderdecker raised an eyebrow. 'I would have thought that was obvious,' he said. 'After all, we are the only people in the world who can do anything — that's if anything can be done, that is. But the Professor can tell us that.'

'You mean because you can't be killed?'

'Exactly,' Vanderdecker said. 'Everything always comes in handy sometime, as my grandmother used to say when she stored away little bits of string, and in our case, it's invulnerability. Well, so far as we know we're invulnerable, but I don't remember the elixir coming with a label saying "Invulnerability or your money back; this does not affect your statutory rights." Remains to be seen, really, now doesn't it? That's why I brought Sebastian with me.'

'But you *mustn't*,' Jane burst out. 'Not if it's dangerous.'

Vanderdecker stared at her, and then began to laugh. He laughed for a very long time, although he seemed to realise that it wasn't going down well with Jane; he couldn't seem to help it. He was still laughing when the Professor came back in.

'Most regrettable,' said Montalban gravely. 'I blame myself, of course.'

Jane scowled at him. 'You mean it's your fault?' she snapped.

'I suppose so,' said the Professor. 'If I had never developed nuclear fission, this could never have happened. Ah well.'

'What's happening?' Vanderdecker asked. 'Was I right?'

'Absolutely,' said the Professor. 'You were entirely correct in your diagnosis. I never knew you were a scientist.'

'It's been a long time, hasn't it?' Vanderdecker replied. 'And you never wrote. But what are they doing?'

'They've evacuated the area,' said the Professor, 'and they're clearing the north of Scotland. But I don't think there will be time. And ideally, one would prefer to evacuate Europe, if one wanted to be on the safe side.'

'Would one really?' said Jane. 'How regrettable!'

'You shut up,' said Vanderdecker, 'you aren't helping. Look, Montalban, is there still time to do anything? Has the situation become critical?'

'I'm afraid so,' said the Professor. In his hand, entirely forgotten, was a stone cold crumpet. He had been carrying it about with him for at least twenty minutes, and the once-molten butter had solidified into a translucent yellow film. 'Although in theory the fire in the main chamber could still be controlled, no human being could survive in there for more than five minutes, even with protective clothing. You see, my latest modifications ...'

'But the fire could still be put out?' Vanderdecker said. 'How?'

'Indeed,' said the Professor, 'how? No fire-fighting equipment could be taken in there; it would simply melt.'

Vanderdecker smiled. 'Aren't you forgetting something?'

'Very probably,' said the Professor. 'What?'

'I'll give you three guesses,' Vanderdecker replied. 'What's the one thing in the whole world that cannot be destroyed?'

The Professor thought for a moment, remembered the crumpet, and took a dainty bite off the rim of it; there was a crunching sound, as if he was eating a clay pigeon. Then he suddenly beamed. 'My dear fellow,' he said, 'you are of course perfectly correct. How remarkably intelligent of you! But,' he added, 'there would be a certain amount of risk. For all I know ...'

'Yes, well,' Vanderdecker said. 'Anyway, don't you think we ought to be going?'

'Of course,' said the Professor. 'Yes. Shall we take your helicopter or mine?'

'Whichever you prefer,' said Vanderdecker. 'Look, I hate to hurry you, but ...'

'Of course. I'll just get a few things. My instruments, and perhaps a flask of coffee ...'

'No coffee,' said the Flying Dutchman. 'No rich tea biscuits, no drop scones, no Dundee cake. Let's just get a move on, and then we can all have tea.' The Professor, slightly startled, hurried away.

'We'll drop by the ship and pick up the rest of the crew,' Vanderdecker was saying. 'I hope his helicopter's big enough.'

'Just what are you going to do?' Jane demanded.

'Put the fire out,' Vanderdecker replied, 'what do you think? I'm not going all that way to a blazing nuclear reactor just to roast jacket potatoes.'

'But you can't,' Jane said.

'Very probably,' Vanderdecker said — how could he be so calm about it all? — 'but it's worth a go, and I've got nothing else planned.'

'You bloody fool,' Jane screamed, 'you'll get killed!'

'Now then,' said the Flying Dutchman, 'don't let Sebastian hear you talking like that. I don't want to raise the poor lad's hopes.'

'I don't believe it,' Jane said, and realised that she was getting over-excited. An over-excited accountant, like the University of Hull, is a contradiction in terms. Nevertheless. 'You actually want to get killed, don't you?' she exclaimed, and then was silent, mainly because she had unexpectedly run out of breath.

Vanderdecker grinned at her. 'Yes,' he said, 'more than anything else in the whole world. In my position, wouldn't you?'

His eyes met hers, and she seemed to see four hundred years of pointless, agonising existence staring out at her; four hundred years of weeks without weekends, without Bank Holidays, without two weeks in the summer in Tuscany, without Christmas, without birthdays, without even coming home in the evening and kicking off your shoes and watching a good film, just millions of identical days full of nothing at all. She sat down and said nothing else, until long after the helicopter had roared away into the distance. Then she started to cry, messily, until her mascara ran down all over her cheeks.

Vanderdecker was not usually given to counting his blessings — not because he was an unusually gloomy person; it was just that he had tried it once, and it had taken him precisely two seconds.

However, he said to himself as the helicopter whirred
through a cloud-cluttered sky towards Scotland, there is
undoubtedly one thing I can be grateful for; I haven't had
to spend the last four hundred odd years in one of these
horrible things. Compared to this airborne food processor,
the *Verdomde* is entirely first-class accommodation.

The journey had not been devoid of incident. For
example, he had been so wrapped up in his thoughts that
he hadn't noticed Sebastian sneakily opening the door and
jumping out as they soared over the Lake District; in fact,
had he not yelled out 'Geronimo!' as he launched himself
into the air, they probably wouldn't have noticed his
departure, and it would have taken even longer to find him
than it did. When at last they managed to locate him, after
several tedious fly-pasts of Lake Coniston, he was lodged
head-first in the trunk of a hollow tree, and they had to
use axes to get him loose.

There was also the smell. Although they were high up in
the sky, their passing gave rise to a wave of seething
discomfort and discontent on the ground below, and they
had had to skirt round the edges of large towns and cities
to avoid mass panic. Even then, an RAF Hercules with
which they had briefly shared a few hundred thousand
cubic feet of airspace had nearly flown into the Pennines.

But none of these trivial excitements was sufficient to
keep the Flying Dutchman from brooding. He was faced,
he realised, with a dilemma, a conflict of interests. On the
one hand, there was a possibility that his wearisome and
unduly extended lifespan would soon be terminated, and
although he prided himself on being, in the circumstances,
a reasonably well-balanced and sane individual, that
would unquestionably be no bad thing. Life had become
one long sherry-party, and it was high time he made his
excuses and left. But, the problem was the great problem
of tedious sherry parties. Just as you can see a way of
getting out without actually having to knot tablecloths
together and scramble out of a window, you meet someone
you actually wouldn't mind talking to — and then, just as
you're getting to know them and they're telling you all
about whatever it is, it's time to leave and the hostess is

coming round prising glasses out of people's hands and switching off the music.

The problem with human life, when it goes on for rather longer than it should do, is boredom. When it's boring and there's nothing to do, it's no fun. Just now, however, Vanderdecker had an uneasy feeling that his life was rather less boring than it had been for quite a number of centuries, and he could fairly certainly attribute the lack of tedium to the influence of that confounded accountant.

He looked out of the helicopter window at Stirling Castle — he had left a hat there in 1742, but they had probably disposed of it by now — and tried to marshal his thoughts. Love? Love was a concept with which he was no longer comfortable. At his age, it did not do to take anything too seriously, and the depressing thing about love was the seriousness which had to go with it, just as these days you couldn't seem to get jumbo sausage and chips in a pub without a salad being thrown in as well. Supposing that a closer acquaintance with Jane Doland could make his life tolerable — that was by no means definitely established, and required the further presupposition that Jane Doland was interested in making his life tolerable, which was as certain as the total abolition of income tax — supposing all that, it remained to be said that Jane Doland would die in sixty-odd years time (a mere Sunday afternoon in Vander- decker's personal timescale) and then he would be right back where he was, sailing round the world, very smelly, with Johannes and Sebastian and Wilhelmus and the lads. Bugger that for a game of soldiers.

That reminded him: the smell. Even if, by some un- accountable perversity in her nature, Jane were to wish to keep him company, what with the smell and all, that could only be done on board ship, and it surely wasn't reasonable to expect Jane to come and live on the *Verdomde* for the rest of her life. And even if she did, would even her unusually stimulating presence be enough to make life on board that floating tomb anything but insufferable? Be realistic, Vanderdecker. Of course not.

Then hey ho for death by radiation. But try as he might, he could not persuade his intransigent and pig-headed soul to accept the force of these arguments. He needed some final compelling reason, and try as he might, finding one proved to be as difficult as recovering something he had put in a safe place so as not to lose it five years ago. The idea that he was doing all this to save the population of Northern Europe from certain death was a pretty one to bounce about in the abandoned ball-park of his mind, but he had to admit that he couldn't find it in him to regard the Big Sleep with quite the same degree of naked hostility as most of his fellow-creatures. There was also the horrid possibility — quite a strong one, if one calculated the mathematical probability of it — that as soon as he and his fellow non-scientists started fooling about with the works of a nuclear reactor, the whole thing would go off pop, drawing a line under Northern Europe but leaving him and his colleagues with no worse effects than profound guilt. That wouldn't solve anything, now, would it?

The Professor had spent most of the journey with a calculator and a small portable Yamaha organ (to him, interchangeable), fussing over some ingenious calculations or other. Now he had put them away and was nibbling at a rock-cake. It was hard to know whether he was frightened, vacant or just hungry. Vanderdecker caught his eye, and over the roar of the rotor-blades, they had their first sustained conversation for many centuries.

'Well then, Montalban,' said Vanderdecker, with as much good fellowship as he could muster, 'what have you been getting up to since I saw you last?'

The Professor looked at him. 'My work ...' he said.

'Yes,' Vanderdecker replied, 'but apart from that.'

'Apart from my work?'

'Yes,' Vanderdecker said. 'In your spare time, I mean. Hobbies, interesting people, good films, that sort of thing.'

'I'm afraid I've always been too busy to spare any time for amusements,' said the Professor, and his tone of voice made it clear that he didn't really understand the concepts that Vanderdecker was proposing to discuss, rather as Vanderdecker himself would have felt if someone had buttonholed him for a serious discussion about the forthcoming world tiddlywinks championship.

'You mean you've been too busy?'

'Yes.'

'Working?'

'Yes.'

'I see.' Vanderdecker didn't see at all. For all his suffer-ings, he had at least had a couple of days off every seven years. He wondered if there was any point in continuing with this conversation, since despite a vague foundation of shared experience he doubted whether he had much in common with his old acquaintance.

'I suppose,' the Professor said uneasily, 'I owe you and your crew an apology.'

Vanderdecker sighed and shook his head. 'Forget it,' he said. 'Two hundred years ago, I might have wanted to break your silly neck for you, but even grudges wear out in time, like Swiss watches. Besides, it was my fault as much as yours.'

'That's very gentlemanly of you,' said the Professor. 'I don't suppose I would have taken such a reasonable view had I been in your position.'

'Think nothing of it,' Vanderdecker said. 'Besides, you are in our position. Well, sort of.' He turned his head and looked out of the window. Sheep. Not exactly enthralling.

'Actually,' the Professor continued, 'there was one thing.'

'Yes?'

'Your life insurance policy,' he said nervously. 'Have you considered ...?'

'Oh yes,' Vanderdecker remembered, 'that. What about it?'

'Well,' said the Professor, 'as you may be aware, I happen to own the Bank that has the risk, and it occurred to me ... If anything — well, unfortunate, should happen at the power station ...'

'I see,' Vanderdecker said, trying to keep himself from grinning, 'Yes, of course, there'd have to be a pay-out, wouldn't there? A bit awkward for you, I suppose. Still, that's the insurance business for you.'

'What I was wondering,' said the Professor, 'was who would be entitled to the proceeds? I don't suppose you've made a will, by any chance.'

'No,' said Vanderdecker with restraint, 'I haven't.
Rather irresponsible of me, I know, but it really did seem a
trifle unnecessary. Well, it's a bit late now, isn't it? Besides,
I never could be doing with lawyers. Did you ever meet a
lawyer whose life you would willingly have saved in the
event of fire? Not me.'

'In which case,' went on the Professor, 'since you have no
next of kin and no testamentary heirs, your estate will
presumably revert to the public treasury of whichever
country you happen to be a citizen of. Would that be
Holland, do you know?'

'Search me,' Vanderdecker confessed. 'I'd leave that to
the experts, if I were you. I see what you mean about
making a will, actually, although I still maintain that forty
quid spent on deciding what's going to happen after you're
dead is a waste of good beer money. Still, it's not really any
of my business, now is it? I mean, I'm not going to be here
to see the fun, so what the hell do I care whether the Dutch
government or the Lombard government . . .'

'There isn't a Lombard government any more,' said the
Professor.

'Isn't there?' Vanderdecker said. 'Oh. Don't mind me, I
only read the sports pages. The Italian government, then,
who gives a damn? Jolly good luck to them, and I hope
they don't fritter it all away on battleships.'

'If you *really* don't care,' said the Professor cautiously,
'then might I suggest that you assign the policy back to the
Bank? It would save a lot of difficulties, you know. With
the economy of the world and everything.'

'Can I do that?' Vanderdecker asked curiously. 'Just say
who I want to have it?'

'Very easily,' said the Professor. 'All you would have to do
is fill in the little panel on the back of the policy document.
Unless you've done so already, of course.'

'I don't know,' Vanderdecker confessed, and he started
to rummage about in his wallet again. This time he found
a ticket stub for the first night of *Aida* (slept), a library
ticket ('Jesus,' Vanderdecker said, 'there'll be some fines
to pay on that'), a membership card for White's Coffee

House and a white five-pound note before he unearthed the document itself.

'Where's this panel you were talking about?' he said, scanning the vellum carefully. The professor pointed. It was blank.

'Just here?' he said.

'That's right,' said the Professor.

'And I just fill it in, do I?'

'Precisely, my dear fellow.'

'Got a pen?'

The Professor produced one from his jacket pocket.

'Something to rest on?'

'Here,' the Professor said impatiently, and thrust a book of mathematical tables at him. Vanderdecker thanked him, wrote something in the panel, and signed his name with a flourish. The Professor peered over his shoulder and then stared at Vanderdecker in disbelief. Although the Flying Dutchman's handwriting was usually about as intelligible as Linear A hastily written with his left hand by a drunken scribe, the Professor could clearly see that Vanderdecker had inserted 'Jane Doland' in the Benefit of Policy panel.

'Now then,' Vanderdecker said, 'we'd better put this in a safe place, hadn't we? It's just as well you reminded me, or I'd have had it in my wallet when we went into the power station, and I don't imagine it would have lasted very long in there. When I think how I've been lugging this thing round with me all these years, it's a wonder it's survived this long.' He thought for a moment, and then put it back in his wallet and went forward to have a word with the pilot.

'That's fine,' Vanderdecker said, as he sat down again beside the Professor. 'I explained to the pilot that if I didn't come back he was to post it to Jane, care of Moss Berwick. I don't actually know her address, but I expect it'll reach her there all right. I mean, if you can't trust an accountant, who can you trust?'

'But ... ' spluttered the Professor.

'It was a good thing you mentioned it, you know,' said the Flying Dutchman happily. 'To be honest with you —

and this is of course in the strictest confidence — I think Miss Doland is getting rather fed up with her career in accountancy and wouldn't mind spreading her wings a bit. A nice little legacy might come in very handy, I imagine, although I assume she'll have to pay tax on it. Oh I forgot, she's an accountant, they know about that sort of thing. That's all right, then.'

'Do you realise,' said the Professor, 'what you've just done?'

'Yes,' Vanderdecker said.

'No you don't.'

'Actually,' Vanderdecker said through a big smile. 'I do. I've entrusted the economic future of the free world — when I was a boy, the free world was anything Philip of Spain hadn't got his paws on yet, and precious little there was of it too; shows how things don't change much, doesn't it? On balance, though, I think Philip was a better bet than you, if you don't mind me saying so. At least he had interests outside his work. I think he collected the bones of saints, or was that Louis the Ninth? — the economic future of the free world, as I was saying, and all that sort of thing, to a singularly clear-headed and conscientious person, who will be able to look after it much better than either of us. No offence intended, Professor, but you've got rather too much of a vested interest for my liking. And most of all you don't have any hobbies; workaholic, I think they call it now. I never could stand workaholics. We must be nearly there by now.'

Montalban quivered slightly, and then sat back on his hard vinyl-covered seat, breathing heavily. 'You're mad,' he said.

'Sergeant Pepper to you,' Vanderdecker replied affably. 'Also, nuts. Is that Suilven I can see down there? Can't be far now. I'm really rather looking forward to this.'

Below them, the coastal mountains of Caithness ranged up into a bleak, wet sky. The first mate, who had slept soundly ever since the helicopter's rendezvous with the *Verdomde*, woke up, stretched his arms and said, 'Are we nearly there yet?'

'Nearly,' Vanderdecker said. 'I can see the sea.'

'Big deal,' grumbled the first mate.

'True,' Vanderdecker said. 'But after it's over I'll buy you a pint. How does that grab you?'

'Thanks, skip,' said the first mate eagerly. 'What exactly is it we're going to do?'

'We're going to put out the fire,' Vanderdecker said.

'Oh.' The first mate frowned. 'Why?'

'Why not?'

'Oh.' The first mate thought about it, and could see no objection. 'And then you'll buy me a pint?'

'If humanly possible, yes.'

'Suits me,' said the first mate. Then he went back to sleep.

Danny Bennett peered through the perspex window of his helicopter and wiped away the little patch of view-obscuring condensation that his breath had formed on it. A BAFTA award, certainly, but probably posthumous. It looked decidedly hairy down there.

It hadn't exactly been easy getting here. Even after he had managed to persuade Neville, the helicopter-flying stockbroker sidekick of megalomaniac academic Professor Montalban, to pilot the spare chopper — the gun had helped, of course, but he had still had to work at it — there had been the problem of persuading the camera crew to participate in the biggest scoop since Watergate. They had been rather less easy to persuade, since they were under the impression that possession of a valid union card made them bulletproof, and he had had to resort to bribery. In fact, he had pledged the Corporation's credit to a quite disastrous extent — tuppence on a colour licence would only just cover it — and had Harvey not backed him up and said he would square it with the Director-General the whole thing would have fallen through. Harvey, clearly, was so overjoyed at the thought of Danny Bennett flying to certain death that he was ready to break the habit of a lifetime and agree to authorise expenditure.

Still, here they were and there was the story, unfolding itself in vivid sheets of orange flame below them. On Danny's knee rested a quite exquisite Meissen geiger counter, borrowed from Montalban's study, and at the moment the needle was still a millimetre or so clear of the red zone. Probably far enough. Danny communicated with the pilot, and told the cameraman to roll 'em.

Danny peered out through the perspex once again. Vanderdecker's helicopter had touched down about half a mile away, just outside the red zone — pity he hadn't been able to get an interview with him, but there it was — and the small party had scrambled out of it and started to trudge towards the distinctly unfriendly-looking power station complex. Even as he wittered frenetically into his pocket tape recorder, Danny's eyes were fixed on his targets, as he expected them at any moment to dissolve into little whiffs of gamma particles (Danny's knowledge of nuclear physics was mainly drawn from reruns of Buck Rogers). He glanced across at the cameraman to make sure that the Aaten was pointing where it should. It was. Would the radiation cock up the film? Well, too late to worry about that now. Better by far to have filmed and lost than never to have filmed at all.

'They're approaching the main entrance now,' he muttered into his pocket memo, his voice as high and agitated as a racing commentator's. 'They haven't been burned to death yet, but surely it can only be a matter of time. And who can doubt that the question on their lips — if they still have lips at this moment, of course — is, what reforms to the nuclear power station inspectorate can the Government propose now if they are to retain any credibility whatsoever in the eyes of the nation? Did anyone in Downing Street know that this was likely to happen? Was there a cover ...?'

Before he could say 'up', there was a deafening roar, and the helicopter was jolted by a violent gust of air as the front part of the power station collapsed in a cloud of smoke and yellow flames. The Meissen geigercounter started to play 'Lilliburlero', which was presumably its quaint, Augustan way of signifying danger. Danny stared but there was nothing to see, just swirling clouds of smoke. He turned away and told Neville to take the chopper out of there fast.

'Did you get all that?' he asked the cameraman breath-lessly. The cameraman looked at him.

'Oh sod it,' he said, 'forgot to take the lens cap off. Only kidding,' he added quickly, as Danny's face twisted into a mask of rage and his hand moved to the butt of the gun. 'Can't you take a joke all of a sudden?'

'No.' Danny snapped. 'That's my award you've got in that thing, so for Christ's sake stop farting around.' The strains of 'Lilliburlero' had died away, and the elegant needle was back out of the red zone. 'Right, Neville,' he shouted at the front of the helicopter, 'let's go back and have another look.'

Neville shook his head. 'No can do,' he shouted back. 'No fuel. Sorry.'

Danny swore. 'What do you mean, no fuel?'

Neville pointed at what Danny assumed was the fuel gauge, although for all he knew it could be the tape deck, and shrugged.

'You clown!' Danny shouted. 'The story of the decade and you choose this moment to run out of petrol.'

'It's not petrol,' said Neville, 'it's aviation fuel.'

'I don't care if it's methylated spirits,' Danny yelled. 'Go somewhere where we can get some more and be quick about it.'

Neville consulted a map. 'Inverness,' he said.

Danny, who had been to Inverness, shuddered, but there was nothing he could do. 'All right,' he said, 'but get on with it.'

As the helicopter turned, Danny peered frantically out of the back window, and could just see the bright glow of a burning power station through a miasma of black clouds.

'Don't go away,' he said, 'we'll be right back after the break.'

Just another day at Broadcasting House. In the rather battered and uncomfortable suite assigned to the lost sheep who run Radio Three, a harassed-looking man in what had been, thirty years ago, quite an expensive tweed jacket told the listening public that they had just been listening to a sonata by Berg. Long ago, when the jacket had been new and the world had been young and not quite such a miserable place, someone out there might have cared.

The harassed-looking man announced Schubert's Unfinished Symphony, took off his earphones and fumbled in his pocket for his packet of peppermints. All gone. Damn.

'George.'

The door of the studio had opened — a curious event during working hours. Had someone lost his way looking for the lavatory? No, for the stranger had spoken his name. George turned his head.

'News flash, George. We interrupt this programme, and all that.'

'Fancy,' George said. 'The last time I did one of these was poor dear President Kennedy. What's up this time?'

'Nuclear power station in Scotland's blown up,' he was informed. George raised an eyebrow.

'Well, now,' he said, 'how dreadful.'

'Indeed.'

'I mean,' George said, 'we'll have to reorganise the whole afternoon schedule. After all,' he explained, 'I'm sure there'll be lots and lots of these little bulletins as the long day wears on, and that'll make it impossible to play the Bartok. Can't play Bartok with holes in it, it's not right.'

'Well absolutely.'

'I'm glad you agree,' George replied. 'Have they come up with a revised schedule?'

'No, George, they haven't,' he was told. 'I imagine they've been too busy playing at being journalists to give any thought to anything so important.'

'Now, now,' George said, frowning, 'there's no call for sarcasm. You'd better leave it all to me, and I'll just have to cobble something together.'

'That's fine, then,' said George's interlocutor. 'I'll leave it all up to you. Let no one say you didn't stay calm and do your bit in the crisis.'

'Thank you.'

'Like the orchestra on the Titanic.'

'Thank you.'

'Don't mention it.' The door closed, and George thought
for a moment. In the background the music played, but the
only effect it had on George was to inspire the reflection
that the Unfinished Symphony would be used to it by now,
and he could safely take it off in a moment to read the
news flash. What could he think of for an impromptu
programme with interruptions?

From a purely aesthetic point of view, it would be appropriate at this stage to describe the interior of the power
station in which Vanderdecker, Montalban, the crew of the
Verdomde, and a cat of indeterminate breed are just now
wandering about. However, there is such a thing as the
Official Secrets Act, and authors don't like prison food.
Take Oscar Wilde, for example.

'What,' Vanderdecker asked as he opened a curtain door
leading to a certain room in a building, 'did you have to
bring that cat for?'

'Guinea-pig,' replied Montalban through the charred
wisps of fabric that had once been a handkerchief held in
front of his nose. The first mate frowned.

'What, to catch one, you mean?'

Montalban stopped in his tracks and turned round. 'To
catch one of what?' he asked.

'A guinea-pig,' replied the first mate. 'Is that why you
brought the cat?'

Montalban smiled. 'No, no, you don't quite seem to
follow,' he said. 'The cat is a guinea pig.'

'No it's not,' the first mate replied, 'it's a cat.'

'That's right,' Vanderdecker said hastily, 'it's a cat, isn't
it, Montalban? Are you still wearing your reading glasses?'

'The cat,' said Montalban slowly, 'is here to perform the
function of a guinea pig.'

The first mate's frown remained as constant as the
Northern Star. 'You mean, running round inside a little
wheel or something?'

'Yes,' replied the Professor; he was a quick learner. 'If
necessary.'

'I see,' said the first mate, and added, 'Why?'

'Because,' explained the Professor, and reached into his

pocket for another handkerchief. Unfortunately, there
wasn't one. Nor was there a pocket. There wasn't, in fact, a
fibre of cloth among the whole party; just hot but invulnerable flesh.

'Stuffy in here, isn't it?' said Wilhelmus. 'Can't we open
a window?'

'Not really,' Vanderdecker said. 'A bit counterproductive, that would be. Look, isn't it about time we started
doing something, instead of just wandering about like this?'

'If you'll just bear with me a little longer,' the Professor
said, 'I hope to be in a position to make a final assessment
of the extent of the problem facing us.'

A large and jagged slab of masonry dislodged itself from
the roof and fell heavily onto the precise spot Sebastian
would have been standing on if Vanderdecker hadn't rather
unceremoniously moved him. Sebastian scowled and
muttered something under his breath.

'Right, then,' said the Flying Dutchman positively. Deep
inside he could feel himself starting to get angry. The last
time he had been angry was many years ago, when, thanks
to a series of accidents and coincidences, he had wandered
into the middle of the Battle of Trafalgar just as the
French were on the point of victory, and a cannonball from
a French ship of the line had smashed a hole in the
Verdomde's last barrel of India Pale Ale. The Flying
Dutchman had felt guilty about what happened next ever
since, and the sight of Nelson's Column always made him
feel slightly ill.

'Where are you going?' Montalban asked.

'Never you mind,' Vanderdecker replied. 'Just lend me
that cat for a moment, will you, and then you can go away
and have a nice cup of tea or something. Cornelius,
Sebastian, you follow me. The rest of you stay here.'

Montalban handed over the cat, which was growling
slightly, and watched helplessly as the Flying Dutchman
stalked off through a door whose existence is not explicitly
acknowledged. The door closed, and a moment later flew
open again as the room beyond it blew up.

'Not *now*, Sebastian,' roared a voice from the heart of
the flames.

'Oh dear,' Montalban said. 'I really don't think he should have gone in there.'

The other members of the crew tried to peer through the cloud of smoke, flame and debris, but it was impervious to sight. They could, however, hear loud banging noises.

'Antonius, Johannes, Wilhelmus, Pieter, Dirk, Jan Christian! Over here, quick as you like!' came a thunderous command. 'Cornelius, grab the cat!'

Montalban was left standing alone in the middle of a burning room. He didn't like it much. It was unnerving, what with the falling masonry and everything, and he hadn't had a rock cake in five hours.

'Wait for me,' he said.

Jane had always hated Ceefax. It wasn't just the way the blasted thing played 'That's Entertainment' on the electronic organ at you while listing the latest casualties in the Mexican earthquake; it wasn't even the mule-like persistence with which it kept giving you a recipe for chicken à la king when you wanted the weather forecast. It was the little numbers at the top of the screen that really made Jane want to scream. She was alone in the house, and there were no neighbours close enough to be disturbed. She screamed.

Then she pulled herself together again and pressed some buttons on the remote control. Back to the index. Yes. Fine. Stay with it. News Update — 351. Key in 351. Today's recipe is Tournedos Rossini. Eeeeeeeeek!

Try the other channel, said a little voice inside Jane's head. It'll be just as bad, but the recipe may be different. She tried the other channel and found the index number for News Update. She pressed the necessary buttons. She got the Australian Football results.

A person could make a fortune, she decided, reinventing the carrier pigeon. Or smoke signals. Craftily, she went back to the main index and keyed in the code for the recipe. There was a flicker of coloured light, the television sang 'I Did It My Way' and she got the Australian Football results. Melbourne, it seemed, was having a good run this season. Come on, you reds.

Perhaps, Jane reflected, it won't be on the news at all. What if Harvey and his colleagues have organised a total news blackout? Was that why he had driven away in such a hurry just after the helicopters took off? Jane was a child of the media age, and there lurked in the back of her mind the instinctive belief that if a thing wasn't on the news, it couldn't really have happened after all. So if Harvey could keep it off the air, perhaps the whole thing could unhappen, like a film projector with the film in backwards. No. Unlikely.

Jane put down the remote control and wandered over to the window. Outside it was raining, that slow, gentle, extremely wet Cotswold rain that once used to turn watermills and was somehow or other connected with the rise of the wool trade. History had never been her best subject at school, and the wool trade had been the armpit of History as far as she was concerned, and so she found it hard to remember the details. What could rain possibly have to do with wool? Did it make the ground so soggy that you couldn't keep cows because of footrot, so you had to keep sheep instead? Was rain connected with the wool trade at all? Had there ever been a wool trade? Yes, because she had met someone who had been involved in it. The Wool Trade, the Hanseatic League, the Spanish Netherlands, all that bit between Richard the Lion-Heart and Charles I, in the margins of which she had drawn little racing-cars. Strange, to think that one man could have seen all that.

There was that song, she remembered. We joined the Navy to see the world, and what did we see? We saw the sea. And the Atlantic isn't romantic and the Pacific isn't terrific and the Black Sea isn't what it's cracked up to be. The poor man. It must have been awful for him.

One thing in history that had registered with her was Robert the Bruce and the spider, because she was terrified of spiders. Back to the Ceefax, then, and let's have one more go. Carefully, Jane selected the required index numbers for the Australian Football results and keyed them in. She got the Australian Football results, while the unseen orchestra played 'They Call The Wind Maria'.

Like St Paul on the road to Damascus, Jane suddenly

understood. Nobody else did, but she understood.
Standing there in her stockinged feet in a sitting room
outside Cirencester, Jane Doland had single-handedly
solved one of the most inscrutable mysteries of the twen-
tieth century. She knew why they played background
music to Ceefax, and the principle by which it was
selected.

All she needed to find now was the Professor's decoder,
but that wasn't going to be easy. Given Montalban's love of
camouflage, it could be anything; the Georgian tea service,
the Dresden shepherdess, the ormulu clock, the little black
box labelled 'Decoder' . . .

With trembling hands, she plugged it in and switched it
on. As the television set launched into 'Thank Heaven For
Little Girls', there was a buzzing noise from the box, a
whistling, a hissing, and then a mechanical Dalek voice
started to speak.

'Melbourne,' said the voice, 'sixteen. Perth nil.'

'Damn,' said Jane, and in a sudden access of fury she
snatched up the remote control and dashed it to the floor.
There was a snowstorm of coloured lights on the screen,
and the news headlines appeared.

Jane peered at them. Latest on Dounreay crisis. Evacu-
ation proceeding in orderly fashion. No cause for alarm as
yet. Questions in the House. So that was how Harvey was
handling it. How terribly unimaginative of him.

Then she caught the subdued muttering of the Dalek in
the black box. It was urging the world to buy. Buy equities,
it was saying. Buy gilts. Buy municipal bonds. Buy short-
dated government stocks. Buy breweries, industrials,
communications, chemicals, entertainments, even unit
trusts. Buy.

Jane's jaw dropped, and then she picked up the remote
control, made a wish, and threw it at the wall. She got the
City News. So that's how it's done.

Share prices, she discovered, were going through the
roof. FT All Share Index reaches all time peak. Dow Jones
explodes in buying frenzy. Hang Seng hangs loose. What,
Jane asked, is going on?

The decoder wasn't much help this time: it just kept on

repeating its command to buy. Buy Czarist government securities. Buy South Sea Company 5 per cent Unsecured Loan Stock. A fat lot of help the decoder was being. Jane shrugged and went to look for a wireless.

She eventually found a portable in the kitchen and tuned it to Radio Three. We apologise for the continued interruption to the scheduled programme, it was saying, owing to the Dounreay crisis. Meanwhile, we continue with our impromptu Gilbert and Sullivan medley, and now let's hear 'Three Little Maids From School' from the D'Oyly Carte company's 1956 recording of *The Mikado*.

The decoder raised its voice to a hysterical scream, conjured the world in the bowels of Christ to buy De Lorean 25p Ordinary Shares, and blew up. Jane shook her head several times, switched off the radio and the television, and went to the kitchen for a cup of tea.

The cat was having a thoroughly rotten time. It was hot, there were no mice, and slabs of pre-stressed concrete kept falling on its head. On the other hand, it had managed to get away from those lunatics with the silly names.

In that ineffably feline way cats have, it arched its back, stretched, flexed its claws and started to stroll quietly, a cat walking by itself. Four centuries of existence had taught it a sort of unthinking optimism. Although the odds against it seemed long, there might be mice somewhere, or birds, or even a decomposing chicken carcass. In this room here, for instance.

In the room there was a table, and on the table was a square white thing which the cat failed to recognise as a computer console. Made of the very latest space-age materials, it had not yet melted. It had been designed to withstand extremes of temperature which would long since have carbonised diamonds. This was necessary, because this was no ordinary playing-video-games computer, but the main instrument panel for the whole complex. Anything that was still capable of working inside this inferno was operated from here.

But the cat wasn't to know that. To the cat, it looked like a nice place to curl up and sleep. With a delicate little hop,

the cat jumped up onto the table and made its way to the
centre of the console, its velvet-padded paws resting ever
so lightly on the many labelled keys. The cat lay down,
turned round three times, and went to sleep.

'Sebastian!' Vanderdecker yelled. 'Over there, to your left.'
   Sebastian looked round and saw the little patch of flame
which was evidently distressing his commander. He
stamped on it until it went out.
   They had been at it for hours, and they weren't making
much headway. It was a big building, and most of it was on
fire, and it takes time to beat out flames with nothing but
your bare hands and feet. Meanwhile the needle on the
Professor's geiger counter (this one was enclosed in a
Fabergé egg) was slowly creeping higher. Not galloping,
just creeping. Not galloping yet.
   'Look, Montalban,' Vanderdecker gasped, 'are we
getting anywhere or not? This is not a time for conventional politeness.'
   'I'm afraid not,' the Professor said. 'The fire is too
widespread. There just isn't time to put it out this way.'
   Vanderdecker nodded. 'So?'
   'Well,' Montalban replied, 'there doesn't seem to be very
much point in our staying here, does there?'
   Vanderdecker shook his head vigorously. 'The hell with
you,' he said. 'There has to be something we can do.' He
jumped on a patch of fire, more to relieve his feelings than
for any other motive.
   'Unfortunately ...' The Professor was suddenly quiet.
The Fabergé egg started to tinkle out 'The Blue Danube'.
'Oh dear,' he muttered sadly.
   'Now what?'
   'Situation critical,' Montalban replied. 'Such a pity.'
   'All right, all right,' Vanderdecker shouted, 'why don't
you do something for a change instead of going all to pieces
like that?' And he looked round for somebody to shout at.
Just then, the first mate came up.
   'Skip,' he said. 'I've lost the cat.'
   'The what?'
   'The cat. The guinea-pig. Whatever.'

'Really?' Vanderdecker growled. 'What a bloody cata clysm! All right, let's go and look for the perishing cat. I'm getting bored just standing here.'

The first mate said that he had last seen it over there, so they went that way. And, in due course, they arrived at the door of the room with the computer console on it.

'What's in here?' Vanderdecker asked, curiously. 'It doesn't seem as badly damaged as the rest of it all.'

'It's the computer room,' Montalban replied. 'Everything in here is the state of the art in heat-resistance technology ... Shoo!'

'Bless you,' Vanderdecker said instinctively, but the professor wasn't sneezing. He was getting the cat off the console.

'That explains it,' he said. 'That dratted animal has pressed all the wrong buttons.' Montalban typed frantically for a moment, but the needle on the Fabergé egg continued to rise and 'The Blue Danube' was getting faster and faster. 'It's switched off most of the failsafe mechanisms,' Montalban explained crossly. 'You *naughty* boy!' he said. The cat looked at him.

'So that's it, is it?' Vanderdecker asked. 'There really is nothing we can do?'

'We could leave,' the professor suggested, 'before the entire complex blows up, with a force approximately nine hundred times that of the Hiroshima and Nagasaki bombs put together. I think in the circumstances that leaving would be extremely prudent.'

'Fine,' Vanderdecker said. 'You just shove off, then. I think I'll stay here for a bit.' He kicked the table.

'Well, goodbye then,' Montalban said, 'it was so nice to have seen you again. Do drop in if ever you happen to be passing.'

The Fabergé egg had stopped playing the Blue Danube and struck up 'The Minute Waltz'. Montalban dropped it, screamed, and fled.

'Here, Captain,' said Sebastian. Vanderdecker turned round and looked at him. He was standing by a small door like a safe-deposit box with a lurid black and red skull and crossbones stencilled on it. 'Pirates?' he suggested.

'Very possibly, Sebastian,' said the Flying Dutchman, 'very possibly.'

'Good,' Sebastian said. 'I always loved pirates,' then he opened the door and walked in. There was a searing flash of blue light, and the world was blotted out.

Half an hour later, Sebastian got up. He looked around, pinched himself, and swore.

'All right then,' he said to the sky, which was visible through a large hole in the ceiling. 'I give up. Forget it. You win.'

He realised he was still holding the handle of the door. The rest of the door was nowhere to be seen. Then he noticed something else. He sniffed.

'Hello,' said a voice from under the fallen lump of ceiling. 'Is anybody there?'

'Is that you, captain?'

'Yes. Sebastian?'

'Captain,' Sebastian said, and his voice was rather shaky, 'I don't think I smell any more. Do you think I smell, skip?'

'I don't know, Sebastian. I'm not sure. Perhaps if you got this slab of concrete off me, I might be able to give you a considered opinion.'

Sebastian thought for a moment, and then went to get the others. This took time, as some of them were similarly covered in architecture, but eventually they were all assembled and together they heaved Vanderdecker out from under the slab.

'Thanks,' he said, brushing dust off himself. 'You're right, Sebastian, you don't. Has anyone seen my egg?'

'Which egg?'

'The shiny stone egg that plays tunes, Antonius.'

'Oh,' said the first mate, 'that egg. Here you are.'

'Thank you.' Vanderdecker looked at it for a moment. 'Well,' he said, 'fancy that. Maybe it's just broken.' He shook it vigorously. The needle stayed resolutely on Normal.

'In fact,' Vanderdecker said, 'none of us do.'

'Do what, skip?'

'Smell, Antonius. The smell would seem to have disappeared. Isn't that jolly?'

There was a ripple of whispering, and the crew of the *Verdomde* sniffed at each other. Then they started to cheer.

All except Antonius, the first mate. He would have cheered, but something was puzzling him. As always, when he was puzzled he consulted his captain.

'Skipper,' he said, 'why don't we smell anymore?'

'That,' Vanderdecker replied, 'is the thousand moidore question. Why indeed? I can only imagine ...'

'Yes?' Antonius said, his eyes alight with anticipation. Vanderdecker didn't reply. He was frowning too.

'Well anyway,' he said. 'I owe you a pint.'

'Why, skipper?'

'I promised I'd buy you a ...'

'No,' said Antonius, 'not that. Why have we stopped smelling?'

'I don't know,' Vanderdecker confessed. 'I really don't. Nor do I know why the power station has stopped burning and the radioactivity has dropped down to its normal ambient level. I'd ask the professor, only he isn't here. It's a real mystery, if you ask me.'

'Oh.' Antonius's face had caved in. 'You *sure* you don't know?'

Vanderdecker suddenly felt terribly guilty. 'Of course,' he said. 'I'm only guessing, but purely off the top of my head it could just be that we took the full blast of the explosion when Sebastian inadvertently opened some sort of pressure lock and triggered off the nuclear reaction, and that all that radiation crashing into our systems carried out some sort of molecular change that counteracted the molecular change that took place when we drank the elixir in the first place. Meanwhile, the sheer force of the explosion, which must have used up all the available oxygen inside the place, just snuffed out the flames and furthermore triggered off some sort of chain reaction which somehow or other reprocesses away all the loose radiation which had escaped previously. And here we all are. Do you see what I'm getting at?'

'No,' said Antonius happily. 'But if that's what you say

happened, that's good enough for me and the lads. Isn't it, lads?'

The lads, of course, hadn't been listening. They were too busy cheering and yelling and generally not smelling horrible to listen to anything. But Vanderdecker had thought of something; what if the reaction had indeed reversed the effects of the elixir? And they were now all mortal again?

'I wonder,' he said to himself.

'What's that, skipper?' Antonius asked, and Vanderdecker pigeonholed the immortality question. He was just starting to realise what life without the 'smell' could possibly mean. So maybe he wasn't immortal any longer. Maybe. There was no need to put it to the test immediately, now was there?

'I was wondering,' Vanderdecker said, 'where we can get a pint or so of beer in these parts.'

'And some clothes, skip,' Antonius said. 'We haven't got any. They got burnt,' he explained.

'So they did,' replied the Flying Dutchman. 'We'd better get some more, hadn't we?'

'Good idea, skip,' Antonius said. 'Where?'

Vanderdecker smiled. 'Tell you what, Antonius,' he said. 'You think of something.'

'Me?'

'Yes, you.'

'Oh.' Antonius considered. 'I don't know,' he said.

'Don't you?' said the Flying Dutchman. 'Sorry, I thought you were just going to volunteer to walk over to the nearest evacuated village, break a few windows, and come back with some clothes for us. Wasn't that what you were just going to suggest?'

'No,' Antonius replied truthfully.

'Well,' Vanderdecker said, 'what do you think of it, as a suggestion? You can be honest with me if you think it's no good.'

'I'll give it a shot, skipper,' Antonius said. 'Which way to the village?'

CHAPTER FOURTEEN

'No,' said Mrs Mackay firmly. 'Go away'.
'Now look,' said the policeman, 'you really will have to leave now, Mrs Mackay. It's just not safe to stay here.'

Mrs Mackay considered this for a moment. 'Have you been listening to my daughter in Edinburgh?' she asked suspiciously. 'Catriona?'

'I didn't know you had a daughter in Edinburgh, Mrs Mackay.'

'A likely story.' Mrs Mackay sniffed. 'She doesn't really want me to go and live with them — not that I would, let me tell you, not if I were starving in the gutter. It's this house she's after, of course; well, you can just tell her that if she thinks she's going to lure me out of my own house where I was born and then put me in a home in Edinburgh ...'

'Now look ...'

'And you should be ashamed of yourself,' Mrs Mackay went on, 'conniving with the likes of her. Call yourself a policeman? Go away!'

She slammed the door, and the policeman closed his eyes and counted to ten. Would it really matter terribly much, said a voice under his cap, if the silly old bag did get burnt to death in a radiation storm?

'Mrs Mackay,' he shouted through the letter box. 'Now I've wasted enough time as it is, so unless you open this door ...'

Just then, a party of naked men walked past.

'Unless you open this door, I'm going to have to break it down, do you understand me? So wouldn't it be much better all round if ...'

'Excuse me,' said one of the naked men. He had a cat under his arm.

'One moment sir,' said the policeman, not looking round. 'Mrs Mackay ...' Then something connected in his brain. He turned round and stared.

'Have you seen a man with no clothes on wandering about looking lost?' asked the naked man. 'You see, we sent him to find some clothes, but he really shouldn't be out on his own, he's not terribly bright. He's about five foot four, black hair ...'

'Dark brown,' interrupted another naked man.

'Thank you, Sebastian, dark brown hair, thick beard, blue eyes — I think they're blue but to tell you the truth I never was very interested, so I may be wrong.'

The policeman rubbed his eyes and forehead. 'Are you from the rigs?' he asked.

'I beg your pardon?'

'The oil rigs.'

'No,' said the naked man, 'no, we're not from the oil rigs. I would imagine they were all evacuated some time ago. I take it you haven't seen him.'

The policeman nodded. It seemed to use up most of his available strength.

'Oh well,' said the naked man, 'thanks anyway. Oh, and by the way, the crisis is over, you can bring everyone back now, it's safe.'

'Safe?'

'Yes,' said the naked man, 'look.' He held up a blue egg-shaped pebble and pointed to it. 'There, see,' he said, 'back to normal residual radiation levels.' He walked over to Mrs Mackay's letter-box, lifted the flap, and shouted through it, 'It's all right now, you don't have to go, panic's over.'

'Are you a doctor?' said Mrs Mackay's voice on the other side of the door.

'No,' said the naked man. 'My name is Vanderdecker.' An idea seemed to occur to the naked man, and he said, 'Do you by any chance have any men's clothes we could borrow? There are fourteen of us.'

The policeman started to protest, but the effort was too much for him. He sat down on the step and looked carefully at the soles of his shoes.

'Fourteen?' said Mrs Mackay. 'Are you the Salvation Army?'

'Not really,' Vanderdecker replied, 'but we would be very grateful if . . .'

'Go away,' said Mrs Mackay.

'All right, then,' said Vanderdecker, 'be like that.'

He came away from the door, and one of the naked men whispered something in his ear. He nodded and approached the policeman.

'Excuse me,' he said. The policeman looked up. 'Now then,' he went on, 'am I right in thinking that you're a police officer?'

The policeman thought hard and then nodded. Vanderdecker smiled.

'That's good,' he said. The policeman thanked him. 'Now,' Vanderdecker continued, 'my friends and I are just going to break into that shop over there.' He pointed to the small, stone-built house across the narrow main street. There was a sign by the gate that read Local handicrafts and tweeds. 'But,' Vanderdecker went on, 'please don't think that we're looting, because we're not. It's just that we lost all our clothes in the power station and we're beginning to feel a bit conspicuous. So that'll be all right with you, now won't it?'

The policeman said that he supposed so. Vanderdecker smiled again. It was a friendly, comforting sort of smile, implying that here was someone who knew what he was doing. The policeman was grateful.

'Right, that's marvellous,' he said. 'And when the proprietor gets back, will you please ask him to send the bill to Professor Montalban, Greathead Manor, near Cirencester, Gloucestershire? Have you got that? Perhaps you'd better write it down.'

The policeman wrote it down in his notebook and looked up at Vanderdecker, as if asking for his approval. Vanderdecker nodded and turned to walk away. Then he checked himself, and said, 'Oh, by the way.'

'Yes, sir?' said the policeman.

'We don't smell funny, do we?'

'No, sir,' said the policeman.

'You're sure about that?'

'Positive, sir.'

'Absolutely sure? You haven't got a cold or anything?'

'No, sir.'

'And you're not just being polite, are you? We won't be offended, you know, if ...'

The policeman shook his head vigorously, then sat down on the step again, buried his face in his hands and started to hum softly. He looked rather tired, and it had been a long week, what with the power station blowing up and his grandmother dying and his wife insisting on a trial separation.

'Fine,' Vanderdecker said. 'Now, Sebastian, Jan Christian, find a stone or a lump of wood, something we can use as a battering ram. Dirk, will you just hold this cat for me? Watch out, it scratches if you're not careful. Come along now, we haven't got all day.'

About twenty minutes later, Vanderdecker and the crew of the *Verdomde* came out of the craft shop. They were all wearing more or less identical clothes — Shetland wool pullovers, hairy tweed jackets, caps and kilts — except that where all the others' pullovers had a design of little white sheep on them, Vanderdecker's had a single black and white panda, like some sort of military badge of rank.

'Now,' Vanderdecker said, 'all we've got to do is find Antonius.'

'Easier said than done,' Sebastian muttered. He had wanted the panda, and he was blatantly sulking.

'True,' Vanderdecker admitted. 'But all we've got to do is imagine we're idiots too, and then we can sort of reconstruct his thought processes.'

Just then, Antonius himself appeared. He was wearing a quiet grey suit under a dufflecoat. He stared.

'Hello, skip,' he said. 'I went back to the power station but you'd all gone. Why are you all wearing those funny ...?'

'Hello, Antonius,' Vanderdecker said briskly. 'Right, now let's all go and have that drink, shall we?' He sighed and walked over to where the policeman was still sitting.

'Excuse me,' he said.

The policeman opened his eyes and shuddered.

'Sorry to bother you again,' Vanderdecker said, 'but can you by any chance tell us where we can get a drink around here?'

The policeman pointed down the street to a building labelled Hotel. Vanderdecker thanked him. 'Maybe you'd like to join us,' he added. 'You look like you could use a drink.'

'No!' said the policeman forcefully. 'Never again.' Then he got up and started to run. Vanderdecker shrugged.

'Be like that,' he said. 'Now then, the drinks are on me.'

The crew of the *Verdomde* hastened away up the street, leaving it entirely deserted. For about five minutes, there was perfect peace and quiet, except for the distant sound of a hotel door being smashed in, and after that, the complete and utter tranquility for which the Highlands of Scotland are so famous. Then there was a clattering, roaring noise as a helicopter swung down low over the village, hovered for a moment, and soared off in the direction of Dounreay Power Station.

Very, very carefully, Professor Montalban picked himself up off the ground and applied his mind.

Being a scientist, he went about things in a systematic and methodical way. He therefore started with his head — yes, that was still there, and it seemed to be functioning properly — then his arms, then his trunk, legs and feet. All present and correct. Good.

Good but extremely surprising. The force of the explosion had been so enormous that he had been certain, in the tenth of a microsecond available for contemplation of the matter, that nothing on earth could possibly have survived it. Well, it only went to show how dangerous it was to jump to purely intuitive conclusions.

Another strange thing was the way the building was still intact. Mostly intact. The huge steel girder that he seemed to remember falling on his head suggested that bits of it had indeed come loose, but what did you expect from modern builders? Nobody seemed to take a pride in their work any more.

Oh, the Professor said to himself, for a cup of tea and a slice of home-made Victoria sponge.

He removed the cinders from his eyes and looked carefully about him. No fire. No smoke. No signs of anything much out of the ordinary. Most peculiar. He wandered away in the direction of the computer room. The sudden violent explosion was puzzling him, and he had a theory he wanted to put to the test.

As I thought, he told himself smugly, examining the wreckage of the plutonium cell. It was his own design, completely revolutionary and top secret; it was also, now, broken. But he didn't mind that.

The question that had been bothering him was what had made the plutonium go off pop like that, and here, it seemed, was the answer. One of the idiots from the ship had opened the door and gone in. There had been nothing between him (or to be precise, the smell) and the plutonium itself. The plutonium had, in combination with the unique carbon compounds found only in the gases comprising the smell, undergone a rapid chemical reaction and evolved into a completely harmless isotope of itself. Now, since to every action there is an equal and opposite reaction (one of his more felicitous sayings, he always thought), it stood to reason that something had happened to the smell-bearer.

Montalban looked round; there was nothing, not a scrap of bone or a fragment of charred scalp. Nothing. They had obviously just disintegrated, turned back into clouds of carbon, hydrogen and oxygen. Kaput.

Oh dear, said Montalban to himself. He was thinking of the Vanderdecker policy. How terribly awkward.

'Our next programme here on Radio Three,' said the horribly plummy voice Jane had got sick of listening to, 'is Wagner's opera *Die Fliegende Hollander,* broadcast in the 1956 Deutsche Gramophon recording with . . .'

It turned out to be a coincidence, of course. Jane had found the Professor's spare decoder in the bathroom (easily done; she just carried the portable radio around the house and waited until something talked back; in this case, the toilet-roll cover) and all it could make of Wagner's early masterpiece was a jumble of incoherent sounds, with the occasional random word, such as Hippopotamus and Canasta, rising above the noise. She switched them both off, tried Ceefax one more time (Adelaide 6, Darwin 5), and gave the whole thing up as a dead loss.

The longer she waited, her reason told her, the better; so far, no clouds of radioactive dust or great searing flashes of heat had interrupted the calm of a wet Cotswold day, which argued that Dounreay hadn't blown up, or at least not yet. But — Jane couldn't help herself thinking, although God knows it wasn't a particularly nice way to think — that wasn't really the point, now was it? When all was said and done, she wasn't all that bothered about Dounreay and the fate of the North of England, or Europe. Not that she had anything against them, and she'd far rather nothing horrid happened to them, of course; but what she was really worrying about was what had happened to one man.

Crazy. Just suppose he did come back; what then? The best way to get rid of the yearning for something, she had always found, was to imagine what it would be like if the dream came true. Once you imagined that, you usually found that you didn't want the happy ending after all, not at any price, and the technique was particularly sound, in her experience, when it came to men. In the past, when she had felt that dreadful, cloying, having-eaten-too-much-Black-Forest-gateau feeling about someone, she conjured up a vision of living with him, ironing for him, holding things and getting sworn at when he put up kitchen shelves. But in this case, for some reason, it didn't seem to work. Perhaps it was because what she was feeling now wasn't anything like eating too much cake; it was more a sort of understanding of what her life had been about all these years. It had simply been Fate's rather cack-handed way of making sure she was there at the right time in the right place to meet Julius Vanderdecker, the Flying Dutchman. And why, Miss Doland, was that such a good idea? Because. No other reason, just because. If he had been handsome or charming or generally wonderful in some other obvious way, it wouldn't be the same thing at all; because when the wonderfulness had worn off, there wouldn't be anything left except a lot of real life. What Jane liked about Vanderdecker was the way she liked him.

Anyway, Miss Doland, your Vanderdecker is quite probably not coming back, so there. And that, after all, was what he wanted; there was no getting away from the fact. Apparently he doesn't think I'm worth staying around for, and who can blame him? Pull yourself together and have something to eat.

Jane was half-way through a cold chicken salad when the sound of rotorblades outside the house made her heart explode inside her. Dumping her knife and fork she sprinted out of the door, quite forgetting that she wasn't wearing any shoes until she set foot on the gravel path.

But only one man got out of the helicopter; one man she'd seen before, and who wasn't quite the same, somehow.

'Professor!' she screamed. 'What's happened?'

The Professor ducked under the rotor blades and walked towards her. He was looking at her rather strangely, but she was too preoccupied to notice.

'Ah,' said the Professor. 'Miss Doland. I'm glad you're still ...'

'Is he all right?'

'He?' The Professor raised an eyebrow.

'Vanderdecker,' Jane howled. 'Is he all ...?'

'Alas,' said the Professor, 'I fear not. A great loss. But I feel sure that ...'

Jane seemed to deflate, like a balloon, and if it hadn't been for her clothes holding her together she would probably have melted onto the ground, like a collapsing candle. The Professor smiled sympathetically and said 'There, there.'

'Were you there when it ...?'

'Not exactly,' Montalban replied, 'but I feel there can be no doubt in the matter. There was quite simply nothing left. It was what he wanted, you know, and he has un- questionably saved the lives of thousands, if not ...'

'Oh go to hell,' Jane snapped. 'It's all your bloody fault, anyway.'

Montalban's avuncular air seemed to wobble slightly, like the picture when a pigeon sits on the aerial. 'May I remind you that were it not for my elixir, he would probably have died in the 1570s. I don't think that he ...'

But Jane wasn't listening. Which was a pity, the Professor thought, as there really was something rather important they should be talking about. Although he understood pretty well everything else in the universe, from the nature of matter to the music of the spheres, the Professor, as he would have been the first to admit, had never known what to make of women. He shrugged his shoulders slightly, smiled again, and went in search of Eccles cakes.

Jane slowly started to compose herself. This is probably how jellyfish feel, she told herself, no bones. They manage, so I suppose I shall have to manage too. A nuisance, but there it is. Back to work tomorrow morning, and that's the end of your holiday. As she started towards the house, the helicopter pilot ran up to her and put something in her hand.

'Here,' he said, 'this is for you. The other one who smelt so horrible said to give it to you. I don't know what it's all about, but the Professor there was mad keen to get his hands on it. Lucky I was flying the chopper, or I think he'd have tried to grab it off me.'

Jane stared at the worn brown wallet the pilot had handed her. She recognised it, and she could feel something tearing at her insides, doing all sorts of damage to nerves and muscles. She thanked him and walked away.

The policy; she remembered now. He had wanted her to have the policy, keep it safe for him. Well yes, but what good was that now, to anybody? She opened the wallet and found the hard, folded vellum sheet, and breathing was suddenly rather difficult. Under the porch light, she opened it out and looked at it, and her eye fell on the coupon on the back. She read her name, and the signature under it, and that was enough to finish her off. But not, strangely, enough to stop her running after the helicopter pilot and having a word with him.

Inside the house, the Professor was talking on the telephone, his mouth full of Eccles cake. He had been

busy; so many people to notify, governments to inform,
evacuations to call off, that sort of thing. Now he needed to
attend to his own affairs, which were shortly going to be in
a rather terrible mess.

He heard the door slam, and put the phone down,
ignoring the Minister at the other end of the line. He could
wait; Miss Doland couldn't. It was vital that they had a
quiet chat immediately.

'Miss Doland,' he called out, 'are you there?'

'Yes,' Jane said, walking into the room. 'I expect you
want to have a word with me. Oh, you've got another gun,
how nice for you. I'm just going to finish my salad.'

She walked into the kitchen, ignoring the menacing
barrel of the Colt .38 that was trained on her, and smoth-
ered her lettuce with salad cream. After a few mouthfuls,
she became aware that she was not alone.

'Do you mind?' she said. 'It's terribly rude to threaten to
kill people while they're eating.'

'Miss Doland,' said the Professor, 'this time I'm afraid I
have to be serious. Unless you hand me that policy document immediately, I shall have no option but to shoot you.'
He cocked the hammer of the pistol and waited for a
reaction. All he got was the sound of crunching radish.

'Wouldn't do that if I were you,' Jane said.

'I'm afraid my patience has run out, Miss Doland,' said
the Professor grimly. 'This time ...'

'You're missing the point,' said Jane, and pointed a half-
gnawed drumstick at him. 'If you shoot me, it'll cost you a
great deal of money.'

'What?'

'Stands to reason,' Jane said, opening a jar of beetroot.
'Now I'm not a lawyer — God forbid — but if I die, I
believe the proceeds of the policy will form part of my
estate. All clear so far? Good. Now, since I haven't made a
will, all my property passes on my death to my next of kin,
which will probably be my parents. If you kill them, it'll
pass to theirs. I have a large family, Professor Montalban,
and if you go around knocking them all off, somebody is
going to notice sooner or later and put you away for the rest
of your life. Given your rather peculiar circumstances, that

all adds up to a hell of a lot of porridge. Have a pickled walnut, they're excellent.'

'No thank you,' said the Professor, 'they give me indigestion. You're overlooking the fact that nobody but you and I know about the assignment of the policy, or even that it exists.'

'Don't count on it,' Jane said through a mouthful of pickled walnut. 'I mean, there's the helicopter pilot, for one.'

'The helicopter pilot?'

'The one who gave me the policy. Nice man. He wrote down the policy number and everything. I also wrote a short letter to my parents enclosing full details, which he said he'd post for me when he got to Yeovilton. He should be nearly there by now. I'm afraid you're stuffed, Professor. Talking of which, have an olive.'

'I do not want an olive, Miss Doland.'

'More fool you, then,' Jane replied. 'It's at times like these you need an olive in order to make sense of things. But I suppose you've been stuffing your face with cakes and biscuits; they're very bad for you, you know.'

The Professor sighed and put the revolver down on the worktop. Then he put the kettle on.

'That's bad for you too, you know,' Jane told him. 'Think of what all that tannin is doing to the lining of your stomach.'

'Academic, Miss Doland,' said the Professor. 'Purely academic. You forget that . . .'

'Hold on,' Jane said, laying down her fork. 'I know you are, and so was he. But you survived.'

'He was nearer the blast than I was,' the Professor said.

'Running away, were you?'

'Yes.' The Professor didn't seem particularly proud of himself.

'Perhaps,' Jane said, 'we could do a deal.'

A tiny part of her, which had been taken by surprise by what her lips had just said, protested; but the rest of her shut it up. Why else, she thought, had he given her the policy? Might as well get it over with.

'Certainly,' the Professor said quietly. 'What had you in mind?'

'Well, for a start,' Jane said. 'About the rain forests . . .'

Simon Courtenay felt in his pocket for his keys, and then realised that he didn't need them. The door of his hotel was open; and not just ajar, or even standing wide. It was unconditionally open, what was left of it.

He swore. Ever since he had sold his house in Surbiton to buy the Highland hotel of his escapist fantasies, he had been waiting for the moment when the very peculiar natives of this area finally lost control and went berserk. He had often noticed them out of the corner of his eye, staring at him and muttering in Gaelic, but he had hoped that they would refrain from actual violence and damage to property. Well, he should have known better.

From the bar came the sound of drunken singing, and the sound of smashing glass. He considered whether he should call the police, but then remembered that they would be Scottish too, and likely to join in and help their countrymen. It was up to him. He picked up a chair-leg — for some reason there were a lot of chair-legs lying about his premises tonight, very few of them with chairs attached — and walked into the bar.

'We are sailing, We are sailing, Home again, Across the sea,' sang the drunkards in kilts lying around the gutted bar. They each had their own personal bottle of his very expensive and select stock of malt whiskies, except for one who was spilling a lot of beer in the attempt to find his own mouth. Pissed as rats, the lot of them. Disgusting.

'We are sailing, Stormy waters, To be . . .'

'That will do,' Simon said, in his very best stiff-upper-lip manner. 'Out, the lot of you.'

The man with the beer looked at his watch — a pity that his watch should be on the wrist of the hand he was holding the glass in — and said, 'Hell's teeth, is that the time already?', in an accent that Simon couldn't exactly place, but which certainly wasn't Scottish.

'Hang on,' said the man with beer all over his kilt, 'it's only ten-fifteen. Drinking up time,' he added. 'Gimme another pint of Guinness, and have one yourself.'

'If you don't all clear out of here in one minute,' Simon

said, 'I'm calling the police.'

'Bloody British licensing laws,' grumbled one of the other drunks. 'God, what a country.'

'Come on,' said the beer-drinker, 'let's be going, I think we've outstayed our ... Christ, is that the time? Look,' he said to Simon, 'is there a telephone here anywhere?'

Simon pointed to an overturned bookcase. 'Under there,' he said grimly.

The man grinned sheepishly. "Fraid we've made rather a mess,' he said. 'Sorry about that, but we've just saved the world, you see, and I promised Antonius a drink afterwards.'

'Really,' said Simon. 'James Bond, are you?'

'No,' said the beer-drinker. 'Vanderdecker. Julius Vanderdecker.'

'And you've just saved the ...'

'Scout's honour. Now, let me just make a quick call, and ...'

Just then, there was the sound of rotor blades overhead, making the whole building shake. It seemed to go on for a very long time and Simon couldn't bear it, not on top of everything else. He sat down on an overturned Space Invaders machine and started to cry.

Meanwhile, Vanderdecker was yelling into the telephone.

'Jane? Oh, it's you. Is Jane there? She hasn't gone? Yes, it's me. Yes of course I'm alive, they don't have telephones in ... Well get her, then. Thank you ... Jane? It's me. Sorry if I've dragged you out of bed or ... Yes, it's *me* and I'm *not* ... You what? Say that again? Oh, oh that's nice. Look, I've just got to find a helicopter and ... Hang on, won't be a minute. Yes?' he added, turning to see who had tapped him on the shoulder. He registered something and turned back to the telephone. 'It's all right,' he said, 'it's that telly bloke, you know, Danny something. Bennett? Yes, that's it. God knows what he's doing here.' He turned away from the receiver again. 'Hey, have you got a ... oh, that's yours outside, is it? Could you get them to turn the bloody thing off, I'm trying to make a call here ... You still there? Good. Listen, Danny's got a helicopter, we'll be with you soon.

Yes, yes, you too. No, there are people listening. Right, see you then.'

He put down the receiver, and stood up.

'I've been looking for you,' Danny said.

'Have you?'

'I thought you were dead.'

'Sorry?'

'I thought you were ...'

'You'll have to speak up.'

'I THOUGHT you were DEAD.'

Vanderdecker laughed, very loudly. 'You too,' he said. 'Fat chance! Come on, let's be going.' He turned and looked round the room. 'You lot,' he said, 'this bloke's giving us all a lift to Cirencester.'

'Why do we want to go to Cirencester?' asked Pieter Pretorius. 'I've been there, it's a dump.'

'That was in 1647,' Vanderdecker said, 'you'll probably like it now. Come on, all of you who're coming.'

There was some grumbling, but the crew slowly picked themselves up and started to troop out. Danny noticed something.

'Hey,' he said, 'you don't smell any more.'

'Thank you,' said Vanderdecker, 'that's the nicest thing anyone's ever said to me. Well,' he added, remembering, 'almost. Look, do me a favour, will you?'

'Sure,' Danny replied, 'what?'

Vanderdecker pointed to Simon and said, 'Write this bloke a cheque,. A thousand ought to cover it.'

'A thousand pounds!' Danny exclaimed. 'Now hang on ...'

'Oh it's all right,' Vanderdecker said, 'I'll pay you back when we get to Cirencester. I have an idea I'll have a great deal of money when we get to Cirencester. Pieter, grab the cat.'

Danny shrugged and wrote out a cheque for a thousand pounds, which he handed to Simon, who stared at it. He was still staring at it a quarter of an hour later, when the helicopter had gone away again and he was alone in a wrecked bar with a lot of broken chairs, a cheque for a thousand pounds and a geiger counter in the shape of a Fabergé egg.

CHAPTER FIFTEEN

I nside the helicopter, the party was still going on. It was a bit cramped, and it swayed about rather more (considered objectively) than the hotel in Dounreay, but it was the considered view of the crew of the *Verdomde* that while there was moonlight and laughter and Scotch and romance, they might as well face the music and get pathetically drunk. It wasn't every day, after all, that you escape from a four-hundred-odd-year-old curse.

'Here,' Sebastian was saying to a bulkhead, 'you remember that time in Nijmegen?'

'That wasn't Nijmegen,' Pieter replied, 'that was Antwerp.'

'No it wasn't,' Sebastian retorted. 'Antwerp was when you and me and Wilhelmus got com-*pletely* ratted and went round smashing up all the watchmaker's shops.'

'Exactly,' Pieter said, nodding vigorously, 'that was Antwerp, not Nijmegen.'

'That's what I just said.'

'You said Nijmegen.'

'Hold on,' Wilhelmus interrupted. 'Nijmegen — *Nijmegen* was when we nicked that old girl's donkey and Jan van Hoosemyr ...'

'*I know,*' said Sebastian angrily. 'That's what I was trying to say. That was Nijmegen. Antwerp was when we smashed in all the watchmakers ...'

'But you just said ...'

The camera crew looked at each other.

'Reminds me of that time in Tripoli,' said the cameraman.

In fact, the only sober Dutchman on board the helicopter was Vanderdecker, and he was beginning to wonder if sobriety and a clear head were a good idea after all. Danny was trying to interview him, and he was finding it rather wearing.

'So when did you first suspect,' Danny was saying, 'that there had been a cover-up?'

Vanderdecker yanked his mind back to what Danny was saying. 'Cover-up?' he said. 'Oh, sorry, I was miles away. What cover-up?'

'*The* cover-up,' Danny snapped. 'When did you first become aware of it?'

'Just now,' Vanderdecker said, 'when you mentioned it. Shows what a good cover-up it was, doesn't it?'

Danny ground his teeth. 'We'll do that bit again,' he said, and wound the tape back. 'Look, will you please try and concentrate on what I'm saying?'

'Sorry,' Vanderdecker said, and realised that since Danny was being kind enough to give him a lift to Cirencester, he ought to say something at least. 'You mean *that* cover-up.'

Danny's hairs bristled. 'You mean there was more than one?' Vanderdecker laughed.

'You bet,' he said.

'Such as?'

'Where do I start?' Vanderdecker said. 'I mean, we are talking yesterday's witness here.' He leaned forward conspiratorily. 'For example,' he whispered. 'I bet you still think Columbus discovered America.'

Danny couldn't believe his ears. 'And didn't he?'

Vanderdecker smiled cynically. 'Don't you believe it,' he said. 'The Portuguese landed in what is now Florida seventy years before Columbus left Spain. But there was this ...'

'Cover-up?'

'Exactly,' Vanderdecker said. 'On the tip of my tongue it was, yes, cover-up.'

'Why?'

'Merchandising,' Vanderdecker said. 'I mean, just think for a moment, will you? Think of all the spin-offs from discovering a new continent. America cart bumper stickers, America doublets, the official America cuddly bison; no, as soon as the Portuguese realised what they'd got hold of, they saw that unless they got the franchising side of it sorted out before the story broke, there was going to be absolute chaos, marketing-wise. So they sat on it while the lawyers sorted out the contractual basis. And you know what lawyers are like; by the time they'd got down to a preliminary draft joint venture agreement, Columbus had landed and the whole thing was up the spout.'

Danny's brain reeled. 'How do you know all that?' he said. 'That was before your time, wasn't it?'

'Or take the Gunpowder Plot,' Vanderdecker said quickly. 'I could tell you a thing about that, make no mistake.'

'Go on,' said Danny, changing tapes. 'I always thought ...'

'I mean,' Vanderdecker went on, 'Guido Fawkes was set up. He was the biggest fall guy of all time. You won't find anything about it down at the Public Records Office, but there was big money involved there all right. Oh yes.'

'So?'

'So it was only a conspiracy by Buckingham and Salisbury to get hold of the biggest monopoly of them all. I mean the big one. None of your fooling about with Rhenish wine this time; I'm talking ...' He stopped, and searched for the right word. '... Megagroats.'

'What was it?'

Vanderdecker looked over his shoulder. 'Milk,' he hissed. 'They were after the milk monopoly. They were going to set up this holding corporation — like the East India Company or something like that — with themselves as the money-men behind it; and this company was going to have the exclusive right to buy all the milk in England and sell it to the ultimate consumer.'

'You mean,' Danny croaked, 'like the Milk Marketing Board?'

'Keep your voice down, will you? Yes, just like the Milk Marketing Board. So now do you see why Guido had to take the fall?'

'I see,' Danny whispered. 'My God, that explains ... But why did they want to blow up King James?'

Vanderdecker sneered. 'They didn't want to blow up the King,' he said. 'If they'd wanted rid of Big Jim, do you think they'd have gone about it like that? Gunpowder, treason and plot? Don't be so naive. Look, just ask yourself this. Why was it that shortly after Guido did the November-the-Fifth bit, the price of clotted cream rose by a factor of seventy-four point six per cent in most of Southern England?'

Danny whistled. 'That much?'

'That's where they went wrong, of course,' Vanderdecker said. 'Too much too soon, you see. And when Hampden and Pym found out ...'

'You mean the Civil War?'

'Do yourself a favour,' Vanderdecker said. 'Take a look at the Putney Debates; you know, towards the end of the War, when all the Parliamentary leaders sat down and tried to make up a new constitution. Is there one mention, one solitary word said about an overall dairy strategy for the 1660's? Nothing. Don't you find that just a little bit surprising?'

Danny's mouth hung open like a dislocated letterbox. 'So the Restoration ...'

'You've got it,' Vanderdecker said. 'All that stuff with the oak tree was just a blind. And then, when you get on to the Glorious Revolution, and after that the Jacobites, it suddenly starts to fall into place. After all, why do you think they called George III Farmer George? He was as sane as ...' Vanderdecker considered for a moment, '... as you are, but ... Anyway, there's the story for you, if you really do want something big.'

Vanderdecker's mouth felt dry with so much talking, and he turned away in search of whisky, but Danny grabbed him by the arm.

'Listen,' he said, 'you've got to tell me. Was the Milk Marketing Board behind the Kennedy assassination?'

Vanderdecker raised an eyebrow. 'You what?' he said.

'The assassination of President Kennedy. Was it them?'

'Don't be ridiculous,' Vanderdecker said. 'That was Lee Harvey Oswald.' He leaned over, plucked a bottle of Famous Grouse from Pieter's hand and took a long drink.

Danny narrowed his eyes. Was Vanderdecker telling the truth? Or was he in on it too?

Below the helicopter Cirencester flickered dimly, and Vanderdecker wiped the spilt whisky out of his beard. The next hour or so was going to be interesting, and he felt that it was probably just as well that he had stayed relatively sober after all. He glanced across at Danny, who was drawing complicated diagrams on the blank pages at the back of his diary, using one of those pens you get from Smiths which has four different colours in it. He was happy, the poor fool.

The crew were singing again:

'We've been together now for four hundred and eighty years,' they sang,

'And it don't seem a day too much.

'There ain't a captain sailing on the sea

'That we'd swap for our dear old dutch ...'

Vanderdecker winced. He hadn't thought about that side of it — he hadn't really thought about any side of it, if he was going to be honest with himself, the implications of getting rid of the smell at last. What was going to happen now? In the end, every community and grouping of human beings (except, of course, the Rolling Stones) drifts apart and goes its separate ways. There was nothing to keep them together now, and God knows, they'd all been getting on each other's nerves. But actually saying goodbye — goodbye after so many years ...

'Hey,' Sebastian protested, 'give it back.'

'Sorry,' Vanderdecker said, and handed the bottle back.

'Some people,' he said. 'That's how we all got into this mess in the first place, remember, you nicking somebody else's bottle. You'd have thought you'd have learned your lesson.'

'Still,' Vanderbecker said, 'it's been fun, hasn't it?'

'No,' Sebastian replied. 'It's been lousy.'

'But we've had some laughs, haven't we?' Vanderdecker said. 'A few good times along the way.'

'When?'

'Well ...' Vanderdecker shrugged. 'Forget it,' he said. 'What have you done with the cat, by the way?'

'What cat?'

'Montalban's cat.'

'Oh,' said Sebastian, 'that cat. It's over there, on the life-
jackets, having forty winks. I spilt some whisky, and it
lapped it up.'

'Fine,' Vanderdecker said. He rubbed his face with both
hands, and tried to think of what he should do next. For
over four hundred years he had been doing all the
thinking, and he was just starting to get a tiny bit tired of
it. Another day, new problems, more of the same old
rubbish; and Captain Vanderdecker standing on the
quarter-deck trying to cope with it, with his usual flair. Let
Julius do it — that was what his mother used to say, all
those many, many years ago: 'Don't trouble yourself with
that, dear; let Julius do it. Julius, put that away and ...'

The helicopter had stopped flying and was just
whirring, hovering tentatively above the grass. Then, with
a rather talentless lurch, it pitched down. Suddenly,
Vanderdecker didn't want to leave; he wanted to stay right
here and let someone else do the coping with things for a
change. No chance of that.

'Hey, skip.' Not you again, Antonius; go away, I died en
route, somewhere in the clouds over Smethwick, go ask
Danny Bennett or someone. 'Is this where we get out?'

'That's right,' Vanderdecker said wearily. 'Right, lads,
show a leg, we're here. Sebastian, bring the cat.'

'Why do I always have to ...?' The rest of the complaint
was drowned out with noise as the helicopter door opened,
and Vanderdecker (lead-from-the-front Vanderdecker)
dropped out onto the grass. Perhaps he was just feeling
tired, but he forgot to duck and the rotor blade hit him just
below the ear. Danny, who happened to be watching,
started to scream, but there was nothing to scream about;
the Dutchman staggered, swore loudly in Dutch, rubbed
his neck and went on his way.

'Well,' he said to Sebastian, 'that's one thing proved
anyway.'

'What?' said Sebastian. 'You never look where you're
going.'

Vanderdecker laughed mirthlessly, shrugged and walked

towards the house. Then he noticed a smallish human figure racing across the grass towards him. He narrowed his brows and wondered what was going on.

'Julius!' said the small human figure, and crashed into him like a dodgem car, jolting him almost as much as the rotor blade.

'Sorry,' he said automatically, and helped the small figure to its feet. The small figure was Jane, and Jane had wrapped her arms around him. He remembered.

'Hello, Jane,' he said.

'Julius, you're safe!' Jane gasped; but there was already a tiny note of doubt, an inflection so slight you would need high-quality scientific apparatus or ears like a bat to register it, but there nevertheless.

'I think we should have a quiet talk,' Vanderdecker said, prising her off gently. 'There's just a few things I've got to do first, and then ...'

'Julius?' The inflection was rather more obvious now. Vanderdecker closed off certain parts of his mind, which were getting in the way, and nodded.

'Won't be long,' he said. 'I've just got a couple of things to see to first, then I'm all yours.' There was something in his voice which belied the words he uttered, and Jane let go of him. She felt all hollow, like an egg with its yolk blown out.

'Such as,' Vanderdecker went on, 'booting a certain professor up the backside. Did you get the policy?'

'Yes,' Jane said. 'I did. Thank you.'

'What for? Oh, I see, yes, well. Where is it now?'

'I gave it to the pilot who brought the professor back,' Jane said. 'He's going to post it to my father as soon as he gets to ...'

'Very sensible.' Vanderdecker said, nodding. 'Perhaps you could just 'phone your father and ask him to send it to my place in Bridport.'

'*Bridport*?' Jane gasped.

'Yes,' Vanderdecker said, 'the fallen-down old dump where you said you found all the bank statements. It'll be safe there.'

Jane was about to say something, but she had forgotten

what it was. Couldn't have been important. 'Right,' she said. 'I'll just go and do that, then.'

'Thanks,' Vanderdecker said. 'Now, then.' He walked off quickly towards the house.

The Flying Dutchman was, when circumstances permitted, a man of his word; and when he said he was going to boot a professor up the backside, he stood by it.

'Ouch!' said Montalban, startled. 'My dear fellow, what...?'

Vanderdecker kicked him again, harder. One of his better ideas, he said to himself. He tried it again, but missed this time and put his foot through a complex piece of scientific equipment disguised as a glass-fronted cabinet full of netsuke. Although he didn't know it, lights flickered in Montreal, Jodrell Bank and Geneva.

'Captain,' said the professor, backing away while still trying to remain dignified, 'what has come over you?'

'Getting me into this mess,' said Vanderdecker. 'I can put up with. Causing me to sail round the world for nearly five hundred years I can take in my stride. Pissing off and leaving me under a ceiling and coming back here and stuffing yourself with macaroons is a bit too much, don't you think?' He aimed another kick at the professor; it glanced off the bunch of keys in his trouser pocket and wasted its force in empty air, making Vanderdecker totter slightly. He regained his balance and his composure at about the same moment.

'Well,' he said, 'anyway, there we are. You will be delighted to know that that gimcrack Friday-afternoon job of a power station of yours is now safe again, absolutely no thanks to you. And you owe me and my lads for a complete set of clothes each. All right?'

'Yes, most certainly,' said Montalban. 'My dear fellow, I am delighted to see you all in one piece. I ...'

'I bet you are,' Vanderdecker said furiously. 'Because if I hadn't been, it'd have cost you plenty. Well, let me tell you that ...'

'And even more delighted,' said the Professor, with all the smoothness he could manage, 'to note that the treatment worked.'

Vanderdecker stared. '*Treatment?*'

'Indeed,' said the Professor. 'Just as I had hoped. The radiation charge has eliminated the smell entirely. My experiments are vindicated. You must be very pleased.'

And grateful, his tone implied. So grateful, in fact, that you really ought to do me a little favour in return. Vanderdecker caught the implication like Rodney Marsh fielding a large, slow football. 'If you think,' he said, 'I'm going to sign over that bloody policy after what you just did to me . . .'

'And what was that?'

'Leaving me there,' Vanderdecker roared. 'Other things too, but just now, mostly that.'

'My dear fellow,' Montalban said. 'I imagined you were — well, dead, to put it bluntly. I could see no sign of you; I feared that you and your companions had been simply atomised by the force of the blast. There was nothing I could do, I came away; my presence was needed here . . .'

Vanderdecker growled softly, but his indignation was leaking away like oil from a fractured sump. The Professor smiled kindly.

'And so,' he said, 'everything has worked out for the best. You have no idea how much pleasure this moment gives me. The unpleasant side-effect of my elixir has successfully been counteracted. My work is over . . .'

The words froze on his lips, and Vanderdecker stared at him as he quietly repeated the words.

'Montalban?' Vanderdecker asked. 'Are you all right?'

The Professor stood there like a dead Christmas tree for a moment and then grabbed Vanderdecker fiercely by the shoulders. 'Vanderdecker,' he shouted, 'did you hear what I just said? My work is *over*! I've finished! I don't have to do it any more, it's finished.'

Vanderdecker stepped back, wondering if the kick had affected the Professor's brain. 'Well,' he said, 'that's wonderful for you, I'm sure. Maybe now you can have a lie-in at weekends, read the paper, that sort of . . . '

Montalban filled his lungs and let out the loudest, least dignified whoop ever heard outside a Navajo encampment. 'It's over!' he screamed. 'Yippee! No more work! No more work!' He danced — literally danced — round the room, kicking things as he went.

'Look, Professor,' Vanderdecker said, 'I'm delighted for you, of course, but could we just have a quick chat about my policy? Then you can dance about all you like, but ...'

"The policy?' Montalban stopped dead, turned round and stared Vanderdecker in the face. 'You can *stuff* your policy!' he squealed. 'That's it, you can *stuff* it! I don't care any more, I'm free.'

Something rather improbable fell into place in Vanderdecker's mind, like the tumblers of a combination lock. 'Professor,' he said, 'are you trying to tell me you don't *like* being a scientist?'

'My dear fellow,' gibbered the Professor, 'I hate it. I hate it, do you hear? It's horrible. It *stinks*. I've always hated it, even when I was a boy and my mother said I was wasting my time composing madrigals and I should grow up and learn alchemy like my father. I've always hated it, and ... and I've had to do it for *five hundred years*! My God,' said Montalban savagely, 'you think you're hard done by, do you, sailing round the world with nothing to do all day? You don't know you're born. Imagine, just imagine what I've had to put up with. I'd have changed places with you like a shot. Day after day after day in a foul, stinking laboratory, fiddling with sulphate of this and nitrate of that, doing equations and square roots and ... and now I'm free. I don't have to do it any more. No more inventing internal combustion and splitting atoms. No more electrons. No more law of the conservation of matter. No more Brownian motion. Dear God, Vanderdecker, you can't imagine how thoroughly depressing it all was, the endless, endless difficulties, five hundred years of them — having to do it all *myself*; nobody — absolutely nobody — to help, all up to me, all that bloody, bloody *work*! I *hate* ... *work*!'

'Oh good,' Vanderdecker said, calmly, 'you won't have to do that any more.'

'No,' said the Professor, quietly, grinning, 'no, I won't. I need a drink. Will you join me?'

'And the policy?' Vanderdecker said.

'Oh, sod the policy,' Montalban replied. 'Now that that's

all done with, I don't need the Bank any more. Just so long
as I never have to do another day's work in my life, the
Bank can go bust for all I care and jolly good luck to it. Let
someone else sort something out, just for once.'

'I know how you feel,' Vanderdecker said gently, 'believe
me.'

'Thirsty?'

Vanderdecker nodded. 'That too. Look, I've just got to
go and deal with something and then I'll be right back.'

'You'd better hurry,' said the Professor, pouring whisky
into a big glass, 'because I'm not going to wait for you.
Tea!' he sneered. 'The devil with tea! I don't have to keep a
clear head any more, I can get as pissed as a mouse.'

'Rat.'

'Precisely, my dear fellow, as a rat. Hurry back!'

'I might just do that,' Vanderdecker said, and he ran off
into the gardens again.

Some time later a car — more than a car; the biggest
Mercedes you ever saw — pulled up outside the front door.
It was full of accountants.

Mr Gleeson got out. He rang the doorbell. After a long,
long time a drunken man in a kilt answered it. In the
background, someone was playing 'My Very Good Friend
The Milkman Says' on the harpsichord.

'What do you want?' he asked.

'Miss Doland,' said Mr Gleeson.

The man in the kilt sniggered. 'You're not the only one,'
he said. He was slurring his words slightly.

'Just get her,' said Mr Gleeson. As befits a high-rolling
accountant, Mr Gleeson had authority and presence. He
was used to being obeyed.

'Piss off,' said the man in the kilt, and slammed the
door.

Mr Gleeson was surprised. According to the latest
charging-rate guidelines, it costs at least fifteen pounds
plus VAT to slam a door in the face of an accountant of
partner status. He rang the bell again.

'I said piss off,' said a voice through the letter-box.

Mr Gleeson muttered something in a low voice, and two

other accountants rang the doorbell for him. This is known
as the art of delegation.

Eventually the door opened again.

'Sorry about that. Can I help you?'

This time it was a man in a kilt with a beard. He
seemed rational enough, and Mr Gleeson stepped forward.
Far away in the distance, a nightingale sang.

'My name's Gleeson,' he said. 'Moss Berwick, accountants. Where's Miss Doland?'

'She's inside,' said the man with the beard, 'but you
don't want to see her. You want to see me. My name's
Vanderdecker.'

For a moment, Mr Gleeson simply stood and stared.
Then he pulled himself together. 'We have to talk,' he said.

Vanderdecker shook his head. 'Perhaps you may have to
talk, I don't know,' he said. 'If it's some sort of obsession
you have, maybe a psychiatrist could help. I knew a man
once ...'

'Please,' said Mr Gleeson. 'This is no time for flippancy.
Have you any idea what is happening on the markets?'

'Heavy falls in jute futures?'

'We must talk,' said Mr Gleeson.

'We are talking,' Vanderdecker replied. Gleeson drew in
a deep breath and started to walk past Vanderdecker into
the house. But the Flying Dutchman put the palm of his
hand on Mr Gleeson's shirt front and shoved. There was a
ripple of amazement among the other accountants.
Vanderdecker smiled. 'So what's happening on the
markets?' he said.

'Massive rises,' said Gleeson. 'The situation has got
completely out of hand. It is imperative that we ...'

'Hold on a minute,' Vanderdecker said, and he stepped
back into the hallway, called out, 'Sebastian! Make him
stop that bloody row, will you?' and turned to face Mr
Gleeson again. Muted grumbling in the background, and
the harpsichord music ceased.

'Sorry about that,' said the Flying Dutchman, 'but I
think you'll find everything will be back to normal on your
beloved markets in a few minutes. The Professor's got
completely ratted and he's started playing things on the

harpsichord, forgetting that it's a computer too. You don't understand a word of that, but what the hell, you're only a glorified book-keeper. Clerks, we called them in my day. Used to shave the tops of their heads and talk Latin at you. I see you shave your head too, or is that just premature hair loss?'

'All right,' said Mr Gleeson, 'that's enough from you. Where is Miss ...?'

But before he could say any more, Vanderdecker had grabbed him by various parts of his clothing, lifted him off the ground and tossed him into a flower-bed.

'Now listen,' Vanderdecker said, 'the lot of you. The phrase "under new management" springs immediately to mind; also, "the King is dead; long live the King." If in future you wish to see Miss Doland, you will have to make an appointment. Miss Doland has left the accountancy profession and has gone into banking. She is now the proprietor of the First Lombard Bank.'

There was a very long silence — if the accountants had had their stopwatches running, about twelve hundred pounds worth, plus VAT — and then Mr Gleeson said 'You what?'

'Miss Doland,' Vanderdecker said, 'has exchanged entitlements as sole beneficiary by assignment of what I believe you meatheads call the Vanderdecker Policy for a fifty-one per cent shareholding in Quicksilver Limited, which is — I hope I'm getting all this right, it's not exactly my field, you know — which I believe is the holding company which owns the First Lombard Bank, Lombard Assurance, Lombard Unit Trusts plc, and all sorts of other money sort of things with the word Lombard in them. The remaining forty-nine per cent goes to me. We've just had a very pleasant half-hour with the previous owner signing stock transfer forms while drinking apple brandy and singing 'Lilliburlero' in Dutch. If any of you people fancy dropping by at about eleven-thirty tomorrow morning, you can help out with the Capital Gains Tax. For now, though, you will kindly shove off before I set the cat on you. Goodnight.'

The door slammed again, and there was the sound of a

chain going on. Mr Gleeson picked himself up, brushed leaf-mould off his trousers and lifted the flap of the letter-box.

'Doland,' he shouted, 'you're fired!' Then he got into the car and drove off.

As the receding-Mercedes noises faded away, the door opened again, just a crack.

'Has he gone?' said a small female voice.

'Yes,' Vanderdecker said.

'Really?'

'Really and truly.'

Vanderdecker closed the door. 'But it beats me,' he said, 'why you're afraid of him. Them, come to that. Glorified, over-fed book-keepers.'

'I don't know,' Jane replied. 'Habit, probably. You know, I used to have these daydreams. The letter would come saying that my long-lost aunt in Australia had died leaving me a million pounds, and then I'd go into Mr Peters' office and say, "Peters, you're a jerk, you can stick your job ..." But even if she had ...'

'Who?'

'My aunt in Australia.'

'You have an aunt in Australia?'

'No.'

'Sorry,' Vanderdecker said, 'forget it, carry on with what you were saying.'

'Even,' Jane said, 'if I'd had one and she had, I still wouldn't have.'

'Because of habit?'

'Habit of mind,' Jane replied. 'Subservience, innate atavistic feudal mentality. You don't go telling your liege-lord he can stick his job even if you're leaving to join the Second Crusade. Purely theoretical, anyway.'

'Not now,' Vanderdecker said. 'You are in exactly that position, thanks to my foresight in taking out life insur-ance all those years ago — my mother wouldn't half be surprised, by the way, she always said I was a fool when it came to money — and yet you denied yourself a moment's extreme pleasure because of habit of mind. Strange be-haviour.'

'Oh, I'm just chicken,' Jane said. 'Anyway, thanks for dealing with it for me. You did it very well.'

'Did I?' Vanderdecker said. 'Call it beginner's luck.'

They were standing in the hall. From the drawing-room came drinking noises. 'Well, then ...' Jane said.

'Well what?'

'Oh, I don't know, Julius ...'

'Do you know,' Vanderdecker said. 'I can't get used to people calling me that again. That Bennett bloke keeps calling me Julius, and I don't know what to make of it. Only person ever called me Julius was my mother. Dad called me son, my master when I was a 'prentice used to refer to me as "hey, you", and then I was captain or skipper for the next four hundred odd years. Being Julius again is a bit unsettling, really. I never liked the name, anyway.'

'Didn't you?'

'No.'

'Do you have another name? A second name, or something?'

'Yes.'

'What?'

'Albert.'

That seemed to kill the conversation for a moment. Then Vanderdecker said, 'You don't like the name Albert, do you?'

'Well,' Jane said, 'not really.'

'Nor me. Good old Dutch name, of course, been in my family for generations. I think it means Elf-beard, which is quite incredibly helpful. Well, too late to do anything about it now, I suppose.'

'Yes.'

There was nothing in particular keeping them in the hall, but neither of them moved. Eventually Jane asked: 'So what are you going to do next?'

Vanderdecker raised an eyebrow. 'Next?'

'Well, yes, I mean, you aren't going to stay here drinking with Professor Montalban for the rest of time, now are you?'

Vanderdecker considered. 'Probably not,' he said. 'On

the other hand, I feel like a bit of a holiday.'

'A holiday from what?'

'From whatever I've got to do next, I suppose.'

'Look,' Jane said sharply, 'you haven't got to do anything next. Or ever.' But Vanderdecker shook his head.

'It's not as easy as that,' he said. 'I really wish it was, but it isn't. It's them.' He nodded his head towards the drawing-room door. Jane stared at him for a moment.

'What, them?' she said. 'Johannes and Antonius and Sebastian and ...'

'I'm afraid so, yes.'

'But what have they got to do with it?'

Vanderdecker smiled, but not for the reasons that usually make people smile. 'I'm their captain,' he said. 'I'm responsible for them.'

Jane stared. 'You're joking,' she said. 'I thought you couldn't stand the sight of each other. I thought that after all those years cooped up on that little ship ...'

'Yes,' Vanderdecker replied, 'and no. Yes, we get on each other's nerves to a quite extraordinary extent, and we can't even relieve the tension with murder or other forms of violence. On the other hand, I'm their captain. I do all the thinking for them. I've had to, for the last four centuries. They've completely forgotten how to do it for themselves. So, okay, maybe we don't have to go back on that boring bloody ship ever again; but I can't leave them. It'd be impossible.'

'Why?'

Vanderdecker was silent for what seemed like an immensely long time, then he turned to Jane, looked her in the eye and said, 'Habit'.

'I see.'

'Set in our ways,' Vanderdecker amplified. 'Old dogs and new tricks.'

'Fine,' Jane replied. 'Well, it was very nice meeting you.'

'Likewise.'

'Perhaps we'll bump into each other again one day.'

'Bound to,' Vanderdecker said. 'Board meetings, that sort of thing. So what are you going to do now?'

Jane shrugged. 'I don't know,' she said. 'I think I'll have

a holiday too. Only ...' Only it won't be the same, not now. You see, Mr Vanderdecker, this freedom you've given me is a fraud. Maybe now I'm free of Mr Gleeson and account-ancy and all that horrible nonsense, but I can't be free of you, not ever. Every man I see in the street, I'll look twice at him to see if it's you. But she smiled instead, and left the sentence unfinished.

'Actually,' Vanderdecker said, 'I'd had this idea of getting a new ship.'

'What?'

'A new ship,' Vanderdecker repeated. 'Only not called the *Verdomde* this time. Something a bit more cheerful. And big. Huge. One of those oil tankers, maybe, or a second-hand aircraft carrier. Only we'd have the whole thing gutted and we'd fit it out like an enormous floating country-club. A separate floor for each of us, with auto-mated and computerised everything. Complete luxury. We could just sail around, landing where we like and when we like, just generally having a good time. I mean.' Vander-decker's voice sounded a trifle strained. 'I think we're all a bit too old to settle down now. Don't you think?'

'You know best,' Jane said. 'Well, I think that's a splendid idea. I really do. Have you put it to them yet?'

'No, not yet. I thought I'd like your opinion first.'

'Yes, you do that,' Jane said. 'And now let's have a drink, shall we?'

They went into the drawing room. The first thing they saw was Professor Montalban, lying on the sofa fast asleep. Snoring.

'Had a drop too much,' Sebastian explained unneces-sarily. 'Not used to it.'

'Fair enough,' Vanderdecker said. 'Now listen, you lot. I've been thinking ...'

And he explained the idea of the oil-tanker. It was well-received, particularly by Antonius, who had been wondering what was going to happen next. They all had a drink to celebrate. They drank the whisky, the wine, the gin, the brandy, the cherry brandy, the rest of the apple brandy and the sherry. At this point, Danny and the camera crew passed out, leaving Jane, the Flying

Dutchman and the crew to drink the vermouth, the Tia
Maria, the ouzo, the port, the bourbon, the vodka, the
bacardi, the schnapps and the ginger-beer shandy.

'That seems to be the lot,' Vanderdecker said, disappointed. 'And not a drop of beer in the whole place.'

'What's this, Skip?' Antonius asked, holding up a cut-
glass decanter. There was no label on it, but it was a
pleasant dark golden colour.

'Where did you find that, Antonius?' Vanderdecker
asked.

'In this little cabinet thing.'

Vanderdecker sniffed it. 'Smells like rum,' he said.
'Anyone fancy a drop of rum?'

Everyone, it transpired, fancied a drop of rum. It must
have been good rum, because it made them all feel very
sleepy.

When they woke up, everyone had headaches, Jane
included. From the kitchen came the smell of frying
bacon, which made them all feel sick. Slowly, Vanderdecker lifted himself to his feet, looked around to see if he
could see where he'd left his head the previous evening,
and went into the kitchen to kill whoever was making that
horrible smell.

It was Montalban, wearing a striped pinny, frying
bacon. He had also made a big pot of coffee, of which
Vanderdecker consumed a large quantity straight from the
spout.

'Why aren't you as ill as the rest of us?' he asked the
Professor.

'I never get hangovers,' said the Professor.

Vanderdecker scowled. 'Clean living, huh?'

'No,' the Professor replied. 'I have a little recipe.'

'Gimme.'

The Professor grinned and pointed to a half-full jug on
the worktop. 'There's tomato juice and raw egg,' he said,
'and mercury and nitric acid and white lead and heavy
water. And Worcester sauce,' he added, 'to taste.'

Vanderdecker had some and felt much better. 'Thanks,'
he said. 'It was the rum that did it.'

'Rum?'

'Vicious stuff, rum,' Vanderdecker said. 'Does horrible things to you.'

'I haven't got any rum,' Montalban said.

'Not now you haven't.'

Montalban was looking at him. 'No, I never keep any in the house,' he said. 'Are you sure it was rum?'

'Well,' Vanderdecker said, 'there wasn't a label on the decanter but it tasted like rum. I think.'

'Which decanter?'

'In a little glass-fronted cabinet thing, by the telephone table,' Vanderdecker said. 'Maybe it was calvados, come to think of it, except calvados always gives me heartburn and heartburn was about the only thing I wasn't suffering from when I woke up just now.'

Montalban was staring now, but not at the bacon, which was burning. 'Large cut-glass decanter in a small glass-fronted cabinet,' he said.

'That's right. Sorry, was it special or something? We just weren't noticing ...'

'That wasn't rum, I'm afraid,' Montalban said. 'That was elixir.'

Vanderdecker's eyes grew very round and his hands fell to his sides. 'You what?' he said.

'Elixir,' Montalban said.

'Oh *SHIT*,' Vanderdecker replied. 'Not again.'

'I'm afraid so,' said the Professor, 'yes.'

Vanderdecker's spine seemed to melt, and he slithered against the worktop, knocking over a glass jar of pearl barley. 'You stupid ...'

'It's not my fault,' Montalban protested nervously. 'For Heaven's sake, I'd have thought you and your friends would have learned your lesson by now, really ...'

Vanderdecker straightened up, turned his head to the wall and started to bang it furiously on the corner of some shelf units. 'Not you,' he said, 'me. Antonius. No, me. Oh hell!'

'It's not,' Montalban said, 'exactly the same elixir as ... well, as last time.'

Vanderdecker stopped pounding his head against the shelves and looked at him. 'It isn't?'

'Well,' said the Professor, 'it's basically the same, but I did make certain changes to the molecular ...'

He stopped short, because Vanderdecker's hands round his windpipe made talking difficult. 'Does it make you smell?' Vanderdecker snarled. Montalban said nothing in reply — not for want of trying — but his lips made the necessary movements to shape 'No'.

'You sure?' Montalban nodded vigorously, and Vanderdecker let him go.

'But,' he added, as soon as he had breath enough to do so, 'it does have side-effects.'

'It does?'

'I fear so.'

Vanderdecker groaned. 'Go on,' he said, 'tell me.'

'You understand,' Montalban said, first making sure that he had the bulk of a chest freezer between himself and his interlocutor, 'that my data is based on necessarily perfunctory and incomplete tests, confined entirely to non-human animal subjects, and that what I say is on a completely without prejudice basis?'

'Tell me.'

'You really must understand that none of this has been proved to the high standards ...'

'Tell me,' Vanderdecker said.

'It makes you go bright green.'

'Green?'

Montalban nodded again. 'Green,' he confirmed, 'and you shine in the dark. There is also an eerie humming noise. Additional limbs are sometimes (although not invariably) acquired, depending on the individual subject's metabolism and whether or not he is a vertebrate to begin with. Also,' Montalban added quickly as Vanderdecker picked up a biscuit-barrel and drew back his arm, 'the effects are strictly temporary.'

'You what?'

'The phenomena I have just described,' Montalban said, 'are exhibited in the short term only, for no more than a few weeks at a time. They do, however, recur; like malaria, I suppose, although on a fascinatingly regular basis.'

'How often?'

Montalban shrugged non-committally, and Vanderdecker threw the biscuit-barrel at him. While he was
reeling and picking smashed pottery and Bath Olivers out
of his hair, Vanderdecker had time to find a spaghetti-jar
and flourish it threateningly.

'My best estimate,' Montalban said, 'at the present time
is that the symptoms manifest themselves on average for
two one-month periods in each calendar year. But I should
stress,' he said, ignoring the spaghetti jar, 'that this is
based on observation of a small nest of field-voles, two of
which escaped, and the tests only cover a three-year
period, which is by any standards ...'

'Why?'

'My housekeeper,' Montalban admitted, 'is terrified of
mice. Green luminous mice especially. So I had to get rid of
them. Since they were immortal and invulnerable ...'

'That bit still works, does it?'

'Most certainly, yes,' said the Professor. 'Since they were
immortal and invulnerable and I couldn't keep them
around the house, they are now manning a small space-
station in orbit three hundred thousand kilometers above
the surface of Mars, providing invaluable data on ...'

'I see,' Vanderdecker said. 'Green, luminous and noisy,
and perhaps an extra arm or two. What happens with the
arms, by the way?'

'The additional limbs,' said the Professor, 'are also
temporary.'

'You mean they fall off?'

'Yes.'

'Moult? Pine needles off a Christmas tree job? That sort
of thing?'

'Roughly, yes.'

'I see,' Vanderdecker said. 'So I'll need a pair of trousers
with a detachable third leg, will I? As opposed to spending
the rest of history going around like a human Manx
emblem. Well, let me tell you ...'

Suddenly Vanderdecker fell silent and he lowered the
spaghetti jar, spilling its contents. He furrowed his brows
and then started to grin.

'Montalban,' he said at last, 'that's marvellous.'

'Is it?' Montalban raised an eyebrow. 'Well, I'm delighted that ...'

'Don't you see?' Vanderdecker said, 'Jane drank some too. A stiff double, approximately. Don't you see, she's going to live forever too. She's going to be one of us! Montalban — oh, look, just stay there, will you?'

He dumped the spaghetti jar in the sink and rushed through into the drawing room. There, Jane was sitting crouched on the edge of a settee, moaning slightly. With one movement Vanderdecker lifted her up in the air, kissed her noisily on the lips and said, 'Guess what?'

'Ouch,' Jane replied.

'You're going to go bright green and luminous, hum slightly, and grow an extra arm,' he said cheerfully. 'What do you think of that?'

'I think I already did,' Jane replied. 'Will you please put me down before my head falls off?'

'Sorry,' Vanderdecker said. 'Now, listen to this. No, better still, have some of the Professor's mercury soup and then listen.'

So Jane went, had some mercury soup, and listened. While Vanderdecker was explaining to her, and inducing Montalban with occasional prods from a rolling-pin to corroborate his narrative, he began to wonder whether Jane would in fact be pleased. He had no idea; all he knew was that he was pleased, very pleased indeed.

'So there you are,' he finished up. 'What do you think?'

Oddly enough, the only thing that passed through Jane's mind for several minutes was the phrase 'Death is a tax holiday,' which she remembered from her tax-planning lectures.

'Jane? What do you think?'

'Death is a tax holiday,' she said.

'I beg your pardon?'

'For the year of death,' Jane said, 'personal allowances against income tax are granted for the full year, regardless of the point in the tax year at which death occurs. There is no requirement to apportion unused allowances. Thus death can be said to be a tax holiday.'

'What?'

'Sorry,' Jane said. 'I was miles away. So I'm going to live for ever, am I?'

'Yes.'

'Ah. Yes, I thought that was what you said. I ...'

'Jane.' Vanderdecker grabbed her by the shoulders. 'Would you like some advice?'

'Yes please.'

'Don't think about it,' Vanderdecker said. 'It's not a good idea to think about it, believe you me.'

'Oh,' Jane said. 'Right, okay then.'

'Secondly,' Vanderdecker said, and then he turned to the Professor. 'Go away.'

'I'm sorry?' the Professor asked.

'I said go away. *Vamos.*'

'Certainly, my dear fellow, certainly.'

'Now then.' Vanderdecker put on a serious expression and looked Jane squarely in the eye. 'Miss Doland,' he said, 'since we are ...'

'All in the same boat?' Jane suggested.

'Precisely,' Vanderdecker said. 'Since we've both been accidentally lumbered with a common misfortune ... Look, do you see what I'm getting at, because this is rather tricky to put into words.'

'Yes,' Jane said.

'Yes, you see what I'm getting at, or yes, you ...?'

'Both,' Jane replied.

'And,' Jane continued, 'some sort of through dining-room in a sort of light Wedgwood blue, with ...'

'Jane.'

'Sorry.'

'That's fine. Now ...'

'And a dressing room,' Jane added quickly. 'I've always wanted a separate dressing-room. In a sort of pinky ...'

'Absolutely,' Vanderdecker said. 'Can you play the harpsichord?'

'No.'

'Pity,' Vanderdecker said, 'because it's years since I learnt, and they've put extra pedals and things on now.'

'Couldn't we have a stereo instead?'

'A harpsichord linked to the computer,' Vanderdecker

explained. 'To control the markets, whatever the hell they are.'

'Oh yes,' Jane said. 'God, you're efficient, aren't you? I'd forgotten all about ...'

'Habit,' Vanderdecker said. 'I've got into the habit of looking after people, remember, making sure they don't get into messes or start fighting each other. While I'm at it, I might as well use the Professor's computer, since he's obviously washed his hands of the whole affair.'

Just then the kitchen door opened, and there was Sebastian. He was looking pleased with himself.

'Hey, skip,' he said, 'it's all fixed.'

'I know,' Vanderdecker said.

'What?'

'Oh, sorry,' Vanderdecker said. 'What's fixed, Sebastian?'

'The ship.'

'What ship?'

'The supertanker,' Sebastian said. 'We've booked one.'

Vanderdecker stared. 'You've booked one?'

'That's right, yes,' Sebastian said. 'We tried Harland and Wolf first, but they thought we were playing silly buggers and put the phone down. So then we tried this Korean firm, Kamamoto-something, Pieter wrote the name down, and they said they had an ex-demo tanker going cheap, low mileage, taxed till April, metallic grey with headrests, and when would we like to take delivery? So we said, can you run it over to Bristol, and they said would Thursday be all right, so we said fine ...'

Vanderdecker smiled. 'Sebastian,' he said.

'Yes?'

'Ten out of ten for initiative,' said the Flying Dutchman, 'but let's say four out of ten for judgement. They were having you on.'

'You what?'

'Pulling your leg,' Vanderdecker said. 'Playing games. Being funny. Laughing up their sleeves.'

'How do you know?'

Vanderdecker widened the smile slightly. 'Trust me,' he said. 'I know. Why don't you just let me ...'

Sebastian shrugged his shoulders. 'Be like that,' he said, offended. 'We were only trying ...'

'Yes,' Vanderdecker said. 'You always are. Very. Go away and count something, there's a good lad.'

Sebastian drifted off, and Vanderdecker turned to Jane. 'You see?' he said. Jane nodded.

'And you still want to come?'

'Yes please.'

Fourteen months later, at half-past four in the morning, the biggest supertanker ever built slithered into the cold grey water of the North Sea and set off on its maiden voyage.

Curiously enough, there were no celebrations to mark the launching of this magnificent vessel (named, for sound fiscal reasons, *Lombard Venturer ID*); no crowd, no band playing, not even a small Babycham cracked against her awe-inspiring bows. Only one camera-crew filmed her departure, and that was because the owners hadn't the heart to refuse Danny Bennett a scoop to make up for the damage that the failure of his latest documentary 'Close The Creamery Door, Lads, There's Blood Inside', had done to his career.

This desire for privacy was understandable, because the owners weren't looking their best.

'I still say it suits you,' Vanderdecker said.

'People will think I'm seasick,' Jane replied.

'Let them,' Vanderdecker said. He glanced down at the instrument console before him; a cross between a huge computer keyboard, the flight deck of an airliner and a Yamaha organ. 'I wonder how you drive this thing.'

'I lent Antonius the manual,' Jane said. 'He asked me what gyroscopic means.'

'Oh well,' Vanderdecker said, and shrugged, 'never mind. It beats hauling in all those ropes, at any rate. Where shall we go first?'

'Rekjavik.'

'Why Rekjavik?'

'Because we have all the time in the world,' Jane answered, 'and I want to save the good bits till later.'

'Good thinking,' Vanderdecker said. 'I can see you're getting the hang of this.'

Through the tinted, double-glazed window they watched the coast receding into the distance. Just briefly, Jane felt her old life slipping away from her, and wondered if she ought to regret it. She was entering into a new timescale entirely now, and the next time she came back to England, perhaps everyone she knew there would be dead. But that was a very big thought, and there wasn't enough room in her head for it; all the available space was taken up with a calm, deliberate pleasure.

'Another nice thing about this ship,' Vanderdecker said, 'is not having to take it to Bridport to be fixed every time something goes wrong with it. God, I hate Bridport.'

'I gathered,' Jane said. 'It can't have been nice having to spend so many of your shore-leaves there.'

'True,' said the Flying Dutchman. 'Mind you, if you go somewhere often enough, you're bound to get sort of attached to it after a time. Even,' he added, 'Bridport.'

'Is that true?'

'No.' Vanderdecker admitted. 'Every time I went there, it had changed, ever so slightly, for the worse. A new car-park here, a fish shop turned into an estate agent there. I really thought it had bottomed out in 1837, but they hadn't built the bus station then.'

'So is it fun,' Jane queried, 'watching history unfold itself? Being a witness to the long march of Everyman? I suppose it's like being a God, really, except that usually you're powerless to intervene.'

'What long words Miss Doland is using,' Vanderdecker replied. 'It's not a bit like that. Hell, you don't notice, it's too gradual; it would be like claiming that the turning of the earth made you dizzy. I don't even feel particularly different, to be honest with you. I think I stopped feeling different when I turned nineteen and stopped growing, and since then I've always been the same. It'd be another matter if I'd gone to sleep and then woken up hundreds of years later, but ... I guess going on a hovercraft must be like that.'

'Haven't you ever?'

'What, been on a hovercraft? No fear. Those things are dangerous.'

Jane giggled. 'But Julius,' she said, 'you're invulnerable and immortal, nothing's dangerous to you. You can't be afraid of hovercraft.'

'Want to bet?'

Jane smiled, and shook her head. Would she be like him in four hundred years or so, or would he always keep this start on her?

'Nice of the Professor to come and see us off, wasn't it?' she said.

'I suppose so.'

'Do you think he ever will get round to finding an antidote?'

Vanderdecker grinned. 'Eventually,' he said, 'maybe. Where's the hurry?'

'There isn't one.'

In the distance, the environmentalist action ship *Erdkrieger* changed course sharply. The ship's Geiger counter had suddenly started bleeping furiously and playing 'Jerusalem' and someone had suggested that the huge ship on the skyline might have something to do with it.

They launched a dinghy and set out to investigate. Business had been slack lately, what with the new initiative (nobody knew where it had started) to phase out nuclear power worldwide, and for once there was no shortage of volunteers.

'Ahoy!' shouted the captain of the *Erdkrieger.* 'You there on the tanker!'

He raised his binoculars and recognised a familiar face.

'Fancy meeting you again,' Vanderdecker replied through the loud-hailer. 'How's saving the world going?'

'Sehr gut,' the German replied. 'Is your ship making the radiation?'

'That's not radiation,' Vanderdecker replied, 'not as such. Completely harmless.'

'If that's so,' said the German, 'why are you bright green and glowing slightly?'

'Too much Limberger cheese,' Vanderdecker shouted back. 'Come on, you know me. I'm a Friend of the Earth too, you know. Me and the Earth are like *that*.'

'Okay,' said the German. 'Sorry to have troubled you. Auf wiedersehen!'

'Auf wiedersehen!' Vanderdecker called back, and added 'idiot' under his breath. He left the bridge and went below to the library. Jane was in the drawing-room, comparing carpet samples. At the moment, she was dead set on a sort of beigy-pink with a faint texture in the pile. As he thought of it, Vanderdecker shuddered, ever so slightly, until he remembered that carpets wear out, eventually, even the best of them. He'd just have to outlive the bugger.

As he walked down the ladder, Vanderdecker paused and looked out over the sea. Very big, the sea, an awful lot of it, like history, or life. The hell with it.

'Skip,' said a voice from above his head. 'You got a moment?'

Vanderdecker sighed. 'Of course I have, Antonius.' He climbed the ladder again.

'Skip,' Antonius said. 'I can't find the mainmast.'

'There isn't one.'

'No mainmast?'

'No mainmast. Propellers instead.'

Antonius reflected for a moment. 'Skip,' he said. 'Yes?'

'How do you get the sail to stay up on a propellor?'

'You don't,' Vanderdecker said. 'It sits in the water and goes round and round.'

Antonius frowned. 'And they call that progress,' he sneered.

Vanderdecker smiled at him, nodded, and went below again, banging his head on a low girder as he did so. I'll get used to it, he thought, in time.

And so he did. And they all lived happily. Ever after.